Also by E.E. Ho

THE WORLD OF THE GATEWAY

The Gateway Trilogy (Series 1)

Spirit Legacy

Spirit Prophecy

Spirit Ascendancy

The Gateway Trackers (Series 2)

Whispers of the Walker

Plague of the Shattered

Awakening of the Seer

Portraits of the Forsaken

Heart of the Rebellion

Soul of the Sentinel

Gift of the Darkness

Rise of the Coven

City of the Forgotten

Shadow of the Brotherhood

Tales from the Gateway

The Vesper Coven (Series 3)

Daughters of Sea and Storm

Keepers of Forest and Flame

THE RIFTMAGIC SAGA

What the Lady's Maid Knew

The Rebel Beneath the Stairs

The Girl at the Heart of the Storm

Keepers of Forest and Flame

Keepers of Forest and Flame

The Vesper Coven

Book 2

E.E. Holmes

Fairhaven Press

Townsend, MA

www.eeholmes.com

ISBN 978-1-956656-21-3 (Paperback edition)

ISBN 978-1-956656-20-6 (Digital edition)

Cover design by James T. Egan of Bookfly Design LLC

Author photography by Cydney Scott Photography

This one's for the mothers, the ones who nearly lost themselves in their love for others. May you find your sparkle again, for you are meant to shine, too, and don't you ever forget it.

"For a witch stands on the very edge of everything, between the light and the dark, between life and death."

— Terry Pratchett

Prologue

Someone was calling my name.

I could hear it inside my head, a whisper of a voice that was as much thought as it was sound. At first, my brain told me it was a dream... or at least, an invitation into a dream. *Just relax,* it told me. *Just take a step forward into sleep and follow it, like walking through a door.*

But I didn't want to walk through a door. I wanted to stay here and find out where that voice was coming from. If I gave in to sleep, I told myself, I would lose my grip on it.

I drifted back toward full consciousness, like a bubble floating to the surface of water. My eyes fluttered open, and I heard it again, somewhere inside myself.

Wren. Wren Vesper.

I sat up and stared expectantly around my little bedroom, a room that was still renewing its place in my heart and my memory as really belonging to me. I was sure I'd see someone standing there at the foot of my bed, waiting for me to wake up. For some reason, this did not scare me. It probably should have, but I felt nothing at all except a feeling of calm expectation. It was only when I found myself seemingly alone that I began to feel uneasy.

A week ago, I would have doubted what I was hearing or at least been terribly afraid of it. I'd have thought I was losing my mind somehow. But I knew better now. I knew that the world—*my* world—was teeming with things I'd never imagined.

Wonderful things. And terrifying things.

But I also knew the most terrifying of them all couldn't touch me here. Here, inside Lightkeep Cottage, I was safe. Spells. Enchantments. Curses. Hexes. Every conceivable method of protection had been employed over the centuries by generations of Vesper women to keep danger at bay within these walls.

A soft mewling sound made me turn my head, and I spotted my black cat, Freya, perched on the window seat. She captured me with her radiant gaze and then turned her head back toward the window with an impatient flick of her tail. The instructions couldn't have been clearer if she'd opened her mouth and suddenly spoken English.

Stop wasting time lying in bed and get over here and look out this window.

For half a moment, I wondered if Freya had been calling my name. A friend had informed me that she wasn't just my pet... she was my familiar. I hadn't had any time at all to understand what that meant, but hearing her little kitty voice in my head didn't feel completely out of the realm of possibility.

I stared at Freya.

Freya stared back. Impatiently.

"Did... did you say something?" I asked her.

She meowed in reply. So, that was a no.

Feeling foolish, I pushed my blankets back and heard it again: my name, spoken both inside and outside my head. This time, Freya's ears perked up, and she turned once again to stare out the window. This time, I hastened to take the hint and ran to the window and peered down into the darkened garden below.

My dead grandmother stared back up at me.

"Asteria!"

Wren.

That was the moment that I recognized the voice that was calling my name. It was her. Her voice. Asteria. It had been more than six years since I'd heard it, but I knew it now.

I bolted from my room and nearly fell down the staircase in my haste to get out into the garden. I pushed open the front door and jumped down off the front porch, losing my footing in the gravel and skinning my palms as I put them down to catch myself. I stumbled to my feet and made a beeline for the garden gate, fumbling the catch with shaking fingers, all the while the same question on repeat in my head.

How can she be here? How can *she* be here?

I ran as fast as I could, dodging the flower beds and skirting the bushes around the side of the house. Any moment now, she would come into view. I leaped a final low shrubbery and skidded to a halt to find...

Nothing. There was no one there.

I spun on the spot, my heart pounding, my breath coming in frantic gasps.

"Asteria? Asteria, where are you?" I whispered into the rose-scented night.

But only the wind answered me, redolent with salt from the nearby sea.

Bewildered, I looked up at my bedroom window, where I saw Freya blinking back down at me. I walked to the very spot I'd seen her standing, refusing to give up.

There. In the dew-dipped grass. The imprints of two bare feet. I reached down with trembling fingers and touched the indentations.

"Asteria," I whispered once more into the silence.

She did not answer.

1

"I'm starting to think that maybe kitchen witchery isn't my thing."

I stood in the kitchen of Lightkeep Cottage, wearing an apron and looking like I'd just fought—and lost—against a sentient sack of flour. The counters were covered in dirty bowls, spilled ingredients, and sticky utensils. The window over the sink was open to coax out the remnants of smoke still wafting up in serpentine tendrils from the oven.

"Now, whatever would make you say that?" asked my aunt Rhi a bit breathlessly. She was sweating profusely and pulling oven mitts from her hands, like a pair of boxing gloves.

I pointed to the counter, where the results of my morning's lesson were laid out on a cooling rack. "Just a hunch."

We both walked over and looked at them. According to the recipe, they were meant to be strawberry thyme scones. According to the evidence in front of us, they were misshapen rocks of dubious origin.

"I'm not even sure they're edible, let alone magical," I grumbled.

"Oh, I'm sure they're fine," Rhi said, but I could hear the false note in her encouraging tone as she scooped up a dishtowel, and began flapping it to help clear the remainder of the smoke.

It was almost impossible to believe it had only been a couple of weeks since I'd first set foot in Sedgwick Cove, because I'd never had so much about my life change in such a short time. Two weeks ago, I was living in Portland, ME, finishing my sophomore year of high school, and looking forward to a summer hanging with my friends and scooping ice cream for minimum wage. Now, I was living in a cottage by the sea in a town populated almost entirely by witches, and was struggling my way through the first few days of my magical education.

Magical education. It still sounded completely unhinged when I said it out loud. In fact, everything that had happened to me in the two weeks since my grandmother had died sounded like fantasy fiction. But it wasn't fiction. It was real. And it all came back to the woman I'd seen standing in the garden last night.

My grandmother Asteria Vesper had been a witch, a descendant of the First Daughters of Sedgwick Cove, who had created their magical community in mid-coastal Maine. A deep, ancient magic had drawn them there, but they were not the only ones. An entity known only as the Darkness had also settled here, feeding on the Cove's inherent magic, and strengthening itself as it did so. Eventually, the Vespers had to come up with a way to bind the Darkness from accessing the deep magic of the Cove. So, they had created a powerful Binding spell, but the only way to seal it and ensure that it would continue to protect the Cove was a second spell called the Covenant. Every generation, three women of Vesper blood had to renew the Covenant, for only if all three of them remained in the Cove would the Binding hold. Asteria had kept that little tidbit of information from her three daughters, including my mother, who had fled Sedgwick Cove when I was just a baby. She'd thought she had time—time to bring her family back together, time to bring them around to their destiny so that they could step in freely and of their own volition. But then Asteria had died on my sixteenth birthday, and when we returned to Sedgwick Cove for the funeral, the truth came out.

My mother was a witch. Her sisters, Rhi and Persi, were witches too. And, despite my current culinary attempt to disprove it, so was I. We had to stay in Sedgwick Cove in order to preserve the Covenant. And honestly, that would have been enough change for anyone—moving to a new place, living with relatives I couldn't remember ever having met, absorbing a new identity and family history—but Sedgwick Cove had more in store for me.

The thing about the Darkness was that it didn't want to be Bound. It wanted to be free, and even more than that, it wanted me. My magic—a magic I wasn't even convinced I possessed. It turned out that the Darkness had tried to claim me as a toddler, and that was why my mother had fled in the first place. Asteria had rescued me, but the damage had been done. It wasn't until just a few days ago, when the Darkness tried to make a bargain with me—my mother's life for mine—that I discovered exactly how much magic I truly possessed. Calling on the elements, I had banished the Darkness, though there was no telling for how long.

"I called on the elements," I mumbled, staring at the scones again. "I commanded the freaking ocean. I made lightning appear from the sky! So why do I now seem incapable of commanding a simple baking recipe?"

"Because," Rhi answered, coughing slightly, "they are two entirely different types of magic. Kitchen witchery is subtle. What you did was..." She paused, struggling for the right words.

"A fluke?" I suggested.

She scowled at me. "Of course not! No one could perform magic like that as a fluke! You just need to gain control over your magic."

"You think I wasn't in control that night on the beach?" I asked.

"In a way, yes. You were in a life-or-death situation. Your magic came to your rescue. But now you have to learn how to do the opposite of that. You need to learn to summon it yourself, and like any other skill, it takes a lot of practice."

I sighed and picked up a scone. "I'm beginning to see that."

"Now, come on, don't get discouraged. I'm sure they're not that bad," Rhi said, tossing aside her dishtowel and picking up a scone. She took a bite and chewed slowly. Her face twitched into a momentary grimace she couldn't quite control. "See? Not bad at all."

I picked up a scone and bit into it. "Rhi, stop torturing yourself. These are disgusting."

Rhi swallowed hard and put the rest of the scone back on the cooling rack. "Kitchen witchery is all about intention. You're focusing too much on getting it right and not enough on imbuing it with your intentions. What were you thinking as you mixed and chopped?"

"Mostly, 'Oh shit, I'm going to screw this up. I can't cook. These are going to be awful,'" I admitted.

Rhi allowed herself a tiny snort of laughter before wrestling her face into a neutral expression. "Well, there you go. Self-fulfilling prophecy."

I raised an eyebrow. "Are you saying they taste terrible because I assumed they would?"

"No, they taste terrible because you overcooked them and screwed up the recipe somehow," Rhi said, patting me on the shoulder. She nibbled the scone again, thoughtfully. "Hmm. Too much salt. And overmixed. But even if you'd gotten it right and they'd tasted delicious, they wouldn't have had the effect that you'd intended."

I sighed, flopping into a chair at the kitchen table. "This is hopeless."

"Of course it's not. We're just trying to do too many things at once," Rhi said, plunking a plate down in front of me with one of her own scones. "You need to learn how to have confidence in the basics of cooking first. I didn't realize how little experience you had, or I would have started with something simpler."

I shrugged. "Mom has never been much of a cook. I can boil pasta and scramble an egg and make pancakes from a box, but that's about it."

Rhi laughed. "Yes, we never could tempt Kerridwen into the kitchen very often. She was too busy running wild on the beach and in the garden."

I tried to imagine my mother, an ER nurse, ever being the kind of hippie little wild child my aunt was describing, but my imagination wouldn't stretch that far. She'd changed so much. Run from so much. Buried so much.

There was a reason Rhi was taking my magical education in hand rather than my own mother, and that reason was fear. The same fear that had sent her running from Sedgwick Cove when I was a toddler had never faded. And in fact, after my recent run-in with the Darkness, it had only increased. Although my mother had agreed to move back to Sedgwick Cove and renew the Covenant alongside her sisters, that didn't mean she was ready to throw herself headfirst back into life as a Vesper witch. I'd barely seen her over the last few days since the Covenant was renewed; and while I knew she had a lot to do to finalize our move to Sedgwick Cove, I couldn't help but feel like she was avoiding the cottage.

No, it was worse than that. I felt like she was avoiding *me*.

In a way, I understood. After all, I was scared, too. Now that I'd accessed my power, it was terrifying to think it had been there all along, and that I had no real idea how to control it. But I also knew that running from it wasn't going to help. I needed to do what my mother hadn't been able to do all those years ago. I had to look in the mirror, embrace who I was, and then start to understand what exactly that meant.

And so here I was. Burning scones. Figuring it out.

I took a bite of Rhi's scone. It was soft and crumbly and ridiculously delicious, but that wasn't the best part. As I swallowed that first bite, a warmth spread through me, rich and dripping like honey, coating my insides in a sense of calm and contentment. I looked at Rhi, wonder all over my face.

"Better?" she asked, smiling.

"Better. How do you do that?"

"Intention combined with the right ingredients. You'll get there. And if you don't, that's okay, too. Every witch has to play to her natural strengths. Much like your mother, you won't find Persi in the kitchen unless she's hungry. Speaking of Persi, I promised I'd drop lunch down at Shadowkeep for her. Would you like to come along?"

I nodded eagerly. I hadn't been to Shadowkeep yet, our family's shop in downtown Sedgwick Cove. All I knew about it was that it sold "witchy" items geared toward tourists who flocked to Sedgwick Cove, the same way they flocked to Salem in Massachusetts. But under the facade of a kitschy tourist trap, Shadowkeep was also a trusted source to the local magical community for the kinds of things witches really needed: herbs, gemstones, books, dousing rods, and all manner of other things I had yet to learn about.

I went and got myself cleaned up, and waited on the front porch while Rhi packed a small basket with lunch for Persi. I stared out over the ocean, watching the waves crash on the sand, and inhaling the sharp, salty air. My heart seemed to swell in my chest, and I knew I would never tire of this view, never wish myself away from this place. From almost the first moment I'd set foot in Sedgwick Cove, a deep, untapped part of myself had woken up and claimed it as home. I didn't really have a choice. We belonged to each other. I wondered for the first time if that feeling had something to do with the Covenant. Did my very blood know it was irrevocably tied to this place? Perhaps the magic of that spell included me, too, tying a string to my heart and tugging me back to the place where I was meant to be.

As this question rolled around in my mind, my eyes strayed to the lighthouse, and I felt my heart rate quicken. I hadn't been down on the beach since that night—in fact, no one had. The section of the beach near the lighthouse had been roped off, and official-looking signs had been posted warning people away. "Falling rocks" was the public-facing excuse, and it was a good one. The cliffs that dropped down toward the sand were very tall and craggy, and it was easy to believe that they could be dangerous if you were a tourist who didn't know any better. For the locals, though, the real meaning of the warning was even more frightening.

Down on that sand was an anomaly of magic and nature, created the night I battled the Darkness, and no one knew yet how dangerous it might be. It was a strange structure made of molten sand created by a lightning strike—that would have been strange enough all on its own. But what we were really concerned about was what may or may not be contained inside it.

The Darkness, trapped and immobilized, its power frozen in grains of sand.

I hadn't seen the Gray Man, sleeping or waking, since that night; but I knew he wasn't gone—whatever power I had, it surely wasn't that impressive. I'd acted out of instinct to protect myself, but I wasn't foolish enough to think it all over, and neither was the Conclave. They were the ones, my mother informed me, who had demanded the beach be cordoned off so that they could examine it safely; and though it had been several days, we'd heard nothing about what they'd been able to discover. Rhi had become increasingly cheerful about it, insisting that "no news was good news." I wasn't quite so optimistic, and from the dark glances I'd seen them throw toward the beach, neither were Persi or my mother.

"Ready, Wren?"

I jumped. I'd been too caught up in my own jumbled thoughts to notice that Rhi had appeared on the porch beside me. I nodded my head, and we set off on a brisk walk toward town.

Main Street in Sedgwick Cove was like something out of a tourist brochure for coastal Maine, but with a decidedly witchy twist. The local microbrewery was called "The Witch's Brew." The little antique store was called "Secondhand Magic." The bed-and-breakfast had a rustic twig broom hanging over the porch rockers with the sign "Come Sit a Spell" dangling beneath it. On the corner was a small black shed with a roof shaped like a witch's hat advertising walking tours. But of all the places that could draw the eye, Shadowkeep was by far the most intriguing.

Shadowkeep comprised a tall, slender, three-story Victorian house painted a vivid shade of lavender, with black shutters and a black slate roof. An intentionally crooked turret thrust its little pointed roof into the sky, topped with a copper weathervane of a witch on her broomstick. A sign in the shape of a bubbling cauldron was adorned with shining gold lettering: *Vespers' Shadowkeep.* The porch was crowded with plants: plants in macrame hangers, plants erupting from vases and pots, plants wrapping their tendrils around the posts and railings. A pair of white porcelain cats stood sentinel on either side of the stairs leading to the front door. I felt a grin spread slowly over my face.

"What are you grinning about?" Rhi asked, when she spotted the look on my face.

"Nothing, it's just... I've never seen a place quite so... Asteria." I watched in horror as Rhi gasped softly and her eyes filled with tears. "Oh God, I'm sorry, Rhi, I didn't mean to—"

"No! Please don't apologize!" Rhi said, brushing impatiently at the tears escaping down her cheeks. "Ignore this, please—I cry at everything these days. It's just that... you're absolutely right, and it makes me so glad to know that you can see it."

"I may not have been able to spend a lot of time with Asteria, but she left a powerful impression," I said. Rhi reached over and squeezed my hand, and then we walked up the steps into Shadowkeep.

A cluster of little bells jangled discordantly as Rhi pushed the door open and stepped inside. The air was redolent with the warm scent of incense and the earthy tang of dried bunches of herbs strung from the rafters between the twinkling string lights. Even though it was a bright June day outside, the interior had a cool, dark feel, as though we'd suddenly gone underground, or else slipped through a little hole in time that led to twilight. Part of the reason for this was all the plants that had crept up outside the window were blocking the sunlight, and the other was the complete lack of overhead lighting. Rather, the whole interior was lit with flickering battery-operated candles in mismatched brass lanterns, and clustered on shelves and tables. The walls were lined with shelves containing books on witchcraft (*Finding Your Inner Witch* and *So You Want to Be a Witch: Now What?* prominent among them); and an array of trinkets and home decor. A pair of women in sun visors were examining a candle in the shape of a skull. A teenage boy was digging through a display of different packages of tarot cards, while his girlfriend gushed over a spinning rack of amethyst pendants carved into animal shapes. A sign on top of the rack said, "Choose Your Familiar!"

Rhi watched me take it all in with an amused expression on her face. "What do you think?" she asked.

"It's... not quite what I expected, actually."

"Oh no?"

I lowered my voice. "Isn't this the kind of gimmicky stuff real witches despise? Like..." I subtly nodded my head at the girl with the pendants who was now squealing, "Look, babe, a love potion perfume! Babe. Babe!" The boy, who didn't seem interested in answering to "Babe," continued to ignore her.

I widened my eyes. "See?" I mouthed.

Rhi laughed heartily and leaned close to whisper in my ear. "This floor is for the tourists. We keep the good stuff upstairs."

At that moment, Persi undulated through the room, tossing her long dark hair over her shoulder. Everyone turned to stare at her—it was impossible not to stare at Persi. She was positively mesmerizing, oozing sensuality and confidence. She leaned in toward the girl now ogling the perfume and whispered in her ear, "If you want to capture his attention, I highly recommend it. I'm wearing it, and I'm still exhausted from last night." She winked at the startled girl and then swept past the tarot display on her way to the cash register. "Babe" lifted his head and started scenting the air like a bloodhound. The girl pressed her lips into a line, snatched a bottle from the shelf, and plunked it down on the counter with a determined expression.

"An excellent choice," Persi murmured. She rang the girl up as her boyfriend stood there, watching Persi with his mouth hanging open. The girl snatched up the bottle, grabbed her boyfriend by the hand, and marched him out of the store without a backward glance.

"Persi, that's not even what you're wearing," Rhi said dryly.

"Yes, well, she doesn't know that, does she?" Persi drawled, and then her eyes fell on me. "Oh, hello, Wren. Coming to do an inspection, in case you want to sell the place out from under us?"

"I—"

"Wren does not own Shadowkeep, as you very well know, Persi," Rhi snapped. "Now stop tormenting the girl and eat your lunch."

Persi smirked at me as she took the basket from Rhi's hands. I tried to look like the joke didn't bother me, but my stomach was roiling with guilt. Asteria had left Lightkeep Cottage to me in her will. It was the house my mother and her sisters had grown up in, and where Rhi and Persi had still been living when we arrived. Of course, it wasn't my fault that Asteria had left the house to me. She'd really done it to tie my mother to Sedgwick Cove—a tactical maneuver to ensure the continuation of the Covenant. But that didn't stop Persi from making snide remarks about it constantly.

I still wasn't really sure where I stood with Persi. One minute, she was giving me a head-to-toe makeover; and the next, she was ignoring me completely. It made my head spin, but I also tried to remind myself that she was trying to process all of this just like I was. We would both need time to figure it out, and in the meantime, I would just grin and bear it.

Rhi had also brought along her own batch of strawberry thyme scones, and was arranging them on a glass pedestal on the countertop near the cash register.

"Is that all you've brought?" Persi asked between bites of chicken salad on a homemade croissant. "I thought you were making a double batch?"

"I was going to, but... well, I wanted to start teaching Wren and we, well..."

"I inherited my mom's cooking ability," I piped up, "so the second batch went straight into the trash."

Persi snorted with laughter and had to cover her mouth to avoid spraying the counter with chicken salad. "Say no more," she said, once she had safely swallowed. "Why are you starting with kitchen witchery, anyway?"

Rhi shrugged, wiping crumbs from her fingers, and placing a glass dome over the top of the scones. "Have to start somewhere," she said.

"Kitchen witchery is so... strict," Persi said, making a face. "You should let her start with something more intuitive."

"Kitchen witchery *is* intuitive for me," Rhi said, sounding almost defensive.

"Of course it is," Persi replied, smiling like a cat with feathers on her lips, "because you like to follow the rules, and I like to break them."

"You say that like it's something to be proud of," Rhi shot back. "Besides, since when have you wanted to weigh in on this topic? I don't see you offering to help with Wren's magical education. If you think I'm doing it wrong, by all means, feel free to take the reins; but I won't hold my breath."

Persi simply shrugged, still smiling, and took another bite of her lunch.

"Come on, Wren, I'll show you where the real magic happens, so to speak," Rhi said, gesturing toward the door behind the counter. There was a sign on it which read, "Staff Only."

I followed Rhi to the door. Just before it swung shut behind me, Persi whispered, "Come find me if you want to learn some real magic."

She winked at me. I just stood there, staring like an idiot, until the door closed behind me.

2

At the top of the narrow staircase was a door painted red, with shiny gold hardware and a tarnished brass plaque on the door that read, "The Vesper Apothecary." Rhi paused in front of it, and tapped the plaque with her pointer finger.

"Before we bought this building and started Shadowkeep, the Vesper witches ran their business out of Lightkeep Cottage. This is the plaque that used to hang on the side porch," she said.

"How do customers find it now?" I asked. "You can't just keep letting them go through the staff entrance. People will notice, won't they?"

Rhi smirked. "Follow me and I'll show you."

And instead of taking me through the door, she squeezed past me back to the landing halfway up the staircase, where there was a small dusty window set into the wall that looked over the side of the building. She gestured me over, and we both peered down into the side garden, which was separated from the sidewalk by a gate and a fence.

"What do you see when you look out this window?" Rhi asked me.

I squinted down through the dusty panes. "I see... grass? And some azalea bushes? A sundial. Sorry, what am I supposed to be looking for?"

"Do you see a way up to this floor?"

I frowned. "I..." I looked again. "No?"

Rhi was grinning now. "Now I want you to think about Lightkeep Cottage... just picture it in your mind in as much detail as you can, and then look out the window, but only from the corner of your eye."

Bewildered, I did as she instructed. I thought about Lightkeep, about the wide sagging porch, the colorful riot of a garden, the little room where I slept, the way the salty breeze from the ocean whistled around the eaves in a familiar song. Then I looked out the window again and, in my peripheral vision, a staircase had appeared running up the side of the house to the second floor. I blinked and turned to look at it head-on, but it had vanished again. Then I turned to Rhi, my mouth hanging open.

"There's an invisible staircase?" I asked, my voice rising to a squeak.

Rhi shook her head. "Not invisible. It's a glamour."

"What's a glamour?"

"A glamour changes your perception of the world, rather than the world itself. Most people think of glamour as related to beauty, and it is often used that way—Persi is particularly adept at glamour spells—but it doesn't always have to do with personal appearance. Often, it simply has to do with desire—what you desire to attract in your life, and what you desire to keep away. In the case of Shadowkeep, we want to keep curious outsiders away from the upper level of the store, while still making it possible for the local witches to find it. So, Asteria put a simple glamour on the building. It's a spell that tricks your eye into not acknowledging the staircase. It's not invisible—it simply deflects your gaze. It's there, but your mind refuses to notice it."

"And everyone here—all the other witches, I mean—know how to find it?"

Rhi nods. "Over time, a witch becomes more adept at recognizing a glamour. There's a certain feeling that comes over you, a tingling sort of sensation, like the way the hair stands up on the back of your neck when you're being watched. It's easy to miss, but if you're on the lookout for it, you can often spot it without too much difficulty. Some glamours are more powerful than others, however, and the glamour on Shadowkeep is particularly so. That's why we have that little trick to get around it."

As she said it, I looked out the window and saw a woman stopping at the gate of Shadowkeep. She looked familiar—it took me a moment to recognize the stout, swaggering form of my friend Zale's grandmother, Davina. She opened the gate and stood near the side of the house, still for a moment. From where I watched her, it looked as though she was examining the large lilac bushes that ran along the side of the shop, their blooms drooping and past their prime. Then, a moment later, she charged purposefully up the stairs, passing right by the window where we stood.

"Come on. We'll need to let her in," Rhi said, and I hurried up the staircase behind her.

Rhi pushed open the red door at the top of the stairs and revealed a room that was, in many ways, the polar opposite of the room below. Now *this* was what I thought Shadowkeep would look like on the inside. Shelves ran from floor to ceiling on two of the walls crammed with ancient books, their spines peeling and stamped with titles in runes and symbols and languages I didn't recognize. Apparently, my four years of public school Spanish had left me ill-equipped for this particular collection. One wall had been turned into a floor-to-ceiling apothecary, with row after row of tiny square drawers. Each drawer bore a circular brass ring as a handle, and also a handwritten label designating the contents. I drew closer to read a few of them: "Powdered Raven's Claw." "Bleached Mouse Bones." "Dried Frog Skin." I swallowed hard and prayed my magical education wouldn't mean I had to actually touch any of those particular ingredients.

There were bins and baskets and pottery bowls full of feathers and precious gems and smooth, polished runestones. One shelf held a collection of mortars and pestles in a variety of sizes and materials. I moved closer to a white one to examine it, and felt my pulse speed up.

"Is this one made of..."

"Bone, yes," Rhi said.

"Human?" My voice rose about an octave and a half on the single word.

Rhi eyed me somewhat warily, as though carefully weighing what she thought I might be able to handle before answering, "Fox, I think."

I tried to keep my face entirely impassive, but my head swam as I moved away to examine something less disturbing. I may have decided to embrace my witchy heritage, but it was obviously going to take some adjustment.

I had barely a moment to take in any more of my surroundings when a second set of bells jangled, and Rhi hurried over to a door in the back corner of the room. She pulled it open to reveal Davina standing on the landing, arms crossed over her formidable bosom.

"Hello, Davina. How are you?" Rhi asked, as she stood back to let Davina through the door.

"Nae bad," Davina said with a shrug. She swaggered over the threshold into the room with an appraising glance around. "I dinnae suppose you've got any more of Xiomara's Florida Water? I've been by to see her, but it's the lunch rush."

"Yes, she furnished us with some new stock just last week, but it always goes quickly. What we've got left is over there by the herb-infused candles. I'll show you," Rhi said.

I was still staring around at all the labels on the apothecary wall when I heard whispering behind me. Davina was a member of the Conclave. Suddenly, goosebumps were breaking out all over my arms, and my heart began to pound so that my pulse thudded in my ears, which made it hard for me to pick up on anything she and Rhi were saying. I had to take several deep breaths before I could catch even a word.

"...cannae tell you any more except that the Conclave has all but concluded its investigation, and Ostara will let you know when she wants to see you."

"Surely you can tell me more than that!" Rhi hissed.

"And risk Ostara's wrath? Not on your life, lassie."

Rhi glanced over at me, and so I started opening the little drawers in the apothecary cabinet, pretending to be fascinated with the contents, and then losing the thread of their conversation when I found myself momentarily distracted by what appeared to be a pile of bird bones. By the time I recovered, closed the drawer, and tried to listen again, they had moved on to another topic. It took a few sentences before my ear adjusted to Davina's Scottish cadences again.

"...cannae decide what we ought to do about Bernadette," she was saying as Rhi nodded along with a solemn expression.

Bernadette Claire. The name sent a shiver of dread down my spine. Bernadette was one of the Claires, the other oldest family in Sedgwick Cove, known as the Second Daughters. When the Vespers had worked to banish the Darkness, the Claires had helped them; but one of their own had fallen to the Darkness and betrayed them all, a woman named Sarah Claire. It was Sarah's ghost, accidentally dragged earthside by Bernadette's well-intentioned but dangerous meddling, who had turned Bernadette's already fragile mind, and weaponized her to kidnap my mother and lure me into a trap. I'd been waiting for news of her for nearly a week, but the Conclave, notoriously tight-lipped at the best of times, had been virtually silent on everything to do with the events on the beach, and that included Bernadette. I shifted myself subtly toward Rhi and Davina, listening hard even as I pretended to still be examining the drawers.

"...but Ostara won't back down," Davina was muttering.

"But surely it's in the best interest of all involved for a Cleansing to take place?" Rhi hissed back.

"Without a doubt, but you know Ostara. Stubborn as a mule, and with a mightier kick," Davina grumbled under her breath. "We'll have to sanction her if she does nae relent, but it will nae be pretty. She's been through the wringer; the whole family has."

I suddenly felt eyes on me and chanced a glance in their direction. Damn it. I'd been too still, listening too hard, and Rhi had spotted me. She raised her voice again and said, "These are what we have left in stock from Xiomara. Did you have a particular scent in mind? I know you've favored the orange and clove in the past, but we're out of that at the moment."

After what seemed like an excessive amount of deliberation, Davina settled on a bottle of Florida Water, and Rhi rang her up at the antique brass cash register tucked into the corner under the window. Shards of shattered rainbow light danced all over her pale skin and wild blonde curls, refracted from the crystal wind chimes hanging behind her. She slipped Davina's purchase into a small cheesecloth bag with drawstrings. She tied it with a ribbon and a sprig of something that might have been rosemary. Davina tucked it into her bag, and with a curt nod in my direction, slipped back out the door and down the hidden staircase.

I pretended to be engrossed in the apothecary drawers so that I could mull over what I'd heard. The Conclave was arguing over what was to be done with Bernadette. It was the first news I'd heard of her since the events of a week ago, despite asking my mom and both of my aunts about it repeatedly. Each time, the answer had been the same: "The Conclave will handle the matter." Well, it sounded like the Conclave wasn't handling it at all. And what was a Cleansing? I hadn't made it past burning scones in my magical education, so it was no wonder I didn't have a clue. I thought about asking Rhi, but decided against it. She hadn't wanted me to overhear her conversation with Davina, so I doubted she would answer my question.

Luckily, I knew a few witches who would. But I would have to wait until after the lunchtime rush.

* * *

THERE WAS no set menu at Xiomara's Cuban Cafe. You showed up, and they were serving whatever Xiomara decided she wanted to cook that day. Today, according to the Instagram page Eva ran for her grandmother, it was classic Cuban sandwiches, black bean soup, arroz con pollo, pork tamales, and tostones. I could smell the mouthwatering aromas from a block away, and as I turned the corner, and the cafe came into view, I understood why. The line to get in was out the door, which had been propped open to allow for the come and go of satiated customers. It also had the added effect of wafting the enticing aromas of Xiomara's cooking out into the street.

Xiomara, like my aunt Rhi, was a kitchen witch. They had a playfully antagonistic friendship, trading recipes and spells back and forth, each insisting the other's were rubbish while secretly enjoying each other's truly magical—and delicious—gifts. As for the hordes of summer tourists, they didn't know that Xiomara's cooking had an element of magic. They simply knew it was some of the best food they'd ever eaten.

I waited for the line to die down, and then slipped inside the cafe to find Eva and another girl handing out to-go orders, and wiping down tables. Eva looked up, and her face split into a grin.

"Hey, there she is—the girl who banished the Darkness!" she said, laughing as she watched my face turn beet red.

"Yeah, I'm thinking about putting it in my social media bio," I said, attempting a level of cool I definitely couldn't achieve. "By day, theater nerd. By night, banisher of ancient evil. What do you suppose the post-graduate job market is like for a skill set like that?"

"Hm. Limited. You should probably study accounting or some shit," Eva said, nodding sagely. "Have you eaten yet?"

She didn't even wait for me to answer, ducking immediately through the door behind the counter and shouting something in Spanish as she went.

I felt the distinct impression of eyes on the back of my head, and turned to see that the younger girl who had been wiping down tables was staring at me. She dropped her gaze the moment I turned, fumbled her bottle of spray cleaner, and dropped it. It rolled under the nearest table, and she ducked down to retrieve it with a squeak of embarrassment. The bottle continued to roll, coming to a rest right against my sandal. I bent down and picked it up, noticing that the girl was still under the table, frozen like prey that had scented a predator.

"Uh, here you go," I said, holding the bottle out to her. Blushing furiously, she reached out from under the table and took the bottle with a shaking hand.

"Thanks," the girl whispered. She had Eva's prominent cheekbones and pointed chin, and looked to be about nine or ten years old. Her hair had been beautifully braided, with blue beads affixed to the ends that clicked together quietly as she moved. I wanted to know if she was Eva's sister, but I couldn't bring myself to ask the question; she looked so flustered to be talking to me. Luckily, at that moment, Eva backed through the door from the kitchen with two heaping plates of food in her hands, and a knowing smirk on her face.

"You know, Bea, if she wanted to banish you too, I don't think hiding under the table would stop her," Eva teased. She set the food down on a table in the corner and wiped her hands on her apron. "Why don't you stop hiding and I'll introduce you properly."

Bea, her face scarlet with mortification, crawled out from under the table, looking anywhere but at me. "I wasn't hiding. I dropped the spray bottle," she muttered.

"Whatever. Bea, this is Wren. Wren, this is Beatriz, the bane of my existence, and also my baby sister," Eva said, but her voice was full of teasing affection.

"Nice to meet you, Bea," I said, smiling warmly, but Bea still looked like she wanted to flee the room. She nodded at me and then returned to wiping down tables.

"Don't mind her; she's just a little starstruck," Eva said, rolling her eyes and pulling out a chair so we could sit together.

"Are you sure that's it?" I asked, watching Bea out of the corner of my eye. "Because it looked more like abject terror."

Eva shrugged as she bit into her sandwich. "What can I say? You're a local badass now."

"But like... is that the vibe now? People are scared of me?" I gasped. "Eva, I can't even follow a magical scone recipe."

Eva batted my words away like insects. "Okay, first of all, baking is hard. Xiomara has tried to teach me, and I just don't have the patience for it. Not all kinds of magic are for all witches, and it's not a reflection on you if you have to try out a few before you find one that vibes with your powers. Okay?"

"Okay," I said, not because I believed it but because she was trying to help.

Eva narrowed her eyes at me like she knew exactly what I was thinking, but she chose to let it go and continued, "And secondly, chill. It's just because the Conclave has been so tight-lipped about everything that happened on the beach. No one knows what's a rumor and what's the truth."

"What kind of rumors?" I asked. My stomach had been rumbling a moment ago, and now I wasn't sure I could eat even a bite of the sandwich in front of me.

Here, Eva gave an uncomfortable little squirm. "Nothing specific. Just... people speculating. You know how people are. They love to form opinions about things they know absolutely nothing about."

"And those opinions are...?" I prompted.

Eva smiled grimly. "That you are some incarnation of or tool of the Darkness, and that your power is unhinged and dangerous, and we should probably all be scared of you?"

I swallowed hard. "Right. Cool. So, normal new kid stuff, then."

Eva reached out and put a hand on my shoulder, shaking it in a congenial way. "People are idiots. And hey, it could be worse. You could be Nova."

Nova Claire was Bernadette's niece. From the moment we'd met, she'd had a certain resentment toward me—a resentment born of the fact that I was one of the First Daughters who had saved Sedgwick Cove, while she was a descendant of the woman who had nearly allowed the Darkness to triumph all those centuries ago. It was an unfair burden to carry, that kind of generational guilt, and having me around was a constant reminder of it. We'd walked away from the events of last week on okay terms—and I'd done everything I could to assure her that she was forging a new legacy for her family, but it had been radio silence ever since. It wasn't that I thought we'd become instant best friends or anything like that, but I had hoped, after everything we'd been through at the lighthouse, that we might find our way to friendship. Now, I felt a sinking feeling in my stomach.

"Are people talking about her too?" I asked.

Eva rolled her eyes. "Very few people have the guts to criticize the Claires publicly—they've got too much money, too much clout. But behind closed doors, yeah, I think a lot of people are judging the whole Claire Coven based on Bernadette's actions."

The shift in conversation opened a direct path to what I'd wanted to ask Eva about in the first place, and so, though I still very much wanted to torture myself with specifics about local gossip, I forced myself to satisfy a more pressing curiosity.

"I just came from Shadowkeep, and Davina came in there," I began.

"You haven't touched your sandwich. Do you want something else?" Eva interrupted.

"No, no, this is great. Sorry, I'm just distracted," I said, picking up the sandwich and taking a bite to appease her. Then I groaned as the flavors exploded in my mouth. "Oh my God."

Eva grinned. "I know, right? Every time she makes them, we sell out. Sorry, you were saying something about Davina."

"Right," I said, around another mouthful. "I overheard her mention something about Bernadette, and how the Conclave hasn't been able to make a decision about her because of Ostara. She said they want to perform a Cleansing."

Eva shook her head, looking disgusted. "Typical. Of course, Ostara would hold them up. Anything to shift the focus off of the Claires. No wonder Xiomara has been so short-tempered. I thought she was worried about something, but when I asked her about it, she just told me to mind my business and make more tostones." She picked up a tostone and popped it into her mouth.

"But what *is* a Cleansing?" I asked. "What exactly are they trying to get Ostara to agree to?"

Eva threw a glance over at Beatriz. She had gone quite still, listening hard while she wiped the same spot on the same table over and over again.

"Bea, why don't you go see if Xiomara needs help with any online orders?" Eva said.

Bea jumped at the sound of her name, and though she threw her sister a frustrated look, she did as she was told.

"Bea's a good kid, but she scares easily. I don't need her crawling into my bed with nightmares for the next week," Eva muttered, watching Bea disappear through the swinging doors into the kitchen.

"Why would a Cleansing give her nightmares? What is it?" I pressed.

"When a space or a person or an object seems to have a negative energy associated with it, a witch will sometimes perform a Cleansing to get rid of that energy," Eva said.

"Oh." I felt almost disappointed. "So like, when people use sage in their house, stuff like that?"

"Sage is a well-known traditional method of Cleansing, yes," Eva said, nodding. "It also happens to be very effective when done correctly. But there are lots of different kinds of Cleansings, lots of different rituals and traditions from all over the world. Sage smudging is a Native American tradition, and other cultures have their own practices. But sweeping away a bit of bad vibes in your new apartment is one thing. The deeper and more insidious the negative energy, the harder it is to get rid of."

I felt my stomach do a flip. "And in this particular case, the negative energy is the Darkness."

To my surprise, Eva shook her head. "I mean, I guess it's possible, but I don't think so. From what we saw, I'm not sure that Bernadette was ever in the Darkness' thrall. It wasn't directly from the Darkness that she was taking orders, remember?"

"Oh. OH." The bit of sandwich I was holding slipped right through my numb fingers and onto my plate. "So then, the negative energy is the spirit of Sarah Claire."

"Bingo," Eva said. "Yet another Claire. No wonder Ostara wants to shift the blame elsewhere."

We sat quietly for a minute or two, listening to the clanking and sizzling sounds emanating from the kitchen, punctuated by snatches of song in Xiomara's rich, husky voice. Another few customers came in, and Eva jumped up to get their orders, which left me free for a few minutes to process everything Eva had told me. I honestly hadn't thought at all of Sarah Claire since that night, which was foolish, I supposed, and yet somehow unsurprising. After all, Sarah had been an almost invisible presence that night. If it hadn't been for Bernadette communicating with her, I wouldn't have even registered that Sarah was there. She hadn't appeared in any sort of physical form. She hadn't made contact with me in any kind of tangible way. She had been merely a theoretical threat—the mysterious spirit that would take over my mother's body once Bernadette had killed her. But once we'd struck our bargain—my life for my mother's—all thought of Sarah Claire had evaporated. She had become, at least for the moment, irrelevant. But if she'd been powerful enough to influence Bernadette and, therefore, help orchestrate the events of that night, she was dangerous enough to still be wary of. I felt her land on the heaping pile of anxieties already crowding my brain, and sighed. I ought to have been worried about her all along. I thought about the past few days: how Rhi had distracted me with books and introductory lessons, how my mom had kept us mind-numbingly busy with packing and unpacking, and finally, I recognized it for what it was.

"That night on the beach, it felt like the end of something scary," I said to Eva as she ushered the customers out and slid back into the seat across from me. "Everyone's been trying to push me forward so that I wouldn't look back, but the truth is that it wasn't the end at all. It was the beginning, wasn't it?"

I looked up and caught Eva's eye. She didn't look away. She didn't even blink.

"I'm no oracle, but I'm afraid so," she said. "Hence why I kick my scaredy-cat sister out of the room every time we talk about it. Everyone's on edge, worried about what will happen next. I know she picks up on it. And she's even more anxious than your average kid because she hasn't really found her magic yet."

"Found her magic?"

"Yeah, you know, her spark, her affinity. I'm sure you're learning all about it now. Every witch is drawn to some kind of magic—think of it like your own personal talent. Bea hasn't found hers yet. It makes her even more anxious, knowing that she can't defend herself the way another witch might be able to."

I swallowed hard. I knew how she felt. Here I was, simultaneously untrained and yet, by all accounts, very powerful. I felt exposed, undefended, like someone trying to navigate their way through a hostile new place with a blindfold on.

There was a pinging sound, and I snapped back out of my thought spiral. Eva reached into her pocket for her phone, and checked her notifications. "It's Zale. He wants me to come help him with Litha pageant preparations."

"Litha?" I asked.

"Midsummer. The summer solstice," Eva said, and her eyes lit back up with an excited sparkle. "Didn't you notice the banner? It's one of Sedgwick Cove's biggest events of the year!"

"Oh, no, I didn't, I... sorry, I've been a bit preoccupied," I said. *Uprooting my entire life. Recovering from a brush with the deepest evil. Seeing my dead grandmother in the garden.*

"Well, don't worry, you'll soon know more about it than you've ever wanted to," Eva said with a laugh. "Why don't you come to the meeting tomorrow night at the playhouse? Zale has bitten off way more than he can chew, and he's gonna need all the help he can get."

Suddenly grateful for a distraction, I nodded. "Yeah, okay! What time?"

"Seven."

"I'll be there. What are you all planning?"

Eva's smile broadened into a grin. "You'll see."

3

I walked back to Lightkeep Cottage, my worries weighing me down like sandbags I had to mentally drag along with me. I'd gone to Xiomara's Cafe hoping for answers, but I only seemed to come away with more questions.

I found myself longing for my life back in Portland. Not Portland itself, or our familiar neighborhood, or the safety and familiarity of my school and my friends and the theater, although I missed all of that, too. No, it was the simplicity of it all—the mundane predictability of our day-to-day existence. I'd woken each day with a baseline sense of security that had been torn to shreds since my arrival here. I'd taken it all for granted—the safety, the banality of it all. And even for the things I worried about, it wasn't anything like the worries I carried around with me now. At this point, I'd have felt relieved to fret about a science test or wonder whether a technical rehearsal would go off without too many hitches. It was almost like I'd been missing out on my real life all along, and now that I'd found it, all the troubles that had piled up in my absence were threatening to bury me all at once.

But then Lightkeep Cottage came into view, nestled against the winding seaside road, as natural in its place as the waving marsh grass and the cliffs and the rolling crash of the ocean. A deep sense of calm washed over me; and I was comforted by the knowledge that, whatever I might have to face, here I was. Despite it all, I was home for the first time in a long time. Lightkeep Cottage was my port in the storm, however new and frightening that storm may be.

I knew from the moment I opened the door that Rhi was at work in the kitchen. The aromas drifting through the house were enough to make my mouth water, despite the huge lunch I'd just eaten. I followed my nose to find her in her natural state: covered in flour and elbow-deep in ingredients.

"Hey, there! How was everything over at the cafe?" she asked, looking up and smudging more flour across her cheek with the back of her hand.

"Fine," I said, because neither of us was emotionally prepared for the real answer. "Xiomara sent this." I handed her a bag that clinked and clanked as she took it.

"Ah, excellent. I've been meaning to ask her to restock her Florida Waters," Rhi said, rummaging her hand through the bottles with a satisfied expression. Then she looked up, her expression almost hurt. "Is that all?"

I grinned. "Nope." And I handed her a paper bag heaped with take-out containers. "It was Cuban sandwich day."

Rhi groaned with anticipation as she took the bag. "Even more excellent!"

I didn't reply, only patting my stomach to indicate I shared her enthusiasm. "What are you working on?" I asked, gesturing to her work surface.

"I was testing out some new cookie stamps I've made using sigils. I thought we could all use some calming influence, so I'm planning to fill the cookie jar."

The word "sigil" tickled the back of my brain, and I tried to remember what I'd read about the word, but my mind came up blank. "Can you... remind me what a sigil is?" I asked, smiling a little sheepishly.

"Don't worry, working with sigils is still a bit advanced for you, but the basics are simple enough to explain. Come here, I'll show you," Rhi said, pointing to the sink in an unspoken command to wash my hands. When I had done that, she patted the stool beside her. I sat, and she handed me a rolling pin. "You roll, I'll explain."

I saluted like a diligent soldier, and then began to work the dough into a flattened circle as she spoke.

"I'm sure you're already sick of me going on about intentions, but it's foundational to your magic, so get used to it. A sigil is a way to represent an intention in the form of a symbol. The way it works, essentially, is to create a statement of intention, remove the vowels and the repeated letters, and then arrange the remaining letters into an abstract symbol."

I smiled down at the dough I was rolling. "That sounds a little like how my friend Poe and I used to create a secret code to pass messages to each other that no one else would understand."

Rhi threw back her head and laughed her throaty laugh. "That's not a bad analogy. There is certainly some element of secrecy with sigil creation —or at least, some element of wanting to protect oneself. As you know, we witches couldn't always practice so openly, and so practices like sigils were integral to our continued spellwork."

"That makes sense. But how do sigils and baking go together?" I asked.

"Well, I created my sigils by carving them into these wooden disks. As you can see, they're basically cookie cutters, except they will not only cut the shape of the cookie, but press the sigil itself into the dough, like this." And she picked up a small wooden disk from her work surface, and pressed it into the dough I'd just flattened. When she lifted it, there was a complex design stamped into the surface of the cookie —a strange, lopsided collection of curves and slashes that made no sense I could understand.

"But... what's the point? Someone will just eat it," I pointed out.

"That *is* the point," Rhi said, smiling again. "There are many ways to charge a sigil so that it is powerful, and one of those ways is to destroy it."

"Destroy it? Seriously? What good would that do?" I asked, confused.

Rhi pursed her lips for a moment as she considered how to answer. Finally, she said, "Wren, let me ask you a question. Let's say I was casting a hex on you, and I wrote your name on a piece of paper and then rolled it up and lit it on fire."

I felt my eyes go wide, my mouth fall open. The words had sent an absolute jolt of fear right down my spine. Then Rhi slapped her hand down on the floured surface, scaring the shit out of me with the sound, and sending a cloud of flour into the air around us.

"You see? Now, why did you react that way? That was a visceral reaction!"

"I...I..." My stammering went on as I tried to analyze what felt like an automatic reaction that any non-witch would have had. "I'm not really sure," I admitted after a moment's pause. "I suppose it's just... well, my name represents me, and so the idea of someone lighting...me... on fire feels like an attack. Something meant to hurt or destroy me."

"That's right! If my intention was to hurt you, that seems like a pretty powerful, symbolic thing to do."

I looked down at the cookie in front of me, wary. "I'm suddenly thinking I might not want to be the one to taste-test these cookies," I said.

Rhi chuckled. "I was just trying to illustrate a point. Destroying something can be powerful in magic, but it's not always a negative thing."

"Oh, okay," I said, the last of the confusion clearing away. "I guess that makes sense."

"Now, back to that idea of lighting your name on fire. Let's take it a step further. Destruction is not the only purpose of fire, is it?" Rhi countered, seeming to really enjoy herself now, the way an expert lights up like a Christmas tree when their subject of expertise comes up in general conversation. "Can't you also cleanse things with fire? Can't you warm them? Light their path forward?"

I suddenly felt completely wrong-footed. "Oh, I... yeah, I guess that's true."

"My point," Rhi said, "is that you can use the destruction of the sigil to enact its intent, even if the intent is a positive one. Fire is one way to do it—the process of baking is nearly that, but as long as my dough recipe is effective in holding the cookie's shape, the sigil will not be destroyed. In fact, it will have gained in strength during the baking process." Rhi reached over onto the cooling rack and plucked an already-baked cookie from among its fellows. She held it up and showed me that the design from the sigil disc was still perfectly preserved in the surface of the cookie. She leaned toward me and lowered her voice. "But can you guess how I intend for these sigils to be destroyed so that the sigil reaches its maximum power?"

"How?" I whispered, almost breathless.

"Like this," Rhi said, and crammed the entire cookie in her mouth, chewing in a loud, exaggerated way.

I burst out laughing and she joined me for a moment before having to stop so she could prevent herself from choking on a mouthful of half-chewed cookie. When we'd both gotten a handle on ourselves, she handed me a cookie with a more serious expression.

"The intention of the sigil, and therefore, the cookie, is to achieve a state of calm," Rhi said, "but without alerting the eater to the fact they've been influenced by the cookie. How did I do?"

I examined the cookie for a moment and then bit into it. Nothing very immediate happened. I took a second bite, waiting for something to take effect; but again, I felt no change. I took the final bite, chewed carefully, and swallowed. Nothing.

I turned to Rhi, unsure whether I should lie or hurt her feelings, and not really wanting to do either, but she held up a finger. "Wait for it," she whispered.

And not a full second later, a wave of absolute contentment washed over me, leaving me with an almost floaty feeling in my head. I shook it, and like the whirl of flakes in a snow globe, the feeling began to spread and settle downward. I felt my shoulders drop, my knees soften. I felt the tension I was holding in my jaw suddenly ease. All of it was subtle and natural, but it made an enormous difference in how I felt.

"Wow," I said, and found I could grin quite easily.

But Rhi shook her head. "'Wow' is not exactly constructive criticism, Wren," she said, sounding a bit flustered. "I need something a little more descriptive than that!"

I tried to dig down under the surface of my newfound contentment to find my real thoughts. "I... well, it works. I definitely feel relaxed. Kind of... lighter, too. Like I'd had a lot of things weighing my thoughts down before, but now they're gone."

Rhi brightened at once. "Oh, I see! Okay, that's helpful!" she chirped, and bent at once over a leatherbound book beside her, where she began to write feverishly. "Anything else?" she asked, as she finished her scribbling and eagerly looked up to meet my gaze again.

"Uh..." I felt the pressure of her expectation, but I tried not to let it bother me too much. I focused on what I'd just experienced and hit on something worth mentioning. "When the feeling first hits..." I began.

Rhi leaned toward me, practically giddy with expectation. "Yes?"

"Well... it comes on kind of strong, sort of like the whole intention hit me in the face at once, instead of creeping up on me slowly. Relaxation doesn't just hit you that way. It takes time."

Rhi was nodding vigorously as she dropped her gaze to the book and muttered, "...less... chamomile..." Then she set her pen down and grinned. "That's very helpful feedback."

"What's that book?" I asked. At first, I'd mistaken it for a cookbook, but once Rhi had started writing in it, I realized that the pages were actually blank except for Rhi's minuscule handwriting and some rough, hand-drawn sketches of some plants.

"Oh, this is my kitchen grimoire," Rhi said. "My working version, at least."

"What do you mean?" I asked.

"I mean, I've gone through at least a dozen of these volumes over the years. Someday, I'll sift through it all to find the winners and compile them all into one volume," she clarified.

"No, I mean..." I swallowed, feeling that shame that can only come from asking for an answer you know you're already supposed to have. "I mean, what was that word you said: *grimoire*? What does that mean?"

Luckily, Rhi didn't scoff at my ignorance. "It means a witch's book of spells," she said with a little shrug. "It's as simple as that. An individual witch will often work on her own grimoire throughout her life as she experiments and grows in her craft. After all, spells and recipes are a helpful jumping-off point, but all magic requires some personalization."

"Does every witch have her own?" I asked as, with a sudden stab of panic, I pictured my own grimoire, completely blank inside except for a series of increasingly messy and frantic question marks.

"Not at all," Rhi said, and her knowing smile made me think I hadn't masked my panic very well. "Many covens have a family grimoire that belongs to the whole, and they all work out of it. Some of them are very old, compiled by generations of witches, each adding her own spells and advice.

"Does our coven have one?" I asked. It still felt so weird to say "coven" in reference to my family, the word awkward as it stumbled off my tongue.

"We do," Rhi said, and reached into a cabinet behind her to pull down a heavy, leatherbound book. She placed it on the counter between us, brushing some flour out of the way as she did so. "You can see the more recent spells and entries are all in Asteria's handwriting, and before that my aunts, my grandmother, my great-grandmother."

"Wow," I said. "How old is it? It looks like it's in pretty good shape," I said.

Rhi smiled. "This one is only about a hundred years old."

"Only?"

"It's not the original Vesper Coven grimoire," Rhi said. "Family legend says that the original grimoire, the one brought to Sedgwick Cove by the First Daughters, was lost in the battle with the Darkness. It was said to contain some of the most powerful magic ever set to paper, magic the First Daughters would not even dare to perform."

"Lost how? What happened to it?" I asked.

Rhi dropped her voice to a spooky whisper. "No one knows. It's a mystery." Then she grinned. "Personally, I doubt it ever existed."

"Why?"

"Well, in the first place, it would have been madness to keep such a book back then. If it fell into the wrong hands, it would have been conclusive proof of our magic, and we would have been burned at the stake. And secondly, it seems like the kind of legend our foremothers would have perpetuated to bolster our magical reputation. No one would mess with us if we could truly perform the kind of magic that grimoire is said to have contained."

I nodded. "I guess that makes sense. But don't you ever wonder what—"

"Rhi? Persi?"

My mom's voice, coming from the direction of the living room, sounded sharp with anxiety. She came around the corner and stopped short at the sight of me.

"Oh! Wren! I didn't realize you were back, honey. I was just about to text you."

"Why? What's up?" I asked.

"If you're looking for Persi, she's still over at Shadowkeep," Rhi said, as she replaced the grimoire in the kitchen cabinet.

"We'll have to pick her up on the way. What are these, anyway?"

"A new recipe for sigil work. It's supposed to produce a calming effect," Rhi said, handing my mom a cookie. We watched in surprise as she crammed it whole into her mouth.

"Um, mom?" I said, suddenly wary. "Pick Persi up on the way to where?"

"Might as well bring that whole batch, Rhi. We're gonna need them," my mom said, before turning to me to answer my question. "We're going to the Manor. We've been summoned."

And she made another cookie disappear in a single, slightly manic bite.

4

I soon discovered the meaning behind my mother's ominous words. In Sedgwick Cove, being "summoned" meant that you had been asked to appear before the Conclave.

Appearing before the Conclave was not necessarily a bad thing, but it was never a trivial matter either. On the drive over to the Claire family home, referred to by locals simply as "The Manor," Rhi babbled almost non-stop about all the times the Vespers had been summoned to the Conclave. I knew she was trying to fill the anxious silence to help me feel less fearful of what awaited me in this gathering. Because I knew, somehow, that this wasn't really about the rest of my family. This was about me.

How I knew this, I couldn't really say—it was simply this intuition that had lodged itself beneath my ribs, causing my heart to race and my breathing to constrict. If I was honest, I'd been waiting for something like this to happen. It was inevitable after that night on the beach.

That night.

If I'd been waiting for the Conclave's summons during my waking hours, I'd been waiting with just as much nervous anticipation for the Gray Man's summons during the hours I lay asleep. I had dreamed of him so many times over the years that I had come to associate him with those murky, nebulous stretches of darkness when my brain dredged up images from the forgotten reaches of my past. But though I dozed off each night with dread nested in the pit of my stomach, my sleep remained dreamless and peaceful. I started to wonder if the strange connection between us had been severed. And now, I wondered if the Conclave might actually have some insight into that.

No one had spoken to me about the events on the beach except for my mom. I knew she had filled in my aunts, and I knew that the Conclave had also been informed of what had happened. I was burning with curiosity about what would happen next, wondering if they would call me in to interrogate me. In my most anxious moments, as I struggled through Rhi's rudimentary magic lessons, I even wondered if they would call me before them and demand an explanation.

Well, how is it you performed such extraordinary magic on the beach, and now you seem powerless?

What incantation did you use? What spells? What potions? Show us!

Prove it. Call the elements now. Command the ocean and the air.

I supposed my real fear was an interrogation because, of course, I had no idea how I had done it. Sometimes, I wondered if that night, too, had been nothing more than a fantastical dream. I almost wished it was. That would have made more sense than what had actually happened... whatever that was.

By the time we had pulled up to The Manor, Rhi's babbling had become so high-pitched and borderline hysterical that Persi couldn't take it anymore.

"For the love of the goddess, Rhi, just shut up already!" she snapped as Rhi killed the engine. Rhi blinked, startled, like her sister had just slapped her physically instead of verbally.

"Oh, I... sorry," Rhi mumbled.

"Persi, that's not necessary," my mom said, her voice weary.

"Well, someone had to do it. Look at Wren. She looks like she's about to have a panic attack."

All three sisters turned their appraising eyes on me, and I quickly tried to look unconcerned. Needless to say, I failed miserably. My mom bit her lip, obviously feeling guilty that she'd been too preoccupied to notice my distress.

"Wren, don't be nervous. I'm sure they just want to discuss the events at the lighthouse."

I nodded, keeping my mouth firmly closed, because that was exactly what I was nervous about.

We walked up the steps and pulled a fancy rope bellpull by the front door. Inside, a bell that was more of a gong resounded through the house. After what felt like an interminable wait, which was probably only about thirty seconds, a young woman in a simple black cotton dress and pearls opened the door and ushered us in.

"They have servants?" I asked my mother in a whisper, as we crossed the entryway. "Like, actual live-in servants?"

"No," my mother replied. "I mean, they have help, but that girl is a secretary for the Conclave. Her name is Iris. She assists with all the meetings, and that includes answering the doors. In fact, she was the person who called to alert us about the summoning."

At that moment, Iris turned, pausing in front of a pair of impressive wooden pocket doors, which I already knew led to the Claire family library. Ironically, I'd already attended a Conclave meeting in that room, as long as we were counting eavesdropping as attending.

"The Conclave is ready for you," Iris said impressively, and pulled the doors wide.

They sat in a semi-circle, their faces all turned expectantly to watch us enter—with the exception of Lydian, whose chin had dropped onto her chest and bounced off it again with a snorting sort of grunt, indicating she'd been asleep. The others—Xiomara, Davina, Ostara, Lydian, and Zadia, watched in silence as the Vespers filed in. My mother took my hand, and I noticed her fingers were trembling slightly. I squeezed them, not sure if I was trying to reassure her or myself. She squeezed back and attempted a tight smile.

"Thank you all for coming at such short notice," Ostara said, inclining her head. She gestured to the chairs that had been placed in the circle for us as we all dropped into them, Rhi and my mother looking wary, and Persi wearing an expression more closely suited to defiance.

"It's not as though we had much of a choice," Persi said, her voice quiet but fierce.

Ostara opened her mouth, presumably to say something dignified and diplomatic, but Lydian had neither the time nor the patience for that.

"Oh, give it a rest, Persephone," Lydian snapped. "You sound like a petulant child."

Rhi smothered a smile behind her hand, while my mother made a valiant effort to disguise a snort of laughter as a sneeze. Meanwhile, Persi glared at Lydian, though I noticed she didn't quite have the courage to talk back again. It was almost unnatural to see Persi back down from an argument, and I had a feeling Lydian was one of the few people who could produce such a response.

"I acknowledge this summons was rather abrupt, and I do apologize for that, but it was for good reason," Ostara went on, as though she hadn't heard the exchange. "We knew that you would be as anxious as we were to know the results of our examination of the lightning sand, and so I sent the summons as soon as we had anything to report."

I'd been tense before, but now every muscle in my body felt coiled like a spring. I'd been right: this was about the events on the beach, and the interrogation I'd feared was about to occur, with my mother and aunts as a captive audience. My stomach roiled with nausea.

When I'd called on the elements that night on the beach, fire had answered my plea with a bolt of lightning. The lightning had struck the sand, turning it instantly molten, and then the liquid sand had risen up and created a sort of cage, trapping the Gray Man inside. It had all happened so quickly, both in and out of my control. To this moment, I had no idea how much of the night's events I could really even claim credit for. It felt as though the power had belonged to the elements themselves, not to me. All I'd done was call for help... hadn't I?

It was all such a blur, such a haze of adrenaline and fear.

"Wren, as I'm sure you remember, the Conclave closed the northernmost stretch of beach so that we could have the time and space we needed to examine the lightning sand. We not only physically roped off the beach, but we took magical precautions to ensure people would steer well clear of the area so that we could keep others safe while we worked, undisturbed."

I had a momentary vision of the five Conclave members there in front of me, dressed like the witches from Macbeth, down on the beach with a massive cauldron over a driftwood fire, and I felt an almost irresistible urge to giggle. For heaven's sake, I had to pull myself together, or they'd all think I was cracking up under the pressure of everything that had been thrust upon me in the last two weeks... and maybe I was. I refocused on Ostara, who was still speaking to me, and tried to pick up the thread of what she was saying.

"...used every protective spell we could think of before we began to examine it in earnest. We feared what might happen if we unintentionally freed the Darkness. All we wished to find, at first, was proof of its presence. Once we had that, we could determine how it was connected to the lightning sand."

"We were so sure of it," Xiomara said, her deeper, more melodic voice picking up the thread of the story now. We all turned as one to listen to her. "We could sense the strength of the Darkness, the power of it. It seemed, at first, that the Darkness itself must be trapped inside, like a beating heart in the cage of a chest."

"What do you mean, at first?" my mom asked, her voice sharp. But I'd caught it, too, the hesitation in Xiomara's tone. It made my heart stutter.

"I mean that it soon became clear that what we were sensing was not the Darkness itself. It was the traces of the magic it left behind," Xiomara said.

I shot a look across the sofa at Rhi, Persi, and my mom. They all looked as bewildered as I felt, so at least I knew it wasn't just me.

"I'm not sure I follow," my mom said. "I thought the Darkness was trapped in that... that sand cage. Are you saying that isn't the case?"

"We must be realistic, not wishful," Zadia said, somewhat sternly. "We would all like the Darkness to be contained somehow, but that was never very likely, was it? Especially when a novice witch was involved."

I felt a surge of guilt and fear. A moment ago, I was worried that I didn't even understand what I'd done—and now, I was scared that whatever I'd done, I hadn't done it right. I opened my mouth—I wasn't entirely sure why, but I expected that I was preparing to apologize. Luckily for me, Persi was easily offended and leaped in before I could so much as clear my throat.

"A novice *Vesper*," Persi said, tossing her magnificent hair and adjusting her posture so that she resembled a queen on a throne. "I think we can all agree that that is nothing to sniff at."

Zadia smiled and inclined her head in acknowledgment, which seemed to satisfy Persi. Ostara, however, proceeded more carefully.

"Naturally, Wren's lineage as a Vesper indicates that her potential is great," she said. "But with no training or knowledge, it is unlikely that her actions on the beach, however admirable or impressive, were sufficient to trap the Darkness permanently. No Vesper has ever been able to do that."

"And no Claire, either," Lydian barked, and Ostara had no choice but to nod curtly in agreement, her expression somewhat sour. I heard a soft exhalation beside me, and saw that Persi was making no effort to hide her smile at Ostara's expense.

"My point," Ostara said, injecting her voice with a ringing note of authority, "is that Wren, whatever her powers, whatever her intentions, was unlikely, on her own, to have trapped the Darkness permanently. We have now determined that she has not. The Darkness is not contained within the lightning sand. The vessel is empty."

This piece of information could not help but chill every person in the room. My mother was so tense beside me that I thought she might shatter with the pressure of keeping herself so tight and still. Unsure what else to do, I raised my hand like I was in school.

"Yes, Wren?" Ostara said, a note of amusement in her voice.

"I was just wondering... if the sand didn't trap the Darkness, then why did everything stop when the sand closed around it?" I asked. "Why didn't it simply keep coming for me?"

Everyone turned to Ostara expectantly, and she suddenly looked like she would have much preferred not to be on the spot.

"We're not entirely certain," she admitted.

"You mean *you're* not entirely certain," Lydian snapped. "I've told you my theory, and I'm damn certain."

We all turned to stare at her. Lydian snorted.

"The older you get, the less people listen to you. I am convinced that Wren's actions were not creating a spell. They were breaking one," Lydian said, speaking too loudly and making everyone jump. She looked around at all of our startled faces, and sighed. "Ah, now I see I've got your attention. Ask yourselves this: why could the Darkness manifest in the first place?"

No one answered.

"It ought to have been impossible," Lydian reminded us. "The Darkness was meant to be Bound, cut off from the deep magic, unable to channel or use it. So why could it manifest in the first place?"

"Asteria's death?" Rhi suggested, sounding both thoughtful and eager. If this had been school, she would have been vying for teacher's pet. "With Asteria gone and the new Covenant as yet unsigned, perhaps we were more vulnerable than we should have been?"

But that couldn't be right, I thought to myself. I'd seen the Darkness in that chosen form before—what I'd taken to be a nightmare all my life had actually been a memory. The Gray Man didn't only appear after Asteria's death—he had appeared to me many years before while she was still very much alive. I began to raise my hand again to point this out, but Xiomara was already shaking her head.

"The Darkness has appeared in other forms throughout the centuries. It is not impossible that it could manifest when there is something it really wants."

Every pair of eyes drifted to me.

"Me. You're talking about me," I said.

"We must consider why that is," Xiomara said. "If we are to understand what happened that night, we must also understand why the Darkness is so interested in you."

It felt like someone had suddenly shoved me into a spotlight. Everyone in the room was not only looking at me now, but examining me —almost as if they were waiting for me to perform a trick, or explode or something. I thought longingly of the door behind me and how much I'd like to flee through it. Before I could make a break for it, though, Xiomara turned her intent gaze from me back to Lydian.

"My apologies, Lydian. You were telling us your theory," she said, giving Lydian a respectful nod.

"No apologies necessary, Xiomara. You've furthered my point. The Darkness wants Wren. When it has wanted something in the past, something it was desperate to obtain, it has used what little magic it can access. It used it again, this time to take a physical form so that it could communicate with her, and lure her to the ocean." She turned to me. "I am assuming that The Darkness spoke to you. What did it say?"

I felt every pair of eyes burning into me. I reached back into the memory, feeling my own resistance. I wanted to bury this memory, not relive it. But I dug the words up anyway, knowing I had no choice.

"It told me that it needed my magic. That I was the weapon it needed to break the Covenant," I said, my cheeks flaming, my eyes on my own violently twisting hands. "And then it told me that when I walked into the ocean, we would become one: the Darkness' eternal state, and my magic."

My words seemed to cast a pall of horror over everyone who listened, all except for Lydian, who clapped her gnarled hands together with a loud "Ha!" of exaltation.

"There you have it! The Darkness planned to use magic—some of it Wren's own—to bind the two of them together. But Wren fought back. She broke the spell—cut it off. When that happened, the Darkness lost its hold on its physical form. It was too weak to remain. Her lightning sand did not contain the Darkness; it simply severed the connection between them."

Lydian looked at each face in turn, waiting for a contradiction that would not come. Her words made sense to everyone, including me. It had never seemed likely to me that I could have defeated the Darkness so simply. But wielding the elements inexpertly, but effectively enough to destroy something—in this case, some sort of connection? That seemed like something I might be able to stumble my way into doing. The others seemed to agree. Heads were nodding, expressions thoughtful as everyone let Lydian's words sink in. Finally, it was Xiomara who broke the silence that followed.

"Lydian's theory is the most likely explanation, and one we will continue to explore. In the meantime, we must assume that Wren will continue to be a target when the Darkness has gathered enough strength for another attack. We have no time to waste. You have begun her magical education, as we discussed?"

My mother looked startled, and then blushed a little as she stole a glance at my shocked face. "Yes, we... well, Rhi has already begun."

I turned to look accusingly at Rhi, who also had the good grace to blush.

"You discussed my magical education without me?" I asked, looking back and forth between Xiomara and my mother.

"We simply impressed upon your mother the importance of understanding your powers as soon as possible," Xiomara said, looking completely unabashed. "The Darkness chose you for a reason, and it would be foolish in the extreme not to understand exactly why that is."

I wanted to argue with that, but I couldn't. My mom took advantage of my momentary wordlessness.

"Wren, listen to me. We discussed it, yes, but I told the Conclave it would have to be your choice. And I gave you a choice, didn't I?"

I nodded grudgingly, though I still felt betrayed somehow.

"And now that you know the Conclave wants you to explore your gifts, does that make you feel any differently about your decision?"

I sighed, all the sudden anger and indignation draining out of me. I felt suddenly tired. "No. I still would have chosen to stay in Sedgwick Cove, and start learning witchcraft."

"And have you made any progress yet?" Xiomara asked, looking back and forth between Rhi and me.

"I... I burned some scones," I volunteered.

Rhi stepped in before I could embarrass myself further. "We've started in the kitchen with some basic exploration of intention and simple spellwork. So far, we've determined that kitchen witchery is unlikely to be her specialty."

"I would suggest an affinity study," Davina said.

"Already?" Rhi asked, raising her eyebrows. "She's just barely started!"

"These are unique circumstances, Rhiannon. She isn't a child. She has already been targeted. It is crucial she understand her abilities as soon as possible, especially now that we know the Darkness has not been contained the way we had hoped."

"Is anyone going to tell me what an affinity study is?" I asked, my voice sharper than I intended in my mounting fear and frustration. Why did they insist I come along to this meeting if they were going to insist on talking about me as though I wasn't even there?

My mother turned to me. "It's a way to understand how your magic naturally works. Every witch has her preferred medium, if you will. Rhi's a kitchen witch, and Asteria was a green witch. It doesn't mean they can only work magic in those ways, but it does mean that their magic will flow most powerfully and naturally in that setting. It's a bit complicated, but I promise I'll explain it better when we get home."

"What kind of w—" I began, too overcome with curiosity not to blurt out the first question I could think of, which was, of course, what kind of witch my mother was. But Ostara seemed to have run out of patience for interruptions.

"To the best of our knowledge, the Darkness has gone to ground again, temporarily banished but by no means gone. It went to great lengths to claim you, Wren. Though your means of defending yourself were truly impressive, I do not believe you have deterred the Darkness permanently. We must be prepared for whatever it may try next, and our best hope for that is to understand why it wants you in the first place. We must understand your magic."

The fear I'd successfully kept at bay over the past few days came flooding back through me. I hadn't truly understood what had happened that night on the beach, but I'd hoped, foolishly, I suppose, that I'd somehow managed to put an end to something.

Now, as I stared around the room of solemn, fearful faces staring back at me, I realized that had been a very naive assumption. The only thing that had ended on the beach that night had been any lingering illusions of safety.

The rest of it—the Darkness and its machinations—was only just beginning.

5

We rode home from the Manor in complete silence.

I preferred it this way. Not because I didn't have a million questions—I absolutely did—but because I wasn't ready to handle the answers to any of those questions. I needed time to think. I needed time to absorb the very frightening fact that had drawn us to the Manor in the first place.

The Darkness was not contained. The Darkness was still out there, and it still wanted me.

I don't know what expression was on my face as I spiraled down through these thoughts, but no one felt the need to press me with questions when we got home. My mom smiled tightly at me, her eyes sparkling with repressed pain and worry, and asked if I wanted to talk. When I told her no, that I needed time to think, she looked almost relieved. Even Persi was subdued as we all trudged into the cottage to stew quietly in our own spaces. Rhi retreated to the kitchen, Persi to her bedroom, and my mom out into the garden. And I went up to my little room, where I found Freya perched expectantly on the end of my bed, like she was waiting for me.

"Hi," I croaked when I saw her.

She cocked her head to one side and then scooted over to make room for me. The invitation unhinged me, dissolved my tenuous grasp on my self-control, and I fell onto my bed, bursting into tears. Freya curled up against me, tucking her head under my chin, and purred softly until I'd cried myself out. She didn't huff or try to wriggle away from me when I pulled her closer to me. I felt her purrs slow to match my breathing as I calmed down, felt her rub her head against my jaw in slow, soothing circles. Gradually, my body relaxed, and the sobs shivered rather than wracked through me, and then stopped altogether, leaving me feeling like an overcooked noodle. Soon, I fell asleep and didn't wake until the next morning, when the light was pale and the shadows still deep, like they were clinging to bits of the night as it slipped away with the dawn. I could still feel Freya's warm body pressed up against me. I pushed up onto one arm and found her looking intently at me, as though to say, "Well? Better?"

"Thanks," I whispered to her. "I really needed to get that out, and I didn't want to do it in front of them."

Freya huffed a little breath and bumped her nose against my cheekbone.

"Yeah, I'm done being dramatic," I told her. "Your tolerance was much appreciated."

She slunk out from under my arm and settled into a little loaf, looking at me expectantly. Apparently, she felt she was entitled to an explanation.

"I'm just scared," I said. "I don't know how to protect myself or anyone else. And I think we're going to need protection. The Gray Man isn't trapped, and he isn't gone."

Freya narrowed her eyes and let out a hiss.

"My thoughts exactly."

Freya sat up on her haunches and looked at me imperiously. Then she walked across the bed and up onto my bedside table. She placed a paw lightly on the stack of books and then looked at me pointedly as she batted the book on the top of the pile right onto the bed. I stared first at the book and then at Freya, who looked calmly back.

"Were you always this helpful, and I just didn't notice?" I whispered.

She sniffed impatiently and began to groom herself.

"Right. Well, thanks. And I think you're right. Whining won't help. I need to start learning." Strange that I needed a cat to call me on my bullshit, but it wasn't the strangest thing that had happened to me in the last few days, so I guess I could take it in my stride. But regardless of whether it was really Freya guiding me or not, I couldn't afford to be self-indulgent anymore. I'd given myself one night of fear and doubt and self-pity. Time to pull it together, or I might as well have just invited the Darkness to swallow me up because, at this moment, I was no more than a sitting duck.

I took a very long, very hot shower, and by the time I'd gotten dressed and brushed my hair, I was starting to feel halfway human. As I gathered up my books to head downstairs, I thought I heard a car pulling away from the house. I looked out the window and saw my mom driving down the road into town. I glanced at my phone to check the time and saw she had texted me.

Didn't want to disturb you. Have to meet with the real estate lawyer in Portland. We can talk when I get back. Love you, honey. It's all going to be fine. Somehow.

I'd known about the appointment, but I'd forgotten all about it. Now I felt my heart sinking as I watched her drive away. That feeling I'd had over the last few days, like she was avoiding me, began to intensify. I'd woken up this morning realizing I had to face my new reality head on, but it seemed like my mom wasn't quite there yet.

Luckily, she wasn't the only witch in the house who could help me.

Rhi was sitting in the kitchen when I walked in, a cup of tea by her elbow and a book open on the table in front of her. She looked up at the sound of my approach.

"Wren! I wasn't expecting to see you so early," she said, marking her place in the book and setting it aside. "Would you like some tea?"

"Sure," I said, sliding into the seat beside her with my own stack of books.

"How are you feeling? After yesterday, I mean?" Rhi asked, her eyes probing me anxiously as she spooned tea leaves from a mason jar into a little metal infuser.

I smiled weakly. "I had a kind of... existential crisis last night, I think. But I think I got it out of my system, at least for the moment."

"I'm sorry you faced that alone," Rhi said.

"I wasn't alone. Freya stayed with me."

Rhi smiled and nodded. "None better than a familiar for a job like that."

"Yeah," I agreed. "Anyway, I've decided to stop feeling sorry for myself, and start learning what I can. I don't want to be an easy target anymore." I patted the books.

"We came to similar conclusions, then," Rhi said, setting the steaming cup of tea down in front of me, and taking her seat again. "After listening to the Conclave last night, I'm also determined to focus on your magical education. But I've also come to the conclusion that I've been going about it all wrong."

I frowned. "Rhi, you can't blame yourself just because I suck at baking."

"That's not what I mean. And you don't suck at it, Wren, you just need practice," Rhi snapped. "But your cooking skills aren't the issue here. It's me. I've started in the wrong place. I've started you out the way I would any young witch who hadn't yet shown any predisposition towards a certain kind of magic. I didn't even really think about it. It just seemed natural to begin at the beginning. But the truth is that you're much further along in the development of your powers than a mere child would be, and I ought to have taken that into account."

"I'm glad you think I've developed somehow, because *I'm* not seeing it," I said.

"Wren, if the events on the beach haven't convinced you that you are a Vesper witch through and through, I'm not really sure what else can."

She said the words gently, but there was steel in them, enough to make me lift my head and look her in the eye. She was staring at me with such intensity that I could feel her intention as clearly as I could when I bit into her baking. She was willing me to believe in myself the way she believed in me.

"It's not that I think I have no power," I finally said. "I *know* I have it. I felt it coursing through me that night. The problem is, it seems to be hiding from me. It feels like it only appeared to save my life, you know? Like an adrenaline rush or something. I feel like one of those people who lifts a car off an injured person in an emergency, but can hardly open a pickle jar the rest of the time."

Rhi laughed —the sound was hearty and hoarse and comforting.

"I'm not trying to make a joke," I pointed out.

"I know you aren't, honey, I've just never heard anyone explain it that way before," she said, still chuckling. "And you're exactly right. Our powers often manifest themselves when our instincts take over. It's almost as though we have to stop thinking in order to connect with them, and of course, when you're trying to learn, it's very hard to do that."

"Learning without thinking," I repeated. "Yeah. That basically sounds impossible."

"Well, I promise you, it isn't," Rhi said, squeezing my arm. "Which brings me back to my original point. Yesterday, the Conclave said we ought to consider an affinity study. Did you understand what that meant?"

"I think so. They want to test me for my natural magical talent, right?"

"Exactly. When I set out to teach you, I started with my own affinity because that's where I'm most comfortable. But that's backward. I need to start with your affinity because that's where you're most comfortable. Does that make sense?"

"Yeah, I guess so. But how do I find out what my affinity is?" I asked.

"You already know it," Rhi said.

I just blinked at her. Rhi smiled again.

"You are most likely an elemental witch," she said.

I blinked again. "I'm going to need you to elaborate on that," I said.

"An elemental witch is very much what it sounds like. Your magic works directly with the elements—that is to say, earth, air, water, and fire. Typically, an elemental witch would find herself drawn much more deeply to one of those elements than the others. A fire witch, for example, would find that she is drawn to that element and that it manifests her power the easiest of the four."

"Are there any other elemental witches in our family?" I asked.

"Yes. Asteria was a green witch, which meant that she was deeply connected to the element of Earth. All you need to do is look at our gardens here at Lightkeep to see how her affinity to that element manifested itself," Rhi said.

Automatically, my eye was drawn through the French doors to the gardens beyond, where the flowerbeds exploded in riots of color, and the trees hung heavy and ripe with clusters of blossoms and fruit. I'd accepted the garden as the wonderland it was at first sight. It felt like such a natural part of Lightkeep Cottage that I had never stopped to consider that it might be magic that made it so lush and enchanting. I allowed one of my vivid memories of Asteria to float to the surface of my mind, and all at once, I felt it: that same energy she always had, that joyous spark, that twinkle in her eyes, it lived in that garden. I looked at Rhi, and I knew she could read the sudden wonder on my face as her smile bloomed as slowly and brightly as one of Asteria's flowers.

"Asteria could make a rose blossom in a snowstorm if she chose," Rhi said, still smiling. "Her salves and teas and potions were always particularly potent because her herbs and flowers and seeds had been tended by her hands, and nurtured by her magic. It enhanced all of their properties, and the resulting spells were always the more powerful for it."

"Who else?" I asked.

Rhi hesitated oddly, then said, "Ostara is an elemental witch. She has an affinity for fire."

"That tracks," I said, and Rhi laughed.

"Yes, she is a bit... well, fiery, isn't she?"

"How do I find out what kind of elemental witch I am?" I asked.

"Well, we'll need to start experimenting, but I... I think... well..." Rhi bit her lip like she was steeling herself to say something.

I felt my heart begin to beat a little harder against my ribs. "What is it?"

"I've been thinking about this since the night on the beach. The fact is that a witch can produce extraordinary magic when her life is in danger — our magic is meant to come to our aid, if only to save the vessel in which it is contained. But what you managed to do on the beach—the calling of four elements and the wielding of them in such profound and powerful ways—I think it might mean that you are more than the average elemental witch."

Rhi paused, almost as though to see how these words had affected me, but I couldn't respond. I was still trying to absorb what she was saying to me.

"Wren?"

"Yeah, I... can you please explain?"

"There is a reason the Darkness has been drawn to you. From the time you were a small child, the Darkness saw something in you that piqued its interest. Its determination has never waned. Asteria never knew exactly why, but she knew it was dangerous. That was why she put that protective spell on you, and as long as she lived, it protected you. But even Asteria knew she couldn't protect you forever. I think she was buying you time, Wren, until your powers were strong enough so that you could protect yourself. And that night on the beach, you did."

"Yeah, but I didn't actually know what I was doing!" I said. The panic was mounting inside me, and I did my best to beat it back, to maintain control over my breathing. "I just... called for help, and the elements answered. It was their power, not mine!"

But Rhi was shaking her head. "It was the call that held the power, not the answer. Not to say that the elements aren't powerful—they have a power we can only dream of as witches. But to summon them like that, and for each of them to respond with such force... I've never seen anything like it."

She was speaking softly, gently, but each word felt like a blow to my body, like being battered by ocean waves relentlessly, each one crashing over me before I'd even picked myself up from the last.

"I think we can conclude, then, that your connection to all four physical elements is powerful. We should test them each individually, to compare them; but I expect we will find your power to be formidable with each one. But even then, our affinity study would not be complete. When non-witches think of the elements, they think only of four: earth, water, air, and fire. But there is a fifth element, Wren, powerful in its own way, and far more ephemeral and rare to connect with. That element is called spirit."

I swallowed in my haste to answer, and felt the hot tea scald my throat all the way down. "Spirit like... like ghosts?" I choked.

"It's a bit more complicated than that, but that's how it often manifests, yes. Bernadette, for example, is an elemental witch who connects deeply with spirit. It's why she was able to communicate with Sarah Claire, the reason she was able, essentially, to pull Sarah across the transom and maintain a connection with her, even after she had closed her circle. It is also the reason behind her remarkable abilities as an oracle. Glimpses into the future and the past can only come from a deep connection to spirit."

I frowned. "Okay. But what does that have to do with me?"

"We all know that the Darkness is interested in you," Rhi began carefully, and then sighed. "Oh, why are we dancing around this. We all know how serious it is. The Darkness went to extraordinary lengths to capture you, and that means you must have powers far beyond the ordinary. It has to be something incredibly rare. I was thinking about your control of the first four elements, and then I wondered: was it possible you could also have a connection to the element of spirit? And if that's the case, you are not just an elemental witch. You are a *pentamaleficus*... a witch of the five."

"I... but no spirits came to help me," I pointed out, trying to keep the hysteria out of my voice. "The other elements did, but it's not like an avenging horde of ghosts showed up."

"Ah, but the other elements showed up because you called them. You weren't aware spirit was one of the elements, so you didn't think to call on it. But if you had... would it have answered?"

I couldn't answer that question. No one could.

Rhi smiled a little at my non-answer. "This is what we must discover. A pentamaleficus is a rare thing—perhaps a once-in-a-century gift. And given the Darkness' interest in you, I think it's a very real possibility." She was keeping her voice deliberately calm and soothing, speaking the words that were shaking me to the core as though they were a lullaby.

My mind reeled, not because I thought her words felt impossible, but because they felt terrifyingly probable. I'd been ready to retort that I had no connection to spirit at all, had never had so much as a brush with activity; but then I realized, with a start, that that wasn't true. Hadn't I heard a voice calling only the other night? Hadn't I seen my dead grandmother from my bedroom window?

"Okay," I said under my breath. "Okay, okay, okay." The word just kept coming, and I wasn't even sure what I meant. That I was okay? I didn't feel okay. That everything would be okay? I didn't really believe that either. Rhi could hear my distress.

"Breathe, Wren, honey," she murmured.

My body took her advice automatically, sucking in huge lungfuls of air, and blowing them out slowly until the room stopped spinning. I looked up at Rhi, ready to tell her that I'd seen Asteria's ghost, but I couldn't bring myself to make her look any more anxious than she already was. Instead, I asked, "So, now what?"

"Now, we need to decide how to test your spirit affinity. I think I should talk to Xiomara. She's the most powerful spirit witch in Sedgwick Cove."

This statement surprised me enough to pull me up out of my panic. "I thought Xiomara was a kitchen witch, like you?"

Rhi smiled. "She is. But her affinity for the kitchen is different than mine. She can explain it better than I can. What would you think about going to see her, maybe tomorrow, if she's available?"

"Sure," I said, and the thought actually calmed me a little. Xiomara had a very commanding presence. I'd found it intimidating at first, but now the idea of talking to her made me feel better. Xiomara was always so sure of herself, so confident in her answers and her abilities. She would know what to do. I looked at Rhi again, and found I could return her smile. "That's a good idea. Will you ask her?"

"Of course," Rhi said. "She'll be busy this early, no doubt, prepping to open the cafe for the day; but, I'll stop by later on my way to Shadowkeep."

"And what should I do?" I asked.

"I found this book for you," Rhi said. "It's all about affinities, and I think it might help if you read it."

I was so relieved that she wasn't dragging me into the backyard to start calling the elements that I snatched the book up gratefully. "Sounds good," I said. "Knowledge is power, right?"

"That's right," she said, with a little nod of approval at my attitude. "And Wren, honey..." She reached over and took my hand, giving it a gentle squeeze. "We're going to figure this out. We're going to do better than protect you—we're going to help you protect yourself. Okay?"

Her face was so fiercely protective that it put a lump in my throat that I had to swallow against before I could answer. "Thanks, Rhi."

"And when I say 'we,' I mean all of us," she said. "Persi, your mom, all of us. Persi can be a bit... well, prickly, but she does care about you. And your mother loves you more than her own self. None of us are going to leave you undefended. Maybe the Darkness has a faulty memory, or maybe it simply didn't learn the lesson of its run-ins with our ancestors, but the Darkness is messing with the wrong coven."

The mention of my mom triggered a memory from the previous night. "Rhi, what kind of witch is my mom?"

Rhi's expression faltered a little. "A confused one, disconnected from her magic," she said finally.

"That's not what I meant," I said, but Rhi put up a hand.

"I know. But I think you should ask her about it. I don't want to overstep any more than I already have," she said. "I couldn't let her drag her feet when it came to your education, but as far as dealing with her own baggage... well, she needs to do that in her own time."

There was a sinking feeling of disappointment in my chest, but I didn't argue.

"Now, how about some breakfast to go with that tea?" Rhi asked.

"Sounds great."

Rhi got up and started zipping around the kitchen, back in her element. I started leafing through the book she'd given me as I sipped my tea, and was glad to find that it had been written with beginners in mind. My phone buzzed against my leg, and I saw that I had two texts waiting for me. The first was from Eva, reminding me about the meeting at the playhouse that night. I'd nearly forgotten about it, but responded that I would be there. The second was from Nova.

I need to talk to you.

I frowned. It was the first I'd heard from Nova since that night on the beach. I was simultaneously relieved to get a message, and anxious about the content.

Sure, what's up? I replied.

Not over text. We need to meet up. Tonight?

I'll be at the playhouse for the pageant rehearsal. Can you meet me there?

Shit, is that tonight? Yeah, maybe. I'll let you know.

I waited a few more minutes, but my phone stayed quiet. I guess I'd have to wait until tonight to find out what Nova Claire had to tell me.

6

Sedgwick Cove was famous for a couple of things. The first, obviously, was for being Maine's version of Salem, Massachusetts —a sort of mecca for witchcraft history and modern-day witchy vibes. The second was the Sedgwick Cove Playhouse.

The playhouse was set on a rocky outcropping overlooking the sea. From the outside, tourists could see miles of scenic coastline, sandy beaches, and several lighthouses. And once inside, they could see some of the best regional theater outside of the major East coast metropolises. For decades, the Sedgwick Cove Playhouse had been the home of The Wandering Mistrals, a theater company known for lush, elaborate musical productions, stunning sets, and headliner talent. All of this was thanks to Vincent Meyers, a flashy Broadway producer who had grown up whiling away his boyhood summers on the beaches of Maine. After falling in love with and marrying a woman from Sedgwick Cove, he decided to buy the land in the 1960s and turn it into a theatrical vacation destination. His connections, talent, and of course, piles of money, meant that he usually got what he wanted. The playhouse had been a tourist attraction ever since, and was still owned by the same family.

I'd known about the Sedgwick Cove Playhouse for a long time. Being a local theater kid, I would have known about it anyway. It had a national reputation, and was way up on my best friend Poe's shortlist of summer stock theaters she hoped to audition for when she was in college. I stopped to snap a quick selfie in front of the place and texted it to Poe, because I knew she'd kill me if I didn't. She responded in about five seconds.

OMGGGGGGGGG I'M SO JEALOUS! Are you seeing a show?!

No, just a meeting for a town festival thing.

Let's see one when I come visit you! They're doing Sweeney Todd this summer, and you know my Sondheim obsession!

Sounds good, I replied. Truthfully, I had mixed feelings as I stared up at the building in front of me. I'd never seen a play there, never even set foot in the place, as far as I knew. But what I did know was that my mother had a very complicated history with the place, for one very specific reason: my father.

My father had never been in my life, and for the most part, I didn't feel the absence of him. After all, it's hard to miss something you've never had. I had gotten curious growing up, naturally, but it took years of wheedling and coaxing before my mother would surrender enough details to piece together the story. My father had been a professional actor, a company member of the Wandering Mistrals the summer before I was born. He was older than my mother by a few years, and apparently he was very dashing, very talented, and very married. Not that my mother had known this last bit until afterward. He decided to keep that little tidbit to himself as he swept her off her feet in a swoon-worthy summer romance. My mom had been working her way through nursing school at the time, and had picked up a part-time gig in the box office; and there he was, with a dazzling toothpaste commercial smile, and a seemingly endless supply of charm.

"And there I was, young and stupid and desperately in love with him from the first time he spoke to me," my mom had said one night, after she had allowed herself a second glass of wine.

"So it was love at first sight?" I had asked in the way only a naive ten-year-old could.

My mom had smiled at me sadly. "I thought so. But infatuation and love are two different things, and I learned that the hard way."

After a two-month fling, my mother had a suitcase packed for New York City. She was sure he would ask her to come back with him when his contract was up, and she wanted to be ready. Instead, he had rumpled her hair like a precocious kid, and laughed off the idea.

"Oh, kid, that's sweet, it really is. I'm flattered," he'd said, like she'd asked for his autograph at the stage door, "but we were just having a bit of fun, weren't we?"

"A bit of fun," my mom repeated in a hollow voice. I hated that voice. I hated it so much that I never asked her about him again.

But I *had* tried to stalk him on the internet. The only place I could find any trace of him was on IMDB, where it listed him in a few small television parts, mostly on soap operas. Then he just... vanished. Nothing listed after 2008, which also happened to be the year I was born. It was an odd coincidence, and made him feel like even more of a mystery. I would sometimes watch commercials and tv shows searching for his face—the face I had memorized in the one headshot I could find of him online. I never saw him anywhere.

Now, as I stood in front of the playhouse, I felt a strange pit in my stomach. How odd that a place I'd never been could hold so much significance in my life. I'd felt that way about the entire town of Sedgwick Cove only a short time ago, but that sensation had been swiftly followed by one of belonging—of rightness. I belonged to Lightkeep Cottage, to that sweeping beach, to the crashing waves and the brine-scented air. But this place, I thought, as I looked up at the front doors... I didn't feel a special connection here.

One of the doors had been propped open with a folding chair, and I slipped quietly into the front lobby. Instantly, I felt my body relax. Okay, I may not have felt drawn to this building, but it was still a theater, after all, and all theaters, from Broadway stages to tiny church halls, are the same at heart. They smell the same: sawdust and paint and hairspray and racks of recycled costumes. The wings are always crammed with the same things: dinged up rehearsal furniture, and boxes of random props and a jungle of ropes, and pulleys and wiring dotted with half-empty coffee cups. I took a deep breath, and felt my body relax. I tried to savor the feeling, because I knew, once I walked through the doors from the lobby to the main theater, I'd be on the defensive again. I might know in my bones that I belong in

Sedgwick Cove, but I still had to convince the rest of the teenage population.

"Can I help you?"

The bored voice seemed to come from nowhere, and I let out a humiliating squeak of surprise. I spun around, and noticed for the first time that there was someone sitting in the box office booth. He didn't even look up from his phone as I approached.

"Uh, yeah, I'm here for the meeting?" I said, turning the statement into a question.

The boy looked up and smirked at me. "You sure about that?" he asked.

"Yes," I said, the word coming out with a snap in it like a mousetrap, partly because I was annoyed at my own lack of confidence, and partly because I was taken aback by his appearance. The boy was lanky and tall, looking like he'd folded himself into the tiny space with difficulty. His features were very angular—protruding cheekbones, a square chin, and a long, slightly crooked nose. Even his mouth, when he smiled, made a sharp slash in his face. But it was his eyes that truly caught my attention, because one of them was the greenish blue of the ocean, and the other was a startling shade of golden brown. I realized that I'd been staring at him for several silent seconds, and I felt my cheeks flood with color as I dropped my gaze to my feet. "Yes," I repeated in a sheepish voice.

"You just need to sign in," the boy said, gesturing toward a clipboard with his elbow, and returning his own gaze to the phone in his hands.

"Right. No problem," I muttered, scrawling my name with the attached pen.

"Straight through those doors," the boy said when I had put the pen down. I mumbled my thanks, and walked straight through the swinging double doors.

The theater was a traditional proscenium space, with a thrust stage on one end and rows of audience seating with those red velvet seats that snap up aggressively when you aren't sitting in them. About two dozen teenagers were spread out in the first few rows, legs dangling over arms of seats, and phones in hands. Zale MacDowell stood up on the stage beside a large writing pad on an easel and three huge Tupperware bins. His face was flushed with excitement, and he kept rubbing his hands together, like an overconfident movie villain. He caught sight of me walking up the aisle, and his face split into a grin.

"Wren! Eva told me you were coming!"

I wished he hadn't said my name out loud. Every head in the room turned, every pair of eyes latched onto me, so I felt like an actor in a blinding spotlight making a dramatic and unexpected entrance from the back of the house. I did my best not to cringe as a hurried the rest of the way up the aisle, and met Zale at the lip of the stage.

"Sorry I'm late," I said, though it couldn't have been a minute or two past seven. "Did I miss anything?"

"No, we're just about to start. Have a seat!"

I turned and saw Eva waving at me. I sank into the seat next to her, still feeling the weight of everyone's gazes. Behind me, a volley of whispering had started up among the other kids.

"Great idea, asking me here. I feel very included and not at all like a carnival sideshow attraction," I said with a big fake smile.

Eva chuckled. "Like I told you earlier, you can either hide away and let the rumors tell the story, or you can show up and help out and let everyone see how boring and normal you are."

"Could we just do a quick demonstration of magical skill and get it over with?" I murmured, thinking about the scones at home. Rhi had tried to salvage them with frosting and placed them on a plate, as though anyone would be tempted by the culinary equivalent of vanilla coated hockey pucks. I glanced around me, and realized I didn't see Nova among the other kids. "Hey, where's Nova?" I asked.

Eva shrugged, and her brows pulled together. "I don't know. I thought she might come, but then she didn't respond when I offered to pick her up."

I frowned. She'd sounded like there was something important she'd wanted to tell me. So why hadn't she bothered to show up? But there was no time to dwell on it as Zale started calling for everyone's attention, flapping his hands like he might take off. When everyone stopped muttering and turned to face him, he smiled again, taking a deep breath.

"Hello everyone! Thanks for coming. When I got voted chair of the Litha pageant committee, I promised that I would make this the best midsummer celebration yet, and I intend to keep that promise!"

"Just for the record, no one voted for you. You won by default, because no one else wanted to do it," called the broad-shouldered guy sitting in the row behind me. I thought his name might have been Sergei, but I couldn't swear to it.

Zale's smile froze on his face, but only for a moment. "Thank you for that clarification, Sergei. Regardless of how I wound up at the helm of this project, it is still going to be the greatest pageant this town has ever seen!" He thrust his fist into the air, as though expecting everyone to shout "HUZZAH!" His exuberant gesture was met with silence.

Someone cleared their throat. Zale sighed and lowered his fist.

"Okay, fine, moving on. To start, I thought that we could—"

The door at the back of the theater swung open and the boy from the box office strolled down the aisle, munching on an apple. He gave a casual sort of wave to Zale, and slid into a seat toward the back of the theater.

"Oh, hey, Luca. Thanks for unlocking the place for us."

"No sweat," the boy called Luca replied. "It's 7:15, so I locked the doors again like you asked."

Eva turned to Zale. "You had him lock the doors? Why?"

Zale rolled his eyes and huffed. "Because obviously I don't want to give away any of the details. I want the town to be surprised. I want them to be blown away!"

Eva opened her mouth to say something snarky, but I interrupted her by asking, "Who is that?"

"Him? Oh, that's Luca Meyers."

"Wait, Meyers? As in the Meyers who own this place?"

"That's right. Hence the keys."

"He wasn't at the bonfire, was he?" I asked, hoping Eva would miss the subtext, which was that if he'd been at the bonfire, I *definitely* would have noticed him.

Based on Eva's smirk, I failed with the whole subtext thing. "He doesn't live here during the school year. They only come up for the summers." She rolled her eyes, as though she couldn't think of anything more ridiculous than someone coming to the beach for the summer.

I had about five hundred more questions about Luca, but I bit them back as someone in the group raised their hand.

"Yes, Petra?" Zale called, looking delighted at the engagement.

"Look, no offense, but what could we possibly give away that everyone in the town doesn't already know?" Petra asked. "I mean, we've used the same script, the same costumes, the same props every single year since... forever."

There was a round of mumbling and nodding. Apparently, Petra wasn't the only one who felt that way.

Zale was not daunted by the general pall of negativity. "I'm glad you brought that up, Petra! You're absolutely right! I know our parents and grandparents insist it's traditional, but let's be honest, this pageant is tired. It needs a new twist. And that's why we're here. We're not just assigning parts and handing out scripts tonight. We're reinventing the pageant!" Zale turned and wrote the words, "Reinventing the Pageant" in big red letters on the easel pad. He embellished it with half a dozen exclamation points, and underlined it three times for good measure. He looked expectantly at the group, who stared blankly back.

"So... how are we reinventing it?" a girl asked.

Zale's smile slipped. "Well, that's... that's what we're gonna figure out. I need your ideas. Let's start brainstorming!"

The answering silence spiraled. Everyone was looking at each other, waiting for someone—anyone—to speak up. Up on the stage, Zale was deflating like a sad balloon. I felt like a kid in class, watching the teacher practically beg for interaction. I'd always been the kid to take pity on the teacher and raise my hand, just to see the hope spring back into their eyes.

I was still that kid. My hand shot up.

"Yes! Thank you, Wren!" Zale sang, the relief palpable on his face.

"Uh..." I swallowed hard, not enjoying the sensation of all the eyes that had now turned to stare at me, and knowing most of them would probably roll when they heard what I had to say. "Sorry, I'm sure everyone else already knows everything about this pageant, but since this is my first summer here in a long time, could you... refresh my memory?" I tried to ignore the sniggering.

"She doesn't even know the story of Litha?" someone muttered.

"I wouldn't mind hearing about it either," said another voice from behind me. I turned to see Luca propping his feet up, like he was getting ready for story time.

"Why would you care?" Sergei asked. He was looking at Luca with a decidedly ugly expression. I was taken aback to see him glare that way, but Luca simply shrugged with an easy smile.

"I don't usually make it up for the summer until 4th of July weekend. I've never seen the pageant before," he said.

But Zale didn't seem to mind. His eyes lit up like they had that night at the bonfire, when he'd taken it upon himself to tell us all the Sedgwick Cove origin story, and I knew he loved any opportunity to geek out about this town.

"Why don't I just give a quick recap for Wren and Luca, and everyone else, start getting your creative juices flowing!"

"Ew," Petra muttered.

Zale cleared his throat theatrically, and the story began.

7

"Litha goes by many names. Midsommar, midsummer, the summer solstice. It's the longest day of the year, marking the start of the shortening of days until Yule, which of course, is the shortest day of the year. It's a time to celebrate fertility and harvest and light and growth. There are lots of ways to celebrate Litha—you'll find not a single coven in Sedgwick Cove celebrates it exactly the same way. But one thing we all do is come together for the pageant.

"The story of the pageant is always the same, the battle of the Oak King and the Holly King. The Oak King represents the sun, the warmth, the time of the year when daylight has the upper hand, and rules over all. The Holly King, on the other hand, represents the darkness—oh, uh... not that Darkness. I just mean like, nighttime," Zale said quickly, perhaps noticing the way I stiffened in my seat, the way my heart had begun to pound. I could feel everyone staring at me again. I tried to ignore them, keeping my attention on Zale, and trying to appear the rapt audience he craved.

Zale went on, "The Holly King rules over the second part of the year, when the darkness rules over the day until Yule, or the Winter Solstice, the shortest day of the year; and the power is returned once again to the Oak King. At dusk on Litha, the Holly King challenges the Oak King to a mighty battle for control of the earth. That's what the pageant acts out—the battle for domination! When it ends, we position the Wheel of the Year at the top of the cliff above the beach, light it on fire, and roll it down to the sea."

Zale looked around at us all expectantly, as though to say, "Is that the coolest thing you've ever heard?" Sergei launched into a sarcastic slow clap. Eva silenced him with a look.

"Why are you even here if you're just going to be an asshole?" Eva asked him.

Sergei shrugged, coloring. "Because if I don't help with the pageant my mother will disown me."

"Oh, so you're here because Mommy said you had to come?" another boy sneered.

Eva rounded on him, too. "Yeah, and so am I. And so are you. Every single person in this room is here because their mother or their grandmother or their auntie said they would hex them otherwise. Now shut up and let us get on with it, Ethan."

The boy named Ethan muttered something under his breath, but no one else argued. Evidently, there was enough truth in what Eva said that no one wanted to contradict her.

"Uh, thanks, Zale," I said into the awkward silence. "That, uh... clears that up. My next question is, what's the usual pageant like?"

Zale cleared his throat, but it was Eva who answered. "Oh, anyone in this room could probably recite the whole thing from memory by the time they were five years old," she said, chuckling. "It's only the cheesiest thing anyone's ever heard. Although, to be fair, when I was little, I thought it was awesome."

A girl stood up suddenly in the row behind me, grinning. "Come forth, oh harbinger of night! I knowst thou art here. Show thyself!" she called in a deep, melodramatic voice.

Three other kids jumped to their feet. "I am no harbinger! I am King of The Darkness, and thou wilt bend the knee or feel my wrath!"

The entire group of kids then shouted at the top of their lungs, "I kneel to no one. Thy shadow crown is naught to me!"

A few tried to keep going, but they'd mostly broken off into raucous laughter, along with some truly terrible fight choreography. Zale seemed to be deflating like a balloon up on the stage, watching his meeting devolve into chaos.

I ignored the full-scale anarchy now breaking out in the seats, and hopped up onto the stage. "What about the props and costumes and stuff? What are we working with?"

Zale drooped even more. "Right here." He popped the top from one of the plastic bins, and lifted out a crown and a robe. The robe was faded purple velvet, with a moth-eaten faux-fur collar and frayed ribbons dangling from the cuffs. The crown had crumbling Styrofoam horns glued to it, and several blank spots where plastic gemstones had fallen off.

"These are..." I searched for a word that could sound complimentary without being a complete lie.

"It's okay," Zale sighed, plopping down on the other bin in defeat. "You can say it."

I sat beside him. "They're in rough shape, but that's not your fault. I mean, if all your families make such a big deal about this pageant, why don't they buy you guys some better materials?"

"Because they're all obsessed with tradition. They like seeing the same dilapidated crap they wore when they did the pageant a hundred years ago," Zale said. "Every year the kids are bored out of their minds, but no one ever does anything about it. I thought, since I was voted director this year, that I might finally be able to convince people to put some effort in and switch it up. You can see how well that's gone, so far."

"Don't give up so easily! I'm sure we can... well..." I looked at the crown still clutched in my hands. Some gold paint had already flaked off onto my skin.

"See? What's the point?" Zale said. "We'll just do the same old thing we've done for a million years."

"There's got to be a way to... hang on." My eyes, ranging out over the seats again in search of inspiration, had lighted on Luca Meyers; and an idea popped into my head. "I'll be right back," I told Zale, as I jumped off the stage and headed up the aisle.

Luca watched me as I approached, and I felt myself suddenly feeling awkward. Why did I walk like that? What was I doing with my arms? Did I always slouch this much?

"Luca, right?" I asked, when I stumbled to a halt beside his seat.

"Yeah," he said. "And you're Wren, right? Wren Vesper?"

I blinked. "How did you know that?"

He smiled. "You signed in at the box office, remember?"

A blush of mortification flooded my cheeks. "Oh. Right. Anyway, I was just wondering, does the playhouse have a costume collection on site, or do you rent everything?"

Luca looked surprised at the question, but readily replied, "There's a whole costume department. Most of our costumes are made in-house, and stored here as well. Sometimes they get rented out to other theaters, but usually most everything is here. Why?"

"How about props and scenery?"

"Generally, unless it's something really complex, all that stuff gets constructed here for each show. We've got full shops out on the other side of the parking lot."

"Do you think it would be okay if we... maybe borrowed some stuff? I'm not sure if Zale has any kind of budget, but maybe we could promote the theater—call it out as a sponsor of the pageant or something?"

Luca shrugged. "I can ask my dad. He's always looking for new ways to drum up publicity."

"Okay, thanks," I said. "Uh... let me know, I guess."

"How?"

"Huh?"

"How should I let you know?"

It was the most obvious question for him to ask, and yet I felt completely blindsided by it. For some reason I couldn't quite pinpoint, the thought of offering him my phone number made me want to sink straight through the floor and never resurface. It was the rational thing to do, by far the most efficient way to pass along information to me, and I absolutely could not bring myself to do it. Instead, I said, "Um, I'll stop by here tomorrow around lunchtime. Will you be here?"

"Sure," Luca said. "Not at the boxoffice, though. My uncle will have me landscaping out near the parking lot."

"Okay, I'll uh... I'll see you there," I said, and for some reason I couldn't fathom, I waved at him like he wasn't sitting five feet in front of me. "Uh, thanks. Bye."

I walked back up to the front of the theater, feeling my face burning and wildly grateful that everyone was too caught up in their ridiculous pageant reenactment to notice me.

"What was that about?" Zale asked.

"I asked Luca if he thought we might be able to use some costumes and stuff from the playhouse. He's going to let me know."

"Hey, that's a great idea!" Zale said, perking up at once.

"Is it really? To be honest, I can't believe no one ever thought to ask that before," I said. "It seems kind of obvious."

Zale snorted. "Too proud. The Meyers family isn't a coven family, they're incomers. Sedgwick Cove is very clannish when it comes to incomers."

"Isn't that kind of a cliche?" I asked. "I mean, the whole little village 'they ain't from here' thing?"

"In other towns, sure, but here it's a matter of safety," Zale said, looking serious now.

"Sure, maybe it was three hundred years ago, but it's not illegal to be a witch anymore," I said. "I mean, he's sitting back there listening to us talk about covens and stuff. What's the big deal?"

"Maybe not illegal, no, but it can still be dangerous," Zale said.

"How could it—?"

"Just ask yourself this," Zale interrupted, his expression quite serious, "Would you ever tell anyone back in Portland what happened at the lighthouse?"

The question startled me, but I thought about it for a moment before answering, truthfully, "No."

"Why not?"

I thought again. "Because I wouldn't want to scare them," I said finally.

Zale nodded with grim satisfaction. "That's right. What we can do—I mean what we can *really* do—would scare a lot of people. And scared people do bad things, sometimes. I mean, what were witch trials but sheer paranoia?

"Patriarchy and religious zealotry?" I suggested.

Zale raised an eyebrow, and I put my hands up in surrender. "Sorry, just a joke. No, you're right. I get it. We have more reason than most to be wary of outsiders. But do you think it's okay if I take a look anyway, if Luca's uncle says yes? Even the tourists come to the pageant. It's not like the pageant itself is a secret. I mean, we advertise it, don't we?"

"Yeah, I'm sure it's fine," Zale said. Then he walked back to the edge of the stage, and tried unsuccessfully for several minutes to get the rest of the kids under control, until Eva took pity on him, stuck two fingers in her mouth, and whistled loudly. Everyone froze, startled.

"Okay, can everyone just chill, please? Wren's got some good ideas for updating the pageant, but we'll need to work out the details. In the meantime, let's get the parts sorted out, and decide when our first rehearsal will be."

Zale read down a list of parts, assigning them to the kids who had shown up. Sergei and Ethan were assigned the parts of the Oak King and the Holly King, which immediately launched a secondary bout of fake fighting.

"I didn't assign you a part because I didn't know you were coming until this morning," Zale said, "but you can always be one of the wood nymphs."

I shot a look at the flower crowns made from plastic leis and shook my head. "It's fine. I'm much happier behind the scenes. How about I be your production manager?"

"I... don't know what that is," Zale admitted.

"It means you just focus on getting the actors into character. I'll handle the other details, okay?"

Zale grinned. "You're hired. I mean, not actually hired, because I can't pay you, but—"

"I know, I know. Don't worry, I'm volunteering my services," I said.

"Great!" Zale launched himself at me in a violent hug, and then went to hand out scripts. I put a hand on his arm.

"Since everyone agrees the script is a bit... well, ridiculous, what do you think about switching it up a bit?" I asked him.

"You mean like, rewrite it? I'm really not good at that kind of stuff," Zale said.

"Hm. I'm not really either. Can I have a copy anyway, though? Then at least I can read it and see if anything comes to me," I said, and he happily handed over to me the entire stack of scripts. Then he set the rehearsal for the next evening, and finally let everyone go.

"See you tomorrow," Luca said, as I passed him to start my ride home. I decided the safest response was just to nod.

As I pedaled along the shore road, my mind was spinning with everything I'd learned about the Litha pageant. If we were counting on that pathetic box of costumes and the theatrical talents of Ethan and Sergei to pull this off, we were definitely in trouble. There had to be a way to reimagine it all, to bring it to life. I didn't have much confidence in my magic, despite what all the other kids thought, but theater? *That* I knew like the back of my hand. My imagination came to life like a movie, as I envisioned an epic battle that would enthrall the watching audience, and make the Midsummer Festival the most memorable of all time. I was so engrossed that I almost sped right past the gate of Lightkeep Cottage.

Inside, my mom and Rhi were sitting on the floor in the living room going through some boxes.

"Hi baby," my mom said as I walked in.

"Hey," I said, tossing my bag on the couch, and coming to sit beside her. "How did it go with the lawyer?"

"Good. Just boring real estate stuff—leases and contracts. But I think it should all be sorted out now. Just waiting on a few things to be signed."

"Were you there all day?"

"No, just for a couple of hours this morning. But then I had some stuff to settle over at the hospital, so that took a while, then I hit awful traffic coming back." She said it all with a slightly desperate air, like she was trying to justify her absence to me.

"Well, that all sounds miserable," I said, trying to sound sympathetic. "I'm glad you're finally home."

The word hit strangely, I could tell, coming out of my mouth. Her face twitched with a momentary expression of distress, but she composed it quickly enough that I could pretend I hadn't noticed.

"Rhi told me you... you talked a little about affinities today?" she asked, sounding tentative.

I tried to catch Rhi's eye, but she was keeping her gaze doggedly on the photo album in her hands.

"Yeah. Yeah, I'm doing some reading about it," I hedged. Had Rhi told my mother about her theory that I might be a pentamaleficus? I had no idea, but for some reason I didn't want to be the one to bring it up, probably because my mother already looked so frazzled that I couldn't bear to be the one to make it worse. Instead, I said, "So I guess we can start testing them, to see how I should study magic moving forward."

"That's... that's great, honey. And I... I promise as soon as I get through all of this... this moving stuff, I'll be right here to... to help." The words were right, but the delivery was wrong. She sounded almost panicked. She seemed barely able to look at me, her eyes darting only sporadically up to my face, focusing instead on the box in her lap. I decided to change the subject before she lost her grip on the remaining threads of her self-control.

"What is all this stuff?"

"Oh, just some photo albums and memorabilia we had in storage. Rhi's helping me sort through it all," she said. She tried to smile at me, but all she looked was exhausted.

"Mom, all this can wait," I said. "Why don't you get some sleep?"

She opened her mouth to argue with me, but a yawn betrayed her immediately, and she stifled it with the back of her hand. "I know, I will. We're almost done."

"You've been running yourself ragged. I wish you'd let me come back to Portland to help you pack."

She waved me off. "Absolutely not. You've got enough to do, starting your magical education. You're behind, and it's my fault. Besides, I broke down and hired movers. They're even going to take the stuff we don't have room for here and store it for us, until we can decide what we want to do with it."

"I'd feel better if you let me help," I pressed.

"And I'd feel better if you started learning to protect yourself," my mom replied, glaring at me.

I sighed. There was no point in arguing with her.

"Where are you coming from?" my mom asked, in a clear attempt to change the subject. I let her.

"I was over at the playhouse. They were hosting a planning meeting for the Litha pageant, and Zale asked me if I would help out."

If I hadn't known my mother so well, I never would have noticed the tiny signs of stress at the mention of the playhouse; the way her shoulders rose just a bit toward her ears, and how her fingers fumbled the stack of picture frames she was organizing.

"That's a great idea," my mom said, in a determinedly even voice. "You're wonderful at organizing shows, and that pageant can use all the help it can get."

Rhi and my mom looked at each other, and burst out laughing.

"I'm missing the joke," I said, looking between them.

"Oh it's just... well, there was one year when Asteria was in charge of the pageant," Rhi said, still laughing, "and she forced Persi to play the Oak King."

"Oh God," I said, trying to imagine Persi agreeing to such a thing.

Rhi was trying to tell the story, but she and my mother were laughing so hard now, that the words were coming out in choked gasps. "And when the battle started... the boy playing the Holly King... hit her in the arm with his staff by accident..."

But Rhi couldn't say anything else. Tears were rolling down her cheeks.

"Persi punched him in the face. Knocked him out cold, in front of the whole crowd," my mother managed to say, between peals of laughter. "And then walked off stage. Two of the wood nymphs had to put the beards on and act out the rest of the battle, while the poor kid was dragged off the platform."

I snorted. "Why does nothing about this story surprise me?" I asked, but Rhi and my mother were lost in their mutual laughter, and I couldn't get another word of sense out of them.

"Okay, well, I guess I'll head up," I said, giving up. "I've got some homework to do anyway."

"Homework?" my mom asked, momentarily distracted and wiping tears of mirth from her cheeks.

I smiled and pointed at Rhi who added, still chuckling, "I found another book on affinities in the library. I've put it next to your bed. You can start on that one after you finish the one I gave you this morning."

I gave Rhi a military salute, which made her giggle again, and trudged up the stairs. The pageant would be a good distraction from all the anxiety about my magic and the Darkness. I needed a project, something I could turn to with confidence, something I knew I could handle at least as well, if not better, than those around me. If I could feel like an asset rather than a liability in this one little thing, I might just get through this summer. I let my imagination begin to wander again, teeming with images of woodland nymphs and frost fairies. It was like Shakespeare's A Midsummer Night's Dream —we had to enchant our audience, like Puck and his love of magic, only hopefully a bit less chaotic. Could we even add a touch of real magic? Was that even allowed? After all, we had a cast full of real witches...

I was so distracted when I opened my door that I'd tossed my stuff onto my bed, and was halfway through pulling my sweatshirt off before I realized I wasn't alone.

Someone was sitting in my desk chair, staring at me from out of the darkness.

8

"GAH!" I shrieked, the sweatshirt still pulled halfway over my head. My glasses, catching as I tugged, skidded across the floor, and landed at the feet of the unexpected figure.

"Calm down, Vesper, it's only me!" hissed a voice. "Stop shouting before someone comes running!"

Though it was hushed and tense, I knew that voice. I extracted myself from the sweatshirt, tossed it aside, and switched on the light.

"Nova? What the hell are you doing here? You scared me half to death!"

Nova Claire bent her silky blonde head, scooped up my glasses, and held them out to me. I took them and thrust them back on my face, my heart still beating so hard I could hear it in my own ears. Nova was one of the last people I'd ever expect to find just sitting in my room unannounced, not least because I wasn't entirely sure she even liked me.

"How did you get in here?" I asked. I couldn't see my mom or Rhi letting someone into my room without even telling me, although I wouldn't have put it past Persi.

But Nova cocked a thumb over her shoulder at the open window, around which the curtains were billowing in the salty evening air.

"Through the side garden, up the rose trellis, across the porch roof, and in through your window. You really should lock that, you know."

"Clearly," I said, sinking on to my bed as my breathing finally began to slow down. "You could have just come down to the meeting at the playhouse if you wanted to see me. It would have been slightly harder to scare the shit out of me, but I'm sure you could have managed it, if you wanted to."

"Look, I'm sorry about lying in wait like a stalker, okay? It wasn't actually my first choice. I was planning to go down to the playhouse, but something came up."

As my eyes adjusted and I was able to see Nova—*really* see her—my heart leaped into overdrive again. "What's wrong?"

"Wrong?" she snapped. "Why should anything be wrong?"

I would have laughed if I wasn't so startled at her appearance. Nova was usually the epitome of cool and unconcerned, a walking poster child for designer ennui. But tonight, in the yellow light from my bedside lamp she looked... well, freaked out. Her eyes were wide and ringed with the purple, bruise-like shadows of sleeplessness. Her hair, usually silky and perfectly straight, was pulled into a messy bun on top of her head, and the strands that had escaped the hair tie hung limply around her face. Her eye makeup was smudged, like she'd applied it yesterday, and hadn't bothered to wash her face. She was also wearing sweatpants in public—I mean it was probably a $500 matching sweatsuit from a well-known designer, but still.

But most startling of all was the spun glass fragility she was trying to hide behind a truculent scowl. She was vulnerable, and she was pissed about it. I thought about what Eva had told me at the cafe the previous day, about how rumors were flying about me and the Claires. I would have expected Nova to face them defiantly, middle fingers flying, but the Nova in front of me looked totally beaten down. She was also sneaking into my bedroom at night, so this was hardly going to be a casual, friendly chat.

"Nova. Seriously. What's wrong?" I repeated.

Nova bit her lip, and jumped up from the chair, starting to pace. "Dammit," she muttered. "I shouldn't have come here. This was a stupid idea."

"Why don't you tell me the idea, and I'll decide whether it's stupid or not," I suggested, sitting down on the edge of my bed. I was burning with curiosity, but I did my best to appear very calm and collected, as a counterpoint to her almost manic energy. It seemed to help. She looked at me as she was pacing, and gradually her steps slowed. She let out a sigh, and leaned against my windowsill, sagging.

"I need your help," she said, the words eking their reluctant way out between her clenched teeth.

I managed not to let my mouth fall open in shock, but it was close. Nova Claire, admitting she needed help? And from a Vesper? If I'd been a less sensitive person, I would have whipped out my phone and recorded the moment for posterity. Instead, I swallowed back my shock and said, "With what?"

Nova pursed her lips, clearly wishing she didn't have to elaborate. Then she blurted out, "It's my mother."

"Okay..."

"You know what she's like. Well, no I guess you don't, but her reputation precedes her in this town, which makes me think you probably have a pretty good idea of what she's like. The Claire name is all that matters to her—protecting it, lifting it up, keeping it polished and shiny and pristine. It's like... a generational trauma response. We fucked up so badly in the lead-up to the Covenant that the Claire matriarch of every generation since has made it her life's work to make up for it. You'd think, over time, they'd get less fanatical about it, but it's only gotten worse."

I experienced a flash of memory of the first time I'd set foot in the Claire family home. There'd been a locked bookcase in their library, where every book on dark or malevolent magic was kept. Nova had told me her mother kept them locked up, because Ostara didn't trust anyone around them. At first, I'd thought Nova was just being melodramatic, but I'd learned better since.

"We've spent a few centuries being pillars of the community, but the way my mother acts, you'd think we were running around hexing everything that moves every time she turned her back," Nova went on. "I don't think there's a single coven in Sedgwick Cove which holds us to the kind of standards we hold ourselves to. Like, they're over it. I'm not really sure why we can't be. But it's almost like she was waiting for something like this to happen."

"Something like...?"

"Bernadette."

"Oh. Right." Everything Nova was saying confirmed what Eva had told me that afternoon at the cafe. The Claires were trying to do damage control on their coven's image.

Nova sighed, and for a moment she looked beyond exhausted. "The problem is that my mother's been so obsessed with maintaining our reputation, she doesn't care if we're rotting on the inside. It's all about appearances, and if things are shitty between our own walls, who cares —as long as no one ever finds out. Not to say we're all a bunch of evil witches cursing and plotting in secret, obviously, but we're like any other family. We're not perfect. We screw up. It's inevitable. We're human beings."

Her voice broke, and I had to swallow against a sudden burst of sympathy. I couldn't imagine what it must be like, having a mother like Ostara Claire. It seemed that Nova had built up her tough-as-nails exterior as a form of self-preservation; and not just from the outside world, but from her own flesh and blood. My mom and I had our differences, and we definitely had our own shit to work through, but I knew she loved me. I was realizing for the first time that maybe Nova couldn't say the same.

"So... what exactly is going on with your mom?" I pressed, after a few moments of silence.

"Huh? Oh shit, I got carried away. Sorry to trauma dump on you. I'm between therapists," Nova said, shaking her head. "So, the Conclave has been meeting almost nightly since everything went down at the lighthouse. They want to perform a Cleansing, which... wait, do you even know what that is?"

I nodded. No reason to tell her I'd only been in possession of that information for a few hours.

"Right. So, they want to perform a Cleansing on Bernadette to make sure that Sarah isn't still somehow able to exert any influence over her. And they absolutely should. The problem is that my mother is fighting them on it."

I decided then and there not to let her know that I'd overheard Davina in the shop. Nova didn't need to know that her mother's truculence was publicly known —she was stressed out enough as it was.

"She's being ridiculous!" Nova went on, swiping ineffectually at the loose tendrils of hair that had fallen down around her face. "She knows there's a possibility that Bernadette is still under Sarah's influence somehow, but she doesn't want to admit it! She wants to sweep it all under the rug. Sarah is the literal reason our family has this dark history, and rather than dealing with her once and for all, my mother wants to pretend she doesn't exist!"

That was the moment I was able to put my finger on exactly how Nova Claire looked. Looking at her with her slightly wild eyes and her manic expression, it was obvious: she looked haunted. I suppose she always had been—her family, at least—but now it was catching up with her.

"For the record, I completely agree with you," I said, still in a determinedly calm voice. "A Cleansing definitely sounds like the right call, just to be safe. But that doesn't explain why you're in my bedroom."

"Oh, right. Well," Nova bit her lip, like she was trying to decide whether she would even tell me the reason for her very unexpected presence in my house. Then she walked over to the chair she had been sitting in when I entered, and picked up a bag I hadn't noticed until she drew my eye to it. It was a backpack, smallish and made of black leather. She unzipped the main compartment and pulled out a pillowcase. Then she opened the pillowcase and pulled out an object. She held it up for me to see, and I recognized it at once.

"What the hell?! Nova... what the actual... are you insane?!" I gasped, backing away from her and the object she now held in her hands.

"I know!" she cried. "I know! I told you I didn't know if this was a good idea or not!"

"Okay, well, let me confirm for you that it is NOT. It is NOT a good idea!"

We both stood in breathless silence, staring at the thing in her hands. It was a mirror: a very old, very spotted and discolored mirror, that no one in the world would have looked twice at, unless they knew exactly what it was; and then, they likely would have run screaming in the other direction.

The mirror was a relic from the Claire family, the only surviving object that belonged to Sarah Claire herself. Once it had hung in the local historical society, but Bernadette had stolen it to use in her misguided attempts to communicate with Sarah. Bernadette used the mirror as a conductor, using Sarah's direct connection to the mirror to clarify their communication.

"Nova," I said, trying to remain calm, even as my body went into full fight-or-flight mode at the sight of the mirror, "Where did you get it?"

"I went to the lighthouse tonight, broke in, and took it off the wall," Nova said, the words tumbling out over each other in her rush to say them, as though getting them over with would somehow make them better.

"The lighthouse that's still sealed off because of the sheer amount of dark magic that was cast over it? *That* lighthouse?" I asked in a hiss.

"I used a masking spell," Nova said defensively.

"I'm not convinced that would make me feel better even if I knew what the hell you were talking about!" I snapped.

"It means I shouldn't have been seen coming in or out."

"Shouldn't?"

"Wasn't. Nobody saw me. Trust me, if they had, Ostara would already have shipped me off to boarding school in a foreign country, right after she disowned me for disobedience."

I narrowed my eyes at her, and she stared defiantly back, her arms crossed over her chest.

"Is it even worth asking you why you would do something so unbelievably dangerous?" I asked, after I had taken several deep breaths.

"Because if my mother isn't going to perform this Cleansing, then I sure as hell will," Nova said.

For a moment, all I could do was stare at her, my mouth opening and closing as my brain struggled to catch up. When I finally did find my voice, it had an audible tremor.

"Is that mirror still connected to Sarah Claire?"

I watched Nova's throat bob before she answered. "I don't know."

"Is it still connected to Bernadette?"

"I don't know."

"Well, is there literally anything you do know that can stop me from flipping out right now?"

Nova bit her lip and began to pace again. "I know that my mother is making a mistake, Wren. I know she's going to put us all in more danger trying to bury this, than I am by trying to bring it to the surface."

For all the gaps in my magical knowledge—and it was mostly gaps, let's be serious—something deep in my gut was telling me to listen to Nova. Maybe this was a flash of my witch's intuition, but as I looked at her, at the earnestness and the fear in her eyes, I knew she was right.

"I'm guessing you didn't come all the way over here just to confess this to me, did you?" I asked, and was surprised to hear that the panic had gone from my voice. I sounded calm, even if I didn't quite feel it.

Nova's lips quirked into a shadow of a smile. "No."

I sighed. "Just say it."

The smile broadened. "I want your help." She paused, and the smile slipped away. "Actually, that's not accurate. I need your help."

"Is it any use telling you that I'll be more of a hindrance than a help at this point?" I asked. "I mean, I failed magical baking 101 this week."

Nova shrugged. "I saw what you did on the beach. Regardless of how we pull off this Cleansing, I'm confident there's no baking involved."

At that moment, Freya slipped through the open window behind Nova as noiselessly as a shadow. She wound around Nova's ankles once before hopping up on my bed, and butting her head against my hand, demanded pets.

"Some guard cat you are," I told her, scratching behind her ears as she lazily closed her eyes. "You're officially fired from sentry duty."

Freya threw me a brief, baleful look before curling up on my pillow and turning her gaze on Nova, her tail flicking pensively over her back.

"So? Are you going to help me or not?" Nova asked, and behind the mask of impatience, I could hear a real plea in her voice. She wouldn't be here if she had another choice, I thought. If she thought she could do this on her own, she'd already have done it.

I sighed. "Fine."

Nova sagged with relief. "Good. Now here. Take this," she said, and held the mirror out to me.

"What?! Why?! I don't want that thing!" I gasped, scooting further from her across my bed.

"For goddess' sake, Vesper, it's not going to bite you," Nova said, rolling her eyes.

"Why do I need to take it, then?" I asked.

"Because my mother is already suspicious that something is going on with me. If she catches me sneaking back into the house, she's going to look through my bag; and if she finds this mirror, I'll be under house arrest indefinitely. Hell, she might throw me in an adjoining cell to Bernadette. It has to stay with you."

I clenched my teeth together. "Fine," I ground out, and held my hand out for the mirror.

Nova smiled and handed it to me. "Good. Bring that with you when we do it." And then she pulled out her phone, and started typing.

"Bring it where? And what are you doing, now?" I asked, exasperated.

"Texting Eva and Zale. Now that you're on board, they'll have to say yes, and we're going to need all the help we can get. I haven't exactly performed one of these before."

"Like, at all?"

"Not when there was an actual entity involved, no," Nova said, not even looking up from her texts.

"Oh, excellent. My confidence in this whole plan is soaring," I said, a note of hysteria in my voice that I didn't even bother to suppress. I shoved the mirror into my backpack and zipped it up. Just the sight of it made me anxious. "Is there anything I can do to help us not royally screw up this whole venture?"

Nova considered for a moment. "Well, I've broken into our collection of banned books, and read everything I can find on spirits and bindings and all of that. I have to assume Bernadette did the same to pull off her scheme in the first place. So now, I just have to pull together everything I can get my hands on about Cleansings, and we'll have to wing it from there."

I swallowed back the almost maniacal peal of laughter that was trying to bubble its way up my throat. "Right. Winging it. Always a good plan when we're dealing with evil forces beyond our comprehension."

"Vesper, you're not cracking up on me, are you?" Nova asked, eyeing me critically as she glanced up from her phone screen.

"Have you looked in a mirror recently? Maybe cut me some slack on the whole 'cracking up' thing, given the several felonies you committed just to get me to agree to this travesty of a plan," I snapped.

Nova raised her hands like I'd just trained a weapon on her. "Okay, okay. You've got a point. Do you think you could find anything here in Lightkeep about Cleansings? I always heard that Asteria's collection of magical texts was extensive."

I took a deep breath. "Yeah, I can look. If I find anything, I'll let you know. When are you thinking you want to do this?"

"Tomorrow night. It'll be a full moon, which can only help the cause. Does that give you enough time?"

"Sure, why not," I grumbled. Asteria only had about a thousand texts in the library, and there was no way I could search them without arousing suspicions from my aunts or my mom. It looked like I wasn't going to be sleeping tonight. "Another question: where do you want to do this? Does the location matter? Because I can maybe get away with creeping through the library collection, but we're not going to be able to stage a Cleansing here."

Nova looked nervous again, and I braced myself for the worst. "Well, that's the other part. The Cleansing will work best if every entity involved is in the same space."

"Meaning?"

"Meaning Bernadette should be present, too."

I stared at Nova, waiting for her to crack a smile and tell me 'Just kidding! You should see the look on your face, Vesper.' I waited. And waited. Her expression didn't change.

"So what does that mean? Where do we have to go?"

Even Nova couldn't disguise the grimness that came over her expression then.

"It means we'll have to go to the Keep."

9

After Nova climbed back out my window, I tried to distract myself with the books Rhi had left on the bed for me, but the sentences all slid together, meaningless in my churning brain. I gave up and tried to look over Zale's script for the pageant, but there, too, I couldn't concentrate. I tossed the pages aside and stared up at my ceiling, letting my myriad new worries chase each other around and around inside my skull, until I was sure that my mom and Rhi had both gone to bed. I didn't think Persi was home, but it was her custom to be out until all hours of the night, and if I waited to hear her bedroom door shut, I might well be waiting until morning. I would just have to risk the possibility that she would find me in the library in the middle of the night. I'd come up with an excuse, but I hardly thought I'd need to use it. I couldn't really imagine Persi showing much interest in anything I did.

I crept down the stairs as quietly as I could, and made my way to the library. It wasn't a particularly large or grand room, but every inch of the walls from floor to ceiling was covered in bookshelves. The sheer number of texts was daunting, and I had no idea where to start. A quick glance was enough to confirm that Asteria had not organized her books alphabetically, and I didn't know enough about magic to know whether they were grouped by subject. I knew I wouldn't be lucky enough to find something called

"Cleansings for Beginners," so I just picked the corner by the door and started scanning titles, pulling anything that looked like it might contain the information I needed. Then I curled up with the first armload of books and started searching.

By three o'clock in the morning, I had only made it through one wall of books, and was nodding off over the tome in my lap. I decided to give up for the night and try to salvage a few hours of sleep. I took three books with me, the only ones in which I'd found any information about Cleansings at all. I wasn't convinced they would be helpful—the information felt very basic, and the only Cleansing spells I had found in them talked about banishing "negativity" and "bad intentions," not "300-year-old ghosts bent on your destruction," but it was a start. I fell into bed fully clothed, and woke with a start to the sounds of shouting. I slid out of bed, crept over to my door, opened it a crack and listened hard.

"—stop shouting, please? Wren is still asleep!" It was Rhi's voice.

"Oh that's right, it's her house, her rules, I forgot," Persi snapped back.

"You're only saying that because you're trying to change the subject! This has nothing to do with Wren, leave her out of it! This is about you, Persi."

I opened the door another inch, just in time to hear Persi sigh like an overwrought teenager. "Fine. You're obviously determined to give me a lecture, so let's have it."

"I'm not interested in lecturing you at all," Rhi said. "Believe me, when Asteria died, I did not relish the idea of becoming the person who has to rein you in. But someone has to say something, Persi, or you're going to land yourself in serious trouble."

"It was just a quick visit. I was barely there an hour," came Persi's sulky voice.

"You shouldn't have been there at all!" Rhi cried. "The Keep is not a social meet-up, Persi, it's a stronghold against powerful magic, and you had no business going there."

"Oh, so now Bernadette is none of my business? You can't honestly be saying that to me with a straight face."

"That's not what I... I know Bernadette means a lot to you—"

"*Meant* a lot to me. Past tense," Persi snapped.

"Oh, come off it, Pers. If she didn't mean anything to you, you wouldn't have bothered to go in the first place. I know you two have history, but that doesn't give you the right to—"

"Rhi, I have every right! She betrayed me! She seduced me and then kidnapped my sister! Ostara might be content to let her rot in there, but I want answers! I need to... to know *why*..." Persi's voice broke on the last word.

Rhi fell silent. I was holding my breath. Finally, I heard a long, drawn out sigh.

"I know. I'm sorry. I just... I don't want to see you get hurt again. That's all."

"If you don't want to see me hurt then leave me the hell alone, and let me do what I need to do to heal," Persi said. Her voice was low, but fierce. Footsteps began to click toward the staircase, and so I pulled my door shut and crept back into bed before she could realize she was being spied on.

So, Persi had visited Bernadette. I wasn't exactly surprised. Persi had never been one for following rules, from what I could gather; and her relationship with Bernadette had been longstanding and messy. And as curious as I would have been to know what passed between them, I was much more curious about how she'd gotten into the Keep. Nova had been extremely vague about it all, probably on purpose, because it certainly didn't sound like the kind of place you could simply stroll into whenever you took a fancy. Knowing Persi had gotten in didn't make me feel any better at the prospect of our impending field trip—after all, there was hardly a rule or a barrier that Persi wouldn't shove aside to get what she wanted. I rolled over and looked at my clock—it was 6:30 in the morning. I closed my eyes, sure sleep would evade me now that I had so much more to worry about, but what felt like a moment later, Freya walked across my face and jolted me awake. The clock read 11AM.

"Shit," I muttered. I'd slept the entire morning away. I hadn't so much as glanced at the script for Zale or the reading Rhi had wanted me to do. On top of that, I now only had an hour before I had to be over at the playhouse to meet Luca, and it would take me a solid half hour to walk there. Maybe Rhi would let me borrow her bike again. I took the fastest shower of my life, dressed, and threw my wet hair up in a bun on top of my head. I paused in front of the mirror as I put my glasses on, and felt a little flop of disappointment in my stomach. If I was the kind of girl who knew how to do makeup, I'd likely have spent an hour and a hundred dollars worth of products on my face to impress Luca, but there was no point in worrying about it. Contouring and blending was as inscrutable to me as kitchen witchery, and I certainly wasn't going to solve that problem in the next fifteen minutes. Poe had once sat me down at her vanity table, and made me up for the homecoming dance. I'd been basically unrecognizable when she was done, and though I thought the girl staring back at me out of the mirror looked pretty, she also looked like a stranger. I didn't feel like myself—in fact, I felt like some kind of imposter.

"When you meet Wren Vesper, what you see is what you get," I told my reflection. "Take it or leave it."

I walked downstairs to find my mom on the phone with our realtor. She waved at me and blew me a kiss as I passed through to the kitchen to see my sad scones were still in a glass covered dish on the counter, alongside a fresh batch of peach cobbler muffins.

"Rhi, I promise if you put those scones in the trash where they belong, you will not hurt my feelings," I said.

"I'm not going to do that!" Rhi said, looking scandalized. "They're your first attempts at kitchen witchery!"

I laughed as I bypassed the scones, and reached for a muffin off the cooling rack. "What are you going to do, bronze them? It's not like they're edible."

"They are so!" Rhi said, and she grabbed a scone from under the glass cloche, and took a bite. It was a testament to her good nature that she barely flinched as she chewed.

"It's your funeral," I said. "I'll see you later. Oh, hey, could I borrow your bike?"

Rhi swallowed—it looked painful— but her face immediately brightened. "I've got an even better idea. Follow me out to the shed."

My curiosity piqued, I followed her out the door and through the garden to the dilapidated shed. It was a slightly lopsided structure, with moss growing on the roof and roses creeping up the windows. Rhi tugged on the slightly crooked door, and it slowly scraped its way open. Then she stepped back and said, "Ta-da!"

A bicycle stood before me, a pale blue old-fashioned one with a white basket slung between the wide handlebars, and a little leather satchel strapped on behind the ivory seat.

"It's adorable!" I said.

"It's yours!" Rhi sang.

I turned to her, my mouth falling open. "Are you serious? Rhi, you didn't have to do this!"

But Rhi waved me off. "Oh, stop, it wasn't expensive. And besides, you needed a proper welcome home present. You also need a little freedom, and since you can't drive yet—"

The rest of her sentence was cut off with an "oof" of surprise as I slammed into her with a hug. She laughed and then put her arms around me, giving me a squeeze in return.

"Thank you!" I said, as I pulled away from her.

"You're welcome," she said, her voice a little husky. She wiped at her eyes, laughing. "Sorry. I don't mean to get all sappy on you. I just... I spent a lot of years not knowing if I'd get to see you again, let alone hug you."

"And now you have to live with me *and* survive my cooking," I said, grinning. "Careful what you wish for."

I PULLED into the parking lot of the playhouse only a few minutes after noon. Rhi had tucked a bike chain and lock inside the satchel, and so I secured the bike to the bike rack near the entrance. Luca had said he would be doing landscaping, but I didn't see anyone out near the parking lot. I did hear a faint buzzing sound, though, so I followed it around the side of the building, and spotted him trimming the edges of the flowerbeds with a weedwhacker. He had oversized headphones on, and though I called his name several times, he obviously couldn't hear me. I crossed the lawn until I was just a few feet behind him, waiting for him to turn, but he was singing along to whatever music he was listening to, completely oblivious to my presence. Finally, when I'd reached my peak threshold for feeling like an idiot, I reached out and tapped him on the shoulder.

"What the hell!" he cried out, dropping the weedwhacker and stumbling backwards. He tripped over the rock border of the flowerbed, and fell onto his back.

"I'm sorry!" I cried. "I've been trying to get your attention for like five minutes."

"No worries," he said, and to my relief he was grinning. "I was in my own world. I usually am." He glanced down at his watch. "Wow, it's noon already? I completely lost track of time. See what I mean? I would have worked right through my lunch break."

"Oh. Well, I don't want to interrupt your lunch break. I can come back when—"

But Luca was already shaking his head. "No, it's fine."

He just stood there, smiling pleasantly at me, until I finally said, "So... uh, did you have any luck? With your uncle, I mean?"

"Huh? Oh, yeah. He said it was fine if you wanted to borrow some of the stuff in long-term storage. It's been in there for years, so he has no idea what's in there, but I can take you over and you can just have a poke around."

"That would be great, thanks so much," I said, feeling relief wash over me that I hadn't gotten Zale's hopes up for nothing. "Is it okay if I text Zale and have him meet us? He probably has a better idea of what would work than I would."

"Knock yourself out. Tell him to meet us at storage building 4."

I shot off a quick text and then set off across the grounds, jogging along beside Luca, who had incredibly long strides. I tried to think of something—anything—to say to make small talk, but my mind felt like it had been wiped clean. Luckily, Luca didn't seem to mind in the least. He was whistling contentedly as he walked, hands tucked into his pockets, completely at his ease. It made me feel even more pathetic. Here I was, stammering like a fool in his presence, and he could not have been less affected by mine. I thought of Persi, of her magnetism, the way she drew every eye everywhere she went and wished, for one wild moment, that I was more like her.

"So you're a Vesper, huh?"

Luca's voice burst in through my thoughts, catching me off guard.

"Uh, yeah."

"So, how is it that you seem to know even less about this festival than I do?" he asked, shortening his stride so that I could walk alongside him.

"Oh. Well, I haven't lived here in a long time. My mother moved us both to Portland when I was a toddler."

Luca's eyes disappeared into his mess of dark hair. "Really? Haven't the Vespers lived in this town since... forever?"

"How do you know that? I thought you were an outsider," I said, and then slapped my hand over my mouth in horror.

But Luca just laughed. "An outsider who's visited all the tourist attractions about a dozen times. I know the local history."

"Sorry," I said, dropping my gaze to my feet, "about the outsider thing. It's just what some of the other kids said last night. I mean... I'm basically an outsider, too. Sort of."

"It's fine. I'm used to it. It's kind of crazy that you can spend every summer of your life in the place and still be considered an outsider, but that's Sedgwick Cove for you. I used to think it was just a money thing, but I don't know. It seems to run deeper than that here."

"A money thing?"

"Yeah, you know, people looking for seasonal second homes, that kind of thing."

"Where do you live during the school year?" I asked.

"Manhattan. My great-grandmother was from Sedgwick Cove originally. That's how my great-grandfather ended up buying this place to begin with."

I had to press my lips together to prevent myself from asking the question I really wanted to ask, which was, of course, whether his mother's side of the family were, in fact, witches. But that wasn't exactly the kind of thing you can just come out and ask someone you've only known for a day. Still, the curiosity burned in me like a coal as we walked around the back side of the theater, and down to a row of low rectangular buildings that looked almost like an army base. Each building was made of concrete, painted gray, with a sloped metal roof and small, high windows. A huge numeral was painted on the side of each building in tan paint to denote which building it was. We walked along the lefthand row to a building marked with a massive number four. A metal sign beside the door read, "Storage 4: Long Storage."

Luca pulled out a ring of keys that would make a custodian insecure, and flipped through them until he found the key to the padlock. He unlocked it and pushed the door wide, gesturing me through. "After you, Miss Vesper."

"Should we wait for Zale?" I asked.

"I'll leave the door propped for him. He'll find us," Luca said.

I nodded and stepped through. Luca followed, and mashed his palm against a bank of light switches.

Row after row of fluorescent lights buzzed and popped to life, revealing aisles of costume racks lined up all along the center of the room, so that the place looked like a fabric maze. The four walls were built out floor to ceiling with heavy-duty shelving that housed an impossible number of bins, boxes, and bags —each one neatly labeled with electrical tape.

"Holy shit," I muttered. "How many buildings do you have?"

"Storage ones like this? Six," Luca said. "Some for costumes, some for sets, some for props. My grandfather kept adding them as the theater grew."

We walked forward, our footsteps oddly muffled by the sheer amount of stuff crammed into the space.

"Any idea what you're looking for?" Luca asked. "I might be able to point you in the right direction. I used to play in here as a kid."

"That must have been fun," I said, thinking of the free rein of a child's imagination loose in this place. "No, I'm not really sure what I'm looking for, actually. Just... inspiration, I guess."

"Okay, well... feel free to just wander. I'll be back in a few minutes—just going to grab my lunch," Luca said, hooking his thumb over his shoulder in the direction of the playhouse.

"Of course. I'll be fine. Thanks for letting me in," I said.

He nodded and loped back out into the blazing sunshine. I felt a stab of pity, watching him go. It must be miserable, doing landscaping work in this kind of humidity. This building, on the other hand, felt almost like a walk-in freezer. Goosebumps were erupting on my arms as I started traversing the rows of costume racks. I supposed they had to keep the air conditioning blasting this time of year to keep the humidity from ruining all the fabrics. I'd never been in a theatre that wasn't either uncomfortably warm or teeth-chatteringly cold—sometimes both at once, depending on whether you were under the stage lights or operating them.

I worried that I might have to dig costume by costume, but I quickly saw, to my relief, that the racks were organized by time period. I bypassed the entire 21st and 20th centuries, feeling the pull toward something older. Surely a pageant about a battle as old as time should have a more historical feel? I drifted past Victorian and Regency era garments, past petticoats and pantaloons, past French revolutionary uniforms and peasant garb, past Musketeer hats and Elizabethan frocks. We were definitely getting closer, I thought. I rounded a corner and found medieval robes and gowns, and several racks of white Greek togas. I dug into them eagerly, but still nothing seemed quite right.

"Wren? Are you in here?" Zale's voice sounded from the direction of the door.

"Yeah, I'm over here!" I called.

We played a bit of Marco Polo until Zale finally found the right aisle.

"I brought reinforcements," Zale said, and Eva appeared behind him.

"Hey, Eva. The more the merrier, because this place is huge," I said. "I never imagined there'd be so much to look through."

"Found anything good yet?"

"Not sure. I'm still hoping inspiration will strike."

"These are definitely a lot better than what we have," Eva volunteered, pulling out a red and gold velvet dress that looked like it belonged in a production of Romeo and Juliet, and holding it up to herself.

"Yeah, but I just keep thinking there must be something bigger and more epic we could do. I mean, we can find the fanciest costumes in here, but when it comes down to it, it's still going to be Sergei and Ethan wearing them, swinging fake swords at each other like a pair of overgrown toddlers," I said.

Eva's face fell. "Good point. Maybe the costumes aren't the biggest problem."

"Let's go check out some of the stuff along the walls," I said. "Maybe we need to think beyond costumes."

We split up and started opening bins and bags and boxes. I soon found that, though they were all labeled, extra things had been shoved into the boxes that didn't necessarily belong there. I was just digging through a box labeled "medieval weaponry" that actually held a fair number of silver tea service pieces, when I heard a shriek and a thump.

"Everyone okay?" I called.

"Zale, you idiot! You scared the crap out of me!" came Eva's grumbling voice.

"Sorry, I just wanted to show you these!"

I walked up the aisle and around the corner to see Zale towering over Eva on a pair of tall black stilts. Eva was angrily picking up handfuls of fake greenery that was spilling out of an overturned bin. Over their heads was a wall of masks and headpieces of all shapes and sizes. Two giant gold comedy and tragedy masks dominated the top row.

It was as though my brain took in each disparate element and synthesized them. My pulse began to race. I gasped out loud.

"Oh my God!"

"It's okay, we'll clean it up," Zale said, still wobbling around on the stilts.

"No, it's not that. It's just... puppets!"

Eva and Zale looked at each other. "Huh?" they both said.

"Look, why does the pageant feel so lame? Because it's supposed to be representing an epic battle waged by mythical monarchs of the seasons, and all we've got is Sergei and Ethan slumping around in some beat up robes. But what if we create versions of the Oak King and the Holly King that are larger than life?"

Zale still looked dubious. "I don't—"

"Look!" I cried. I dragged a step ladder over from the corner and clambered up it until I could reach the gold comedy mask. With a grunt of effort, I managed to get it off the wall. It was big and awkward, but not heavy, as it was made of papier mâché. I climbed down and handed the mask to Eva.

"Hold this," I told her, and then ran down the nearest aisle of costumes until I found the Victorian era ones. I pulled a long black cloak that looked like it may have been worn by the Ghost of Christmas Future, and ran back with it.

"Zale, totter your way over here for a second," I said, throwing the cloak over my shoulder, and climbing back up the ladder.

Zale still looked mystified, but he did what I asked. I draped the massive cloak over his shoulders, and then held my hand out for the mask. Eva handed it to me, and I placed it carefully on Zale's head. Then I pulled the hood up over his head.

"Hand me some of that greenery!" I said.

Eva's face broke into a grin as she caught on to what was happening. She started handing me long flowering vines and trailing garlands of ivy. I wound them around Zale's arms and draped them from his shoulders.

"How about this!" Eva shouted, running for a display of headpieces. She lifted one down that looked like deer antlers dipped in gold, and I placed it, with a final flourish, on Zale's head.

"Holy shit!" I said.

"Lemme see!" Zale demanded.

Between us, Eva and I held up the cloak and the trailing vines so Zale could rotate himself and look into the full-length mirror on the opposite wall. He looked like some kind of strange apparition.

"It needs some work, but you can see it, right?" I asked eagerly. "We paint the mask, use seasonally appropriate greenery, find a big gnarled staff? Maybe give him some big branchy arms that people can operate with sticks?"

For a moment, Zale didn't move or speak. I felt my heart sink. Did he hate it?

"I mean, it's just an idea, we can just use the stuff we—"

"THIS IS GOING TO BE THE BEST PAGEANT EVER!" Zale shrieked. Eva yelped and jumped away from him, which made him lose his balance. He toppled to the floor, still laughing with excitement in a heap of fabric and fake leaves.

Eva looked at me and grinned. "I think he likes it," she said.

As Eva and I helped the still giddy Zale extract himself from the makeshift costume, Eva's phone went off. She pulled it out of her pocket to check the notifications.

"Oh, it's Nova, reminding me about tonight," she said.

"Nova?" My head snapped up. I'd been so caught up in thoughts of the pageant that I'd completely forgotten about Nova.

"Yeah. She asked if Zale and I could help her with something."

"Is that what she said?" I asked.

"Yup," Eva said. "She was kind of sketchy on the details, to be honest, but we told her we'd come. I mean, she's basically been in hiding for a week."

"Dammit, Nova." I groaned, and Zale and Eva both looked at me.

"There's a reason she's being sketchy about the details," I said.

"Wait, are you going, too? Do you know what she wants help with?"

I hesitated only a moment. I didn't want to betray Nova's confidence, but at the same time, I couldn't let Zale and Eva go into Nova's plan blind. I'd only agreed to it out of guilt, and probably because I didn't know enough about magic yet to realize how dangerous it was going to be. But Zale and Eva were lifelong witches. They deserved to know what they were getting themselves into.

I sighed. "You'd both better sit down," I said. "There's something I need to tell you."

10

"Please tell me this is a joke," Eva said. "Like, some YouTube influencer is about to pop out from behind one of these boxes and tell us we're being pranked, right?"

"Unfortunately, no," I said. "She's doing it tonight, whether we go with her or not."

"But not to tell us what she's planning? Just texting us to hang out? Is she out of her mind?" Zale asked weakly.

"She knows we'd never show up if we knew what she was doing," Eva said.

"Does that mean you're not coming?" I asked.

Eva raised her eyebrows at me. "Does that mean you are?"

"Well," I began, fumbling around for the words. "Nova... it's not like we're friends, but she put herself on the line for me last week on the beach. I mean, you all did. And so, when she showed up in my room and begged for my help..."

"You agreed because you felt guilty," Zale finished.

"Well, partly, yes. I'm also probably just an idiot, because let's be honest, I don't actually know what I'm getting myself into. I don't even know what the Keep is."

Zale and Eva looked at each other. "It's down in a cavern near the beach," Eva said. "It's sort of our version of jail around here."

"We also have, like, normal jail," Zale added. "We've got a tiny police station with a couple of holding cells for when the tourists get feisty. But when a witch needs to be contained, we bring her to the Keep."

"That sounds... ominous," I said. "And a bit dramatic."

"It's almost never used," Zale said as Eva nodded. "There've only been two witches held in there since we've been alive. And the other one hadn't done anything terrible, like Bernadette. She'd just been experimenting with love potions and went off the deep end. It was only temporary, but they had to leave her in there until the effects wore off, because they thought she'd do something crazy."

"You'd have to be an absolute fool to mess with love magic, even if you do know what you're doing," Eva said, shaking her head.

"But the point is, sometimes when magic gets out of control, we need a place to contain it," Zale said. "And Bernadette was definitely out of control. A danger to herself, and others."

"But what kind of place is it?" I asked. I kept picturing a Rapunzel-type situation, a tall windowless stone structure that can only be entered if the trapped princess lets down her hair.

"I know, it sounds all Alcatraz, but it's not that impressive. It's basically just a structure built into the underside of the seawall. A lot of the kids like to brag that they've been out to it, and even broken into it, but they're all full of shit. The truth is, hardly anyone knows what it's like inside, because only the members of the Conclave are allowed to go in and out."

"So, how does Nova expect to pull this off?" I asked, incredulous now. "She made it sound like this was a place we could just walk into!"

"I have no idea, but if she thinks we're just going to go in there without a plan, she's lost her damn mind," Eva said, crossing her arms over her chest.

"Have either of your grandmothers mentioned anything about all this?" I asked, looking between them. "About Ostara refusing to perform the Cleansing?"

Zale frowned. "Hm. She has been grumbling about Ostara more than usual, but she's kept quiet about the details."

"Xiomara and Ostara have never really gotten along, but yeah, things seem especially tense right now. I assumed it had to do with the Darkness; but as usual, the Conclave keeps all its cards very close to the chest," Eva said.

"Can't the other members overrule her or something?" I asked. "I mean, it doesn't seem fair that one member can prevent all the others from making the right decision."

"Ostara's been the High Witch of the Conclave for more than a decade," Zale said. "If they want to overrule her, they would have to call for a meeting of the covens to have her voted out of her position. They'll do it if they absolutely have to, but I'm sure they're trying to avoid it at all costs. The Claires are a powerful coven with a lot of allies, and the fallout from an ousting—whether it was successful or not—would be really nasty."

"So while everyone plays politics, Bernadette could still be connected to this spirit that wants to destroy us all and feed us to the Darkness? Excellent. What could go wrong?" I said, and there was a definite note of hysteria in my voice now.

"I think your family is one of the only ones who could challenge her seriously," Eva said. "After all, Asteria was High Witch before Ostara. But I don't get the impression that either your aunts or your mom want that kind of responsibility."

"Definitely not," I said, biting anxiously at a fingernail. "I had to drag my mom back here. There's no way she wants to run the place. Rhi just wants to be in her kitchen, and Persi... well, I don't think she..."

My voice trailed away as I remembered the conversation I had overheard that morning between Rhi and Persi. Persi had gone to the Keep to visit Bernadette. That meant she knew how to get inside. Was it possible that she could help us? It was a fleeting thought at best, and my brain dismissed it almost immediately. Persi's attitude toward me was mostly resentment—I couldn't imagine gathering the courage to ask for her help any more than I could imagine her offering it.

"Wren?"

"Huh?"

Zale and Eva were both looking at me expectantly.

"You were saying something about Persi?" Zale prompted.

"Oh. Yeah, sorry. My mind is spinning with all of this. I was just going to say that I can't imagine her being responsible enough to be in a position like that. I haven't known her that long, but she doesn't seem very interested in things like rules."

"I think Sedgwick Cove at large would agree with that assessment," Eva said, nodding. "No offense, but she's always been a bit of a loose cannon."

"None taken," I said. "Like I said, I barely know her."

"Well, look, it sounds like Nova is going to attempt this regardless, so why not at least meet up with her like she asked, and try to talk her out of it," Zale suggested. "Maybe if we all gang up on her, she'll realize what a truly insane idea this is."

"I'm down," Eva said, nodding. "We've got to try to stop her."

I bit my lip. I really didn't want to go back on my word to Nova. But Eva and Zale knew a lot more about this stuff than I did. If they were so against it, it probably was as terrible an idea as it sounded. I wasn't sure if Nova would forgive me for backing out on her, but it was a risk I would have to take.

"Okay," I said finally. "I'm not really sure what other choice we have. Let's finish finding what we need here, so Luca can lock up."

Zale retrieved a second pair of stilts where he'd found the first, and then carefully lifted the oversized tragedy mask off the wall, while Eva and I gathered big piles of spring and winter greenery into some empty bins. Then we dug through the costumes for another long robe, and found one made of gauzy gold material. There would still be more accessories to gather, but we had a good start. We dragged the items we were borrowing to the front door, and found Luca outside waiting for us.

I started at the sight of him, wondering how long he'd been there, and if he'd been able to overhear any of our conversation. Eva threw me a sideways look that told me she was thinking the very same thing.

"All set?" Luca asked, looking between us with an easy smile on his face.

"We've got enough to get started," Zale said. "Do you think we might be able to come back again?"

"Sure, sure," Luca said. "Just let me know. I'm here most days."

"Doesn't sound like much of a summer vacation," Eva commented.

Luca shrugged. "It could be worse. I get to the beach a lot. It beats summer in the middle of the city any day."

He handed Zale a clipboard, and Zale wrote down everything we were borrowing. We asked if we could alter and paint things, and Luca assured us that it was part of the deal.

He walked us back to the parking lot, hefting one of the big plastic bins onto his shoulder to help us bring it all back in one trip. I stopped for a moment, remembering that all I had was my bike, but saw with relief that Zale was pulling a set of car keys from his jeans pocket. Luca helped us load the bins into the trunk and the back of the car, and waved us off.

"Thanks for your help," I told him as Zale and Eva got in the car. I noticed Eva watching me from out of the corner of my eye, and felt my cheeks turning pink.

"Any time. Maybe I'll see you down on the beach. You know, we outsiders need to stick together." He winked, which I would have sworn was the cheesiest thing someone could do, but for some reason he pulled it off.

"Uh, yeah, sure. See you around," I mumbled, practically forgetting how to form words. I jumped on my bike and pedaled away before I could find another way to make a complete fool of myself. Before I'd even made it out of the parking lot, my phone buzzed in my pocket.

Looks like someone's got a crush.

It was from Eva. The problem was, I couldn't tell if she was talking about me, or Luca.

* * *

When I arrived back at Lightkeep Cottage, my mom was there. She looked exhausted, but she raised her hands into the air in victory when she saw me.

"The apartment is officially empty, and everything has gone to storage," she said with a genuine smile.

I plopped down next to her on the sofa, and hugged her. "That's great, Mom. But you know, you don't have to act happy about it for my sake."

She frowned at me. "Act happy? If I wasn't so tired I'd be throwing a party right now."

"I know you're glad to have all the packing done, that's not what I mean," I said, shaking my head. "I mean the whole moving thing. I know you didn't want to come here. I know you love your job in Portland. I just want you to know it's okay to be honest about it."

My mom reached over and rumpled my hair, like she did when I was a kid. "Thanks for that, Wren. I know you think I needed to hear it. But honestly, I'm relieved."

"Relieved?"

She took her time before answering. "I ran from Sedgwick Cove, not because I didn't love it here, not because I didn't think of it as home; but because I was scared that you were in danger. I should have realized we would always be tied to this place, but I didn't want to admit that at the time. It's exhausting, denying who you are at your core. For all the worries I still have, I'm glad we're back. It's... I think it *will* be... good to be home."

I felt a warmth flooding through me. Home. Hearing that word from my mom's lips, knowing that she meant it, that we both felt the same ties to this place—it felt like one more unbreakable thread binding us all together. The Vespers.

"Where were you off to? Rhi told me about the bike," my mom asked.

"Pageant stuff. The costumes are just so pathetic, Mom, I don't know how anyone can take the pageant seriously. So I asked Luca Meyers if we could borrow some stuff from the playhouse. They've got buildings and buildings full of costumes and props they don't even use."

"Did you have any luck?"

"Oh, yeah, we did. I came up with an idea to create larger than life versions of the Oak King and the Holly King—sort of like puppets on stilts. I think it will be really cool, if we can pull it off."

"Well, that sounds great, honey," my mom said, stifling a yawn. "It's about time someone jazzed up that pageant, and I can't think of a better person for the job than you."

"Personally, I wish Charlie was here," I said, referring to one of my best friends from home, who was a brilliant costume designer. "But I'll do the best I can."

"I'm sure it will be wonderful. I can't wait for Sedgwick Cove to see what you can do, Wren." She kissed the top of my head.

I smiled half-heartedly. The problem was that Sedgwick Cove *had* seen what I could do—or heard rumors about it, at least—and now they were all wary of me.

The hours until midnight dragged by. I tried to fill the time by reading the books Rhi had given me, but I couldn't focus. I found myself reading the same paragraph over and over again, without absorbing a single word. Every time I looked up at the clock, I was sure it would be time to go; and instead, I would see there was still an interminable wait left. I threw the book aside in frustration, and picked up the pageant script instead, but I might as well have just stared at the tiny spider weaving a web in the corner of my ceiling for all the progress I made. It wasn't that I wanted to go—I simply wanted to get it over with. Rhi, being such an early riser, was also in bed well before ten o'clock, and my mother was so exhausted, she'd been snoring in the room beside me since eight-thirty. So at least I didn't have to worry about climbing out of my window to make my escape. Nova might be competent at scaling trellises, but I'd never had the chance to hone that particular skill, and I didn't much feel like breaking my neck in the attempt.

I put a few things in my backpack—a flashlight, my phone, and all the notes I'd made for the pageant. If we were caught, the pageant was a passable excuse why we might all be meeting up together. I saw the mirror tucked down at the bottom, and shuddered involuntarily. If there was any way I could convince Nova to take that thing back to the Manor with her, I would try it. I changed into all black clothes—I had plenty of them from working backstage— and slipped as quietly as I could down Lightkeep's creaky old staircase, and out the front door. I'd stashed my bike around the side of the fence rather than locking it back up in the shed, so that I'd have easy access to it. I wheeled it carefully through the gate, hopped on, and took off down the road toward town. I tucked the flashlight under my arm to light my way until I reached the part of the road that had streetlights, and made a mental note to invest in one of those little lights I could strap to my handlebars. I had a funny feeling this was not going to be my last clandestine bike ride in the middle of the night.

I felt a stab of guilt as I glided into the deserted downtown. Every decision my mother had made, ill-conceived or not, had been to protect me; and here I was, sneaking out in the middle of the night. Of course, I reasoned, I wasn't doing it to get into trouble. I was doing it to get someone else *out* of trouble. And the only reason Nova was even attempting this ridiculous scheme was because the Conclave wasn't doing its job. If the adults were handling things the way they were supposed to, instead of playing politics, we wouldn't be in this situation.

Nova asked us to meet her outside of Shadowkeep which, tucked as it was down a narrow street with two other shops but no houses, meant there was little chance that we'd be seen by anyone. As I rounded the corner, I saw that Eva and Zale were already standing there, huddled together against the surprisingly cold wind rolling up from the harbor. I pulled my bike up, leaned it against a picket fence, and pulled my hands into my hoodie sleeves as I joined them.

"Any sign of Nova?" I asked.

"Not yet," Eva said, pulling out her phone.

"What are we going to do if we can't talk her out of it?" Zale asked. "Like, what if she just decides to go through with it anyway?"

"Look, I'm not here to be a snitch," Eva said. "I might not want to participate, but Nova can do what she wants. If she wants to get herself caught interfering in Conclave business, that's on her. I'm not risking Xiomara's wrath because the Claires can't get their collective shit together, but I'm not going to rat her out either."

We stood there together in the cold, waiting. Zale's teeth were chattering. Eva was bouncing up and down on the balls of her feet, trying to keep the blood flowing. The temperature had dropped considerably that night, due to a storm that was rolling past the coastline out to sea. The minutes ticked by, and the anxious knot in my stomach twisted tighter. Where was she? What was taking her so long to get here? I could tell the others were thinking the same. Eva was glancing at her phone every ten seconds, waiting for a text, and Zale was pacing the block, peering down in the direction of the Manor.

"Something's wrong," I finally whispered, when a glance at my phone told me it was one o'clock in the morning, a full half-hour after Nova had asked us to meet. "What should we do?"

Zale was still looking up the street in the direction Nova should be coming. "Should we go to her house?" he asked.

"And do what, throw rocks at her window? I'm just going to text her," Eva said, and began typing. At that moment, all our phones buzzed: a group text message.

There's been a complication. Talk to you tomorrow.

Eva expelled a sigh of relief. "I guess that's it, then. She's not coming."

"What do you think happened?" Zale asked.

"Probably got caught trying to sneak out. The last time Nova snuck out after curfew, Ostara grounded her for a month," Eva said. "Hopefully she only found out that she was sneaking out, and not *why* she was sneaking out, or we won't see her again for the rest of her natural life."

"Speaking of getting caught, let's all try not to," Zale said. "Can you both come by tomorrow to help with pageant stuff?"

"Let's do it at my house," Eva suggested. "Xiomara will have leftovers from a catering gig, and we can use my mom's art supplies. She's got a sort of workspace up in the attic where we can lay everything out."

"What time?" I asked.

"I'll have to be at the cafe for the lunch rush. So... how about three?"

We all agreed. Zale and Eva headed off in opposite directions toward their houses. I stood at the fence getting ready to mount my bike, when a sudden flare of light caught my eye. I looked up, and saw that the light on the top floor of Shadowkeep had just turned on.

"What the hell?" I murmured. I hastily rolled my bike a few feet so that I could conceal both it and me behind a massive hydrangea bush, and continued to watch the upper windows. There was a figure moving around up there, silhouetted against the cream-colored shades that had been pulled down over the windows. My heart began to pound. Had someone broken into the store? Were we being robbed? And what did someone even do if they found out the secret part of their store was being robbed? It's not like I could just call the police, could I? I could see it now: me standing in the side garden with two bemused officers, trying to explain about the invisible staircase, and then getting carted off to an in-patient mental facility. Unless the police here understood enough about the secrets of this town that they'd actually believe me? I didn't know for sure. No, I'd have to handle this by myself.

I toyed with the idea of sneaking up the stairs to catch whoever it was red-handed, but dismissed it almost at once. Whoever was up there was clearly a witch, because they knew about the second floor; and if they were willing to use magic to break into Shadowkeep, I was sure they wouldn't hesitate to use it against me if I confronted them. And so, I did what every teenager does when they want to document something: I whipped out my phone and started recording. I decided to wait and catch footage of whoever this person was sneaking back out of Shadowkeep, and then I could bring the evidence to Rhi and let her decide what to do with it. Of course, that would mean I'd have to explain why I was outside of Shadowkeep at one o'clock in the morning when I was supposed to be at home in bed, but I would cross that bridge when I got to it. Shadowkeep meant everything to Rhi and Persi, and I couldn't just pretend I hadn't witnessed this.

I shrouded myself further back into the bushes, and trained my camera on the upstairs window. The figure moved swiftly, but I was fairly confident it was a woman from the silhouette. As I recorded, the wind from the harbor numbing my fingers, the light in the upper level suddenly went out. I heard a creaking sound, followed by the shutting of a door, and then the footsteps down the hidden staircase. I waited for the person to come around the corner of the house and into my view, so that I could catch them on camera. My hands shook, and my lungs burned with the breath I was afraid to release. At last, I heard the creak of the gate, and the figure emerged from the shadowy garden into the golden pool of a street light.

It was Persi.

My first feeling was one of utmost relief. We were not getting robbed, and no thief was going to find me in these bushes. But that initial relief was followed by an intense wave of curiosity. Persi was wearing all black clothing—not totally off-brand for her, but these weren't her usual style. She wore a pair of black leggings, a black sweatshirt with a hood, which she was now pulling up over her hair, and a pair of black sneakers. She carried a black backpack slung over one shoulder, which she was hastily zipping up as I watched her. She raised her head, looked warily down one end of the street, and then the other, before hurrying off down toward the harbor.

Go home, Wren. Just go home. It's none of your business.

I hesitated only a moment and then, abandoning my bike in the bushes, I followed after her.

11

My brain seemed to be completely disconnected from my body. I was shouting inside my own head to simply go home and mind my own business, but my body just kept plunging forward heedlessly. There was something inside me that was more instinct than logic, and I couldn't help but obey it in this moment. About halfway down the narrow side street, I stopped fighting it. I was listening to something deeper... something more innate in me, something I wouldn't have trusted before that night on the beach, but which I now recognized as intuition. Was this part of what Rhi had been telling me? That I needed to trust myself more?

I doubted she'd approve of the scenario, but I was going to take her advice regardless.

The narrow cobbled street we were on sloped down and met up with Harbor Street, which ran the length of the waterfront. Beyond the sea wall, boats bobbed in the dark water like corks under a star-sprinkled sky. The remnants of the old boardwalk jutted up from the waves, like skeletal fingers pointing out the constellations. I crept silently along, keeping a wide distance between myself and Persi as she walked purposefully down the street. For someone who looked like they were up to something shady or possibly illegal, she certainly didn't carry herself that way. We'd traveled maybe half a mile down Harbor Street when Persi took a sharp turn, and disappeared through a gap in the sea wall. I quickened my steps, afraid I would lose her. When I reached the spot where she had vanished, I realized that it was the top of a staircase that led down to the rocky lip of ground that only appeared during low tide. I began to descend the stairs, which creaked with age; luckily, that creaking was swallowed up by the sound of the ocean, and the wind that whipped loudly against the sea wall.

The moment my feet hit the ground, I felt a sharp yank on the back of my sweatshirt. I yelped in surprise, but a hand clamped down over my mouth, smothering the sound. I was dragged backward into the deeper shadows underneath the staircase, and began thrashing in panic until I heard a voice whisper harshly.

"Stop flailing, Wren! It's me."

I recognized Persi's voice, and forced my panicking body to go still. As soon as I did, Persi removed her hand from my mouth, and turned me by my shoulders so that we were looking at each other face to face.

"What the hell are you doing?" she asked. "Why are you following me?"

"I thought we were being robbed!" I said, feeling defensive.

"So you followed a potential criminal down a darkened street to a secluded beach?" Persi asked, incredulously. "Good God, child, has my sister taught you even a modicum of self-preservation? If it was anyone but me, you could be dead right now!"

"Okay, fine, not my most brilliant moment, but what are you doing, looking like you're burgling your own store?" I asked.

"What are you doing outside the store at 1 o'clock in the morning?" Persi snapped back.

"I asked you first!"

"I'm an adult!"

"Well, you're not acting like one!"

She glared at me for a moment, and I glared right back. A second later, the corner of her mouth twitched into the merest suggestion of a smile, and I knew I had scored a point somehow. She dropped her hands from my shoulders, and sighed.

"You are infuriatingly like your mother sometimes, you know that?" Persi said.

I had no idea whether I should be offended or not, but it sounded like she was trying to insult me, so I crossed my arms over my chest and waited.

"I'm visiting Bernadette, okay?" Persi blurted out after a few seconds of expectant silence.

"I... you are?" I asked, my hands dropping to my side.

"Yes, and if you snitch on me, I'll hex you into oblivion. Now it's your turn. What the hell are you doing out here?"

"Nova wanted to perform a Cleansing on Bernadette, and she wanted my help. I came here to talk her out of it, but she didn't show. I think maybe she got caught sneaking out, but I don't know for sure," I said. The words were out of my mouth before I'd even really decided to tell her the truth. But she'd been honest with me, and so I felt like I owed it to her.

"Nova Claire?" Persi asked, her mouth falling open in shock.

"There can't possibly be another Nova living in this town," I said, before second-guessing myself. In a town like Sedgwick Cove, all bets were off.

But Persi shook her head. "No, it's just... I never thought I'd live to see the day when a Claire broke ranks."

"You are literally sneaking out to visit a Claire in prison, Persi," I said.

"Bernadette's different. You have to be *in* the ranks to break ranks, and she never bought what Ostara was selling. She was always determined to forge her own path, and they all resented her for it. They would have kicked her out of the coven if they weren't so worried about appearances." Persi's words were fierce, and I could tell that, in spite of everything, she was still fiercely protective of Bernadette.

"Quite the path she forged," I said.

"I don't... that's not what I meant. They were terrified of her gifts, and they didn't let her explore them the way she wanted to," Persi said.

"Yeah, and when left to her own devices, she brought back a servant of the Darkness and kidnapped your sister," I said quietly.

"She wasn't herself! She was... she's still..." Persi stammered.

"What are you really doing?" I asked. "I know you visited her already; I heard you and Rhi arguing about it."

"So, you're eavesdropping now?" Persi spat.

"No, you were shouting in the living room," I shot back. "It's not my fault you were too worked up to keep your voices down."

"I don't have time for this," Persi said. "I've got a small window here, and you're wasting it. So let me ask you this: If Nova had insisted on going through with the Cleansing, would you have ratted her out, or helped her?"

I hesitated. I thought about Nova, how she had been so distraught in my room, so sure that her mother was making a terrible mistake. I thought about the weight of the books in my backpack, the books I had snuck from the library in a rudimentary attempt to help. Would I really have left her to figure it out on her own, if I couldn't talk her out of it?

"I probably would have helped her," I admitted. "But she's not here, so I don't see the point of—"

"Fine, then. You can help me," Persi said, before turning on her heel and marching off down the beach. She was at least ten paces away before my brain caught up, and I started running after her.

"Help you with what?"

"You said you were down for a Cleansing, so you can help me."

"I didn't say I was... what are you talking about?"

Persi stopped and rounded on me so suddenly that I stumbled backward, and landed on my butt in the sand. "So, you'll help Nova Claire, but you won't help me?"

"Are you... you can't possibly... what?!" I gasped, as I scrambled to my feet.

"Your little friend isn't the only one who's been paying attention. The Conclave is in shambles. They're so caught up with infighting over Ostara's behavior that they're not doing their job. There's no longer a Vesper in the Conclave, or this would have been handled. So I'm stepping in."

"There's no way you and Nova were both independently planning a Cleansing on the same night," I said.

In reply, Persi swung her backpack around to her chest and unzipped it, revealing a book, candles, rope, and a number of other items I couldn't even identify. "I didn't want to use anything from the cottage, in case Rhi or your mother noticed it was missing, or caught me heading out the door. So, I took all this stuff from Shadowkeep instead. So what do you say? Are you in?"

I stood there for a moment, frozen with indecision.

"Why?" I finally asked.

"It was a yes or no question, Wren. I don't have time for this."

"I understood why Nova wanted to perform the Cleansing. I still don't understand why you do."

Persi's intense eyes bore into me, but I held my ground. It was a question I deserved an answer to, and she knew it. I held my breath, waiting.

"Bernadette is important to me. I know she's not well. I need to know how much of this was because she chose it, and how much had to do with the manipulation and control of Sarah Claire."

And I realized. All the words might have been about Bernadette, but this wasn't about Bernadette. Not really.

"You need to do this for you," I said.

Persi looked startled, but the look faded to one of resignation. "I do."

She looked at me and I looked back at her, this woman I shared such a deep connection with, through blood, through power. She was a stranger to me, and yet she didn't have to be.

"Okay. Let's do it."

Persi looked absolutely stunned, and I realized in that moment that she had not expected me to agree.

"Seriously?"

"Yes. And if we get caught, I'll tell them I was trying to stop you, and that you forced me to help," I said.

Persi's face split unexpectedly into a grin. "Noted. Now let's go. There's not a lot of time."

With that, she took off down the beach with surprising speed, and I struggled to keep up with her on the uneven terrain. She'd clearly walked this path before, picking her way expertly between the larger rocks, and avoiding the slippery places. I did my best to follow her exact route so that I wouldn't sprain an ankle, but it was no easy feat in the dark. We kept to the shadows where the beach met the sea wall, avoiding the pools of brightness where the streetlights from Harbor Street stretched down toward the water. At first, I thought Persi was being paranoid, saying we didn't have much time; but as I glanced out at the fishing boats anchored in the harbor,

I realized she might be right. Surely, fishermen set out incredibly early in the morning. We would want to be far from the beach before we had to start worrying about fishing crews spotting our flashlights bobbing around on the shore.

Nova hadn't explained where the Keep was exactly, just that it was down near the water; and so, I had no idea what to expect as we moved further and further down the beach. We made our way under the remains of the old boardwalk, and then under the structure of the new boardwalk to where the sea wall ended, and the cliffs began to jut up, separating the beach below from the waving dunes of sea grass, above. At last, Persi came to a stop where three large, jagged stones rose up in front of the cliff face. I came to a stop beside her, panting.

"Where is it?" I asked, when I had caught my breath somewhat.

"This is it," Persi replied, gesturing toward what appeared to be a solid wall of stone.

"I'm missing something."

Persi was already rummaging through her backpack. "It's got a spell of concealment on it, called a glamour. You probably haven't learned what—"

"Actually, I have," I said quickly, relieved not to be totally ignorant. "Rhi explained to me about glamours when she brought me by Shadowkeep the other day."

Persi nodded. "Well, this one can't be broken with just simple foreknowledge of the location. It requires another step."

"Isn't there, like... a guard or something?" I asked. "How can they expect a prisoner to stay secure with no guard?"

"They've used magic to secure it. Bernadette can't leave. I can't get into her cell or try to engineer her escape in any way, and I would be foolish to try," Persi said. "But a Cleansing should work. At least, I think it will."

"Why would a Cleansing work when other forms of magic won't?" I asked. My pulse was beginning to race, imagining that we were about to set off some kind of magical alarm system.

"Well, in the first place, we are Vespers," Persi said, and I could hear the ringing note of pride in her voice. "Our magic helped to fortify this place, and magic recognizes its origins."

"You mean the spells will... know us? Trust us?" I asked.

"Something like that, yes," Persi said. She was lighting a candle now with a tiny lighter that looked like a tube of lipstick. "And secondly, a Cleansing is something that ought to have been performed already, and has been performed on other prisoners in the Keep in the past. The fortifications allow for that type of magic, because it was anticipated that such a spell might be required." She turned and looked at me with a serious expression. "Bernadette is not the first witch to be locked up here due to the influence of dark forces."

"You mean, if Ostara would agree to a Cleansing, it could be performed right here, with Bernadette still in the Keep?" I asked.

"Correct," Persi said. "We're only doing what ought already to have been done. And if Ostara doesn't like it, she can take it up with me in front of the whole gathering of Sedgwick Cove covens, and she can explain to all of us why she hadn't already done it herself. I promise you, I am far more prepared for that scenario than she is."

"But you're not a Conclave member. I thought only Conclave members could get in."

"And all Conclave members have one of these," Persi said, holding up a silver amulet on a chain, which swung wildly from her fingers. "Asteria still had hers. I simply borrowed it. Now stop with all the questions. I need to concentrate."

Persi took a tall taper candle from her bag, and wrapped the chain of the amulet around it three times as she lit it. Then she reached into her pocket, and flung what appeared to be a handful of salt into the air. She muttered an incantation under her breath, and blew out the candle flickering between her fingers. I looked at the cliff face in front of me, waiting for something to happen. Then I blinked.

When my eyes opened again, the door to the Keep had appeared. Well, it was less of a door, and more of a jagged fissure in the rock that hadn't been there a moment before; but I recognized it for what it was: an invitation to enter. Persi moved forward with purpose, and I followed, trying to take comfort from her confidence.

I was expecting something like a cave, with rough, damp walls and a sandy, rocky floor; but as we passed through the opening, I gasped audibly. Inside the confines of the cliff itself was an almost modern chamber. The walls, though made of stone, were smooth and cleanly carved. The floor transformed from beach to concrete. Narrow metal pipes ran along the ceiling over our heads, and industrial lighting hung down from them, illuminating the room with a surprisingly warm glow.

"It's not all magic," Persi said, flicking a light switch, and illuminating still further along what I now recognized as a corridor. "The electricity is run down from above on Harbor Street."

We walked along the corridor to a door, which Persi unlocked. I raised an eyebrow at her, and she shrugged. "Asteria still had a key, too," she said.

"Not for long," I murmured, and Persi snorted.

The door swung open on loud, rusty hinges, and we were met with a gust of warm air from the room beyond. Just from the name "the Keep," I'd dreamed up manacles chained to the walls; but the place in which we stood looked much more like a modern jail might look. There were three cells along the far wall, separated from each other by cinder block dividers, and separated from us by a wall of bars. The outer room contained little except for a few stackable molded plastic chairs for visitors, a bench along one wall, a small trash can, and a row of hooks on the wall, presumably for people to hang coats. Inside the cells themselves, there were metal bed frames made neatly with tan blankets and pillows, toilets, and a sort of shelf that pulled down from the wall, and could be used as a desk when one sat on the bed. The cells were empty except for the one in the middle, where Bernadette sat, blinking at us in surprise.

Bernadette looked thin and haggard. I reminded myself that she had been thin before she'd been relegated to the Hold, but it didn't soften the shock of seeing her. Her eyes, always large, appeared to be bugging out of her skull, with deeply purple shadows sunken beneath them. Her hair was matted and tangled, hanging on either side of her hollow-cheeked face in great clumps. I swallowed hard against a lump in my throat, and then against the anger that followed it. This woman had held my mother hostage —had been content for my mother to die so that some ghostly ancestor could take her place. How dare she elicit my pity?

"Are you okay to be here?" Persi asked, and I turned my head sharply to see that she was watching me intently. "I'm sorry," she went on, and her expression was the softest I'd ever seen it. "It was pretty thoughtless of me to invite you here to do this. I should have realized it would be hard for you to see her."

"I'm fine," I said, not because I actually was, but because I was grateful to her for recognizing the position she had put me in; and also because I wanted it to be true. I wanted to be fine. I wanted the woman in front of me to hold absolutely no more power over my life. Even if it wasn't true yet, I was determined to make it true, out of sheer stubbornness.

"Are you sure? Because you don't have to—"

"I said I'm *fine*," I replied through gritted teeth.

Persi nodded once, and I was relieved to see that she accepted my answer. In a strange, unexpected way, I felt part of the wall between us crumble in that moment. I couldn't really process it right then, while staring into the face of the other woman in the room, the one who had tried to kill me, so I pushed it to the back of my brain.

As we had this hushed conversation, Bernadette was watching us with a curiously hungry expression. Persi stepped forward, and Bernadette cooed at the sight of her, wrapping her arms around her midsection.

"I knew you couldn't stay away," Bernadette said in a sing-song voice that made the hairs on my forearms leap to attention. "But who have you brought along with you?"

I stepped forward to stand beside Persi, and watched the exact moment when Bernadette's confusion turned to recognition. Her already enormous eyes grew even wider, and she slid down to crouch on the very end of the bed with an almost animal motion.

"Wren Vesper. You're here," she whispered. Her voice was raw and scratchy, like she'd been deprived of water, though I could see a glass of it sitting on the fold-down table beside the bed.

"It's not a social call," I said, the words coming out staccato as I practically choked on the anger surging up my throat. The sound of her voice, casually speaking my name, burned away the pity I'd felt at the first sight of her. How dare she talk to me? How dare she speak any words to me that weren't an apology?

"But I've been asking and asking to speak with you and they... they wouldn't allow it. How did you change their minds?" Bernadette asked.

Persi was frowning. "No one changed their mind. This isn't a sanctioned visit. We came on our own."

She tsk-ed loudly, and Persi flinched at the sound. "Breaking rules, as usual."

"Do you remember what we talked about yesterday, Bernadette?" Persi asked. Her posture was as languid and unbothered as usual; but her knuckles, I noticed, were white—she wasn't nearly as relaxed as she let on. I wondered if Bernadette could sense it, too. After all, she knew Persi much better than I did.

"Oh yes, I remember. Why did I do this, why did I do that? Why, why, why?" sang Bernadette. "Such an exhausting conversation. It seems to be the only question you know how to ask."

"It's the most important question, in my opinion, and yet you can't seem to answer it," Persi said, "and so I keep asking it."

"Oh, but I did answer it," Bernadette said, running her fingers back and forth across the bars. "You just didn't like the answer."

"I didn't like the answer because I don't think it's yours," Persi said, her voice still admirably calm. "I think it's Sarah Claire's."

Was it my imagination, or did something shift in Bernadette's eyes? There was a momentary flash, like a change of color, and then it was over, like a trick of the light. I had just decided that I'd imagined it when Persi muttered out of the corner of her mouth. "Did you see that? In her eyes?"

"Yes," I murmured back. "What is it?"

"It's why we need to do the Cleansing. There's more than Bernadette inside that cell."

12

Her words sent a shiver skittering down my spine. "Persi, what do you..."

"Shh," Persi said, for Bernadette was now rising from the bed and coming closer to the bars, head cocked to one side, as though curious about our whispered conversation.

"It's not nice to keep secrets," Bernadette sang from inside her cell.

"Do you hear it?" Persi asked, ignoring Bernadette's words as she placed her backpack on the table, and started rifling through it. "When she speaks, do you hear it?"

"Hear what?" I asked, but Persi just shook her head and then cocked it toward Bernadette, who was now pouting and talking to herself on the other side of the bars. I paused for a moment, and listened hard.

Now that Persi had pointed it out, there was something very strange about her voice. I barely knew Bernadette—I think I had spoken to her a total of three times before she was arrested, and even then, I was hardly making a study of her voice—but even I could hear it, now that Persi had drawn my attention to it. There was something in the cadence, something... antiquated. The only way I could explain it was the difference between listening to an actor in a contemporary movie, and then listening to that same actor perform in a period drama. There was a different style, a different lilt and rhythm to the words that sounded, to my ear, to belong to another time. And I was quite sure it hadn't been there when I'd spoken to Bernadette before.

I looked at Persi again, and she was watching me, watching that realization kindle in my eyes.

"Do you understand now?" Persi asked.

I nodded, because the pieces had fallen into place. Ostara's fear was true, and Nova had been right. Sarah Claire was somehow attached to Bernadette.

"We will never understand how culpable Bernadette is until we untangle this mess of spiritual coercion, and that means we have to sever the ties between them," Persi said.

"Persi." I waited until she was looking directly at me before I continued. "Even if this Cleansing works, even if we're able to completely separate the two, there is every chance that Bernadette was a willing participant in all of this. You may do all of this, and find out that that was the case all along. Are you okay with that?"

There was a muscle jumping in Persi's jaw as she stared back at me. Then she let her eyelids flutter closed, and took a long slow breath in and out before opening them again.

"Yes," Persi said, and I heard no defiance, no defensiveness—only acceptance. "I have had to make my peace with worse things. Not many, but still. I will be fine. I still want to know. I need to know. I can't move forward unless I do, and I will move forward regardless of the answer."

She may have been looking at me, but the promise she was making was to herself, and we both knew it. I also knew—and I wasn't sure how I knew—that she would keep it.

"Okay," I said. "Then let's do this."

Persi smiled at me—it was quick and small, but sincere. Then her face dropped back into a furrowed expression of concentration as she emptied the contents of her backpack onto the table. There would be no more bonding tonight. We had work to do.

Persi handed me a fragrant bundle tightly wound in string, along with her lipstick lighter. "Light this, then count to ten and blow it out, so that it smokes, but you can no longer see any flame."

"What is it?" I asked, fumbling with the lighter.

"Lavender, rosemary, and cedar," Persi replied.

Behind the bars, Bernadette had gone very still. She was no longer talking and singing to herself, and she had lost the almost playful attitude she had been exuding from the moment Persi had entered. It was as though Bernadette had been playing a game, in charge of the rules, and suddenly Persi had pulled the rug out from under her. The game had changed, and Persi was now making the rules. Bernadette watched unblinkingly as I lit the bundle and counted.

"Now what?" I asked.

"Walk in an unbroken pattern around the four corners of the room, waving the bundle up and down. Start here, in the north corner. The idea is to touch as much of the room as possible with the smoke."

I did as she instructed, taking slow and careful steps, and watching the tendrils of smoke curl up into the shadowed recesses of the corners. A rich, heady fragrance began to fill the room, and my eyes began to water; but I continued doing as Persi had instructed me. As I walked past the cell where Bernadette was sitting against the bars, I felt her eyes on me.

Don't look at her. Whatever you do, don't make eye contact.

I couldn't explain to myself why this directive was so strong in my head, but it was as though I was screaming at myself. What was this feeling? I didn't remember feeling this way when I'd seen Bernadette in the lighthouse that night. I was much more frightened of the poisoned knife she had clutched in her hand than I was of her personally. Had I been too distracted, or was something different about her now? I certainly wouldn't have blamed myself—or anyone else there that night—for being too caught up in the chaos to notice something subtle, but strange, lurking in the back of Bernadette's eyes. Had it even been there yet? Had Sarah already curled up inside Bernadette like a hibernating creature, or had that come later, after the Darkness had been defeated? I finished my walk of the room's perimeter, and arrived back beside Persi.

"Lay it here," she said, pointing to a small bowl, like a mortar. "And let it burn out on its own." I did as she instructed, laying the bundle carefully in the bowl, where it continued to release curling smoke like spectral threads up toward the ceiling.

I watched as Persi reached into a leather pouch, and extracted a handful of coarse sea salt. She tossed the salt into the four corners of the room, her lips moving in a constant but silent incantation. For the first time, as the salt hit the floor with a soft shushing sound, Bernadette reacted. An undulation rolled through her body, like a wave toward the shore, and a strange hissing sound escaped her lips. The sound seemed to startle her, and for the first time, her expression shifted. Initially, she had seemed only curious about what we were doing. Now, there was a tentative wariness to the cock of her head, and the lines around her mouth.

"There she is," Persi whispered.

"There who is?" I asked.

"Sarah Claire. We've lured her out," Persi said. There was a deep, ringing satisfaction in her voice, the kind of satisfaction that can only come from being proven right in a crucial moment.

The name, meanwhile, acted like a trigger for Bernadette. She slammed her hand down against the bars, and the sound echoed brightly through the room.

"This isn't about Sarah Claire. This is about me!" she said.

"You're right, Bernadette, if that's even who I'm talking to," Persi said, not bothering to look up from her preparations. "It is about you. It's about finding you in all of this."

"You can't do this," Bernadette hissed through clenched teeth.

"I am already doing it," Persi replied.

"There's nothing to find. I've done what I've done, and I'm proud of it. Why does everyone feel they must take away my agency, simply because they don't approve of what I've done? Are my own actions no longer mine? Am I not allowed to own my mistakes?" Bernadette asked.

"If I'm wrong, which I'm not, then this Cleansing will do absolutely nothing. You will still be yourself, in full control of your words and actions, and you will have all the agency you could ever desire," Persi said. "You'll be able to confess and take responsibility, if that's what you want to do, and I will personally lock the door and throw away the key."

"You won't," Bernadette cooed. "You won't do that. You love me. I can see it in your eyes."

Persi looked up and met Bernadette's eye then, her expression calm and steady and edged just a little by grief. "I do love you. But I will no longer allow myself to be exploited because of it. And yes, I do promise you, I will do it. I will not do it happily, but I will do it, and you would be smart not to test my resolve on that point."

Bernadette's top lip curled into a snarl, and she beat her hand against the bars again.

"Be careful," I whispered to Persi. "You're pissing her off."

"No, I'm pissing Sarah off. There's a difference," Persi said, still with an admirable facade of calm, even as the tiniest of tremors crept into her voice.

"Aren't you worried that she's going to... I don't know, fight back?" I asked.

"She can't. The spells on this place have utterly decimated her powers, and Sarah is powerless without a living witch to carry out her bidding. Her connection to Bernadette is the only thing keeping her here. It's time to sever the connection between the two, and send Sarah back beyond the veil where she belongs."

"But once Sarah is disconnected from Bernadette, what will stop her from just... I don't know, hopping straight into you or me, like an empty Uber?" I asked.

"It doesn't work that way," Persi said. "Once she exits Bernadette, we will trap her in an object. Then we destroy that object. That should send her back beyond the veil."

"What's the veil? What does that even mean?" I asked.

"It's the only thing that stands between us and the beyond, and Sarah Claire is on the wrong side of it. But after this Cleansing, we will have cut her ties here. The beyond will claim her again."

I felt like my head was spinning. I had to push a swirling mass of questions about the afterlife away for the time being, because Persi was now rolling up her sleeves to perform the next part of the Cleansing spell; and I suddenly found I wanted to have all my wits about me for whatever the hell was about to happen.

"What object are you using to trap her? Can you just use... anything?"

"No," Persi said. "You have to use something that has a blood or life connection."

"Meaning?"

"Meaning either something the spirit handled while alive, or something handled by a member of their bloodline," Persi said, and she tapped her finger on a book she'd pulled from her bag.

"What is that?" I asked.

"A book from the Manor. I took it from the library when we were summoned there. Unexpectedly helpful, that summoning. Instead of inventing some kind of pretext for entering the Manor, I was invited."

"You mean you stole it?" I asked.

Persi gave me a withering look. "You mean did I take one of Ostara's own items to solve a problem that she created? Yes, I did."

But I was hardly listening. I'd just remembered what I had sitting in the bottom of my backpack. Something else stolen.

"Persi, would something that Sarah Claire actually owned work better?" I asked.

Persi rolled her eyes. "Almost certainly, but we don't have anything that she—"

"I do," I replied, as I reached into my bag. I pulled out the mirror and laid it on the table.

For a moment, Persi could only stare at the mirror in undisguised shock. Then she looked at me with something akin to wonder. "Should I even ask how you came to have this sitting in your backpack?"

"Probably not. It was Nova. I told you she was determined to see this through."

Persi smirked. "I knew I liked that girl. Okay, well, we'd better get started. Dawn isn't far off."

"Is this safe?" I asked her.

"Should be," she replied.

"*Should* be?"

"Well, I've never actually performed one before—not like this," Persi said. She caught my eye and then added, "I've performed many Cleansings. I've just never specifically Cleansed an angry centuries-old spirit from the body of an ex-girlfriend, and frankly, neither has anyone else I know."

"So, you're saying this isn't typical Sedgwick Cove relationship drama? I'm so glad to hear that," I laughed, my voice rising a full octave.

"Wren. Get a hold of yourself."

"Sorry," I said, and took a steadying breath. "Seriously, though, what happens when the—bond or connection or whatever it is between them—is broken? Will Sarah just be hanging around, ready to attach to someone else like a parasite?"

"No, she'll be drawn out of Bernadette and into this mirror," Persi said. "And then we'll destroy the mirror. Once that's done, she'll be sent back to the other side of the veil, where she belongs. And she knows it. That's why she's trying to hide."

Persi then reached into her bag and pulled out a long, thin braid of white, blonde hair. At the sight of it, Bernadette let out an angry hiss, like a cat. Persi looked over at her, her expression almost amused.

"Oh, do you recognize this? I would hope you do. You gave it to me when you swore we would be bound together in love for all of this earthly life. I was besotted enough with you at the time that I tucked it away, like a treasured possession. I nearly burned it when you betrayed me, but I thought better of it. I knew there had to be a better use for it. At the time, I was seeing red and thinking only of revenge; but then I realized I could put it to much better use in another way."

Persi then took a bundle of ribbons from her bag. She began to wind them, one by one, around the braid of hair. "These ribbons represent the dark manipulations of Sarah Claire. They are the hold she has upon you, Bernadette Claire, the source of her power over you. They are the choking weeds that throttle you, the puppet strings that control you. They are the manifestation of her influence, her energy, and her power."

Persi held out the hair, now tightly bound in different color ribbons, and dangled it in slow, deliberate circles —first clockwise, then counterclockwise, over the still smoking herbs in the bowl. I watched, entranced as the smoke curled and danced around the hair, how it seemed to circle and snake itself around each knot, each twist. Behind the bars Bernadette—or perhaps Sarah—was actually snarling with anger. She beat her hands against the bars again, her palms red with the fruitless effort.

Next, Persi pulled a tiny dagger from her bag. She pulled it from its leather sheath to reveal a slightly curved, wickedly sharp blade. Then she held up the bound braid of hair, and slipped the point of the dagger beneath the first ribbon.

"I release you from this dark energy," she murmured, and sliced neatly through the first ribbon, which fluttered away to the floor. My eyes darted toward Bernadette, who was now howling with anger, and throwing herself against the bars.

"Persi, she's going to hurt herself," I muttered.

"A few bruises are a small price to pay to get her soul back, wouldn't you say?" Persi replied. Still, the next time the bars rattled, she flinched; and I knew she didn't like the idea of Bernadette injuring herself.

"I release you from this dark energy," she whispered again, and cut through a second ribbon.

Bernadette had now jumped to her feet, and was making furious swipes toward us with her thin but powerful arms. The sounds escaping her sounded like an incantation of her own, something lilting but dark, in a language I didn't recognize.

"I release you from this dark energy," Persi repeated once, twice, three times more. At last, she sliced through the last of the ribbons.

Bernadette let loose a screech of rage, and then fell to the ground in a heap, like a marionette whose strings had been cut. As she hit the ground, a cloud of dust rose up around her, dark and almost sparkling, like soot. The cloud hovered, swirling like mist, and my breath caught in my throat.

"Is that... that's not..."

"Sarah Claire," Persi breathed. "Or what's left of her. Quick, the mirror!"

I held up the mirror, and Persi began to tie the ribbons to it, her fingers sure. As I watched, I looked into the mirror and saw something in the reflection that caught my attention for just a moment. A word, carved into the stone of the wall behind where Bernadette now lay: Kildare. I'd barely had time to register it before my attention was drawn away again, this time to the strange sparkling, smoke-like cloud that was Sarah Claire. The cloud shifted, forming, for a brief moment, an almost human shape before shooting across the room, and directly into the mirror. Persi yelped and dropped the mirror, which landed with a clatter on the table, looking old and innocuous as ever.

Persi and I stood motionless, hardly daring to breathe, waiting for something else to happen. When nothing did, Persi sagged beside me with a sigh of relief.

"I think we did it," she murmured. "I think she's gone. Can you feel it?"

I thought I understood what she meant. The entire atmosphere of the room was lighter somehow. It was as though a gust of fresh air had swept through, and took the mustiness and the decay and the dark, heavy energy of the place with it. I turned to Persi and felt a smile spread slowly over my face. Persi, on the other hand, darted forward to where Bernadette still lay in a motionless heap against the bars of her cell. She reached through, snatched up Bernadette's hand, and pressed her fingers to her wrist.

"Pulse is steady and strong. I imagine she'll sleep for a long time now," Persi said, slumping into a seated position with a sigh. "If she's been fighting against Sarah at all, she will be exhausted, mentally and physically. We won't know until she wakes how much she remembers."

"What if she tells the Conclave about this?" I asked. "Won't you get in trouble for coming here, and doing this without their permission?"

"I won't give her the chance," Persi said. "I'll go to the Conclave tomorrow and demand an audience. I'll tell them exactly what I did, and why." She looked at me, almost as an afterthought. "Don't worry, I'll leave you out of it."

"But won't you be in huge trouble?" I asked. Surely what Persi and I had just done was the witchy equivalent of a felony? I didn't yet know much about how the Conclave functioned in Sedgwick Cove, but I knew they were powerful enough to make life difficult for anyone who disobeyed them.

"Most of the Conclave were pushing for this to happen," Persi said, rising to her feet now, and brushing the sand and dust from her leggings. "They'll make a show of admonishing me, but I doubt I'll get more than a caution, maybe an official writ of warning, if they're feeling spicy. Either way, I don't care. Whatever happens now, whatever she says, whatever she does, I know it's her choice. Even if she breaks my heart again, I'll know she meant to break it."

She stroked Bernadette's hair once more, tenderly, and then turned to me.

"Come on. Let's get out of here."

I followed her out of the Keep, back down the improbable hallway, and out onto the rocky shoreline. We retraced our steps to the pier, but this time, Persi didn't turn to ascend the steps back up to Harbor Street. Instead, she began climbing the stairs that led to the pier.

"Persi? What are we doing?"

"We're sending Sarah Claire right back through the veil, where she belongs," Persi huffed.

I followed breathlessly behind her as she charged down the pier and, when we had reached the very end, watched as she hurled the mirror with all her strength. We watched it shatter on the rocks before being swallowed up by an incoming wave. Only when it had disappeared did Persi let out an exhalation of relief, her shoulders sagging with exhaustion.

She turned to me. "We've done what we can do. It's time to go home."

13

"What's Kildare?"

"Huh?"

We were flying back along the road toward Lightkeep Cottage, Persi behind me, using the leather satchel on the back of my bike as a makeshift seat.

"I saw it carved into the wall behind Bernadette's head, in the cell. What does it mean? Is it like, an incantation or something?"

"No, it's a name. The Kildares were a coven that lived in Sedgwick Cove a long time ago—close to two hundred years ago, I think."

"Why's their name carved into the wall of the Keep?"

Persi laughed humorlessly. "Probably because they saw it as a badge of honor to be locked up in there. They were a nasty bunch, or so the stories go."

"Really?"

"By all accounts, they made no secret of their affinity for dark magic. They rose quickly when they came, gathering allies and challenging hierarchies. Soon it became clear that they were not content to simply coexist in Sedgwick Cove —they wanted the deep magic for themselves. They even tried to summon the Darkness, like Sarah Claire had once done.

When their attempts were discovered, they were banished, but not before they spent a bit of time in the Keep."

It surprised me to hear of another coven doing what Sarah Claire had done, but I supposed it really shouldn't have. I was beginning to understand that the deep magic was a temptation that brought out the worst in those who sought it. Absolute power corrupts absolutely, or whatever the saying was.

We managed to make it in the door, and up to our rooms without arousing any suspicion. I fell into bed fully clothed, and didn't wake up until well past ten o'clock. My mouth felt like sandpaper, and my head was pounding. I'd never been hung over, but I thought this might be how it felt. I really needed to start sleeping on a normal schedule again.

The door to Persi's bedroom was closed, and the room on the other side of the door was quiet. I didn't have the courage to knock, though I wondered how she was holding up. Other than answering my questions about the Kildares, she'd been silent the whole way back from the Keep — the kind of silence that demands to be respected rather than broken. So I had taken my cues from her, and we had not discussed Bernadette or Sarah or anything that had transpired that night. I wondered, in the light of day, if she had any regrets. Maybe, given how late I'd slept, she was already gone, off to turn herself in and confess everything to the Conclave. I supposed I'd hear about it one way or the other. It would likely be all over Sedgwick Cove within an hour of her walking out the door. I didn't know a whole lot about my hometown yet, but I did know that gossip spread like wildfire, and that Persi frequently made herself the subject of that gossip.

My mom wasn't in her room, or anywhere in the cottage. I decided not to text her or try to hunt her down. My relief over the successful Cleansing was already fading, and I was ready to dive back into my studies. I ate my breakfast with one of my introductory magic books propped up against the pitcher of orange juice. I spent the next couple of hours reading and taking notes, and then heading out into the garden and seeing how many of the plants and herbs I could identify by sight. The answer was not a lot, so I started taking pictures of them all, and storing them in an album on my phone, so that I could flip through them almost like flash cards. Then I started making a map of how they were all laid out that I could study. I'd only just begun this, though, when Rhi came running out to the garden.

"Wren, there you are! I was looking for you everywhere!" she said, slightly out of breath.

"What's up?" I asked, rising from the grass and brushing the dirt from my knees.

"Do you think you might be able to come down and help at Shadowkeep for a little while this afternoon? Persi is... well, she's got something she needs to deal with." Rhi attempted a smile, but it was forced and slightly manic.

I kept my expression as neutral as possible. "Sure, no problem."

"You won't be by yourself, I'm headed over, too. I just need someone to keep an eye on downstairs when I need to pop up to the second floor."

"I think I can handle that," I said. "I'm supposed to meet Zale at six for pageant stuff. Do you think we'll be done by then?"

Rhi nodded. "Shop closes at five, except by appointment on the second floor. I wouldn't ask, but with tourists coming in for the Solstice Festival, we're busier than usual this week."

"It's fine. I'm glad to help," I said, clamping down on the urge to ask more about Persi.

"Great. I'll just change clothes and we can head over there," Rhi said, glancing down at her flour-sprinkled overalls.

Despite her usually chatty nature, Rhi hardly spoke a word as we rode side by side into town on our bikes. She kept her eyes locked ahead of her, and she was chewing anxiously on her lower lip. I could only conclude that Persi had done as she said she would, and gone to confess to a member of the Conclave. What would happen now? She'd said she would keep me out of it, but would she really be able to do that? Would she even want to? Persi and I had been together—cooperated with each other—during a very vulnerable moment for her. Had she woken up today and remembered how much she still resented me? If so, I was likely to be in nearly as much trouble as she was. My palms were sweaty against the handlebars of my bike, and I could feel nervous perspiration starting under my arms. Despite this, I told myself I didn't care. I told myself that I had done the right thing by helping Persi, and I still believed it. If I had to face consequences for that, so be it.

The door to Shadowkeep had been locked, and a sign had been hung in the front window: *Gone for a Spell. Be Right Back.* I smirked at the pun, but quickly sobered my expression as Rhi fumbled with the keys, swearing under her breath. She pushed open the door, flipped the sign, and checked the register as I followed behind.

"Can I do anything for you while I'm here?" I asked Rhi, as she paced absently behind the counter, looking like she'd forgotten something.

"Huh? Oh, no thanks, honey. Why don't you keep on with your studies? I'll give you a shout if I need you."

I shrugged, and settled on a velvet green settee in the back corner of the shop that was piled with decorative pillows that said things like, "I'm Here for the Boos," and "Are You A Good Witch or A Bad Witch?" I settled in and pulled out the pageant script, feeling guilty that I hadn't really looked at it much, but had only managed to read a few pages when the bell for the upstairs echoed down the stairs.

"I'll be right back," Rhi said. "Are you sure you'll…"

"I'll be fine," I said, tossing the script aside, and coming around behind the counter.

"We're not really digitized. It's part of the charm, or so Asteria thought," Rhi said, smiling weakly. "Just punch in the prices on the tags, and the register will total it for you. And this button opens the till."

"No problem, I've had to make change before," I said. "I'll figure it out. Honestly, I'm fine."

Rhi hesitated, but a second ring of the bell sent her scurrying upstairs instead. I slid onto the stool, opened my book again, and tried to pick up where I'd left off, trying to find some semblance of concentration. I listened to the gentle music of wind chimes out on the porch. I breathed in the herb-scented air. An antique clock ticked up on the wall. Rhi's footsteps and the muffled hum of conversation echoed overhead.

And then I heard my name.

At first, I was so lulled by the atmosphere of the shop that my brain took a moment to catch up. It was almost as though I expected the sound, like it was a natural part of the soundscape of Shadowkeep. This was my family's shop. My name belonged in this place as fully as I did. Then, I heard it again, and it sounded... insistent.

I looked up toward the ceiling, my heart beginning to race. Surely it was just Rhi, talking to the customer upstairs, and happening to mention me. That made much more logical sense than what my intuition was screaming at me. Surely the simplest explanation was the correct one. I should have realized by now that that particular adage didn't apply in a place like Sedgwick Cove.

Wren. Wren Vesper.

This time, I felt the words inside my head even as I heard them outside of myself, and once again, I felt a pull toward the window. I abandoned the script on the counter, and approached slowly. I knew who I would see. I knew who would be waiting for me.

Asteria stood in the garden, looking at me. Her expression was at once warm and loving, but also somehow mournful. She looked not-quite solid, and yet there was no mistaking her. She wore the dress I had last seen her in, a colorful confection of patchwork and lace. I'd nearly convinced myself that she'd been a dream that night I saw her standing outside my bedroom window, but now there she stood again, in broad and shining daylight; and I knew I had no more dreamed her then than I was dreaming her right now. Every part of me was awake, drinking her in.

"Asteria," I whispered.

She raised a single hand in a gesture that seemed to speak at once of greeting and farewell. I raised my own hand and pressed it to the glass, feeling the longing for her to sing in my bones, and knowing that even if I ran out to her, she'd be no closer or further away than she was to me in that moment.

Wren. Tread carefully, my love.

"Why?" I whispered.

They still seek you. You must—

The bell over the door jingled brightly, and I spun away from the window with a startled gasp to see Luca Meyers freeze with one foot over the threshold of the door.

"Oh, shit, sorry. Did I... I didn't mean to scare you," he said, looking warily around the inside of the shop, like he was unsure if he should walk the rest of the way in. He hooked his thumb over his shoulder at the door behind him. "The sign says open."

"Luca! No, it's fine, I... we are open, I was just... distracted. What are you—come on in," I said. I'd been about to ask him what he was doing there, but then I remembered it was a shop. Why did anyone walk into a shop? I tried to pull myself together as I chanced one last glance out the window. Asteria had vanished again.

If Luca noticed my awkward greeting, he didn't show it. His face split into an easy smile as he loped in.

"Hey, Wren. So, you've got your family putting you to work this summer too, huh?"

"I guess so," I replied. "Can I, uh... help you find anything?"

"No, I'm just—" he gestured over his shoulder, and at that moment a woman walked in through the door behind him.

She was a strikingly beautiful woman—the sort of woman that usually only seems to exist in the pages of fashion magazines. She was tall and statuesque, with impossibly long legs, made longer by four-inch stiletto heels. Her pale pointed face was surrounded by a cascade of dark curls, and her full lips, when she spotted me, curled into a smile.

"—here with my mom," Luca finished.

I did my best not to gawk at the woman while she removed an oversized pair of designer sunglasses to reveal grass green eyes, fringed with thick lashes.

"Luca, do you know this young woman?" she asked, looking curiously back and forth between the two of us.

"Uh, yeah. Mom, this is Wren Vesper. Wren, this is my mother."

"Veronica Meyers," the woman said, extending a perfectly manicured hand, which I hurried forward to take. "It's a pleasure to meet you."

"You, too," I said, feeling suddenly self-conscious about my bitten fingernails, not that Veronica seemed to take the slightest notice. She was smiling at me pleasantly, and I did my best to smile back.

"And how did you two meet?" Veronica asked, looking back and forth between Luca and me. "I hadn't realized Luca had had any time off for socializing. His uncle's got him working all kinds of hours." She leaned toward me conspiratorially, like she was inviting me to share in some private joke. "I told him he should just enjoy his summer, but he's determined to work himself to death."

Luca squirmed uncomfortably. "I told you, Mom. I'm saving up for a car."

"And I told you I would buy you one," Veronica said, looking absolutely bewildered.

"I know, and I appreciate it, but that's not what I want," Luca replied. It was the first time I'd ever seen him look anything but utterly relaxed. His face was bright red, and he was staring at his feet, his hands shoved deep into his pockets. "I want to do it myself."

Veronica rolled her eyes. "He's got his heart set on this rusty old relic, and then he wants to spend months and thousands of dollars to restore it. Boys and their toys," she added with an airy laugh.

Luca's tight smile was his only response. I felt a pang of pity for him. It was obvious just from Veronica's handbag that they were loaded. He probably could have had any car he wanted, brand new. He was probably used to having things handed to him. I had to admire that he wanted to work for something on his own, without his parents' help.

"Sorry, we got off track. How did you two meet?" Veronica asked again.

"Wren is in charge of the Litha pageant," Luca said.

"Actually, my friend Zale is directing it," I said hurriedly. "I'm just helping out. Thank you again for letting us borrow the old costumes and props and stuff."

Veronica waved my thanks away with a casual flick of her hand. "Heavens, no need to thank me, I've hardly ever set foot in that place. It's my brother who keeps it running. I should be thanking you for putting some of that old junk to good use. I keep trying to convince my brother to clean those storage buildings out, but he's such a packrat. Can't bear to throw anything away, in case they might need it for a future production."

"I think that's like, a requirement for theater," I said, laughing. "Every theater needs a lowkey hoarder in charge of inventory. At least, the amateur ones do."

"Well, I can't say I know anything about it," Veronica said. "This is the first summer I've spent here since I was a little girl. Such a quaint little town. So... kitschy." She reached out and picked up a candle shaped like a witch hat, and gave an amused if bewildered sort of sigh. I felt a sudden rush of defensiveness until I remembered that the Shadowkeep she was seeing wasn't the real Shadowkeep. The kitschiness served an important purpose, and if she thought these silly souvenirs were all there was to our family's shop, then they were doing their job.

"So, what is this festival all about, then? The town seems abuzz with it," Veronica said.

"It's for the summer solstice. There will be a sort of sidewalk festival, with food and shops setting up stalls outside. And then at night, they have the pageant, which sort of dramatizes an old story about the solstice. That's the part I've been helping with," I said.

"Fascinating," Veronica said, with the air of someone listening to the mating habits of extraterrestrials, rather than the details of a town fair. It grated on me just a little, and I had to remind myself that I'd likely have thought it all rather strange only a few short weeks ago.

"Yeah, if only the script was fascinating," I said, picking it up and brandishing it, "instead of cringy and badly written."

"Oh, dear. Yes, I imagine these quaint small town productions leave something to be desired. If only we were hosting the playwrights' festival this summer, you might be able to get some help with it."

I sighed. "We'll just have to deal with it, I guess. None of the adults seem to mind that it's trite and corny. It's a tradition, apparently," I said. "It's the first one I've ever been a part of that I can remember. I haven't lived in Sedgwick Cove since I was a baby."

"Well, you know, my grandmother came from Sedgwick Cove; but as far as I know, she never had anything much to do with all... this." Again, she gestured around at all the merchandise with a dismissive flick of her hand. "Couldn't wait to get out of this place, by all accounts. Small town girl desperate for big city life. She worked on Broadway, you know. Never a big star, but my grandfather made sure there was always a part for her somewhere. I don't think she ever looked back."

I just smiled, unsure of what to say.

"Still, I can see why the tourists like it, and thank goodness they do, or the playhouse wouldn't still be thriving," Veronica said, and then glanced at her Rolex. "Speaking of which, your uncle will be waiting for me, Luca. I'm sorry we can't keep sightseeing. Can you bear to carry on without me?"

Luca rolled his eyes. "I think I'll survive."

Veronica threw him an air kiss and winked at him. "Don't let her put a spell on you!" she said, and with a tinkling laugh, she swept from the store.

It took Luca a full five seconds to raise his eyes from the ground. "And there you have it. The Veronica Meyers experience. Sorry about that."

"What are you apologizing for?" I asked. "She seemed... nice."

"If by nice you mean overbearing and condescending, then sure, she's nice," Luca replied.

I suppose I must have looked surprised because Luca sighed and shook his head. "I'm sorry, Wren. I shouldn't be unloading my frustrations on you."

"It's fine," I said automatically.

"It's really not. It's just... I came here this summer hoping to sort of... get a break from her, you know? She was telling the truth. She's been here maybe twice in her whole life. She's never shown the slightest interest in coming out here and leaving the city. She always has a million events and galas and business functions to attend for the family. I thought I could just have a quiet summer—hang at the beach, earn some money, just... find some space, you know? But then suddenly, a week ago she shows up in my room with a suitcase, and announces she's coming, too."

"Just the one suitcase?" I asked, smirking.

It worked. Luca's face broke into a real smile. "Well, no. More like a nine-piece set of matching luggage. But you get the idea."

"Look, I get it. This isn't the summer I had in mind either," I told him.

He raised his eyebrows. "Really?"

"I thought I was going to spend my summer scooping ice cream and hanging with my friends in Portland. And now I'm here, permanently. My grandmother passed away. She sort of left me her house."

"She left you her house? Aren't you, like..."

"Sixteen? Yeah."

"Whoa."

"I know, right?"

Luca puffed his cheeks out, running a hand through his hair. "When my grandfather died, he left me a pocket watch and a coin collection."

"Yeah, it was pretty intense, bequest-wise," I admitted. I could have gotten into all the family drama it had caused, but I didn't want to dump all my problems on him, either.

"So you just moved into it? By yourself?"

I laughed. "No, my mom and I moved in. And my aunts were already living there, so now we're all there together. We've got a lot of history here—my family, I mean, the Vespers. And once we came back... well, let's just say that Sedgwick Cove is one of those places that gets a hold on you and doesn't let go."

Luca nodded, not like he totally understood, but like he was trying to. "So now instead of scooping ice cream, you're... casting spells?" he asked, pointing to the array of pre-bottled potions on the shelf behind me.

I smiled. "Not casting them. Just selling them," I said. "Are you in the market?"

"Hmm. Got anything for overbearing mothers?" he asked.

I laughed. "Not in stock at the moment, but I'll let you know if we get any in."

He sighed theatrically. "Okay, well, I guess I'll see you around. Will you be at the theater this week?"

I felt a little flutter in my chest, even as I told myself it was a completely normal question to ask someone. "Yeah, I'll be there. We have just over a week to pull this together. Just listen for the sound of Zale having a mental breakdown, and I'll probably be there."

"Cool. I'll see you around, then."

"Yeah. See you," I replied.

He smiled again and walked to the door. I forced myself to turn around and pretend to be busy at the counter, so that I wouldn't just gawk at him as he walked down the street. I looked up at the wall behind the counter, and right into the gilt-framed mirror that hung there. A perfectly unremarkable face stared back: gray eyes behind tortoiseshell glasses, thin lips, narrow, freckled nose, and a messy bun piled on top, like a lopsided crown.

"Get real, Vesper," I whispered.

14

When I arrived back at Lightkeep Cottage later that afternoon, it was to find the house empty, except for Persi. She hadn't returned to Shadowkeep, and Rhi had stayed behind to close up. Persi was sitting on the front steps as I pulled up on my bike.

"Hey," I said.

"Hey, yourself," she replied, the words muffled by the clove cigarette dangling from her lips.

"Rhi told me you were... dealing with something," I began, as I approached the stairs to sit next to her, "and I was just wondering if—"

"If I ratted you out to the witchy powers that be?" Persi asked, raising an eyebrow. "No. But I did go to the Conclave and tell them about the Cleansing, minus your involvement."

"What happened?" I asked. "I mean, you're here, so at least they didn't throw you in the Keep."

Persi smiled and blew a smoke ring. "Not this time, at least."

"Well?" I finally prompted when she showed no signs of going on.

"I thought they were furious at first," Persi said. "I'd expected that. But it soon became obvious that what I was getting was fury from Ostara, and a show of fury for her benefit from the others."

"Really? They didn't vote to... I don't know, excommunicate you or something?"

Persi chuckled. "Hardly. When I'd explained it all, Xiomara thanked me. Said I'd saved them all the trouble of having to go over Ostara's head. Ostara didn't like that at all, but what can she do about it now? It's done with."

"She should be happy, shouldn't she? Or at least hopeful? Finding that Sarah had attached herself to Bernadette means there's a chance Bernadette wasn't acting of her own free will."

"Ostara is never happy when she isn't in complete control. But yes, I think, because of that, she let me off with only an official warning." Persi looked at me and smiled her most winning smile. "I have a talent for getting out of trouble to match my talent for getting into it."

"Useful."

"Very."

"Hey, you haven't seen my mom around here anywhere, have you?" I asked. "I feel like I've barely seen her in the past couple days. It's almost like she's avoiding me."

To my surprise, Persi looked uncomfortable. "Yeah, she's around," she said vaguely.

"Around... where?" I asked.

Persi sighed. "Ugh. I don't want to... look, you're partly right, okay? Your mom isn't avoiding you, but she's definitely avoiding something."

"What do you mean?" I asked.

Persi was literally squirming now. "It's not my place, but... well, your mom is having a sort of witchy existential crisis. You know, being back here, dealing with her own magic. I think she's struggling—not that she's confided in me about it."

"No offense, but you aren't really the confiding type, are you?" I said.

Persi shrugged. "I can be. We used to be a lot closer, Kerri and me."

I thought about my mom, and wondered if this return to Sedgwick Cove had driven a kind of wedge between us, me ready to embrace my magic and her...

"What kind of witch is my mom?" The question popped out before I could stop myself.

Persi looked at me, indecision all over her features. Then she said, "The walled garden."

"I don't... huh?"

"A minute ago, you asked where your mom is. The walled garden. I'm not the person you should be getting your answers from. Go talk to her."

It wasn't really a suggestion... more of a command, and one that I was more than willing to obey. I stood up and walked out into the garden, winding through the familiar sections that bordered the house, to find the lavender door set in the stone wall. I'd been in this part of the gardens only once before, when my mom and my aunts had used a spirit board to summon Asteria's spirit. Asteria had left it for them, knowing they would need it to connect with them. Was that because none of them were elemental witches with a connection to spirit? And if that was the case, what did it mean that I'd seen Asteria twice now without using a spirit board? The first time, I'd practically written it off as a dream. But the second time, at Shadowkeep... there was no question of dreaming then. Did I have an affinity for spirit after all? Because if so, Rhi's theory that I might be a pentamaleficus might just turn out to be true.

These questions carried me almost unconsciously to the lavender door in the garden wall. As it had been the last time I'd been here, the door was partially open. I slipped sideways through it, and into the garden beyond. Almost at once, I spotted her in the center of a clump of bushes.

"Mom?"

I'm not sure why I hesitated, like I wasn't sure it was her. But for a second, it hadn't *seemed* like her. Something about her felt different, or maybe it was several little things. Her hair, usually up in a messy bun on the top of her head, was falling in thick brown waves around her shoulders. Her usually ramrod straight posture had a relaxed droop to it. And her expression, which seemed permanently harried and stressed these days, was softer. She looked... well, maybe not happy, but peaceful somehow. Content.

The first time, the word had come out as little more than a whisper, easily carried off on the breeze. The second time, I made sure she would hear me.

"Mom!"

She peered up from the rose bush she was examining, looking almost guilty —like I was the parent, and I'd caught her doing something she knew she shouldn't be doing. But then the expression softened again, and her lips curled into a rueful little smile.

"Wren. You found me," she said. "I was... hiding."

A sharp emotion shot through me, something with an edge of pain to it. "Oh. I'm sorry, I didn't mean to... I can go."

"No, sweetie, don't go. I just... I wasn't sure how I'd feel, having you here."

I frowned. "I've already been here, remember?"

"Yes, but you didn't know what this place was then, and I didn't tell you. A holdover from all those years of secrecy, I guess," she said with an embarrassed little shrug. She pointed to a tree just to her left. There was a plaque affixed to it, one I hadn't noticed the last time I was here, sneaking around and spying in the dark. It said, "Kerridwen's Garden."

"Oh. This... this is *your* space."

"It used to be," she said, her voice little more than a broken whisper.

"Mom, seriously, it's fine. If you want to be alone, I totally get it," I said, wanting to run from the vulnerability on her face. I didn't want her to have to open up parts of herself she wasn't ready to open, just so I could peer inside. She didn't owe me that. Well, maybe she did, but I wouldn't collect. I'd already forgiven her for lying to me.

"No," she said, and the guilt was gone. She sounded a little more in control of herself. "No, it's fine, Wren, honestly. I do want you to see this place. I've been working up the courage to ask you to come here with me— I guess that's what I was trying to say. So, thank you for finding me here. If we'd waited for me to work up that courage, you might never have seen it."

I'd been so focused on my mother that I'd barely glanced at our surroundings, other than the plaque. Now I took a long moment to gaze around me, and my mouth fell open.

The word "garden" could hardly do justice to the beauty of this place. Gardens were neat and orderly, trimmed and pruned and mowed. This place felt like the wild version of that kind of garden; a place where the plants themselves decided where they loved best to grow, and were just free to do it. Vines tangled up trees, and draped from their branches. Peonies were poking their fluffy heads up between the branches of rose bushes. Herbs seemed to spring from the ground in bouquets, a dozen fragrant plants all mingling happily.

And the colors... oh my goodness, the colors.

A memory shot to the surface of my mind. I was six years old, and my mother snuggled up with me on our worn sofa and introduced me to The Wizard of Oz. Now, I was a kid of the modern world: every video I'd ever seen was in color. But when Dorothy left the dull, dreary sepia tones of Kansas behind and stepped into the vibrant Land of the Munchkins, I was awestruck, like it was the first time I'd ever seen color on a screen.

That's what I felt like in this moment: Dorothy stumbling into Technicolor.

"Does this mean that your magic is... that you're a..."

"A green witch, like Asteria was? Yes. It seems, despite my best efforts, that is still true," she said. There was the strangest tone in her voice, a searing combination of wonder and sadness. She reached out a tentative hand, and touched a rose that hovered an inch or two from her fingers. As she did, another layer of brilliant petals unfurled around it. It put a lump in my throat that I had to swallow against before I could speak again. But my mom continued before I had the chance to fully compose myself.

"I spent almost all my time in this garden, Wren. As a girl, I followed Asteria around her gardens, tending to the plants and my budding magic at the same time. I know Asteria was so happy that one of her daughters had finally inherited her gift. She would never have admitted it out loud, but I knew she was disappointed that Rhi and Persi had never shown any inclination for the garden. I couldn't get enough of it. Sometimes, I would fall asleep under a bush or in a tree, and Asteria would have to come find me and carry me inside to bed. But when she woke in the morning, my bed would be empty, and I'd be snoozing in the branches somewhere. Eventually, she gave up trying to bring me inside, and just brought me a blanket instead."

She smiled, and it wasn't as sad now. I found I could smile back. It sounded like the kind of mad thing Asteria would do, letting a toddler sleep in the flowerbeds all night.

"When my gift began to emerge, Asteria decided I needed a garden of my own. The one next to the house—that was hers. It was full of her magic. There was no real way to know what I could do unless I could start with a blank canvas. And so she gave me one. She walled off this little patch of land for me, and set me free in it. There was instruction—it wasn't complete chaos all the time, though probably more often than not. She let me experiment. She let me test and practice and plant and tend and dig up and try again. This place was... my little magical laboratory. All mine."

I could see it in my mind, my mother as a wild, barefoot child with dirty fingernails and flushed cheeks, flowers tucked in her curls, vines wound around her limbs like living jewelry. I felt the smile spread across my face. My mother saw it, and smiled back, as though in acknowledgment of that same little girl she used to be.

"It went on that way for years, me and my garden, all wrapped up in each other. My sisters were older, already entangled in the deeply personal process of unraveling their own gifts. We had each other, but we were each, for a little while, consumed with ourselves; Rhi with her recipes and her ingredients, Persi with her potions and charms. It's inherently selfish, this exploratory stage of magic." She hesitated, biting her lip. "Maybe not selfish, that's not quite it... self-involved? Self-centering? In any case, though we loved each other, and loved Asteria, our magic was the most important thing as we discovered it. The most important thing... until you came along."

She smiled at me, a softer smile than the mischievous grin of a moment before. I returned it, eager for the smile to carry us into the next part of this story she was telling me.

"It was a gravitational shift, Wren. I can't say that I had planned for you. You were a surprise, as you know... the best surprise. But when you arrived and the midwife laid you in my arms, the center of my universe moved outside of myself. My world no longer revolved around the magic in my veins. It revolved around you. The shift was instant and irreversible. You became the most important thing to me. I hadn't expected it. Or at least, I hadn't expected the force of it." She smirked. "This is the part where you get to scoff and say I'm being dramatic and mushy."

My eyes had filled with tears. The fact that I had to wipe them away made the exaggerated roll of my eyes slightly less effective. "Seriously pathetic, Mom," I said, in the most sarcastic teenage tone I could muster under the circumstances. She smiled, appreciating my efforts.

"In any case, you became the new focus, Wren. My magic became... well, not unimportant, but secondary. My sisters underestimated that, but Asteria never did. I think she knew that you were more important to me than anything else, even more than my ties to this place. It's why she tried to protect you herself that night. It's why she didn't tell me what had happened until I confronted her."

My heart sped up. She was telling me so many things that I'd always wanted to know, but had been too afraid to ask.

"The night the Darkness came for you, I wasn't with you at the house." She said it like each individual word was being painfully ripped from inside her. "I was here, in this garden, trying to find a small portion of peace for myself. I'm not sure if anyone's ever told you this, but being a mom is kind of hard, and no toddler is a picnic. I was tired and feeling a bit burnt out. I came here to... to be a little selfish again, I guess. To reconnect with myself. And in that couple of hours..." She shook her head, unable to continue.

I took a step toward her, wanting to comfort her. "It's not your fault, Mom. The Darkness was waiting. If it hadn't come that night, it would have come another night. And another after that. Even the most attentive parent can't be watching 24/7."

She sighed. "I think enough time has passed that I know that. Logically. But then? When it happened? Wren, you can't begin to imagine the guilt, the horror I felt when I walked back in the house to find Asteria had you in that protective circle. I... think I lost my mind for a short time there, I really do. I held you all night in that circle. And only at dawn, when Rhi and Persi came to relieve me, to insist I eat something and get some sleep, only when they had you guarded between them did I leave that circle. But I didn't go to the kitchen to eat, or to my bed to sleep. I came here. I came here, to the place I built entirely with my own magic, and I destroyed it."

I must have looked skeptical. I glanced around me, but I couldn't imagine a place more vibrant, more... alive.

My mom interpreted my expression perfectly. "Asteria," she said, shaking her head. "She rebuilt it for me, during the years we were gone from Sedgwick Cove. I never asked her to. I never wanted to think about this place again. But she knew what I didn't know, of course. She knew about the Covenant. She knew we'd have no choice but to come back one day, and when we did, she wanted this place to be waiting for me." What started as a laugh ended in a sob. "I really didn't deserve her. It wasn't this place I was mad at. It was me. My magic."

I realized I was holding my breath, and let it whoosh out of me. I felt almost dizzy with the weight of all she was telling me.

"The other thing I didn't know then, Wren, was that the Darkness was after your magic. After all, we had no idea what your magical gifts would be. Vesper witches are traditionally powerful, but not always. One of Asteria's cousins never really managed much magic at all, never developed a clear affinity. So, it does happen, even in families like ours. But even assuming you would someday be a witch of potent magical ability, my mind couldn't fathom that the Darkness wanted you for you. I thought the Darkness wanted you to get to us. I thought it wanted the Vespers. And that meant that my magic had put you in danger."

I pressed my lips together. Just because I thought I should respond didn't mean I had any idea what to say.

"It wasn't just that I wanted to run from this place, Wren. I wanted to run from myself. From my magic. I wanted to sever myself from the thing that put you in danger. It seems ridiculous now, but I was crazy with fear. I thought I could do it. I thought I could walk away from my magic. I thought if I never used it, if I let it wither on the vine, if you'll pardon the plant analogy, that it would shrivel up and drop away. I wanted to starve my magic. So that's what I did."

"You moved us to a city, somewhere that didn't have many trees or green spaces," I said.

"That's right. I never had plants in the house. Not even cut flowers. I told you it was because I was allergic, that I had a black thumb, that I was too busy or tired to take care of anything but you. But of course, the truth was that I didn't want to tempt myself. I didn't want to give my magic anything it could work on."

"How did that make you feel?" I whispered. "Wasn't it hard?"

"It was, harder than I ever could have imagined, but I didn't allow myself to acknowledge it. I was a mourner who was completely burying her grief. It… wasn't healthy. It's one of the reasons I would get so angry when Asteria came to visit. It wasn't just that I was worried that she'd let something slip to you. It was because she was the living embodiment of what I'd chosen to leave behind, and I… I resented her for it. I was jealous."

My mother was revealing herself to me, layers of delicate petals peeling back to reveal what was in her heart; and though some of it made perfect sense, I never, in a million years, would have thought my mother jealous of Asteria. I couldn't reconcile that emotion with what I'd seen pass between them, but then, I'd never understood any of it until Asteria was gone.

"I'm sorry you had to… to choose between me and who you are," I finally managed to say.

My mother's face crumpled. "Ah, shit. This is one of the reasons I kept putting this off, Wren. I knew you would find a way to blame yourself, and that's the last thing I want. This whole mess is my fault, honey, not yours. These were my choices, and I… well, I wouldn't say I don't regret them. Let's face it, this whole situation is messier than that." My mom passed a hand over her face, and sighed deeply. "I regret running away from Sedgwick Cove because, in the end, it didn't protect you. I should have known that it wouldn't. Asteria certainly knew, but I couldn't bring myself to listen to her. And now here we are without her. What I wouldn't give to be able to take her advice now."

My heartbeat stuttered. Should I tell her that I'd seen Asteria just this afternoon, standing in the garden of Shadowkeep? Surely not. What purpose could it serve? Asteria certainly wasn't here now, and I had no idea if I would ever see her again. No. Best to keep my mouth shut, at least for now. If I saw Asteria again, then maybe… well, I would cross that bridge if I got to it.

"Thank you for telling me all this," I said instead. "That was… you really didn't have to."

"Yes, I did," my mom said. "I've owed you an explanation for a long time, Wren. You didn't get the full story even after the lighthouse, and that's inexcusable. And so, I'm offering you another apology as well. I know moms are supposed to have it all together or whatever, but… well, I hate to break it to you, but moms are just people stumbling through life like everyone else. We only pretend to have it all together so you'll listen to us."

"I'm gonna remind you that you said that," I teased.

"Good. Maybe it will keep me humble, and help me stop and think before I do something else as monumentally stupid as abandoning this place," she said, gesturing around her.

I followed the path of her hand through the air, taking in the garden again. "You said Asteria took care of this place for you?"

My mom nodded. "The most remarkable thing about it is that it still feels like *mine.* She fixed it but, magically speaking, she left hardly a fingerprint. Now that's a skill I have yet to attain."

"Maybe you should start practicing," I suggested.

And then at last, my mother *really* smiled: a full, uncomplicated smile that lit up her face and made her look, for a moment, like the girl who had once brought life and color to this place. She reached a hand out for mine, and I took it.

"Maybe I should."

15

I could happily have spent hours in that garden with my mom. Seeing her perform her magic was as strange and wonderful as anything that had happened to me since arriving in Sedgwick Cove. I couldn't find it in me to be angry that she'd never shown me this side of her—I was too happy to watch her embrace it again. I wondered if this was what it had been like when she was a girl, watching Asteria bring color and growth, with nothing but the power tingling in her fingertips. But though I was impressed with each and every mesmerizing bit of green magic, it was clear my mom was frustrated.

"I suppose I couldn't neglect my magic for thirteen years, and expect everything to come flooding back to me," she said, sighing over a wilting hydrangea blossom. "Looks like you and I will both have some practicing to do."

But that practicing would have to wait. I had a stop to make before I went to Eva's house.

I pulled my bike up in front of the Manor, my heart pounding. I'd texted Nova several times, but she hadn't replied to me. I was starting to think that maybe she'd had her phone taken away. I checked with Eva and Zale, too, but no one had heard from her. The Conclave knew about the Cleansing now, but that didn't mean that Nova did.

My whole body was buzzing with anxiety as I walked around the side of the house. I knew Ostara wasn't home. I'd overheard Rhi on the phone with Xiomara, talking about the Conclave and how they were at the Historical Society for final approval of the exhibits for Litha. I wasn't sure how long they'd be there, so there was no time to waste. I didn't know who else might be home, but I wasn't going to risk them turning me away at the door. I counted the windows along the back of the house, until I was under Nova's room. Then I picked up a small pebble, smooth and rounded by the sea, and threw it toward her window. It took three failed attempts and three successful ones before Nova's face appeared. I watched her eyes go wide, and then she opened the window.

"Wren? What the hell are you doing?"

"What does it look like I'm doing? I'm trying to get your attention!"

"Why didn't you just ring the doorbell? I'm the only one home."

"Well, how was I supposed to know that?" I asked.

Nova rolled her eyes. "I'm coming down. Meet me at the front door."

I stomped back around to the front of the house, grumbling under my breath. So, it was okay for her to break into my bedroom like a thief in the night and scare the shit out of me, but I was ridiculous for tossing a few pebbles? I had half a mind to get back on my bike, and not tell Nova a damn thing about the Cleansing. But as I rounded the corner and saw her standing on the front porch, her thin arms wrapped around her midsection, her face tight with worry, I sighed and felt all my aggravation whoosh out of me with a breath.

"Look, I'm sorry I bailed on you," Nova blurted out, before I could say anything. "My mom caught me sneaking out, and grounded me. I was lucky to get that one text off to you all before she took my phone. I thought you'd put two and two together, so I didn't bother to—"

"Nova, this isn't about that. The Cleansing happened without you."

Nova just blinked at me. "You don't mean... Wren Vesper, did you seriously try to do that all by yours—"

"Are you out of your mind? Of course not!" I said, and launched quickly into an explanation. The longer I spoke, the wider Nova's eyes got. By the time I'd finished, she looked like she'd forgotten how to blink.

"Oh my goddess! My mother is going to lose her ever loving shit when she—"

"She already knows," I cut in. "Persi went to the Conclave today to confess everything. They didn't even go hard on her. She said she got an official warning."

"Unbelievable. And here I am, grounded for the next month."

"Seriously?"

"She won't even let me out to help with the Litha pageant, and that's like a local cultural requirement." Nova exhaled sharply, her nostrils flaring. Then, all at once, her shoulders sagged, and all the fight went out of her. "Bernadette's okay?" she asked in a small voice.

"Yeah. Well, I think so. In any case, she's herself again," I said. "And now they'll be able to question her without Sarah's interference."

Nova's voice dropped to a hoarse whisper. "I hope she wasn't... I hope she didn't know that..." She couldn't finish, but she didn't need to.

"I know. Me, too."

We both jumped as the phone rang shrilly inside the house.

"Probably Ostara checking to make sure I stayed put while she was gone," Nova ground out. "I've got to go. Tell the others I'm sorry? You know, for the lying and for not being able to help with the pageant."

"I will, but seriously, don't worry about it, Nova. They understand."

Her face twisted with an emotion she couldn't repress. "I don't think they do. But, thanks."

And she ran into the house, closing the door behind her, a little harder than was strictly necessary.

* * *

The Marins lived in a beautiful old house right on the corner of Main Street and Hecate Lane, less than two blocks from the cafe. It was bright yellow, with shutters and a door painted robin's egg blue. A Cuban flag and an American flag fluttered enthusiastically on the pole jutting out from the porch, and pots of flowers and herbs crowded the railings and windowsills. From that porch, I could see the beginnings of preparations for the Midsummer Festival. A few shops had already begun erecting stalls on the sidewalks, and a stage was being constructed on the grass in the middle of the town's only roundabout. A huge banner fluttered above Main Street, and brightly colored flyers had been stapled to all the light poles, and taped onto shop windows. Soon, the steady trickle of summer tourists would become a horde, and the quaint and quiet street would come alive with the bustle and magic of a Sedgwick Cove celebration.

"Hey, Vesper. Come on in!" Eva called from inside, before I could even knock. I supposed she could see me through the big picture window by the front door.

I pushed the front door open, and let myself into the living room. It was as cheerful and colorful as the outside of the house, with coral-colored walls and flowers everywhere. Eva was standing in the doorway to the kitchen. She had a bottle of soda in her hand.

"I was just grabbing a drink, you want something?" she asked.

"Sure, thanks. Whatever you're having," I said, pulling off my shoes and placing them by the door, where a small pile of shoes was already sitting.

Eva pulled another bottle from the fridge, and closed the door with her hip. Then she popped the tops off with a bottle opener that hung on the wall, and handed one to me.

"Xiomara makes this herself. It's delicious," she said.

I didn't need convincing; everything Xiomara made was delicious. I took a sip, and sighed. Flavors of ginger, citrus, and tarragon burst on my tongue.

"Is that Wren?"

A woman appeared from the room beyond the kitchen, a tall woman with full lips and sharp cheekbones, like Eva's. Her hair stood out in a beautiful natural halo all around her face.

"Yeah, Mama, this is Wren. Wren, this is my mom, Maricela."

"You can call me Mari. Everyone does," she said, holding out a hand for me to shake.

"It's really nice to meet you," I told her, taking her hand. It was warm, and her handshake was firm.

"I told Eva you could use my workshop for the pageant costumes,"

Mari said. "And I told her I could help with the sewing, if there's any to do."

"I'm happy to hear that, because I don't know how to sew at all," I admitted. "I was kind of hoping we'd be able to do all of this with a glue gun and duct tape."

Mari's smile widened. "Well, if that turns out not to be the case, you girls can give me a shout. I know no one in the Conclave will say as much, but I'm glad you're trying to overhaul this pageant. It's been sad and tired for decades."

"It has not!" came Xiomara's voice from the room beyond the kitchen. "You just don't know how to appreciate tradition!"

Mari rolled her eyes. "Aren't you supposed to be communing?" she called.

"Yes. The ancestors told me to pass that on," Xiomara called back.

"*Ay, Dios mio, mama.* No, they did not!" Mari grumbled.

"You young people and your need to shake everything up. *Hasta el ultimo pelo.*" Xiomara went on.

"What do you mean, communing?" I asked.

"Oh, she's been unsettled like the rest of us with... well, I surely don't need to explain it to you, do I?" Mari said, with a knowing look. "So she's been trying to commune with the ancestors, to get some insight into what's happening."

My face must have been full of confusion, because she clarified.

"My mother has that gift—to communicate with the deceased. She uses that gift sometimes to seek guidance."

I nodded slowly, even as my mind spun. Rhi had told me that Xiomara was a powerful spirit witch, but seeking guidance from our deceased relatives? Was that something witches could do? Could I? And moreover, was that why I'd seen Asteria twice now? Was she trying to give me guidance, and I was just too unskilled to receive it?

"Wren? You ready?" Eva asked, frowning a little at me.

"Huh? Oh, yeah. Let's get to work," I said. "Nice to meet you, Mari."

"You, too, Wren. We're glad you and your mom are back in Sedgwick Cove, where you belong," Mari replied.

"I... me, too," I said, and quickly turned to follow Eva up the stairs.

"Shh," Eva said, as soon as we'd reached the top of the stairs. "Come to my room first, I need to talk to you."

I followed Eva down a short hallway and into her bedroom. Her mom had clearly given her free rein to decorate how she wanted —the walls were the color of the Caribbean, and she had drawn and written all over them: song lyrics, poetry, quotes, and doodles, blossoming across the walls like living, growing things. Her bed in the corner was draped in mosquito netting hung with tiny, white fairy lights. She had an altar on a shelf over the bed; and her bookshelves, bedside table, and desk were piled with seashells, driftwood, little bowls of sand, and jar after jar of...

"Is that water?" I asked, approaching the shelves so that I could examine the jars more closely. They were all labeled in a hand so rushed and crowded, it was barely decipherable.

"Yeah, I collect it for spell work; rainwater, moon water, stormwater, ocean water, they all have their uses," she said.

I must have been staring because she smiled. "We've never really talked about affinities before, have we? At least, not mine. I'm a water witch."

"Really? I had no idea," I said. "What exactly does that... mean?" I asked.

"It just means I'm drawn to the water. My magic works best when I'm working with water, or near water. Lucky for me, really, that we live right by the ocean," she said with a smile that quickly faded. "Now what's going on? I overheard my mom and *abuela* talking about Persi and Bernadette. What happened, do you know?"

I sat down on the edge of her bed, and sighed. "You should have popped some popcorn for this one." And for the second time in an hour, I told the whole story of the Cleansing. Then I explained my visit to the Manor.

Eva let out a low whistle. "Persi took a huge risk."

"I'm still only just getting to know her, but I think that's kind of her thing," I said. "Being ungovernable."

"Well, at least this time, it paid off," Eva said. "So what happens now?"

I shrugged. "I don't really know. Sarah Claire can't interfere again, but that doesn't mean it's over. It feels like I'm just sort of... waiting for the Darkness to try again."

Eva grinned, and nudged me with her elbow. "You don't think the Darkness learned its lesson, messing with you the first time?"

I laughed humorlessly. "I think that was mostly luck, and the Darkness knows it."

Eva's grin faded down to a grim smile. "That was more than luck, Wren. I know you're raw and untrained, but you are powerful."

"I don't feel powerful."

"Doesn't change the fact that you are."

"But how can I—"

Thump. Eva and I both turned to the sudden sound which came from the direction of her closet.

"What was that?" I asked, but Eva had already stomped over to the closet door, and yanked it open.

"Bea! How many times do I have to ask you not to hide in my room!" Eva shouted.

Bea was crouched on the floor of the closet, staring back at her older sister with a mixture of embarrassment and defiance on her face. "How else am I supposed to find out what's going on around here?" she demanded, in a small but steady voice. "No one tells me anything!"

"No one tells you anything because you're still a kid," Eva said, and though she still looked aggravated that her privacy had been invaded, her tone softened just a little. "I know it's frustrating. I've been there, Bea. Truly, I get it. But there really is stuff that a kid shouldn't know about—that they aren't ready for. And there's a lot of that going around at the moment."

"You're still a kid, too," Bea shot back, not backing down.

Eva almost smiled, but managed to smother it. "True. But I'm a big kid. You're still a little kid. And there's a difference, Bea, as much as you wish there wasn't."

Bea pressed her lips together around whatever retort she was longing to throw at her older sister. However, at that moment, Eva's mother called from downstairs.

"I'll be right back," Eva said to me, before rounding on Bea again. "When I get back, I want you in your own room, where you belong."

Bea stuck her tongue out at Eva's retreating back, flinching when Eva slammed the door on her way out.

The silence expanded to fill the space left behind by Eva's absence. At last, I felt compelled to break it.

"She's just trying to look out for you, you know," I said.

"She thinks I'm a baby," Bea said, pouting; and then, realizing that pouting was rather a babyish thing to do, tucked her lower lip in and sat up straighter, trying to look dignified.

"Maybe," I said with a shrug. "I don't have any siblings, so I should probably mind my own business." At that moment, Bea shifted her position on the floor, and I noticed for the first time what she held in her lap. "What's that?" I asked her.

Bea's complexion darkened with embarrassment, and she made to hide the object behind her back. "Nothing."

"Oh, come on," I said, smiling and winking in what I hoped was a conspiratorial way. "Is it Eva's? A diary, maybe? Come on, let's see."

Bea looked almost affronted. "I wouldn't read Eva's diary, even if I knew where she hid it," she said. "It's... it's mine."

"Your diary?"

"No. My sketchbook," Bea replied, dropping her gaze to the book she had tucked behind her leg.

"You like to draw?" I asked.

Bea nodded, and I watched as something kindled in her eyes. "I love to draw," she amended.

I slid off the edge of the bed, and came over to sit on the floor in front of the closet. "I wish I could draw, but I can barely manage stick figures. What kind of stuff do you like to draw?"

That spark I'd seen in her eyes ignited, and the words burst from her, as though she'd waited since the day she was born for someone to ask her that very question. "Everything! The ocean. Plants and animals. People. People the most. But not as they really are."

"What do you mean? How do you like to draw them?" I asked. At first, I'd just been trying to cheer her up, but now I was actually curious.

"I like to draw people the way I imagine them. How they *should* be," she explained solemnly.

"How they should be?"

She frowned. "It's sort of hard to explain. No one really walks around as their true self. They walk around being the person other people want them to be. That always makes me sad. So when I draw someone, I draw them the way they really are. On the inside."

I blinked, and did my best to swallow my astonishment. Instead, I attempted a casual nod and said, "You must be a talented artist, then. Would you let me see one of your drawings?"

Bea narrowed her eyes at me, as though she was sizing me up, judging whether I was worthy of this most prestigious honor. She hesitated so long that I wondered if she'd ever shared her drawings with anyone at all, even her own family. At last, she nodded slowly, once, and leaned closer to me, her voice a mere whisper.

"I can show you one. But you have to promise not to tell anyone," she said.

I quickly raised a hand, like I was swearing in before a judge—in a weird way, it felt like the same thing. "I promise. I give you my word as a Vesper."

Bea seemed to take those words as seriously as I meant them. She pulled out the notebook that had been concealed behind her leg, and placed it on her lap. She thumbed through the pages before laying it open to a portrait.

"This is Xiomara," Bea said, in the tiniest of voices.

I stared in awe at the creation in front of me. It looked exactly like Xiomara—that much was obvious to anyone who had ever met her. Bea had, in relatively few strokes of her pencil, captured the high cheekbones, the wry mouth, the wise eyes. But it wasn't just that it looked like Xiomara —it *was* Xiomara, just as Bea had said. Xiomara was in the details—the towel thrown over her shoulder, the spoon held so naturally in her grip, the proportions of her hands, which had conjured and cooked and nurtured themselves into a gnarled shape that was, in itself, poetry. Around her, hovering over her shoulders, were a dozen vague, shadowy shapes that lacked true definition, and yet were unmistakably people. I thought about what Eva had told me, that Xiomara's food was so wonderful because it was as though she had the ancestors whispering in her ears.

"You're absolutely right, Bea. That *is* Xiomara," I murmured.

Bea nodded again, as though she knew every detail that had just flashed through my mind. "I don't show these to a lot of people. I don't think they would understand. And it feels like... like giving away other people's secrets."

"Because you see them in a way that other people don't?"

"Yes. I think sometimes I see things that they would rather hide. That they do hide. Every day."

I looked down at the sketchbook in her hands, and was suddenly burning with curiosity. What did little Bea see that other people didn't? Who else had she drawn, and what had she revealed about them with a few strokes of a pencil? I longed to look through every page to see what else I might be able to learn about the people around me. Maybe even...

"Have you ever drawn me?" I asked.

I expected Bea to look embarrassed again, but she didn't. She nodded solemnly at me instead, never taking her eyes from mine.

I felt unaccountably nervous. "Is... that something you would ever let me see?" I asked.

Bea tilted her head to one side, considering. "Maybe. But not today."

I nodded. It might have been a drawing of me, but I certainly didn't feel entitled to it, no matter how curious I was. It belonged much more to Bea than it did to me; and anyway, for all it might reveal about me and how she saw me, it would surely reveal almost as much about her, and that had to be her choice.

Suddenly, Bea sighed, her face crumpling.

"What's up?" I asked.

"I wish I knew what it meant."

I waited for her to clarify, and a moment later, she obliged.

"My drawing. Sometimes, I wonder if it might have something to do with my magic."

"What do you mean?" I asked.

Bea chewed on her lower lip, considering. "I know everyone is waiting for me to find my affinity. They expect it to be something flashy and exciting. When Eva first showed her affinity, she almost flooded the whole house."

I laughed out loud. "The tracks," I said.

"But it seems to be that way for everyone—the first time they show their affinity, it's obvious. Sometimes I wonder if I have any magic at all." This last statement came out in a whisper, a confession she was almost ashamed to speak out loud.

I felt a pang, not just for her, but for me. "You know, Bea, I've worried about the same thing?"

Bea's eyes went wide. "You? But... the beach... I've heard my sister talk about it, when she thought I couldn't hear."

I nodded. "Did you know that was the first sign of magic I ever showed?"

I had the satisfaction of watching Bea's mouth fall open. "Ever?"

"Ever."

"But... how?"

"I'm not really sure. I'm sure part of it was that my mom never let me near anything related to witchcraft. I didn't even know about our family history. So, I never really had a chance to test my magic, and see how it manifested. It wasn't until that moment on the beach that I felt the spark, and I realized what I could do."

Bea didn't seem capable of replying. Her mouth was still hanging wide.

I pointed to the sketchbook in her hand. "There's magic in there, Bea. I can feel it. Can't you?"

Bea looked down at her sketchbook. "I... I don't know. Sometimes, I think I can."

"Trust yourself," I told her. "Magic doesn't have to be flashy. It doesn't have to be big to be powerful, and it doesn't have to look like everyone else's to be real. Be patient with yourself. If you asked me when I was ten if I had any magic, I would have laughed in your face; and now half of this town full of witches is terrified I'm going to call the elements to destroy them. And can I tell you a secret?"

Bea nodded eagerly. I leaned in, dropping my voice to a whisper.

"I have no idea how I did it."

I had told her because I wanted her to feel better, and yet saying it out loud made *me* feel better... lighter, somehow. It was a confession I needed to get off my chest, to someone who wouldn't just brush it off. In a weird way, Bea was the perfect person to tell.

"We're all just figuring it out as we go... the big kids, too," I told her.

Bea's lips curved into a smile. Then she said, "I wasn't just spying, you know. I was trying to help. With the pageant."

"Oh! Well, you've probably noticed we could use all the help we can get. How did you want to help?"

"I saw all the stuff you got from the theater, and I thought... well, the masks are cool, but they could be cooler if we painted them."

I looked over at the giant gold comedy and tragedy masks propped against Eva's wall.

"Painted how?" I asked.

Bea flipped ahead a few pages in her sketchbook, and held it up for me to see. She had created two images, one of the Holly King and one of the Oak King. It was clear she was inspired by what we'd already borrowed from the theater—the figures were dressed in long cloaks and had the greenery and the headpieces like the ones we had found, but she had pulled it all together into something cohesive and arresting. The masks were detailed now, not just in solid gold, but painted to look like terrible ancient faces. She had added other details I hadn't thought of—icicles and frost to the Holly King, and a collar on the Oak King's cloak that looked like the sun rising behind his head.

"These are amazing, Bea!" I gasped. "Do you think you could actually paint the masks to look like this?"

Bea nodded. "I love to paint, too. And I thought we could use—"

At that moment, the door opened, and Eva walked back in carrying a tray of snacks. Bea snapped her mouth shut with an audible click, clamming up at once under her sister's frustrated gaze.

"Bea, I told you to—oh," she said, stopping short. She looked surprised to see me sitting on the floor of her closet.

"It's my fault," I told Eva. "I held her up. We were just chatting."

Eva looked at me, her eyes full of questions, but she nodded, accepting the excuse.

Bea, meanwhile, had risen to leave, but I held out a hand to stop her. "Show your sister your ideas for the pageant."

Eva's eyebrows shot up, and she shifted her attention to Bea. "What ideas?"

"It's nothing," Bea said, digging her toes into the carpet.

"Oh, come on, Bea, it's not nothing!" I cried. "It's brilliant! Come on, let Eva see!"

Bea threw a non-committal glance my way, and I smiled encouragingly. Finally, she sighed, opened to the sketch, and turned it around so Eva could see it. I watched with satisfaction as Eva's eyebrows rose, and her mouth fell open.

"Bea, what the hell?" she gasped. "These are... did you seriously come up with this?"

Bea was trying very hard not to look too pleased with herself as she nodded.

"We have to show this to Zale. Bea said she could paint the masks to look just like this," I added.

"And we could add these to the cloaks," Eva said, looking excited now as she pointed to the icicles. "Glass ones would be too heavy and loud, but I bet we could make them out of glue and some serious glitter."

I turned to Bea, whose tentative smile was slowly blossoming with every word. "I think you're hired, Bea. Welcome to the design team!"

"Let's go down to the theater," Eva said. "Zale should be down there rehearsing everyone. He needs to see this." She turned to her little sister and gave a playful flick to one of her braids, causing the beads to clack against each other. "I guess I should let you eavesdrop more often, *hermanita*."

Bea raised her chin. "I guess you should."

16

Over at the theater, Zale looked ready to pull his hair out. He stood on the lip of the stage as Sergei and Ethan attempted to toddle around on the stilts we'd found in the storage building. They were supposed to be learning to walk on them, and instead, they kept trying to sweep them out from under one another, and make the other fall.

"Will you two stop dicking around, and learn how to use those things already!" Zale shouted, looking close to tears.

"We are learning to use them," Ethan insisted, as he lurched dangerously to one side and took a vicious swipe at Sergei's knees, which Sergei successfully dodged, but then lost his balance and toppled backward into the curtains.

"Not as weapons!" Zale shouted. "We have the staffs for that!"

"Yeah, and we don't even get to carry them!" Sergei complained, as he disentangled himself from the curtains. "The whole reason I took this part was because I get to do the fight scene, and now you're telling me someone else is going to be controlling the arms on these things? What's the point if I don't get to hit someone?"

"The point is to put on an entertaining performance!" Zale snapped.

Off to the side of the stage, four of the girls stood holding staffs and the branchy arms Zale had built for the puppets. They looked bored and aggravated, and kept rolling their eyes at the boys on the stilts.

"Are we ever going to get a chance to do anything?" Petra whined.

"Not if we have to wait for those two to grow up," Kaia grumbled.

"I'm not going near them until they can keep their balance," a third girl added. "I don't want to get trampled."

Zale's hair was sticking straight up from the number of times he had run his hands through it. He turned toward us as we walked up the aisle, looking like a mad scientist with anxiety.

"How's it going?" I asked.

Zale let loose a hysterical cackle of laughter in reply.

"That good, huh?" Eva asked, grinning.

"My goddess, they are so pretty, but so impossibly immature. Like, what minor deity did I piss off to be born attracted to them? At this point, I'm seriously considering giving them each a real sword, and letting them take each other out so I can recast them," Zale huffed.

"You're telling me you think you can get someone else to play these parts?" Eva asked.

Zale opened his mouth to retort, but I interrupted him.

"Bea has something to show you."

"Oh, hey, Bea. What's up?" Zale asked.

Reluctantly, and with much mumbling and blushing, Bea explained her sketch to Zale. As I predicted, his face lit up like a Christmas tree.

"Are you serious? Do you think we can really make these?"

"We need some more supplies, but yeah, I really think we can," I said. "Bea's gonna do the painting, and Eva and I will add these details to the costumes. Do you think the Meyers family would let us dig around for some more stuff to borrow?"

"Probably," Zale said. "We could text Luca and see if..."

At that moment, a door to the left of the stage opened, and Veronica Meyers stepped through it, a ring of keys in her hand.

"Oh, hello, Wren."

"Hello, Ms—"

"Veronica, please," she said with a smile. "Ms. Meyers always makes me feel like I'm turning into my mother. What are you... oh, that's right, of course. You're helping with the pageant. You mentioned that when we met. I'm sorry, I forgot."

"Yeah, and we were actually wondering if it might be possible to borrow a few more things? Bea came up with some awesome designs, but I'm not sure we'll be able to pull them off with what we've got."

"Do you mind if I take a look?" Veronica asked, smiling down at Bea.

Bea did not return the smile. She seemed to have retreated into herself, reverting to the shyness that had caused her to hide under the table the first time we'd met. Bea took half a step behind Eva, looking very much like she would like the floor to swallow her up. I guessed she hadn't expected she would need to share her artwork with so many people, and certainly not with a stranger. I tried to catch her eye, to give her an encouraging smile, but she just kept looking warily at Veronica.

Eva sighed impatiently. "Sorry, she's a bit on the bashful side. Here," and she plucked the sketchbook from Zale's hand, and held it out for Veronica to see.

Bea took a step forward, like she meant to snatch the sketchbook back; but she restrained herself, swinging her hands behind her back, and clasping them tightly together.

"My goodness, what a talented young lady you are," Veronica said, looking down at the sketch. "Did you really come up with this all on your own?"

Bea nodded her head once, tensely. "I've seen that pageant lots of times," she said.

Veronica smiled gently. "Of course, you have. And you realized that what it needed was a healthy dose of childhood imagination. Not that you're a child anymore, of course," she added quickly. "I can see that you are, in fact, quite the grown young lady now."

Bea's lips twitched into the suggestion of a smile, and Veronica's smile broadened, recognizing her victory.

"Now, as I told Wren, I've spent very little time here at the theater," Veronica went on. "But as I'm here this summer, I've made it my business to get to know the place. In fact, I've spent quite a bit of time in our costume shop as they prepare for the coming season, and I think we might have just what you need. Come on, I'll show you."

Zale's face lit up, and we all turned to follow Veronica up the aisle toward the front lobby of the theater. "Take five, everyone," Zale called. "And for the love of the goddess, try not to kill each other."

"No promises," Ethan shouted, as he took another lunge at Sergei on his stilts.

Veronica led us on her clacking heels out of the main theater, and through the front doors, to the first building that stood to the right of the theater.

"I think you'll find everything you need in here," she said, as she unlocked the door. "This is where the costumes are designed and constructed."

We walked into a huge space full of bolts of fabric, racks of trims and ribbons, cutting tables and sewing machines, and a long row of dress forms standing at attention like half-dressed soldiers. One wall was hung with rows of design sketches, each accented with swatches of fabric pinned to the corner. Another wall was covered in wooden pegs from which hats and headpieces of every variety hung above several rows of wig heads, bearing every hairstyle I could imagine, from every conceivable time period. My very first thought, as I took it all in, was that if Charlie could see this place, they would squeal with uncontainable delight, like a kid on Christmas morning.

"Wow," I whispered.

Veronica smiled, looking pleased. "This was always my favorite place to come when I was a little girl. I think I liked it better than watching the performances," she admitted. "Now let's see if I remember where... ah, yes. Here we go." She opened a large cabinet to reveal hundreds of jars of craft and fabric paints, bottles of glue, cans of spray glitter, and all manner of craft supplies. "I imagine this should be sufficient to get you started."

"Wow!" Zale murmured, and started toward the cabinet. I reached out an arm to stop him.

"This is amazing," I said, "and we're so grateful; but I really wouldn't want to use up anything that the designers will need for the current season."

"That won't be a problem. Just write down what you use here," Veronica said, handing me a clipboard, "and I'll make sure it's replaced."

"This is really generous of you," I said, taking the clipboard.

"Nonsense. This town has been our theater's home for decades. A bit of glue and glitter and fabric is the least we can do. Ah, you've discovered our wig collection, I see," Veronica added, her gaze falling on Bea. I turned to see Bea taking a deliberate step away from the nearest wig head.

"I didn't touch anything," she said quickly, looking mortified.

"Whyever not?" Veronica asked, smiling. "That was my favorite thing to do as a child." She walked around the nearest cutting table, so that she stood right beside Bea. "Go on. Which one is your favorite?"

Bea barely glanced at the wigs. "I... I don't know."

"Oh, come now. There must be one you like! I think I'll pick... this one," Veronica said, seizing a wig that looked like it might have rolled right off Marie Antoinette's neck when she was beheaded. She shook her own glossy hair back from her face, and slipped the wig on her head, tucking and adjusting it in the mirror until it was just right. "There now. What do you think?"

Bea couldn't help but smile just a little. She gave Veronica a thumbs up, and Veronica laughed.

"Now it's your turn. There must be one you'd like to try on!"

Bea hesitated another moment and then, her smile widening, she pointed to a wig on the far end of the display. The long, shiny hair was a kaleidoscope of colors—turquoise and seafoam green and vibrant lavender. Starfish and seashells had been woven into a few of the scattered braids. It looked like the hair of a mermaid or a water sprite.

"Excellent choice," Veronica said, clapping her hands in delight. She pulled it from the wig head with a flourish, and helped put it on Bea's head. She straightened and adjusted it for a moment before turning Bea by the shoulders to face a mirror on the wall. As Bea's face split into a real grin, so did Veronica's. "You see? It's like magic!" she said.

For the next hour or so, Eva, Zale, and I collected the necessary materials, while Bea and Veronica continued to try on wigs. Finally, when we had found everything we needed, we recorded it all on the clipboard, and loaded it into a pair of cloth tote bags.

"Oh, are you finished already?" Veronica asked. She and Bea were wearing identical blonde pageboy wigs.

"Yeah. Thanks again," Zale said. "I should really get back up to the rehearsal. Goddess only knows if they've all just fallen off their stilts and broken their necks. I suppose I'm not that lucky."

"Are they really that hard to manage?" I asked.

"It's like herding kittens, Wren. I don't know what we're going to do."

"Do you think it would help if I came to tomorrow's rehearsal? I can bring the finished costume pieces and help you wrangle everyone," I offered.

"Could you really?" Zale asked, looking relieved. "I could really use the help. This whole directing thing is a lot harder than I thought it would be."

"I'd be happy to," I said earnestly. "Don't worry, Zale. I've never let a show go up without everyone being whipped into shape, and I'm not going to let you, either. Have you had any luck improving the script?"

Zale rolled his eyes. "No, and it's probably too late to do anything about it. By the time I manage to write anything worth performing, there won't be any time to learn it. I think we're probably stuck with the script we've got."

"Well, we'll do our best with what we've got, then," I said, "and hope that the costumes are cool enough to distract from the words."

* * *

Back at Eva's house, we worked for several more hours on the costumes, doing our best to bring Bea's vision to life. Maricela came up to join us, assisting with some stitching and hemming, while Bea was hard at work painting the masks. By the time I left, we'd made good progress, and we agreed to meet up again the next day to finish what we could before the next evening's rehearsal. It was important to rehearse in the full costumes as much as possible, to make sure the actors could maneuver the way they needed to without tripping, or getting tangled up.

Bea was as talented with a paint brush as she was with a pencil. The masks, when she had finished with them, were truly works of art. The face of the Holly King was that of a silvery, apple-cheeked Father Christmas, with a beard made of glittery cotton batting that we tucked twinkle lights inside of, so that it looked like a storm cloud impregnated with lightning. Icicles made of glue dangled from the tip of his nose and the line of his jaw.

The Oak King was the embodiment of the forest in summer, all greenery and blossom and trailing vine. His hair and beard were braided of fiery red, orange, and yellow, and his crown looked like the sun coming over the horizon of his head. Even Sergei and Ethan stopped goofing around long enough to look impressed when we carried it all into the rehearsal that night. It was an arduous process, getting all the pieces to work together – tying and pinning and adjusting, until before us stood two apparitions of the seasons, at once beautiful and terrible, looking like they had sprung to life from the pages of a children's storybook.

"I think I'm going to cry," Zale said, when we were finally able to stand back and admire our handiwork.

"Try to hold off until they start moving around in them," I said. "Depending on how it goes, you might really want to cry."

Maricela entered with the costumes for the wood nymphs and the frost fairies. All the girls started squealing over the trailing, glittering skirts and the tiara-like headpieces. They immediately pulled out their phones, looking up makeup tutorials that would compliment their costumes, and comparing hairstyles accented with bright flowers or wintry snowflakes.

"I've got just the right palettes to do these," Kaia promised, and for the first time, the cast looked excited rather than apathetic. It was precisely the shift in attitude we needed to start practicing again. I'd seen it a hundred times: the magic of seeing oneself transformed into a character that suddenly feels real. It always breathed new life into the homestretch of rehearsals, reinvigorating everyone's enthusiasm. And we needed all the enthusiasm we could get, because we had a lot of work to do in a short amount of time.

We spent the next three hours working through the choreography step by step. The nymphs and the Oak King had to move as one unit, matching the swing of the arms to the teetering steps of the body. The frost fairies and the Holly King had to do the same, and all of it with a smoothness and synchronicity that made the onlooker forget they were watching a puppet and a group of puppeteers. We kept them motivated by taking videos of their progress and then playing them back for them, so they could see from an audience's perspective how it would look. Then Luca saved the day by drawing open the black backdrop to reveal a wall of mirrors. Now the actors could watch the effects of their coordination in real time, and they improved much more quickly. Zale had chosen sweeping instrumental music to play under the action, and the addition of beats they could count helped to keep them all moving together. In just a single rehearsal, we managed to evolve from chaos to some semblance of working together. It wasn't nearly ready for an audience, but it no longer seemed impossible that it could be by the end of the week. Even Sergei and Ethan allowed themselves to express a modicum of enthusiasm for the performance. The subtle shift in their behavior revealed that, though they loved fooling around in rehearsals, they didn't actually want to look like fools in front of the whole town.

"All right, that's all we can do for tonight," Zale called when Luca appeared to lock up at ten. "Same time tomorrow, and don't forget to practice your lines!"

"Everyone, hang your costumes up! The hangers are labeled; find the one with your name! And all props go back on the prop table!" I shouted, as everyone broke into conversation. "Don't forget to check the list of things you need to bring with you for tomorrow's rehearsal. It's posted on the door at the back of the house!"

There was the general scrum around the costume rack, followed by the milling about as people gathered their belongings, and made their noisy progress out of the theater. I sighed and went over to tidy the rack, which, despite the clear instructions, looked like a jumbled mess. Luckily, I'd labeled everything with the actors' names, so they were easy to identify when they inevitably fell off the hangers.

"That was really awesome," said a voice much too close to my ear. I spun with a gasp to see Luca standing behind me, arms folded over his chest. "I caught a little of the performance at the end. Those puppets are really something else."

"Thanks," I said, and silently cursed the blush that was creeping up my neck. "It's starting to come together, I guess."

"I might actually go down and watch this year," Luca said. "I think the outsiders will be impressed." He winked, grinning, and I felt the blush creep all the way up to my hairline.

"Oh yeah, you... you should definitely come down. I mean, everyone should..." I babbled.

"Maybe we can watch it together... you know, unless you have to be backstage or something."

"I... oh, yeah, that would... I mean, no, I don't have to be... I think I can watch...but I'm not really sure. I'll have to check with Zale to see where he needs me..." *Oh my God, Wren, shut up, like literally just stop making sounds.*

"Sure, sure, just let me know. I'll probably come down to watch it anyway. Well, see you tomorrow," Luca said, and loped off the stage and up the aisle.

I stuck my head in among the costumes on the rack, like an ostrich hiding its head in the sand. "Kill me right now."

"Excuse me? Why are we killing you?" Eva's voice cut through all the layers of fabric.

"Because I'm a babbling idiot," I moaned.

"Explain."

"Luca basically just asked me if I wanted to go to the festival with him, and I short-circuited. Like, my brain stopped working."

"Okay, well, rewire yourself and try again tomorrow," Eva said with a shrug. "We've all gone to pieces in front of a beautiful human before. It happens."

I groaned again. I couldn't imagine Eva going to pieces in front of anybody. She always seemed to know exactly what to say. "He literally just wanted to stand next to me in public, and I couldn't even say yes. I'm such a useless coward."

"Do you always talk about yourself that way?" Eva asked, looking suddenly stern.

"Huh? What way?" I asked, my voice still muffled.

"*That* way," Eva said, "like you can never do anything right."

"I... didn't realize I was talking about myself that way."

"Well, you do, and frankly, it's starting to piss me off," Eva snapped.

I blinked, a little shocked, and pulled my face out of the fabric to see Eva, arms crossed over her chest, glaring at me. "I... I'm sorry?"

"Good. You should be sorry. I don't let anyone talk about my friend like that," she said, and then ruined her stern expression by winking at me.

I nervous laugh escaped me. "For a second there, I thought you were actually mad at me."

"Oh, I am mad at you. I'm furious," Eva insisted. "How can you call yourself useless after everything you've done for this pageant!"

I felt my cheeks burn. "Eva, I've barely done—"

"Wren, for the first time ever, we won't be a total laughingstock, and that's all down to you! You really have a creative eye! You knew exactly what this pathetic little pageant needed, and now, for the first time, someone besides Zale is excited to be a part of this thing!"

"I've just hung around a lot of shows, that's all," I muttered, still feeling embarrassed. "I wasn't even in them. I just sat backstage calling cues because I was too much of a coward to audition."

"Bullshit. You were definitely doing more than that. You get how what makes a show work. You know how to put the pieces together so that they create exactly what you envisioned. You don't have to be in the spotlight to play an important role, you know."

"Yeah, I know," I said, feeling a smile trying to break through my embarrassment.

"And as far as you being a coward... well, I don't know who you're talking about, but I watched you that night on the beach, and that girl was no coward."

"Okay, okay, oh my GOD," I said, sure my face must be purple at this point. "I can't take any more pep talk; it's literal torture. I promise I won't talk about myself like that anymore. Can you please *please* just let it go..."

Eva pursed her lips. "Are you sure? Because I can also give a lengthy speech about how beautiful you are, if that's another area of self-confidence that you strugg—"

"YES. YES, I AM SURE," I yelled. God, why did floors never swallow you up when you wanted them to? There was a full five seconds of silence. Then Eva's face broke into a grin.

"Do you react like this any time someone tries to compliment you?" she asked, sounding positively giddy at the prospect.

I was wary now. "Kind of?"

The grin widened. "Oh, I am going to abuse this power so, so much."

I groaned again, and walked away from her to find Zale putting the top on the old box of costumes and props we were no longer using.

"After tonight, I think it's safe to say we won't need these again," he said cheerfully, tapping the box with his hand.

"Well, let's make it official, then," I said, and picked the box up. "I'm taking this to the dumpster."

"The perfect place for it!" Zale agreed, laughing.

I walked up the side aisle and out the fire exit door halfway up the house, which I knew led to the back side of the building, where the dumpsters were located. As I walked, I tried to shake off the rest of my embarrassment over Luca. Instead of focusing on my mortifying response, I should be focusing on the fact that he asked me to hang out. Wasn't that the point? That he seemed interested? It wasn't a sensation I had much experience with. For a moment, I allowed myself to imagine what it would be like arriving at the festival, and seeing him standing there, waiting for me. His face lit up with a smile when I appeared, and me, confident enough to return that smile without turning the color of a ripe tomato. Maybe even his hand reaching casually out to take mine as we walked. Looking over to sneak a glimpse of his face, only to find he was sneaking a glimpse at mine...

"Oof!"

I was so lost in my daydream that I didn't see the small pothole in the pavement walkway. I caught the toe of my shoe in it and stumbled forward, losing my grip on the bin and falling painfully on my side.

"Shit, ouch!" I gasped, as I pushed myself into a seated position and examined the damage. My left palm was scraped up from where I'd thrust it out to catch myself, and I could tell my hip and thigh would be bruised before I could even get to my feet. Grumbling at my own clumsiness, I hobbled over to the overturned bin, and began shoving all the scattered items back inside. I vented my feelings by breaking one of the Styrofoam antlers off one of the crowns. As I snatched at the moth-eaten old Holly King cloak, something small and dark tumbled out of the folds, and I picked it up.

It was a book, small and old-looking, bound in deep green fabric, with a faded illustration on the front. There was no title, but it reminded me of old editions of Grimm's Fairytales I'd seen in used bookstores. Curiously, I opened it, and began to skim the words. "Holly King"... "Oak King"... it was the story of Litha, I realized, in book form. There were color plate illustrations between the text pages, somewhat faded, but still beautiful in their details. I flipped forward a few more pages, and came to what looked like a poem. I started to read it...

"We are the Keepers of Forest and Flame!
We are the beacons of sun! Of Spring!
Wielding our power, to grow and to survive
We cast you out Darkness, so hence Light can thrive!"

A tingling excitement ran over me, like an electric shock. I turned the page, reading another passage.

"We are the keepers of Darkness and Ice!
We are the bastions of frost, and of sleep!
We blanket all nature in a mantle of white,
And wrap all the world in endless dark night!"

I forgot all about my bruises and scrapes, and I jumped to my feet. It was all I could do to chuck the bin and its contents into the dumpster before running back into the theater, my heart pounding.

"Zale! Eva! Look at this!" I cried, as I bolted back down the aisle to the stage where the two of them stood, looking alarmed. "Have you ever seen this before?"

Zale and Eva both examined the little book, each shaking their heads.

"Where did you find it?" Zale asked.

"It was in the bottom of that bin of old costumes," I explained.

Eva snorted. "Where it's probably been for like fifty years."

"It's... a children's book?" Zale asked, flipping through it. "About Litha?"

"Yeah, but look here at the end. Read this poem and tell me it isn't a million times better than that script we've been using."

They huddled together, Eva's chin on Zale's shoulder as they read. I watched with satisfaction as their eyes grew wide, and their faces split into smiles. Finally, Zale looked up, looking both thrilled and devastated.

"Wren, this is amazing, but... the pageant is in four days. How is anyone going to learn this that fast?"

"They don't need to!" I said. "We need a narrator, someone offstage, like a voiceover."

"Oh, that's a good idea!" Eva gasped.

"But who would—" Zale began, but Eva immediately cuffed him on the head.

"What do you mean, 'who'? Isn't it obvious? It's you, Zale. It has to be you!" she said.

"Me?"

"Yes!" I agreed eagerly. "Zale, you are the resident storyteller around here! You had everyone captivated at the bonfire when you told the story of Sedgwick Cove. It was spellbinding! Even the story of this pageant sounded cool when you explained it! So instead of assigning lines and hoping people can stumble through them, just tell the story yourself and let the others act it out!"

"We could put a cool vocal effect on the microphone," Eva added. "And maybe these parts," she pointed, "we could have everyone recite together just before the battle begins, like a chorus in a musical. It's only a few lines. They can learn that much."

Each word we spoke seemed to illuminate Zale's face more and more, until he was positively glowing with excitement. "This was it!" he crowed. "The final piece of the puzzle we were missing! Do you really think I should—"

"Zale, you are the only person for the job," Eva said firmly. "Your voice is a spell in itself —that's what Davina has always said. If you tell the story, it will be sure to enchant the whole audience."

The last of the doubt vanished from Zale's face, and he clutched the book to his chest, grinning. "Sounds like I've got some rehearsing to do!"

17

As hopeless as we'd all felt watching Sergei and Ethan stumble around on stilts, delivering their lines in monotone mumbles, we were now wild with anticipation for the pageant. Seemingly overnight, our whole production had been transformed, first by the costumes, then by the replacement of the script. No one could help but stop and listen when Zale spoke in his clear, musical voice; there was no choice but to be swept away by the enchanting images he conjured, just on the rise and fall of his intonation. It no longer mattered that our actors were a bunch of apathetic teenagers with no stage experience—with Zale giving them voice, and the puppets giving them form, all they had to do was not fall over. Kaia and Petra came flying into the next evening's rehearsal to show off the makeup looks they'd created for the frost fairies and the wood nymphs. The final touches on the costumes also added to the magic—and nothing could have made me happier than watching the proud smile on Bea's face when she saw her masks atop the towering, almost mythical figures of the Holly and Oak Kings.

Despite how excited we were, we kept all of the details of the pageant a secret. Aside from Eva's mom, whose help we had enlisted with the costumes and whom we had sworn to secrecy, no one else knew what we had in store for Sedgwick Cove on the night of the festival. Zale felt that the element of surprise would be the final flourish to enchanting the crowd —if their expectations were low, they'd be all the more impressed when they saw what we'd created. As for me, it was hard to keep my mouth shut.

"Really? You can't give us any hints?" my mom asked on the eve of the festival, as we stood on the cliff above the water.

"No. I promised," I said.

All of the Conclave covens had gathered together to decorate the sun wheel, another traditional element of the festival. Unlike the pageant, the sun wheel was inherently impressive. Enormous and constructed of wood, it was positioned at the top of the sloping path from the cliffs to the beach. When the pageant was over, the crowd would progress in a sort of parade up to the cliff, where the sun wheel would be lit on fire, and then released. Then the crowd would watch as the sun wheel, flaming and smoking, rolled all the way down to the sea, marking the official triumph of the Holly King and the beginning of his reign until Yule, when the Oak King would wrest the power away once more.

"I don't even want to know," Rhi said. "The surprise makes it more exciting."

My mom pouted a little, and then winked at me. "I'm sure it will be wonderful," she said. She was tucking blossoms into the spokes of the wheel, and securing them with floral wire. Then she laid her hands on each blossom, one by one, so that they brightened and grew more lush beneath her fingers."

"What spell is that?" I asked her.

"Just a little something to make sure they don't wilt between now and tomorrow night," my mom said, smiling at me.

"Can you show me?"

She smiled. "Come here."

I walked around the wheel to stand beside her. She took my hand in hers and wrapped it gently around a peony she had just finished wiring to the frame. "Take a moment to connect with the blossom," she said, "Let yourself feel the life still pulsing through it."

I closed my eyes and concentrated all my energy on the flower, trying to find that ephemeral "life" my mother was talking about. I was mentally prepared to grope and search fruitlessly, which was why I gasped with surprise only a moment later when I felt it: an unmistakable something running under my fingertips. It was warmth, but not warm; light, but not visible. It writhed and expanded, though it did not move. It was more that I could feel the potential of all of it—warmth, light, growth—all contained in a little beat, like a pulse, running from the petals to my fingertips.

"You feel that?" my mom whispered.

"Yes!" I said, still not quite able to believe how easily I'd done it.

"Now imagine pouring from yourself into that blossom, like filling a cup. Give it your energy."

I did as she said, trying to envision that same pulse, but in me. I imagined it flowing through my veins. Then I imagined a little offshoot—a place from which I could siphon off that energy, so that it could pour from me to the blossom. I heard my mother gasp and opened my eyes.

The peony, slightly drooping a moment before, now stood with every petal at attention. The solid white color of the petals was now tinged with pink at the center. I dropped my hands to my sides in shock.

"It... did I actually do that?" I whispered.

My mom laughed. "You certainly did!"

"Are you sure you didn't cheat? Give it a little nudge of your own while I wasn't looking?" I asked, narrowing my eyes at her.

She lifted her hands in surrender. "Cross my heart! That was all you!"

I looked back down at the peony in wonder, and then sighed. "Oh, man."

"What?"

"This is one of the first bits of magic I've managed to produce on purpose, and we're literally going to light it on fire," I grumbled.

My mom laughed, and threw her arms around me. "It doesn't need to last forever to be magic, Wren. You're doing great."

I thought of what I'd done on the beach the night the Darkness tried to take me. The magic had come through me suddenly, as bright and powerful as the bolt of lightning that answered my call. I looked down past the cliffs to the beach where, still hidden under the white tent, the cage of lightning sand still stood, proof that it had all really happened—a testament to my power. I remembered Eva's scolding words at the theater. Why did I doubt myself so much? Why couldn't I admit that the only thing standing between me and my power was... well, *me*?

I felt a tap on my shoulder and turned to see Persi beckoning me away from the sun wheel. I dropped my handful of wire and roses, and followed her.

"What's up?" I asked. Persi was looking shifty. Her eyes kept darting to the other adults as she reached into a little pouch slung around her waist, and pulled two small vials from it, each one sealed with wax.

"Here," she said, thrusting the vials into my hands.

"What are these for?" I asked, staring down at them. Their contents had a slight iridescence to them, like they might glow when darkness set in.

"It's a little something to help make your pageant special," Persi whispered. "Magic isn't allowed to be used in the pageant, strictly speaking —no one wants to tip off the tourists about what really goes on around here. But this is just a bit of fun."

I looked over my shoulder, too, to make sure the others were occupied. "But what are they?"

"Pour this one with the blue wax on the Holly King's staff. And this one," she pointed to the other vial, sealed with gold wax, "you pour on the Oak King's staff."

"What do they do?" I asked.

Persi smiled. "Nothing, until the staffs hit each other. Then they'll create a little... special effect for you."

"Are you gonna tell me what the special effect is?" I asked.

"No, I don't think so," Persi said, smirking.

"This is why everyone in this town is half-afraid of you, isn't it?" I sighed, pocketing the vials.

"Probably," Persi admitted, and sauntered away.

* * *

The morning of the Midsummer Festival dawned bright and beautiful, to no one's surprise. Though Rhi insisted that the witches of Sedgwick Cove could not control the weather, she nonetheless admitted that they had never had a rainy day for the festival in the entire history of the celebration, which led me to believe they had more collective influence than they were willing to admit.

Main Street had been blocked off from traffic. Shops and restaurants were spilling out onto the sidewalks with tables and tents and booths, all decorated with suns and balloons and bright yellow flags. Banners had been strung up across the street, welcoming the influx of tourists who began to trickle in first thing in the morning. A large field to the west of Main Street had been cordoned off with cones and yellow tape, and cars were lining up in shiny rows, like beetles. Street performers had staked their claims to their corners, and were busy setting up their acts. The celebration in the air was palpable as I rode my bike through the growing crowds, and came to a stop in front of the stage in the center of the roundabout. Zale was already there, ordering around the sound crew, and making sure the wires were taped down in front of the stairs that led to the platform.

"Hey, Mr. Director," I said, as I approached him. "How are you feeling about tonight?"

Zale looked up with that slightly manic look I knew so well—the look of a director who is constantly mentally cycling through his to-do list, while also contemplating all the myriad ways the performance could go off the rails. "Does the day of the show always feel like this?" he asked.

"Like what?"

"Like you're going to simultaneously implode and explode with stress?"

I considered a moment. "Yeah, pretty much. What can I do to help?"

He looked at me, wild-eyed and frazzled. "I don't... I can't..."

"Zale. Rule number one of surviving opening night: delegate. Now, what's that?"

"It's a list of all the props and costumes that are supposed to be in the bins that came over from the theater," Zale said.

"Give it to me," I said firmly. Zale held it out but didn't let go of it.

"Where are the bins?" I asked.

He pointed to the left side of the stage, where I could see several large plastic storage bins peeking out from under the platform.

"I'll go through and double-check everything, okay?"

Zale sighed and finally let go of the clipboard. "Okay. Yes. Thank you."

"Breathe," I instructed, watching as he took a slow, deliberate inhale and then went to check on the bins. I'd packed them myself, so I knew everything was in there, but this wasn't really about the bins. It was about preserving Zale's sanity.

Once the speakers were set up, the inventory complete, the microphones tested, and the set decorations hung, I told Zale I would stop over at the cafe to get us some lunch. It was hard to tell if he heard me; he was too busy pacing back and forth across the stage, mouthing the words from the book that had become our script. I left him to it, no longer able to ignore my rumbling stomach.

The cafe was bustling with people, queued up outside at a little food cart that had been set up on the sidewalk. Maricela stood at the cart, taking orders. She waved me past her and inside. "Eva was just about to go look for you," she said.

I walked in to find even more customers lined up at the counter. Eva waved at me, indicating I needed to give her a minute to take care of the influx of orders. Over in the corner, Bea was sitting at an empty table, bent over her sketchbook.

"Hey Bea," I called.

"Hi Wren," she said, and I was rewarded with one of her elusive smiles.

"Oh, Wren! Hello!"

I turned back to the line of customers to see Veronica and Luca standing in it. Luca gave me a friendly wave, but it was Veronica who had spoken.

"Hi, Ms. M— sorry, Veronica," I said. "Nice to see you."

"I had to come down and see what all the fuss was about," she said, gesturing vaguely back out to Main Street. "It's a much bigger event than I realized!"

"Me, too," I admitted. "But at least we'll have a good-sized audience for the pageant later."

"I asked where the best spot for lunch was and was told repeatedly to come here," Veronica said. "I had no idea your family owned it, Eva."

Eva smiled and took Veronica and Luca's order. Veronica stepped away from the counter so the next customer could order, and spotted Bea over at her table.

"Bea! I almost didn't recognize you without your mermaid hair," Veronica teased. "How are you? Excited for the pageant?"

Bea looked startled at being addressed, and though she had met Veronica before, she seemed wary to talk to her. She snapped her sketchbook closed. "Not really," she said, her voice little more than a mumble. "It's always so loud and crowded. I like the quiet days better."

"But surely you'll enjoy seeing your creations up on the stage," Veronica enthused. "Luca, did you know Bea designed the masks for the play?"

Luca's face split into a grin. "No, I didn't. I saw the cast rehearsing in them. They're awesome, well done."

Bea took compliments about as well as I did. "Thanks," she muttered, retreating to her sketchbook again.

"What are you creating now? Can I take a look?" Veronica asked, and crossed the room to where Bea sat. Bea hesitated a moment, then opened her sketchbook again, allowing Veronica to gush over her artwork.

"Looks like it's coming together out there," Luca said to me, nodding his head toward the stage. "You guys need any help?"

"No, unless you've got some Valium we can borrow for Zale," I said. "There's a good chance his head might explode before showtime."

Luca chuckled and patted his pockets. "Sorry, don't have any on me."

"Damn. Well, it was worth an ask."

We talked for another couple of minutes, until Eva handed Luca their food.

"I'll catch you later then?" Luca said.

"Yeah, I'll be here. Just follow the sounds of Zale having a panic attack, and that's where you'll find me," I replied.

Luca laughed. "Mom, you ready?"

Veronica patted Bea on the head, and wished us all luck, before following her son out the door.

"Here," Eva said, handing me a paper bag. "Sustenance. How's Zale?"

"Melting down. We should go feed him," I said.

Eva checked her watch. "Yeah, I'm officially off for the afternoon. Let's go."

"See you later, Bea!" I called.

Bea stifled a yawn as she waved goodbye.

It was a full-time job between lunch and evening time, keeping Zale distracted. After we fed him, the cast arrived for a quick walk-through on the outdoor stage. It went fairly well—no one fell off their stilts, and the choreography for the fight scene went smoothly with no injuries, accidental *or* intentional. Everyone took their costumes and accessories so they could get ready before our call time at 7:30pm. We took Zale for a walk along Main Street, checking out all the stalls. A walking tour was making its way up the street; I recognized Phoebe from the Historical Society in a pointy black witch hat, pointing out the sights. She winked at us as she passed. Little stalls were selling merchandise that celebrated the sun—sun-shaped pinwheels, sunglasses, hats and masks, and windchimes and flags. Restaurants were selling street food in the theme as well—round hand pies full of strawberries, and cookies decorated to look like flowers, suns, and candles. There was a tangible joy in the air on this, the longest day of the year. It felt as though the town itself was collectively trying to squeeze as much celebration and joy into the hours before the sun went down, and the waning of the year began.

Zale and I found some dinner while Eva went to change into her nymph costume, and at last, the time came for the cast to return. They arrived in twos and threes, looking every bit the wood nymphs and frost fairies they were supposed to be, thanks to the revamped costumes and Kaia's makeup design. For once, the teenage apathy wasn't strong enough to burst the bubble of excited anticipation. Even Ethan and Sergei looked both excited and nervous as we helped them climb into their costumes. Without telling anyone, I took out Persi's vials and applied the contents to the staffs, before handing them off to the nymph and the fairy who would be swinging them.

While we got ready, Ostara herself took the platform to welcome the visitors to the festival and to explain, in layman's terms, what the Litha festival was all about. The crowds milling up and down Main Street began to corral themselves together near the platform, drawing in closer to where the action would clearly be starting soon. I spotted my mom and my aunts in the crowd, waving at me. Children were being hoisted onto shoulders so they could see over the heads of the adults. Someone was lighting tiki torches up and down the street, bathing the festival in a warm, golden light, even as the sun was drifting closer to the horizon. Finally, the clock in the tower of the library chimed 8 o'clock, and it was time for us to begin.

"Break a leg," I whispered to Zale, and kissed him impulsively on the cheek as I handed him his microphone. I turned to the platform to make sure everyone was in place. Eva waved down at me, her face aglow with excitement. I gave her a thumbs-up, and went to join my mom and my aunts in the crowd.

"Here we go!" I whispered breathlessly to my mom as the music began, and Zale's voice sang out from the speakers.

18

The words had drifted over the gathered crowd like snow, landing softly and silently, and transforming the landscape. Curious faces turned rapt. Confused faces turned content. Bored faces turned mesmerized. The movement of the performers fell into a rhythm, almost like choreography. The arms of the wood nymphs swayed and fluttered in perfect synchronicity. The frost fairies seemed to be floating around the Holly King like they really had swirled down from the dark of the sky in a kind of twirling dance. The lights that glowed from their fingertips darted and dipped through the gathering twilight, like lightning bugs. Whether it was the excitement of having an audience or simply sheer luck, our modest pageant had transformed into something much more than a reluctant group of teenagers going through the motions. I felt the thrill that only a theater kid can feel, the feeling that your performance has transcended the mess and frustration and monotony of rehearsal, and has been elevated to something more—something cohesive and enchanting. Something magical.

I tore my eyes from the performance and turned to grin at my mother and aunts, sure that they were as surprised and impressed as I was, but none of them were looking at me. They were staring, utterly entranced by the performance as well. My grin widened, and I enjoyed myself for a minute watching their expressions. Then I leaned over and spoke into my mother's ear.

"So where would you rank this year's pageant compared to the year Persi beat up that kid?" I asked, chuckling.

My mother didn't answer. She was still staring at the pageant.

I laughed. "Hello? Earth to Mom! Come in, Mom!"

She didn't reply, and I felt the smile slide off my face.

"Mom?"

I waved my hand in front of her face. She didn't so much as flinch.

Unease pooled in my stomach, cold and congealed. I reached out and took her by the shoulder, shaking her roughly. "Mom!" MOM!" My voice had risen to a shout now, but I didn't care. Something was wrong. Was she having a seizure or something? A stroke? "Rhi? Something's wrong with Mom!" I cried.

I was so focused on my mother that it took me a moment to realize that Rhi hadn't responded. I turned to see her staring with the same rapt attention as my mother, her eyes following every movement of the performers on the platform. I stepped past my mother and tugged on Rhi's arm.

"Rhi? Rhi!"

She didn't react at all. It was as though I didn't exist.

Heart hammering now, I turned to Persi. Though a glance told me she was unreachable, like Rhi and my mom, I shook her shoulder anyway, my fear spilling over into something like frustration. I had to stop myself from slapping her. I whirled on the spot instead, searching the crowd before grabbing the arm of the woman in front of me. She was clearly a tourist, sporting a sweatshirt that said, "Get Spooked by the Sea in Sedgwick Cove." She turned to glare at me, and I recoiled from her, dropping her sleeve at once.

"What's your problem?" she snapped at me.

"I'm so sorry," I replied breathlessly. "I... I thought you were someone I knew."

The woman narrowed her eyes at me before turning around again. I began to scan the crowd more carefully now. Nearby was a family with three small children. At first glance, they seemed to be caught up in the performance, too; but after a moment, the toddler in the stroller began to fuss, having dropped his sippy cup on the ground, and the man behind the stroller bent to retrieve it. The other man, who had one of the children on his shoulders, turned to see that all was well. The little girl on his shoulders caught my eye and smiled shyly at me when she saw me watching. Beside this family was Phoebe, who I remembered meeting on my first day in Sedgwick Cove. She was the woman who ran the Historical Society. I hurried toward her and tapped her on the shoulder, holding my breath. She didn't turn.

"Phoebe?" I said once, and then again, louder. She didn't respond. Nothing existed for her but the pageant. I may as well have been a ghost.

I turned my head, my thoughts whirling faster than my body, as I found one familiar face after another: Davina, Ostara, Maricela. Every person I knew from Sedgwick Cove seemed to be entranced in the same way, utterly unable to pull their eyes from the performance, even as the tourists around them chatted and laughed and munched on concessions.

It's a spell, I realized. *It's some kind of spell, and the only people affected by it are the witches.*

Except for me.

The realization caused the cold dread in my stomach to spread like ice water through my veins, until the tips of my fingers and toes tingled with it. I didn't know what to do or what to think. Would the enchantment—or whatever the hell it was that held them all in thrall—break with the end of the pageant?

The idea shot through me, sharp and clear. End the pageant.

Throwing one last anxious look at my mother and my aunts, I began to weave through the packed crowd as quickly as I could, mumbling apology after apology to anyone I jostled. At last, I reached the edge of the platform. It was about waist high, and I used my arms to boost myself over the lip of the stage. I ignored the angry shouts of the audience members nearest me, and shook off the grasping fingers of a man who attempted to pull me off the stage. I darted around to the side of the stage, masking myself behind the swaying mass of wood nymphs. I was looking for one nymph in particular, and after a moment, I spotted her in the middle back row.

"Eva! Hey! Eva!" I called in an exaggerated whisper. Eva didn't turn.

She continued to sway and wave her foliage-covered arms in perfect synchronicity with the other nymphs. I tried again, louder this time. Finally, throwing my last remaining bit of caution to the wind, I ran across the stage, ducking down so that I would be hidden by the other performers until I reached her.

"Eva!" I cried, taking the sleeve of her costume between my fingers and tugging on it. "Eva, can you hear me? Eva, answer me!" I took her by the arm and pulled, forcing her to face me, but though she twisted her body in my direction, she continued to chant the words, to wave her arms as though she was a sleepwalker in the depths of a dream.

"We are the keepers of forest, of flame! We are the beacons of sun! Of spring!" she repeated over and over again, her voice going hoarse, her eyes glazed as though she had a fever that had rendered her incoherent. Her gaze was vacant, devoid of reason or understanding. Again, I felt like a ghost, invisible and silent, no matter how loudly I screamed. I released her, and she whirled right back into sync with the others. Tears were pooling in my eyes, and I couldn't force them back. They spilled down my cheeks as I allowed myself one moment of panic. Then, I brushed them away impatiently. Falling apart now would solve exactly nothing. Instead, I made use of my new vantage point, peering through the frolicking nymphs to examine the crowd of upturned faces in front of me. Surely, there must be one witch, just one, who was unaffected by this madness like I was.

My eye was drawn to a little figure standing apart from the crowd. I don't think I would have noticed her at all in the gathering darkness if it wasn't for the sudden, violent flares of light emanating from the nearby tiki torches. Something about the figure was familiar, tickling my recognition like a breeze, until a particularly bright flash of firelight glinted off the colorful beads on the ends of her braids.

It was Bea. And she wasn't staring at the pageant like everyone else.

Hope swelled in me, sudden and strong. I waved my arms frantically over my head, but it wasn't enough to attract her attention. I let my hands fall to my side, a strange new sort of anxiety rising in me as I watched her. She wasn't paying the slightest attention to the spectacle on display only a dozen yards from where she stood. I scanned the shadows that hemmed her in for a sign of Xiomara or Maricela, but they were where I had last seen them, in the midst of the crowd, faces blank and hypnotized by the pageant. Why wasn't she with them? Why wasn't she, like the other witches, in a trance?

At that moment, the Holly King and the Oak King came at each other, their staffs meeting mid-swing with a loud crack, sending a shower of sparks and snowflakes drifting up into the air. The crowd cheered in reply, and Bea threw her hands up over her ears at the burst of sound. Her eyes were bright, and I realized in the flash of light that it was because they were full of unshed tears. Then she shifted her gaze away from the giant puppets, and her eyes found mine at last.

She looked at me. I looked at her. Then, something shifted in the shadows behind her.

No, not something *in* the shadows: the shadows themselves. They peeled away from the ground, from the trees, from the walls of the building she stood in front of. They pooled and swirled and then spun upward into a sort of dervish, before settling into a recognizable shape: long and thin, human, and yet so terribly not.

The Gray Man.

"Bea, behind you!" I tried to cry out, but the fear was smothering my voice, choking me, and the words came out in a strangled, breathless whisper.

As though she had sensed the danger, Bea turned and saw the figure standing there. *She's going to run,* I thought. *She's going to scream. Bedlam is about to break out, and this whole festival is about to disintegrate into panic. Maybe that will be enough to break the spell.*

The Gray Man reached out and extended a hand toward her. Bea stood motionless. I couldn't see her face, couldn't understand why she wasn't backing, stumbling away. Was she, like me, immobilized with fear? Was she as helpless in her shock, as incapable of self-preservation?

And then, before I could do more than open my mouth to call out to her again, my breath stopped. My heart stopped. Everything around us seemed to stop. All except for Bea, who reached out her hand and placed it in the Gray Man's. I watched his long, smoky fingers curl around hers, saw his ghost of a face twist into the suggestion of a grin. And then they turned together at a run and were almost instantly swallowed by the dark.

"Bea!" I shouted after her, but it was useless. The tumult in the street overpowered my voice completely—I could barely decipher it in my own ears.

It had to be magic, the way Bea and the Gray Man had melted through the throngs of people. No one had even glanced at them, too caught up in the music and the lights and the spectacle of it all. Without thinking, without caring that I was running toward the very thing that wanted to claim me, I bolted after her. Because what choice did I have? There was no one else who could help her.

"Bea! Wait!"

I leaped from the edge of the stage and hit what felt like a solid wall of people. With no other choice, I started shoving my way through. I ignored the startled and angry shouts, spewing a steady stream of preemptive apologies that I wasn't even convinced anyone could hear. I didn't want to apologize. I wanted to scream so loudly and so fiercely that every person around me would stop in their tracks, and turn to listen. So that everyone would have a taste of the terror licking its way up my bones, burning away my self-control, my logic, my self-preservation.

I couldn't let Bea go where the Darkness would lead her, wherever that may be. I couldn't let it happen.

I ducked around families with overstimulated, sticky-faced toddlers in strollers, and groups of tourists in masks and gaudy witch hats. I could smell booze and incense and greasy street fair food, all wrapped in the constant pungent scent of smoke from the torches, and it made my head spin. Laughter and shouts and music and the constant discordant jangling of bells assaulted my ears from every direction, disorienting me. I suddenly found I couldn't stand to be in the crowd another moment. I stumbled through a sudden gap in the crush of bodies, only to find myself on the edge of a circle that had formed around a secondary pair of street performers.

I was momentarily blinded, throwing my hands up in front of my face in terror until I realized what I was looking at: they were juggling flaming torches, faster and faster, so that the individual flames became glowing circles suspended in the air. I stared in frozen wonder, my eyes dazzled for a moment before my adrenaline surged again, reminding me why I was running in the first place; and I took off again across the circle, skirting the performers who called out in alarm that I'd gotten too close. People were shouting at me, but I couldn't care. I had to get to Bea. Perhaps the terror was as clear on my face as it was in my head, because the people who made up the opposite wall of the crowd hastily jumped out of my way, parting like the sea at my frenzied approach.

Once I'd emerged from the other side of the wall of people, I stared around again, wildly scanning the street for any sign of her—of him. Was it possible I was the only person who had seen him? Bea certainly had. But why would she go with him? Didn't she know what he was? But then I thought of Eva, of how overprotective she was.

Bea's a good kid but she scares easily. I don't need her crawling into my bed with nightmares for the next week.

What could possibly be more nightmare-inducing than The Gray Man —the Darkness itself? Whatever sanitized details Eva and her family had chosen to share with Bea, the Gray Man certainly could not have been among them. Bea had no idea whose hand she had just taken, and somehow, that made it all immeasurably worse. As I ran, dodging, pushing, and weaving to find a clear path out of the festival, I feared I would lose them entirely and then... I shuddered, refusing to allow my brain to complete the thought. I didn't know what the Darkness wanted with Bea, but I knew that whatever it was, it wasn't good. I plunged heedlessly onward.

How could such a tiny town hold so many people? They seemed to have multiplied now that I had to fight my way through them. Desperate not to lose Bea, I climbed awkwardly up onto the base of a street lamp so that I could see over the seething mass of people, my eyes scanning the darkness for some sign of them. At last, I spotted them disappearing around a corner from Main Street down one of the side streets that would, I knew, lead them down along the harbor. Dread flooded through me as I watched Bea's tiny form slip out of sight. I couldn't let the Gray Man take her anywhere near the ocean. What if he tried to walk into the water with her, to steal her, like he had with me? The very thought felt like a punch to the gut, causing what little breath I'd managed to maintain while running to huff out of me. My head spun as I jumped down off the lamppost, and I had to grip a stranger's arm to right myself before mumbling a half-apology, and tearing off down the street again.

The worst part, as I weaved and dodged and tripped through the crowd, was that I couldn't shout out for help. What could I say that anyone would believe? And if they did believe it, that in itself would present a new kind of danger—a danger to the carefully hidden secrets of Sedgwick Cove, and the families who lived there. I could be putting even more people I loved in harm's way by calling out, but by keeping silent, I might be making it possible for the Gray Man to... my mind wouldn't let me finish that thought. If I allowed myself to imagine what Bea's fate might be, I would lose what little grip I had left on my self-control.

At last, with a grunt of effort on my part, and a chorus of annoyed shouts and dirty looks from those around me, I managed to force my way through the rest of the crowd. I broke into a real run as I darted around the straggling groups on the outskirts, which became fewer and fewer the further I got from the pageant stage. I skidded to a stop at the corner where Bea and the Gray Man had turned and paused a moment, both to ease the burning cramp in my side, and to peer cautiously down the street from a concealed spot behind a clump of bushes. I could no longer see either of them. I stared wildly around for the street sign, and saw that it was Hydrangea Street—this was definitely the road they'd taken, but how had they traversed it so quickly? Had the Gray Man used some kind of magic to transport Bea more quickly? But he shouldn't be able to access that kind of magic. The Covenant was designed to prevent that—so how was this even happening? It ought to have been impossible.

But I knew what I saw. And I also knew that the word impossible likely didn't apply in a place like Sedgwick Cove.

Suddenly, a figure came out from between two of the houses on the lefthand side of the street, loping with an easy stride, hands in pockets. A cheerful whistle drifted up the street. As I watched, wondering if I should hide from the figure, it passed under a pool of light from a streetlamp, and recognition hit me like a slap to the face.

"Luca!"

His name burst from my mouth before I had even decided whether I should call attention to myself or not. He looked up, startled, and then spotted me. His face broke into that slow, broad smile, and he waved a hand.

"Hey, Wren! What's going on?"

How could I even begin to answer that question? I replied with one of my own instead.

"What are you doing here?"

Luca gave me a strange look. "I thought I'd come down and check out the festival after hearing you all talk about it so much."

Oh right. The festival. The event of the year had turned into little more than an obstacle in my path, as I'd fought my way through it to find Bea.

"You know, I'm pretty sure you're going the wrong way if that's where you're headed, too," Luca said, his smile tentative as he nodded his chin toward the main road I'd just come from.

"Oh, yeah. I mean... no, I was already there. Listen, did you see a little girl and a... um, well, a taller person... come down this street just now?" I asked, stumbling over the words as I struggled to make them sound even slightly normal.

Luca frowned at the obvious tension in my voice. "Hey, are you okay?"

"I'm fine, I'm fine," I gasped, though I knew I sounded anything but. "I need to know if you've seen—"

"I did see a little girl come down this way, but she was by herself," Luca said, and I could see a bit of my own tension reflected in his face now. "Why?"

I hesitated. It had to have been Bea—it was too much of a coincidence. Had the Gray Man still been with her? Was it possible that Bea could see the Gray Man, but Luca couldn't? Maybe he was only visible to witches? I didn't have the time to work out the details.

"It's my friend's little sister. We can't find her, and—"

"She looked like she was maybe eight? Braided hair with beads?" Luca said.

"That's her! Did you see which way she went?" I said.

"Yeah, she turned left down at the end there," Luca said.

"Thanks," I cried, and took off in the direction he'd pointed.

"Wait! I'll help you look!" Luca said, and started jogging after me.

"No, you don't have to do that. Go enjoy the festival," I called over my shoulder, but he ignored that.

"I won't be able to enjoy it if I think some kid's gone missing. Let me help," Luca said.

I didn't have the time or energy to argue. Finding Bea had to be the first priority. And if we found someone—or something—else with her... well, I'd cross that troubling bridge if and when we got to it.

"Okay, fine. Come on."

We hurried all the way to the end of Hydrangea Street, pausing only long enough to peer down the narrow cobbled alleyways that ran between some of the houses, but there was no sign of her. Finally, Hydrangea spilled out onto Harbor Street, the street that ran the length of the wall along the water, toward the cove and the beaches. The street was completely deserted, with the exception of one couple sitting on a bench facing the water, and I didn't bother asking them if they'd seen which way Bea had gone. Frankly, they looked too preoccupied to notice anything at all. I looked frantically down the street in both directions, but saw no sign of Bea or the Gray Man.

"Shit. Shit!" I hissed between teeth that felt glued together with stress.

"We can split up," Luca said, coming to a stop so silently beside me that I jumped at his nearness. "I'll go left, and you go right."

"But how will I—"

"Have you got your phone?" he asked.

"Yeah."

"I'll call you if I spot her."

I bit my lip, hesitating again. I really didn't want to drag Luca into this. He was so nice, so... normal.

"Wren?" he prompted, looking confused.

"Uh, yeah," I said, shaking my head and deciding on the spot. "Yeah, fine. Just... Luca, be careful, please."

Luca grinned. "It's an eight-year-old kid, I think I can handle it."

"Please, Luca. She's... she's shy. If she sees you chasing after you, she might... might take off or hide or something, and then we'll never find her."

Luca's smile folded into a frown. "You're worried she's in trouble."

I nodded, my fear choking me.

"Okay. I'll keep my distance if I can," Luca said, and with a reassuring nod, he took off at a run, headed north up the shoreline.

I watched him for a few moments, heart in my throat, wondering if I should go after him, before dragging myself back into the present moment. No. Bea was the one I needed to focus on right now. She was the one in immediate danger. Finding her had to be the priority, even if it meant... well, I just had to hope that Luca could take care of himself.

19

I ran as fast as I could down the street, pausing every now and then to bend over the sea wall and scan the beach for any signs of movement. The dark was deep and velvety down on the beach. The noise and commotion of the festival were just a faint echo now, kept at bay by the wind that was whipping in off the water. The houses and restaurants that faced the water were all dark as well, their windows blank and empty, looking like jack-o-lanterns whose candles had been blown out. Everyone was at the festival.

No. Not everyone. A single square of golden light hovered over the shore in the distance, like a moon who didn't know what shape she should be. It hung too high to be one of the squat cottages that lined that stretch of beach, and that meant it came from the Manor. I jogged toward it, knowing that it marked the southernmost border of Sedgwick Cove. As I drew closer, I pulled my phone from my pocket and texted Eva and Zale to let them know what was happening. It was a desperate action—they'd never see it. I wasn't sure if they'd ever see anything again. Whatever the spell was that had been triggered by the pageant had been powerful—a fever dream. I didn't really have a hope that a text would somehow find its way through to them. Still, maybe when it wore off... *if* it wore off. Tears began pricking the corners of my eyes.

"Wren?"

I yelped at the sound of my own name, spinning on the spot to see where it had come from. Nova was walking down the front steps of the Manor toward me. I'd never been so relieved to see anyone in my life.

"Nova!"

"Making a run for it already? I told you that pageant is borderline torture."

I broke into a jog again, and as I got closer, I finally reached another streetlamp. Whatever that light revealed playing across my face was enough for Nova.

"Wren, what's going on? Why aren't you at the festival?"

I couldn't help it. I burst into tears. As I stumbled to a stop in front of her, I sank to my knees, out of breath and out of hope.

"Wren? Wren! Hey, what happened?" Nova asked, dropping into a crouch and putting a tentative hand on my shoulder. "Hey, are you okay?"

"No. No, I'm n-not okay," I replied, the words catching on the sobs that kept ripping their way up my throat. I struggled to catch my breath, while Nova patted me awkwardly on the back, looking alarmed. "It's the pageant... something happened..."

With many starts and stops, I managed to explain what I'd witnessed at the festival —how the words of the pageant had acted as a sort of incantation, and how every member of Sedgwick Cove's magical community seemed to be in its thrall.

"Hmmm... it sounds like an enchantment. It needs a powerful incantation."

"There was no incantation! Not that I heard. They just... performed the words on the..." My voice trailed off as a fresh horror took root.

"I don't understand. We've been using that same stupid script for like a million years," Nova said. "How could it possibly enchant anyone?"

"It's not the same script," I whispered. "There was a book... a very old book, about Litha. It had a poem in it, and Zale decided he wanted to use that instead."

Nova groaned. "Oh my God, was he out of his mind? He should know better than to use something he found in a book! Where did he find it?"

"It… it was me. I found it. In the bin of old costumes and stuff," I said. "I had no idea what it was… no one seemed concerned."

"Well, they should have been! Words have power, and using words when you don't know their source or their intention?" She shook her head, looking uncharacteristically grave.

Guilt was squirming inside me like a living thing, but I pushed it down. There was no time to dwell on how this was, apparently, all my fault. "It's not just that the whole damn town is under a spell, Nova," I said, and explained about Bea.

Nova frowned again. "But why wasn't she under the spell? That doesn't make sense at all. She's a witch, too."

Impatience was swelling inside me. "Nova, I don't know, okay? I don't know anything! I'm surrounded by spells and enchantments and glamours, and I don't know how any of it works! All I know is that Bea went with the Gray Man, and I need to find her!"

Nova bit her lip. "Sorry. I'll help you." She jumped to her feet and held out a hand. "Let's go."

I took her outstretched hand gratefully, and got to my feet. It wasn't until I'd given in to my fear that I realized how tired my body was. My legs shook under me as I tried to stand up, my muscles fatigued and aching with the effort of the chase.

"Thank God you were grounded," I gasped. "How did you see me coming?"

"I've been sitting on the porch listening to the music coming from Main Street, and I spotted you stumbling toward the house. I thought you were a drunk tourist at first."

"But you didn't see Bea or the Gray Man?"

"No, there hasn't been a soul on the beach or the road that I've seen."

I swore under my breath. "They must have gone the other way."

"Well, then let's follow them!" Nova said.

At that moment, my phone buzzed, and I fumbled it out of my pocket. "It's Luca," I muttered.

"Luca? Luca Meyers?" Nova asked, eyebrows raised.

But I was already answering. "Luca?"

"Wren, I saw her!"

"You did? Where is she?" I gasped.

"How the hell is Luca Meyers involved in this?" Nova persisted, but I waved my hand impatiently at her. I didn't have time for stupid questions, not with how much time we'd wasted already.

Luca's voice was cutting in and out, so I was only catching every third word.

"That... girl... you...name... I saw... the theater... inside..."

"Luca, I can barely understand you, what—"

"...in the playhouse..."

The call dropped. I turned to Nova.

"I think he said she went in the playhouse."

"You told him what happened?" Nova looked aghast.

"No, I only told him that Bea had run off. He had just seen her and offered to help me look."

"But he's not supposed to know about—"

"Nova, there was no one else!" I shouted. "Everyone who can help us is enchanted!"

Nova bit her lip and then said, "Screw it. Let's go. If Xiomara has to whip up something to make him forget some shit, so be it."

I nodded, and turned to start running again, but Nova caught my sleeve. "Wren, it's like two miles to the playhouse. Let's take the car."

I hesitated. "Are you allowed to—?"

"No, of course not, but I'm already grounded, so who the hell cares?!" Nova snapped, starting to sound like herself again. I didn't bother arguing, and just took off after her in the direction of her driveway.

Within moments, we were speeding along Harbor Street entirely too fast. Nova's knuckles were white on the steering wheel as we screeched around the curves. I was too terrified for Bea to have any room left for fear over our speed. All I could think was that it was still taking too long, that anything could have happened to Bea by now.

At last, the playhouse came into view around the curve of the road. Nova swung the car across two parking spaces, and had barely shifted it into park before I threw my door open, and started pelting toward the playhouse's main entrance. Nova caught up with me just as I tried the door handles.

"It's locked," I said.

"Where's Luca?" Nova asked.

"I don't know," I grunted, still tugging fruitlessly at the door handles.

"There's another door around this side," Nova said. "It's where they load in the sets and stuff. Come on." She grabbed my hand, and pulled me away from the doors, and through the grass to the side of the building. The outdoor security lights were on where the huge double doors stood at the base of a long driveway. I felt my pulse quicken at the sight of the lights. If they were motion-activated, that meant someone had come this way. We skidded to a halt in front of the doors, and Nova put a restraining hand on my arm. She put her finger to her lips. I nodded.

I tried the handle, and it turned easily in my hand. I pushed it slowly, cringing as the hinges gave a prolonged squeal; but though we stood for several seconds, listening, we were met with only silence. Nova pulled out her cell phone, and turned on the flashlight as we crept into the darkened hallway.

Could Bea really have ventured through this dark, creepy hallway? Not by her own volition, I decided, with a quickening pulse. The thought of how scared she must be spurred me further into the building. Amorphous shapes lined the walls, and though I knew they were likely just random set pieces and props being loaded in for the next production, I couldn't help but cringe away from them. I wished I knew this place the way I knew the theater back in Portland, where I'd memorized every nook and cranny, every pulley and rope and ladder. I'd have felt so much more confident maneuvering around in the dark. Where the hell was Luca? He knew this place inside and out. He'd know where to look. Maybe he was already in here somewhere. Did I dare try to call him? What if the sound of the phone alerted the Gray Man to my presence? But before I could make a decision on whether we should try to stay hidden, Nova decided for me.

"Bea?" she called out. "Bea, are you here?"

Her voice expanded like an explosion through the building, echoing and re-echoing in the cavernous spaces that lined both sides of the hallway. We shone our light into each doorway, revealing a woodshop, a prop shop, and a half dozen storage and rehearsal rooms. Each appeared to be completely empty, and though Nova continued to call her name, Bea didn't appear. Finally, we reached the end of the hallway, a dead end. To the left, a staircase led up to the main level of the building, where the stage and lobby were located. To the right was another door, this one marked "custodial supplies," which was partially open. Nova walked over and pulled the door wide, flashing her light around inside.

"Empty," she replied. "Now what?"

"Upstairs, I guess?" I whispered, biting at my lip. "Maybe she's not here at all. I couldn't really hear what Luca was saying. He mentioned the playhouse, but—"

We both froze as a voice called my name. It was distant—if we hadn't been whispering, I was sure we wouldn't have heard it at all.

"Was that... that wasn't Bea," Nova mouthed, barely making a sound.

I shook my head. It hadn't been a child's voice; I was sure of that.

"Wren!"

Nova and I both jumped, and Nova's hand shot out to grab my wrist. We both looked toward the closet she had just searched.

"Did that just come from..."

Nova swallowed hard. "I think so."

We both crept back to the door of the closet, and Nova raised her phone again in a trembling hand, shining it into every corner of the tiny room. Shelves full of cleaning products, a floor polisher, a mop dangling limply over the edges of a bucket.

"What the hell?" Nova whispered. "Where's it coming from?"

As we stared, mystified, into the tiny space, we heard my name again, faintly, and there was no doubt it was coming from the supply closet, but how? Nova, her expression determined, stalked back into the closet and began shoving things aside.

"What are you doing?" I asked.

"We both heard it, Wren. It's coming from this room. There has to be... ha!" Nova turned to me, triumphant, her finger pointing into the corner of the room. Low on the wall, below the bottommost shelf of cleaning products, was a vent. It was small and about two foot by two foot square, set flat into the wall. As we moved closer, dropping to our knees in front of it, we heard my name again, more distinctly this time; and there was no arguing the point anymore: the sound was definitely coming from that vent.

Nova and I threw each other one wary look before scooting forward in tandem to examine the vent. I ran my fingers along the edges, probing.

"There are screws missing here," I said, pointing to the top and bottom right corners.

"See if you can open it!"

I bit my lip. "This just doesn't make sense. Why in the world would Bea come to this theater, open a custodial closet, and climb into a vent?" I asked.

"She probably didn't. There must be another way to... wherever that vent leads. But do you really want to keep wasting time searching the building for it?"

"I don't know! I don't know what to do! I'm just afraid that..." But my voice died in my throat as the flashlight beam reflected off something on the ground, next to my left knee. I plucked it from the floor of the closet with trembling fingers, and held it up. Nova shone her flashlight on it so that we could both see it properly.

It was a bead. A shiny, cobalt blue bead, from the end of one of Bea's braids.

"Wren!"

My mind was churning, so full of Bea that it took me a moment to realize that it was Luca's voice I was hearing. It sounded panicked. There was no more time to deliberate or reason. It was time to do something, and damn the consequences.

I dug my fingernails between the vent and the wall, and tugged. I put more force into it than was necessary, and fell onto my backside with a huff of surprise as the vent cover swung easily out from the wall. Nova trained her light on the opening, and we saw a silver metal vent extending forward, disappearing into darkness.

"Hecate preserve us; we're climbing down that thing, aren't we?" Nova muttered.

"We sure are," I replied.

A grin flitted over Nova's face. "After you," she said.

I was too anxious to retort. Besides, I was the one who had enlisted her help, not the other way around. It was my name echoing up from the gloom. I should be the one to go first. I heaved in a deep breath and, before I could talk myself out of it, shoved my head and shoulders through the opening of the vent. I slid in easily, though there wasn't much room on either side of me. It was also stiflingly hot. I didn't think I was claustrophobic, but I was definitely about to test that theory. I scooted forward on my stomach in a sort of army crawl, my hands clasped in front of me.

"Here." Nova's arm snaked in beside me, and handed me the phone. I took it gratefully, holding it out in front of myself, and swinging it right to left in the narrow space to get a better look. The vent itself was coated in dust except for a wide, shiny stripe down the middle.

"Someone's been down here recently," I said. "The dust has been disturbed."

"We must be on the right track then," Nova said. "Keep going!"

I inched forward, alternating my elbows to propel myself. Once I had managed to get my whole body inside, I heard Nova crawl in after me, cursing quietly.

"Holy shit, it's hot! Where does this thing empty out, the ninth circle of hell?" she hissed.

"Let's hope not," I whispered in reply.

Inch by inch, we moved forward, the flashlight beam jerking and swinging with my movements. I had no concept of how far we'd traveled, thinking it couldn't have been more than thirty or forty feet before the vent suddenly widened. We saw another, smaller vent to the left, through which the hot air seemed to be pumping. Once we had passed it, gasping with the intensity of the heat, the metal on all sides gave way to damp stone that sloped gently downward. The heat we'd felt in the first part of the vent began to dissipate as we descended, slipping a little on the dampness of the stone, which increased as the passage became colder and clammier. Soon, we were barely able to keep ourselves from sliding straight down into the darkness. I had to brace my hands and feet against the walls to slow my progress. I panted with the effort, terrified that I'd lose my grip and go barreling down the passage, and right into the arms of waiting danger. Behind me, Nova was making quiet sounds of distress as she, too, tried to control her progress down the passage.

Suddenly, as I shifted my weight to ease a cramp in my leg, my shoe lost its purchase, and I tumbled downward. My hands scrabbled desperately against the walls for a handhold, but I found none, and landed with a gasp and a thump on the floor. A squeal of alarm was the only warning I got before Nova slid down as well, and landed in a crumpled heap right on top of me.

"Sorry! Are you okay?" she asked, in a voice that was little more than a breathless whisper.

"I'm fine," I lied, as I crawled out from under her, wincing.

Nova fumbled for a moment with her phone, which had landed on the ground beside us. The space in which we found ourselves was dimly illuminated. It was a small, round chamber—I could have reached out with both arms and touched the walls on either side of me simultaneously. The ceiling was unexpectedly high; how far had we descended? I was too panicked and sore to try to estimate the distance, but I knew we were well underground. The thought only made me more anxious. This was a theater, for goodness sake. Why the hell did it have a creepy subterranean passage? As though she had read my thoughts, Nova whispered in my ear.

"What is this place?"

"I have no idea, but if the Gray Man brought Bea here, I'm sure it's not anything good," I replied, my voice barely more than a breath.

Directly across from where we had spilled out of the vent, a door was set into the wall. It looked old and damp, like everything else around us —a door built from wide wooden planks, and held together with rusting metal hardware. In place of a doorknob, there was a heavy metal ring. Nova and I looked at the door for a long, silent moment, and then turned to look at each other.

She shrugged. "It's the only way through, unless you want to crawl back up that vent," she said.

I wasn't even sure I could crawl back up the vent again, and anyway, I wasn't turning back now. With a deep breath, I stepped forward, took hold of the metal ring, and pulled.

"Help me!" I gasped, and Nova leaped forward. Shoulder to shoulder we grabbed onto the ring, and pulled together. The door dragged grudgingly open with a grating, grinding noise against the floor.

With my heart pounding like a jackhammer in my chest, I stepped into the room beyond.

20

The word "room" was entirely wrong for the place in which we now found ourselves. A room was a box, straight walls, a ceiling, a floor. This place was a cavern—a space hollowed by the gentle but relentlessly greedy fingers of the ocean tide, weathering the rock away, millimeter by millimeter, over centuries. The floor was damp stone, polished smooth by the sand dragged over it by the undulating surf. The walls were pock-marked and twisted, a creation of jagged edges and sharp crevices. The air was briny and moist, moving in and out of my lungs like a tide as I gasped, trying to take it all in —to understand.

At the center of the room was what once might have been a stone dais, but was so worn down and broken apart, that it was now only an echo of itself. And upon the remains of the dais was a crumbled pile of ancient stone, built up into two piles, about waist high. It had once been something taller and grander, something... mystical. It was more knowledge than feeling, somehow. I felt no surprise or confusion upon seeing it. It was as though some deep part of me expected to see it. It felt at once like something humans had made, and somehow also something endemic to the location, forming from the ground the way mountains did.

But it wasn't only its physical form that drew my eye to the stones. There was something absolutely magnetic about it. It drew my gaze, and I didn't know how to look away. It was as though it was calling to me, over and over again, asking a question in a language I couldn't comprehend, and yet was desperate to answer. I took an involuntary step toward it, but Nova grabbed me.

The feeling of her frantic fingers on my arm was like the breaking of a spell. I tore my eyes from the dais, and once I had, everything else about the room came rushing back to me. The cold, the damp, the sound of dripping water. Nova wasn't looking at me. Instead, her gaze was fixed on the far side of the room, where two figures stood. The first was Luca, his posture relaxed, hands thrust into his pockets, an easy smile on his face. The second was Bea, looking frightened and withdrawn, her arms wrapped tightly around herself. The sight of them wrenched a cry of relief from my throat.

"Bea!" I cried.

"Wren!" The reply echoed around the space, so that it took me a moment to understand that both Luca and Bea had answered. They'd both said my name at the same time.

"Are you all right? I was so worried!" I said.

"Of course, I'm all right," the answer came again; and again, both Bea and Luca answered.

I started forward, but Nova grabbed my arm again, holding me back.

"What are you doing?" I asked, trying to shake her off, but she held me fast.

"Something's wrong," she whispered. "Something is very wrong."

"What are you talking ab—"

Nova held up a finger, silencing me mid-question. Then she turned to Bea and Luca and said, "What is this place?"

Both of them simply stared at me, as though Nova hadn't even spoken.

"Now you ask," she whispered, nudging me.

"I don't—"

"Wren, just do it!"

I turned to Bea and Luca. "What is this place?" I asked.

"I don't know! I'm scared!" came the answer, again from both mouths at the same time, in an identical intonation. Bea's expression matched her words, but Luca's was all wrong. He was still smiling, still looking as cool and casual as he had when I'd first seen him lounging in the ticket booth, upstairs.

"Do you see it?" Nova asked.

"I... what is it?" I asked, keeping my voice low now, even as fear began to skitter up my spine.

"I don't know, but something's up," Nova said. "They only answer you, and they only answer together. It's like I'm not even here. Does that seem normal to you?"

I turned back to them, biting my lip. "Bea, is that you?" I asked, and it was a struggle to get enough breath to raise my voice.

"Of course it's me, Wren!"

Two voices. Two figures speaking to me, and only to me.

Dread exploded in the pit of my stomach.

"What's happened to you, Bea?" I whispered. "Luca, what's going on?"

And then suddenly, both figures laughed, a long, harsh laugh that sounded strange in their voices, and looked even stranger as their expressions did not change. They laughed and laughed, like I'd just told the funniest joke.

"My goodness, that was easier than I expected," they both said to me, as their laughter died away. "Honestly, it was almost too easy. I'm rather disappointed."

Nova's fingers on my arm tightened, as we watched a third figure emerge from the shadowy corner of the cavern. The figure stepped into view with slow, measured strides, that nonetheless had a feline fluidity. Watching the figure come closer was more like being stalked, than approached. As the figure moved forward into the light, it revealed itself, piece by piece, like a puzzle clicking together in my head. First, the long, slender legs, then the sparkling, bangle-clad arms, then the shining halo of hair surrounding the flawless face of Veronica Meyers.

"Ms. Meyers?" I mouthed. There wasn't enough breath in my lungs to say the words out loud, and yet she seemed to understand me perfectly. At the mere suggestion of her name, she twitched with annoyance, as though a fly had landed on her.

"I do believe I told you to call me Veronica," she said, hitching her smile back in place at once.

"I don't understand," I said. My brain felt slow, like every thought was wading through molasses. I looked from Bea to Veronica to Luca, desperate for the pieces to fall into place.

"Oh, that much is very evident. I never imagined I'd be up against such an utter ignorance of magical knowledge. I mean, I knew you were unpracticed, but *wow*."

"Up against?" I asked. "Why would you be up against me? What are you even doing here? Did Luca call you?"

"Dear Luca," she looked at her son beside her, his expression impassive, almost blank. "He did provide me with an in, however inadvertently. I really must remember to thank him when I see him."

I looked back and forth between Luca and Veronica, feeling like someone had put my brain in a blender, and hit the button. "What do you mean when you see him? He's... he's right there."

Veronica looked at the figure beside her, and then back at me with a pitying look. "My dear, you are even further behind than I thought." She then bent over to whisper something in Luca's ear. As she did so, she rested a single hand on his arm. A moment later, Luca was simply gone—crumbled away to nothing, like sand in the wind.

I cried out, taking a step forward, and raising my hands as though I thought I might be able to gather all the tiny particles, and reassemble him. The impulse died as quickly as it flared, and I froze where I stood, horror bubbling inside me.

Luca hadn't been real. But then...

My eyes drifted over to Bea.

"There we are. Catching on at last," Veronica said, and she crossed the space between her and Bea in a single long stride. She reached one long, slender finger out, and cocked it under Bea's chin, pulling Bea's face toward her, and then puckering her lips and planting a gentle kiss on the tip of Bea's nose.

With a shiver and a *whoosh*, Bea vanished as well.

Veronica then turned to me, cocking her head to one side. "Surely, you recognize a glamour when you see one? Your family's shop is crawling with them, after all."

I turned to Nova, and she nodded, answering the question in my eyes. How could I have been so stupid?

I'd thought Bea and I had been the only two witches who hadn't been affected by the spell at the festival. But now I understood: Bea wasn't Bea at all. The real Bea was probably somewhere in that crowd back on Main Street, still hypnotized by the pageant. This Bea—the one I had followed here—had been nothing but an illusion, a piece of bait dancing on the surface of the water. And like the most gullible of fish, I leaped for it. And yet...

"I still don't understand. How do you know about... about glamours and... You're not even a..." I felt almost dizzy with confusion. I must have swayed because Nova put out a hand to steady me. When I locked eyes with her, she looked just as bewildered as I felt.

"Not even a witch?" Veronica finished my sentence for me, her lips exaggerating the final word. "I'm afraid that was just an assumption on your part, and a foolish one at that."

"You're a witch," I repeated, and the words sounded wrong.

"That's right. Do try to keep up."

"I... how?" I asked, utterly unable to form a more coherent question.

"The very same way as you are a witch, Wren. I was born one. Surely you heard the story of the playhouse? That Victor Meyers fell in love with a girl from Sedgwick Cove, and then bought the playhouse. Did you never think, perhaps, that the woman he married might have been a witch?"

I blinked. No, I hadn't considered it. I glanced at Nova, and she looked as surprised as I felt. Everyone in Sedgwick Cove considered the Meyers family outsiders, regardless of who might have married into it three generations ago.

Veronica clicked her tongue. "My, my, how soon we were forgotten. I'd have thought our coven had made a bigger impact than that. After all, the Kildare name once struck fear into the heart of this town."

A memory stirred. The Keep. The name carved into the stone. Persi's words echoed back to me: *By all accounts, they made no secret of their affinity for dark magic. They rose quickly when they came, gathering allies and challenging hierarchies. Soon, it became clear that they were not content to simply coexist in Sedgwick Cove; they wanted the deep magic for themselves. They even tried to summon the Darkness, like Sarah Claire had once done.*

Nova replied before I could. "The Kildare coven was driven out of Sedgwick Cove centuries ago."

Veronica turned her eyes on Nova, giving her an appraising look. "And who are you?"

Nova swallowed hard but lifted her chin, looking for a moment exactly like her grandmother. "Nova Claire."

Veronica's pursed lips widened into a smirk. "A Vesper and a Claire? Well, if this isn't poetic justice."

"What do the Kildares have to do with the Meyers family?" I asked impatiently. I was sick of feeling clueless, tired of trying to catch up.

"They are one and the same now. Nova is correct; the banishment of the Kildare coven is common knowledge among the residents of Sedgwick Cove. What is much less well known is that the Kildares came back."

This pronouncement was met with total silence. Veronica seemed to enjoy the shock she was inflicting on us. She paused a moment to savor our dumbfounded expressions, before continuing.

"The Kildares were patient—their lust for power was for their coven, not themselves; and so, they waited. They knew they would have to bide their time, would have to let generations slip by, before they could dare try to set foot in the Cove again. And so they did. But then my grandmother Paulina, and her sister Valerie, stepped into their power, and it was clear to the entire coven that it was time. My grandmother was incredibly powerful, and her sister almost equally so. Before they had even reached womanhood, they were wielding spells of such power, that even those closest to them feared them as much as they loved them. The coven gathered, calling the spirits of their ancestors, and made a decision. Paulina and Valerie would return to the Cove, and seek the source of the deep magic there.

"They changed their last name to Jaques and invented a back story. They arrived in Sedgwick Cove, claiming to be refugees from a coven in Europe, escaping the devastation and poverty that had laid waste to their homeland after the war. They were accepted with open arms, and spent several years working their way into the community, gaining trust and forging connections. They were very good at their deception. Before long, it was as though the Jaques sisters had always been a part of the magical fabric of the town. Only then did they dare begin their search.

They could only work at night, in secret; and even then, they had to be wary of other witches, and their nocturnal practices. After a few nearly disastrous failed attempts, they managed to forge a connection to the Darkness. They were able to rouse it from its slumber, just enough to gather some clues about the deep magic. And at last, the Darkness led them to the source."

Here, Veronica paused, her eyes fever bright, ignited with the passion of the tale she was retelling. It reminded me of that night up on the cliffs, when Zale had told the story of the founding of Sedgwick Cove. Veronica knew every syllable of this story by heart, and had probably heard it a thousand times, just like the kids sitting bright-eyed around that bonfire, their lips mouthing the words like the chorus of a favorite song. Another origin story of this place.

"So where was it?" Nova's voice sliced through the silence like a knife: sharp, quick, and dripping with skepticism.

Veronica raised an eyebrow, looking amused. "You're looking at it."

And all three of us together let our gazes drift to the dais, to the pile of rubble that had so captivated me when first I'd seen it. Now that I had turned attention to it, I could feel it again, the lure of it, almost like... an invitation.

"This?" Nova asked, and again, her voice sounded sharp, but this time with badly suppressed fear. "This... pile of rocks?"

"I understand your skepticism," Veronica said, and her smile twisted into something more vicious. "After all, the Second Daughters sought this power as well. To know that another coven discovered what you could not... it must be galling."

"One." Nova snapped.

"Excuse me?"

"One Second Daughter sought that power. Only one. And she does not define us."

I reached over and took Nova's hand. She didn't look at me, but she squeezed my fingers in acknowledgment.

"Pity," Veronica said. "To think what you all could have achieved if you'd had the courage to follow in her footsteps. Still, I should be grateful. My grandmother certainly was when she realized that the source of the deep magic had been safe all those years, since our coven's banishment. But almost as soon as she and her sister discovered this place, that safety was threatened.

"The town was struggling financially at the time. Tourist dollars were being exhausted before they reached Sedgwick Cove, as the southern coast of Maine became more and more developed. I mean, why drive four hours from Boston for some quaint Maine seaside charm, when you can get your fill of it barely two hours away? They had to find a way to bring in revenue, and so they voted that this piece of land could be developed," Veronica explained. "It was a contentious decision. The population of the town was very divided over it. My grandmother thought it must be the work of adversarial magic. How else could such a decision be made at the same moment she had made this crucial discovery? But she didn't give up—she couldn't. She simply needed to find a way to secure the property herself. The prospect seemed, at first, impossible. But my grandmother was a tenacious woman. The only thing that stood between my grandmother and what she wanted, was money. And so, she set her sights on the easiest way for a woman in those days to get some: a man."

She smiled as though this particular detail of the story was her favorite, like a favorite chord in a familiar song.

"And so, she made her way to the seaside resorts, and started flirting with the vacationing businessmen. It didn't take her long to catch the attention of Victor Meyers. He was a Broadway producer, with an overflowing wallet and a wandering eye. He fell so hard for my grandmother that the love potion she'd brewed for the occasion was almost irrelevant. She used it as a bit of insurance, but Victor, my grandfather, was smitten almost as soon as he'd laid eyes on her. We've always had a certain something, the women in my family." Veronica tossed her hair, looking matter-of-fact rather than self-satisfied.

"Anyway, he proposed right out there on the rocks, but not before she'd convinced him of the beauty of this place, the potential it possessed, the money it could generate. Victor was more willing than she could have believed, but it wasn't only his love for her that made him leap at the chance to buy this property. He'd passed over an opportunity to purchase a floundering resort in the Catskills, and the friend who had bought it instead had turned it into a goldmine. Victor was bitter. He wanted to make his mark in a whole new place, somewhere no other producer had been. My grandmother convinced him that Sedgwick Cove was that undiscovered gem. He made an offer that the town couldn't refuse, and they began construction on the playhouse as soon as Victor and his bride returned from their whirlwind wedding and honeymoon.

"Paulina feigned interest in the theater itself so that she had the excuse to be here on site, overseeing the building project while really trying to unravel the mystery of the source. She was able to use her persuasion and magic to ensure that a secret entrance was created so that she could reach this cavern, while the men who built it immediately forgot about it. Once this had been done, she was free to come and go as she pleased, and she could begin the grueling work of unraveling the secrets of this place."

"And how did that go for her?" Nova asked, the effectiveness of her sarcasm marred by the slight tremor in her voice.

"Oh, very slowly, at first. The Darkness was still bound by the Covenant, and could not access the deep magic. Paulina tried every method of magical discovery she could find, but she, too, remained unable to connect to the magic. Her frustrations grew, but so did her determination. Paulina decided she had to convene with the Darkness again, and try to learn more. She did not expect the Darkness to give her all the answers she was looking for—she was not so naive about the creature she was dealing with. But she did hope it might tell her enough that she could come to understand the nature of the source—and through that understanding, she thought she may even be able to access the deep magic directly, without involving the Darkness at all.

"On the summer solstice, under the light of the full moon, she drew a circle and convened with the Darkness. What she learned within the boundaries of that circle changed our coven's course yet again. The Darkness sensed Paulina's greed, but did not seem to fear it. In fact, it laughed at her. What did it matter if she coveted what neither of them could have? Paulina was deeply troubled by this. 'What do you mean by this?' she asked, expending a great amount of magic—of herself—so that the question became in some way a command. The Darkness had no choice but to answer truthfully.

"The source remains impenetrable until such a time as a pentamaleficus of the first blood walks this shore again."

Something was tugging at the frayed edges of my attention, trying to draw me away from Veronica, even as I sensed it had everything to do with her tale. My brain was trying to make a connection, but I was too slow, too confused, too scared...

As though she had heard my thoughts, Veronica's faraway gaze became focused again, and she turned to look directly at me. Her eyes were penetrating, as though they could peer into the very corners of you, the hidden places you barely acknowledge to yourself, let alone anyone else. My blood felt sluggish in my veins as I looked into those eyes, trying to remember and not to remember something all at the same time.

"Come now, Wren Vesper. Haven't you put it together yet?" she whispered.

And like a rubber band twanging, all the disparate parts of the situation snapped back into place, so that I could see it for what it was. It felt like a good, cold slap across the face, at once painful and necessary.

The pentamaleficus was an elemental witch who could command all five of the elements, including the element of spirit. I had recently shown an affinity for all five elements, the first four on the beach while facing down the Gray Man, and the final one just in the last couple of days, having encountered my dead grandmother's ghost repeatedly. The Darkness told Paulina they needed a pentamaleficus to access the source of the deep magic. The Darkness had tried, repeatedly, to lay claim to me and my power since I was barely old enough to walk.

I was staring at the completed puzzle, and the picture it presented crashed down upon me, all at once.

"Whoa, Vesper! Stay with me here!"

It was Nova's voice, and it was coming from above me. Without realizing it, I had fallen to my knees, which I supposed was better than falling on my face. My arms, which were trying to hold me up despite having turned entirely to water, wobbled dangerously beneath me. My stomach gave a lurch, and I had no choice but to fold forward and rest my cheek on the cold, damp stone of the cavern floor.

"Got there at last, have you?" came Veronica's indifferent voice.

"What is she—" Nova began, but she was pulled up short as the truth burst out of me.

"It's me. I'm the pentamaleficus the Darkness was talking about. That's why it found me when I was just a child. That's why it found me again, as soon as my grandmother's spell of protection died with her. It's why it almost walked away with me into the sea. It needs me. It needs my... my power, to access the deep magic."

There it was. I had said it out loud, and I couldn't take it back: the truth at the heart of all of this.

I looked up and found that Nova's eyes had gone black as her pupils expanded, until it seemed they would swallow her whole face. Every bit of the horror I felt was reflected back to me in those eyes.

What do we do? those eyes seemed to ask me.

I don't know, my eyes answered back.

"Now you understand. My grandmother couldn't complete the work she had so faithfully begun. But still, the Kildares did not lose hope. We waited—perhaps not patiently, but diligently, and while we waited, we prepared. We studied our craft in secret. We taught our daughters and their daughters. We stayed in this place and ensured its survival, so that the source would remain protected. And we waited. We waited, of course, for *you*, Wren Vesper."

The words now caused only a dull echo of the shock I'd felt a few moments before, but my body still trembled with it. Nova was now gripping my arm so tightly it was tingling.

"How did you know?" I asked, the thought slipping out of my mouth unintentionally.

"How did I know what?" Veronica asked, her voice smooth and polite, like a teacher clarifying a point in front of a class.

"How did you know who I was? That I had... arrived?" I asked.

"Oh, that was simple enough. We had bound ourselves to the Darkness so that we would know when it had awakened to your presence. Think of it as a magical alarm going off. It was my mother, the matriarch of the coven, who made her way to Sedgwick Cove then. She expected to find a powerful witch, fully attuned to her power, ready to become either a willing ally or a fearsome adversary. What she found instead... was a mere child."

"It became clear, as she watched and waited, that our time to claim you had not yet come. Your grandmother saw to that. She was a powerful witch. She protected you exceedingly well, in more ways than I think anyone but we, who were trying to penetrate her defenses, could comprehend. Still, we had waited so long. What was a few more years? When you had matured, her protection would be useless. You would step into your power, and then step into our waiting arms. We could be patient a little while longer."

"And then I came back," I whispered.

Veronica's smile widened, a cat-in-the-cream smile. "And then you came back."

21

I looked at Veronica. She looked back at me. I'm not sure what was on my face, but hers was alight with triumph.

"I knew I had to be careful. I didn't want to be hasty and squander the opportunity to get you on your own. The first step was to offer the theater as a rehearsal space for the pageant. I knew all the covens would participate—it's a Sedgwick Cove rite of passage, and so I thought the chances were good that you would be involved. And sure enough, when I checked the sign-in log the day after the first rehearsal, there was your name. I can't tell you what a thrill it gave me to see it there. To know that you had been here, so close to where I needed you to be."

This knowledge that had so thrilled her sent a shiver of horror up my back. Beside me, Nova had gone statue-still with stress. I'd now lost all feeling in my fingers, and had to gently pry her hand away from my upper arm. Veronica was too caught up in her own story now to notice what we were doing. It was clear, now that she had a captive audience, that she was enjoying herself. This story was centuries in the making, and she was the one who got to tell it.

She went on, "The more I considered it, the more I thought the pageant was the key to everything. It would bring the entire town together. If I could separate you from all those who might be able to protect you, I would have a better chance of success. And so, I put the pageant at the center of my efforts. I also wanted to meet you, and so I suggested to Luca that we do some sightseeing in town. It was strange seeing you for the first time and realizing how... insignificant you were. How unimpressive. Just a little mouse of a thing, aren't you? Just utterly forgettable."

She laughed, and there was no malice in her voice. It was more... incredulity than anything else.

"And then you told us about the script, how it was so terrible, and that you were looking to improve it somehow. That provided the opening I'd been looking for. The next step was planting the book. It was almost ludicrously easy, with Luca working here every day. I simply told him that his uncle had found the book left behind on the stage and to put it in the prop box. He did so gladly, unaware of the magic the book contained." She sighed. "I had to put a spell on it so that it would make its presence known to someone. Imagine my delight when that someone turned out to be you."

Guilt, sharp and hot, bubbled in my stomach. I was so stupid, so gullible. I'd played right into her hands, and delivered the one thing she needed to carry out her plan. I wanted to scream. Sure, Zale had been immediately on board, but he had been desperate to make his mark on the pageant. He would have done anything, even ignore the most basic of magical safety guidelines, in order to make that happen. And I was too ignorant to warn against it.

"Don't be too hard on yourself," Veronica said, as though she could hear what I was thinking. "You really didn't have a hope once you opened the book. It would have ensnared you all at once."

We'd all been ensnared, I thought. After the cheesy, hackneyed lines of the old script, the book had breathed fresh life into the pageant. We'd all agreed to use it. Perhaps if Nova hadn't been grounded, she would have had the good sense to stop us, but somehow I doubted it. We were damned from the moment we opened it.

"I'd enchanted the words so that when they were spoken on the solstice, they would turn every witch within its hearing into a waking dreamer. All except for one." She smiled at me again, a smile that seemed almost... loving. Like she somehow thought she was doing all of this for me instead of for herself. It was the most disturbing thing I'd seen from her up until that very moment. She went on, "But once everyone who could protect you was neutralized, how to lure you here? I toyed with the idea of asking Luca to do it, but in the end, I decided against it. That boy is not as obtuse as his father, a trying complication I hadn't considered when I married the man. Men usually can't seem to help but love me, but Luca... well, he never really warmed to me."

Despite my terror, a bubble of hope rose in my chest. "Luca's... not your son?"

"Surely you knew that," Veronica snorted. "I was under the impression he couldn't wait to out me as the evil stepmother."

Relief flooded through me. Luca wasn't a Kildare. Luca hadn't known anything about this. He hadn't been a knowing participant in this plot to lure me here. I was so relieved that I almost missed what Veronica said next.

"...like I said, too perceptive to be useful. He would question me. I couldn't risk it. But then I thought, hmmm, maybe I could use him in a different way."

My breath froze in my lungs and the relief drained away, to be replaced with an icy fear. "What do you mean, use him?" I asked. "You better not have... if you hurt him..."

Veronica laughed, a high, tinkling sort of giggle that made me shudder. "For goodness sake, stop being so melodramatic. You'd almost think I was some kind of villain; but I'm not a monster, Wren, whatever impression you might have of me right now. I'm explaining all of this to you so that you can start to understand your place in all of this—how we got here. No, Luca is just fine. Working on his car out in the garage when I left. It's a very powerful spell, the glamour I used to create the illusion of him. If you'd touched him, he even would have felt real to you. But in order for it to work, I needed his essence. A hair or two taken from his hairbrush was enough."

"What about Bea?" Nova asked. I jumped, having almost forgotten she was right beside me. "How did she get wrapped up in all of this? How did you get her essence? Felony kidnapping?"

Again, Veronica laughed. "My goodness, you are determined to think the worst of me, aren't you? As the day of the festival grew nearer, I saw that Wren was much more involved in the production of the pageant than I had originally thought. She had all but taken it over. I thought it unlikely that Luca would be able to pull her away with a simple invitation to walk the beach with him, even if she did have the crush on him that I suspected she had." She raised her eyebrows at me, as though asking the silent question.

I kept my mouth shut, but the blood flaming in my cheeks answered for me.

She looked gratified. She turned back to Nova, and continued to answer her question. "Well, as I said, I couldn't count on her going with him. She'd put a great deal of effort into the pageant. She'd likely want to stay and see the fruits of her labors. And so I had to think of another way, something more compelling. And then she showed up at the theater with Beatriz. I had to assess the relationship quickly, but I'd always been gifted when it came to understanding the ties that bind people. I could see that the girl was very timid, and painfully shy. I could also see that Wren felt protective of her. Something had formed there—a kinship of sorts. I knew I could use that to my advantage. I offered to let the girl try on some wigs and hats, and in the process, I procured the necessary hairs. Of course, I had to make sure to find a way to keep Beatriz from the festival, or Wren might have seen her in the crowd and ruined everything. A simple charm cast while picking up some lunch at the restaurant that day did the trick."

Anger flared in me as I remembered that moment in the cafe, and Veronica, sensing it, turned her attention back to me. "I already told you, Wren. Beatriz is perfectly safe. I wouldn't harm a hair on that girl's head... though I might steal one or two." She smirked wryly. "Beatriz simply will have found herself unable to keep her eyes open as the afternoon went on; and by evening, she will have been so tired, she would have no choice but to go to bed. She had expressed a dislike for the noise and crowds of the festival, which led me to believe that no one would be too suspicious if she didn't want to go. She is no doubt sleeping soundly, and will wake feeling refreshed and perfectly herself."

Nova looked like she wanted to say something, but she just chewed viciously at the inside of her cheek. I could tell she still wouldn't trust Veronica as far as she could throw her, no matter how Veronica tried to make herself sound like the rational adult in the room. Veronica was in league with the Darkness. That was all either of us really needed to know.

"And so, with the real Luca happily building his car, and the real Beatriz enjoying sweet dreams, there was nothing left to stand in my way. It all unfolded smoothly. The pageant began. The spell took effect. My one moment of fear came when I thought you might turn to an outsider for help—so recently returned as you were, I wasn't sure if you knew better than to betray the magical population to the outside world; and even if you did, I thought there was a chance you might be desperate enough to do it anyway. But again, my luck held. You were braver and smarter than I had given you credit for. You chased after Beatriz alone, isolating yourself from the others. Then I sent the Luca glamour to meet you, and lead you in the right direction. The only complication I hadn't foreseen was you." Veronica turned to look appraisingly at Nova, as though she still hadn't decided just how big of a complication she was.

"So sorry to spoil your plans," Nova said, a sneer in her voice.

Veronica smiled pleasantly. "You haven't spoiled anything as of yet," she said.

"I've only just arrived," Nova said. "Give me time."

Veronica's smile widened. "Oh, I will. And I'll give you a choice. What you do with that choice will be your own business. You will decide your fate, Second Daughter, not me."

"What the hell does that mean?" Nova shouted, and though her tone was angry, I knew that it was actually fear that was driving her words.

"What I mean is that I've told you all there is to know. There is no more reason to delay. We've reached the moment when we all must decide what part we will play," Veronica said. "Wren is here. She is the pentamaleficus of the first blood, the long-awaited key to opening this lock. So now she has a decision to make."

"You're saying I actually have a choice?" I asked, incredulous.

"Of course you do," Veronica said, and then turned her attention to the dais in the middle of the room, her eyes sparkling with a covetous light. "But surely this place has been calling to you, as deeply and consistently as it has been calling to me. You are the only one who can accept its invitation.

You must have been longing to find it from the moment you knew of its existence."

It seemed pointless to contradict her. The truth was that I had never given the source a second thought. I'd had a little too much else on my mind since arriving in Sedgwick Cove. Even Nova, who had known about the deep magic all her life, looked skeptical and a bit wary.

"My grandmother spent the better part of her life trying to understand it. My mother did as well, though in the end, she despaired of ever comprehending its true nature," Veronica said, her voice little more than a murmur that nonetheless carried in the echoing cavern. "But like both of them before me, I must admit it is a mystery to me. Still... can you *feel* it?"

Nova and I turned, almost simultaneously, to stare at the dais. The longer I concentrated on it, the more attuned I became to the energy that seemed to roll off of it in waves. There was a lure to the stones. I could almost—no, not almost. Undoubtedly. I could *undoubtedly* hear them whispering to me, like each tiny chip of rock was calling my name in an irresistible tone that I could not ignore. It felt like a string tied to my ribs, trying over and over again to tug me forward, to answer this call that I didn't comprehend, and yet wanted desperately to. It begged to be answered. I turned to Nova, the question on my face, but her expression was puzzled, almost frustrated. It was at that moment that I understood: it didn't call to her the same way it called to me, the way it called to Veronica. What did that mean?

Rather than shying away from the call, I leaned into it, focusing every particle of my being on the steady, bone-deep pull of it, the way it ached and soothed all at once. It was like something inside of me already knew it, and had been waiting to answer it since the moment I'd begun my existence. I wanted to laugh and cry, to run far from it and right into its arms at the same time.

"Wow," I whispered.

"What's wow?" Nova hissed. "What are we supposed to be feeling?"

I tore my eyes from the stones to stare at Veronica, whose eyes gleamed with the depth of her understanding.

"What is it?" I asked her.

Her eyes flashed. "Do you not know?"

"No. How could I? I've never felt... it's so..." I shook my head, utterly incapable of finding the words.

Veronica's expression fell. "I was so sure you'd understand."

The people-pleasing part of me wanted to apologize, but I bit back the words. I had nothing to apologize for, certainly not to the woman now standing eloquent with disappointment in front of me.

"So you can't tell me anything at all about these stones?" Veronica asked.

"No," I replied. *And I wouldn't even if I could,* I added silently.

Veronica's bottom lip began to tremble. Was this grown woman about to burst into tears, like a child denied a treat? I felt an edge of anger in my thoughts again, and welcomed it. Whatever was happening here, I should be focusing on finding a way out of it. There would be time for understanding later.

"It's no matter. The Darkness will know what we must do. And that is why you must call it."

Every particle of air in the room seemed to crystallize. "What?"

"You must call the Darkness. Summon it here, to this place," Veronica said, more loudly this time, as though the problem was that I simply hadn't been able to hear her.

"Why the hell would I do that?" I asked, panic dragging my voice up half an octave.

Veronica blinked. "Because we've found it. The source of the deep magic. The very thing that has drawn our ancestors to this place over the centuries, the thing that strengthens our gifts. The Darkness knows how to draw upon it. We need that knowledge to do the same."

She said the words so matter-of-factly, as though stating the solution to an equation. She could comprehend no differing opinion here, no hesitation or uncertainty. To her, it was a foregone conclusion that we would want this power for ourselves, just as she did.

"I don't want to draw upon it," I said, speaking slowly and clearly so that there could be no misunderstanding. "And I don't want the Darkness to draw on it, either."

Veronica's eyes went flat. The change was immediate and startling. A moment before, she'd been alight with a kind of euphoric fervor. Now, she looked as empty and hollow as the glamours she'd used to bring me here.

"Don't be a fool, Wren Vesper. Ask your friend here. A Second Daughter would never pass on an opportunity like this, isn't that right, Nova? After so long in the shadow of the Vespers, surely you cannot pretend this magic isn't everything you've dreamed about?" And Veronica actually reached out a hand to Nova, expectant.

I glanced at Nova. A muscle was jumping in her jaw, and her hands were clenched into fists at her sides. For one wild second, I thought she was going to reach out and take that hand. I thought I saw her finger twitch. But then she shook her head. "I will not deny that there have been Second Daughters who have dreamed of it. But we all woke up. All except one, and I assure you, that one is not me."

Veronica's hand lowered slowly, until it hung limply at her side. "Very well. If you insist on being ordinary, that is your choice to make. But you," she turned to me now. "I'm still going to need you to summon the Darkness."

I laughed a sharp, short bark that tore at my throat on the way out. "Look, I know everyone's got this impression that I'm some powerful elemental witch, but I don't know what I'm doing. I'm failing Witchcraft 101, okay? I don't know how to summon the Darkness, and even if I did, I'd probably just screw it up."

"Don't downplay your powers. I heard about what happened on the beach. You clashed with the Darkness, and you won. That is not the work of some clueless novice," Veronica said, impatient now.

"That's exactly what it was!" I cried, feeling a week's worth of frustration at my own ignorance bubbling over all at once. "I have no idea how I did that! I'm not... I don't... it was just instinct!"

"Well, then, use your instincts now!"

"It's not the same! I was in fear for my life! I... it was probably just adrenaline and luck and..."

But Veronica's face brightened with understanding. "Yes, of course. The circumstance triggered the magic in you. I should have... well, never mind. That is easily remedied."

And before either Nova or I could do more than yelp, Veronica had lunged forward and caught Nova by the arm, simultaneously pulling a small handgun from her coat pocket. She cocked the hammer and put the gun against Nova's temple.

"No, stop, stop!" I cried out, raising my arms over my head like she was pointing the gun at me. "What are you... leave her out of this, okay? Nova has nothing to do with this. You should be pointing that gun at me, okay?" My voice was shaking so badly I could barely understand my own words.

"Oh, no, I'm afraid that won't work, Wren," Veronica said, pulling Nova slightly closer to her. "You know I can't kill you. I need you. But I don't need her."

"So much for not being the villain," Nova said, and though her voice was calm, her eyes were wild with fear.

"An utterly unnecessary escalation, born of your own stubbornness. I was perfectly happy to ally with you, but I will not let you stand in my way," Veronica hissed at Nova before turning back to me. "Now summon it, Wren."

"I don't... I... why don't you do it?" I blurted out, desperately playing for time. "Your grandmother and your mother convened with the Darkness! Surely, they must have taught you how to do it!"

"Of course they did!" Veronica shrieked, the final threads of her composure snapping and startling us all. Her face contorted. "I followed their instructions to the letter. I did it over and over and over again. But my grandmother's spell won't work. Your protective spell is getting in the way."

"What protective spell?" I asked, pulled up short. I dropped my hands from above my head. Nova gave a little whimper.

"The magic you used to escape the Darkness. You thought you trapped it in the sand, but you know now that that's not true. No doubt your Conclave told you that."

"I... how do you know all of this?" I gasped.

"Davina. I visited her shop and performed a bit of... persuasion. She doesn't remember that she spoke to me, let alone all the details she'd given me. I know all about the night on the beach, the lightning sand, the fact that it's empty, even the form the Darkness takes when it comes to you. It's how I was able to make my glamour so effective—producing the very Gray Man that lured you to the ocean, twice."

I wanted to scream. No one had suspected her, an outsider. Everyone's guard had been down.

"Does it really matter how I know? It is enough that we understand. What you did that night was protect yourself. You created, unintentionally, it seems, a barrier between yourself and the Darkness. Haven't you wondered why you haven't felt its presence? Why the Gray Man hasn't been standing under your window every night?"

Yes, I'd wondered. But I'd never thought... never stopped to consider... that I'd been protecting myself all along, without realizing it.

The play of these thoughts across my face was evidently answer enough. Veronica went on. "What your grandmother had done for you, you have unwittingly been doing for yourself. But that must end now. Your spell is standing between the Kildare coven and what we want. And that is a very, very dangerous place to stand." She shook Nova by the arm, and her resultant whimper snapped me back to the reality of the situation we were in. To the reality of a gun against the head of my friend. Despite my best efforts, my eyes began to fill with tears.

"Veronica, I am not trying to play you. I am very, very serious when I tell you that I don't know how to do what you're asking me. I didn't even know that I had cast a protection spell."

"And yet you did it," Veronica said, the words tight. "And so, for the sake of your friend, I suggest you *try*."

I swallowed hard. I looked at Nova, who shook her head, even as tears streamed down her face. "Don't do it," she whispered. "Don't let the Darkness free."

"Shut up!" Veronica screamed, and for the first time, her expression matched the madness of her scheme. She looked deranged and unstable—centuries of generational trauma coming to a head before my eyes.

"Okay, I'll... I'll try," I gasped, raising my hands again. Veronica pressed her lips together, making a clear effort to calm herself again.

"Go on, then."

Heart pounding in my chest, I closed my eyes, trying to reach back into my memory, to the night of the lighthouse. What had I done? How had I called my power? The details of the night swirled and blurred, spinning like an out-of-control carousel. I was panicking. I was failing Nova. I didn't know how to...

Wren.

My eyes flew open. I knew that voice. And I had never been more grateful to hear it. But though I scanned the room eagerly, I did not see Asteria.

"What? What is it?" Veronica asked eagerly, craning her neck to look around as well.

"I... nothing. I'm just... I'm trying to focus," I mumbled.

Wren. Listen to me.

This time, the voice came distinctly from the center of the room, from the dais itself, or at least, the space around it. And I was the only one who could hear it.

Wren, the source of the deep magic is not safe, came Asteria's voice, urgent as a scream, yet quiet as a whisper. *You must protect it.*

"I don't know how!" I whispered.

Help is coming.

"What do you mean?" I asked the question inside my own head, so that only Asteria could hear it. "How do I get out of this? I can't summon the Darkness, but I can't let Nova die! What do I do?"

There was a pause, then I thought I heard a ghost of a laugh.

Duck.

"Huh?"

DUCK.

My brain was still questioning her, but my body obeyed. Without warning, I threw myself on the ground, covering my head, just as something large erupted through the wall behind me.

22

Veronica and Nova screamed. The room exploded in a choking haze of dust and sand and rock. I lifted my head, and looked toward the source of the sound, just as a cold, salty wind whipped at my cheeks.

Three figures stood silhouetted in the gaping opening that had been blasted through the side of the cavern. The Vesper Sisters, bathed in moonlight, looking at once beautiful and terrible, their hair tossed around their faces like boats on the sea that crashed behind them: Rhi, on the right, her hands clenched at her sides, her tiny figure, yet somehow intimidating in her power. Persi, looking like an avenging siren that had just stepped from the waves, magic sparking in her fingertips like sparklers. And my mother, Kerridwen Vesper, her long hair loose, her face transformed with rage and fear, her hands extended out in front of her, fingers wide. And all around her, vines and branches were writhing and twisting and blooming like a pit of snakes, forcing their way through the stones across the floor.

"Wren!" Her voice called out sharply, cracking.

"I'm here!" I tried to answer, coughing and choking on the debris still settling all around me. "Nova! Where's Nova?" My heart was in my throat. I hadn't heard a gunshot, but the explosion had been so loud...

I heard an answering groan, and turned to see Nova crawling out from behind a huge, jagged piece of the wall. She was coated in dust, but I could see the blood on her forehead.

"Nova! Are you... did she...?" I choked, trying to crawl toward her just as my mother reached me, and pulled me around to face her, shaking my shoulders.

"Wren, speak to me! Are you okay? Are you hurt?"

"I... no. I mean, yes, I'm okay. No, I'm not hurt. I'm worried about..."

But Rhi had already crossed the cavern to help Nova to her feet, examining her wounds and fishing in her pocket for a handkerchief to help stop the bleeding.

"Wren, are you okay?" Nova was calling, shakily, as she blinked blood out of her eyes.

"She's fine, honey, it's you we're worried about," Rhi said. "Now, stay still so I can get some of my calendula salve on it." Nova yelped. "Did I mention it stings a bit?" Rhi added apologetically.

"There's another entrance back here," Persi called from somewhere behind the rubble. "Damn it all, I think she's gone!"

"Are you sure?" my mother called sharply. "All that rubble. Are you sure she's not..." But she couldn't bring herself to complete the question.

Persi understood, however. "I've cast a detection spell, but it's still very —ugh, Kerridwen! Calm down!" Persi had to yank her ankle out of the curling tendrils of a nearby plant that was attempting to climb her.

"Sorry, sorry. I'm out of practice, I... damn it, hang on." My mother shook her head as though to clear it and closed her eyes, taking several long, slow, measured breaths. As she did so, the rioting vines and branches slowed their spreading until, after maybe ten seconds, they had stilled entirely.

Ensured that she wouldn't be strangled by a wayward vine, Persi was able to concentrate on her own spell. She held a hand out over the rubble, and began to walk slowly from one end of the pile to the other, murmuring an incantation under her breath. We all watched, no one daring to move or make a sound. My lungs felt like they'd been restricted to pinholes; I couldn't seem to get any air into them at all. Was Veronica under there? Was she... had she actually...?

"No," Persi said with a level of certainty that no one would even consider questioning. "I don't know where she is, but it's not under this debris; more's the pity."

I didn't know whether I should feel relieved she wasn't dead, or alarmed that she had escaped. I gulped, swallowing back some monstrosity born of emotional turmoil, a hysterical peal of laughter, or perhaps an onslaught of sobbing. I never found out which. I fought it off, choosing instead to try to stay in the moment.

"Pers, you have to get Ostara on the phone. Or Davina, or Xiomara, whoever you can get," my mother ordered. "They need to know who—"

"I know, I know, I'm on it," Persi said, striding across the room to the gaping opening, her phone already at her ear.

"Rhi, can you go check on—?"

"Yes, yes. I don't see any reason to think Miss Claire here won't be perfectly fine after a hot cup of tea and a soak in the bath," Rhi said, tucking her tins and beakers into her apron pocket, and guiding Nova gently toward the dais. "Here you go, dear heart. Sit back against this and keep holding that gauze there, all right?"

"No!" I cried out, and Nova stumbled back in alarm, falling into Rhi, who only just managed to keep her feet.

"Wren, what in the world...?" Rhi gasped.

"I don't... don't think we should touch it," I said, trying to sound calm, but unable to quell the note of hysteria in my voice.

"Why? What is it?" Rhi asked.

"It's the reason she lured me here," I answered.

Rhi's eyes widened, and she took an awed step back from the dais, staring at it as though it had materialized right out of the ground in front of her.

"Rhi, please!" my mother said, and Rhi seemed to snap out of her fixation.

"Right, yes. Sorry. I'll make sure she's...I'll be right back." Rhi helped Nova take a seat on a different lump of rock, one a good ten feet from the dais, and then scurried from the room. I thought I heard her call something out in the night, but the wind made it hard to hear. When I could no longer see her, I turned to my mother instead, the unanswered questions pouring out of me now.

"How did you know where to find me?" I asked.

My mom held up her cell phone. "I just tracked your location. See? Not just handy for lost pets."

"But—"

"The tracker led us to the playhouse, but we couldn't find a way inside. While Rhi started trying to pick the lock and Persi was trying to find a good sized rock to hurl through the nearest window, I circled the building, looking for another entrance. When I came around the far side of the building, closest to the rocks, the signal on the tracker got stronger, and so I followed it until I saw what looked like an HVAC vent. I'd barely bent to examine it, when voices started drifting up out of it. I heard her threatening you, Wren, and I just... I couldn't wait for locks or broken windows. I focused my magic on the bushes and plants on all sides of me, and gave them one command. *Take me to that voice.* And they did." She looked at the vibrant instant garden that had literally exploded into life to help her and smiled a fond, wistful smile. She stroked the petal of a nearby Rose of Sharon blossom, and then looked past it to the crumbling dais, her expression turning grave once again. "You said that's why she brought you here," she said, pointing at it. "What did you mean? What is this place?"

"How much did you hear?" I asked.

"I knew she had a gun, and that Nova was down there with you, and that she was threatening you, and..." my mother shuddered at the pain of the memory, and hugged me again.

"Well," I said, "according to Veronica, we're looking at the source of the deep magic."

I wouldn't have thought my mother could go any paler, but somehow she managed it. Her eyes widened, her lips pressed into a tense, stressful line. It took what felt like a very long time for her to answer.

"The source?" she verified.

"Yes."

"Well, that's... probably not good," she concluded.

No, it was decidedly *not* good. But there was no unknowing it now.

"I guess we'd better tell Persi to pass along the message and get the whole Conclave down here." My mom shook her head. "Veronica Meyers, of all people. I just don't understand."

"She's only a Meyers in name," I said, shaking my head. "It's the mask she wears to hide the fact that she is actually a Kildare."

My mother's mouth dropped open. "But the... how do you know about—"

"Persi mentioned them to me," I said vaguely. There was no need to explain the exact circumstances under which I'd learned of the existence of the Kildare coven. There would be time for that later.

"It sounds like a lot unfolded before we found you," my mom said.

"There's so much to tell you. But..." I threw an uneasy look at the dais, felt the tugging of its strange lure, heard what could have been whispers. But what I no longer felt was Asteria's presence. The cavern suddenly felt sinister again, even with Veronica gone. "Can we get out of here?"

My mother shuddered and nodded. "Yes. I think that's an excellent idea. And we'll need to stop at Xiomara's house on the way."

Xiomara's name flicked some switch in my brain, and I felt a sickening wave of fear all over again. "Wait, Mom! Bea! Someone needs to check on Bea! Veronica put some kind of sleeping spell on her and—"

"Bea's fine. She's more than fine. In fact, she's the reason we're here," my mother said, managing a semblance of a smile.

"What do you—"

But there was no time to finish my question. At that moment, Rhi walked through the opening to the cavern and holding her hand, looking at once cautious and pleased with herself, was Bea. She smiled at me, and I smiled back.

"How?" Nova asked hoarsely.

"I think I'd better let Bea tell you that. She's had quite the night herself."

* * *

Back at Xiomara's house, everyone had crowded into the too-small living room—the Conclave, my mom and her sisters, Nova, Eva, and Zale. There had been no trace of Veronica anywhere around the theater. The Conclave had instructed Sedgwick Cove's tiny police force to set up a perimeter and search for her, both near the playhouse and up at the

Meyers' palatial beach house. It was a formality; no one really expected to find her. Veronica had shown her hand, and now she had no choice but to hide herself for the time being, unless she was a fool and, as Lydian wisely observed, "the Kildare coven didn't produce fools."

It was a long night. Eva, Zale, Nova, Bea, and I sat in Eva's room, all of us bleary-eyed and exhausted, as the Conclave met —calling us in one at a time to tell our parts of the story, so that they could piece it all together from multiple angles. It was a little like waiting with your friends outside the principal's office after you'd all gotten in trouble. Not that I'd ever been sent to the principal's office—I'd been a bit of a goody-two-shoes before I started waging magical war with ancient evil entities. While Nova was downstairs being questioned by her own mother, we all sat around and listened to what had happened to the others.

"I knew something was wrong the moment we started reciting," Eva said. "Something was almost imperceptibly different, like seeing the world in a mirror or something. Everything was right, and yet it was wrong. It was disorienting and weird, but once we started, it was already too late. We couldn't stop."

"I think I felt something, too," Zale said, shaking his head ruefully. "But I couldn't swear to it. I was such a nervous wreck about the pageant, wanting everything to be perfect, that I chalked it up to nerves at the time."

"And then?" I prompted. I'd been incredibly eager to hear what it was like to be under the spell on the stage.

"And then... nothing," Zale said, with a shrug. "Absolutely nothing."

"Seriously?"

"Me, too," Eva confirmed, nodding. "I think I heard the music start, the part right at the beginning with the pan flute? And then the next thing I remember is having to cover my ears because of the feedback from the speakers, and there was Bea right next to me."

"It was like I blinked, and the entire pageant was over," Zale wailed. "All that work, and I don't have a single memory of it. And all anyone could say was how amazing it was!"

"Everyone else was under a spell, too," Eva said, shrugging. "Maybe it was terrible, and they were all hexed into enjoying it."

Zale gasped and then geared up to retort, but I cut him off. "Not everyone was under the spell," I explained. "It was designed to affect all the witches present, except for me. Everyone else was riveted, Zale, trust me. And so was I before it all went to hell. I promise."

Zale gave a whoop of glee. Eva rolled her eyes.

"Sure, the whole thing was a ploy to hijack the festival and hand Sedgwick Cove over to the Darkness, but the important thing is that they *clapped*," she grumbled in disgust.

"But they did!" Zale said. "I heard that part."

"So what happened next? After you all woke up, or whatever?" I prompted.

"All of the witches were really confused when they snapped out of it," Eva said. "We didn't have any trouble convincing them they'd been under some kind of spell, too. They believed it right away."

"Why do you think that was?" I mused to myself out loud, not really expecting that anyone would know the answer, but Eva laughed. I looked at her in time to see her reach out a finger and playfully flick at one of Bea's braids. "We all knew Bea would never come down to that festival alone, unless it was a real emergency. The second I saw her face, I knew there was some serious shit about to go down."

I turned to face Bea, who was doodling quietly on the corner of one of her sketches, her lips fighting a smile that would have given away how pleased she was with herself. "Okay," I said, nudging her knee with my foot. "Now I want to hear it from the hero of the hour."

Bea's complexion darkened as she blushed. "I'm not a hero," she muttered.

Eva rolled her eyes. "Bea, just tell us what happened, okay?"

Bea bit her lip, then set her pencil down, and watched her own fingers while she spoke. "I knew something wasn't right about that lady. I knew it the first time I met her, over at the pageant rehearsal. I wasn't sure exactly what it was, but I knew I didn't like her."

"Neither did I much, but I figured it was just the rich yuppie thing," Eva muttered.

"But I didn't think about it again, until she came to the restaurant at the end of the lunch rush today," Bea went on, her little brow furrowed as she sifted through the memory for the relevant details. "She came in with that tall boy, her son..."

"Luca," I said automatically, and then felt my own cheeks flush. I hoped no one noticed. I felt a pang of pity for him. What must it be like up at his house, the local police officers searching for his step-mom, having no clue what was going on...

"Right, Luca. *He* seemed nice," Bea qualified. "He waved at me and smiled, but that was it. But then *she*," she shaped the word like it was a curse, "came over to me and wanted to see what I was drawing. I got really scared, because, well... I'd started drawing her while she was standing at the counter, talking to *abuela*. I... I didn't want her to see, so I turned the page."

"Yes, I remember that," I said, nodding. "I remember her talking to you."

"She was so close to me. She was trying to lean over to see my sketches, and she felt so... so wrong. Too close. Too cold."

I frowned, not really understanding, but also not wanting to disrupt her story.

"Then after she left, I started not to feel well. Mama kept asking me what was wrong, and I didn't really know how to explain it. I just knew that I was so tired, I could barely keep my eyes open. Mama kept checking my forehead to see if I had a fever, but I guess I felt normal. She got worried about me, though, so she left early and took me home. She asked if I wanted her to wake me up to go with them to the festival, but I said no. All I wanted to do was sleep. I don't really like the festival anyway. So loud. So crowded."

I didn't wonder about Bea's mom letting her sleep at home by herself. You could see the pageant from Bea's bedroom window. It was right in the heart of downtown. It would have been easy for her mom to walk a couple of houses down, watch the pageant, and come back before Bea had so much as started snoring.

"I was laying in bed, and my eyelids were getting heavier and heavier. I rolled over onto my side, and that's when I felt it. There was something in my pocket. I couldn't remember putting anything in there, so I reached in and pulled it out. It was a charm bag. I got scared. I ran to the window, opened it, and threw the bag out into the yard. I guess it's probably still down there."

"And how did you feel when you'd gotten rid of it?" I asked.

"As soon as it was away from me, I felt normal again. Well, not right away, but it faded after a few minutes. I stood at the window, taking some deep breaths, and that's when I started paying attention to the festival outside my window," Bea said. She shuddered. "I felt scared all over again. If that lady put a spell on me, who else did she put a spell on? I wanted my mom. I wanted Xiomara. I wanted to make sure they were okay. So, I went down to the festival to find them."

"And when you got there..." I said.

Bea swallowed hard, her throat bobbing convulsively. "Something was wrong. Everyone was under some kind of spell. Mama and *abuela* couldn't even hear me. They couldn't stop watching the pageant. Then I ran to the stage and tried to get Eva's attention, but she couldn't see or hear me either. Everyone, *everyone* was under a spell." Her eyes filled with tears, and she brushed them away with the back of her hand.

"That must have been so scary," I whispered, as Eva threw her arm around her little sister, and pulled her in so that she was tucked in the crook of Eva's arm. Bea accepted the contact, snuggling into it and availing herself of the comfort her sister provided.

"It felt like I stood there for a long time. I didn't know what to do. I wanted to sit down on the ground and cry, but I knew that wouldn't fix anything. Then I..." Bea hesitated.

"Then you what?" Eva prompted.

Bea hesitated, throwing a quick, surreptitious glance my way before answering. "I decided to interrupt the pageant," she said.

The words were decisive, and yet I was positive that it was not all that she had meant to say when she first opened her mouth. And what was more, I felt as though she *meant* for me to know it. That scrap of a look that had passed between us felt heavy with meaning. But when I started to ask what it meant, she widened her eyes and shook her head the merest fraction of an inch in either direction. I swallowed my question.

Bea's shoulders relaxed a little, and she went on, "I was freaking out, but after a few minutes, I realized no one was coming to help me, but I guess it needed to sink in. I stopped crying. I kinda got... calmer. I paid more attention. I looked all around the stage. I listened to the performers. After a few more minutes, I heard it."

"What did you hear?" It was Zale who asked now, looking absolutely riveted. Here, at last, was someone else who had seen at least part of the pageant he couldn't remember performing.

"No matter what the big tall kings were saying, the fairies and the nymphs kept repeating the same words over and over again."

"Yes, I remember noticing that as well," I said, feeling the gentle tug back into the memory of the pageant.

"It was almost like a song," Bea said, "Sometimes it sounded like one. But after a minute, I felt myself start to get, well, kinda sleepy again, and I covered my ears. I thought the words might be the spell... like an incantation."

"That's exactly what it was," I said, forcing myself to say the words. "Veronica as good as told us that." I didn't look at Zale or Eva. I couldn't bear to see the accusations in their eyes, knowing that I was the one who passed along the book in the first place. So, instead, I kept my attention on Bea and said, "What happened next? You interrupted the pageant somehow, didn't you?"

Bea nodded, and raised her chin just a little. "I used the speakers. There were these microphones on the front of the stage, and they were attached to two really big speakers. I watched them this morning when they were setting up for the pageant." She pointed at Zale. "During the sound check, one of the speakers started squealing, and Zale said they needed to move the microphone because it was too close to the speaker and was causing feedback. I thought maybe if people couldn't hear the incantation, it might not work anymore. So, I just grabbed the microphones and caused some feedback." She shrugged as though anyone would have thought of doing the same.

"How long did it take?" Zale asked. "Until we snapped out of it, I mean?"

"Oh, not long at all. The crowd started shouting and complaining. The actors stopped dancing around one by one. Nearly everyone was blocking their ears, so the words lost all their power. At least, that's what it seemed like."

"Okay, Bea, I know you didn't like us calling you a hero," Zale said, shaking his head in disbelief, "but how would you feel if we called you a genius instead?"

Bea squinted for a moment, thoughtful. Then her face settled into a placid expression. "I'll allow it," she said, and Zale burst out laughing.

"Eva! Zale! Can you come down here, please?" Xiomara's voice called from the bottom of the stairs. Eva and Zale traded one anxious look, and then both slid off the bed and walked out the door.

I counted three quiet breaths, waiting for the sound of feet on the stairs to fade, before I turned back to Bea.

"You left something out, didn't you? Something you didn't want to say in front of Zale and Eva?" I asked her.

She nodded, looking tense.

"Did you tell the Conclave? Or your mom?"

This time, she shook her head. "I didn't think they'd believe me."

I swallowed hard, trying to keep my voice calm and even. "Would you like to tell me?" I asked.

Bea played with her fingers, clasping and unclasping them in her lap. "I think... I think I'm *supposed* to tell you."

I raised my eyebrows. "Supposed to?"

Bea nodded again. "I think she... she wants me to."

"Who wants you to?" I asked, my voice cracking with the strain of trying to remain calm. I was wound so tightly, I thought I might snap.

In answer, Bea picked up her sketchbook and flipped back through the pages to the very last sketch. Then she held it up for me to see, and as determined as I was to remain placid, I couldn't help but gasp in surprise.

It was Asteria. Asteria, in her flowing skirts and her boundless curls. Asteria, whose wise and often mischievous face was folded into planes of worry... perhaps even fear.

"You've seen her too?" I whispered.

Bea's eyes widened. "You?"

I nodded.

"I... I didn't know you could. I didn't even really know that I could." Bea whispered.

"At first, I thought I was dreaming," I admitted. "Seriously. Because as far as I knew, Asteria wasn't... still here. There was also the fact that I didn't believe in ghosts at all. Then again, my life has become one long string of things I probably wouldn't have believed a month ago, so I'm getting used to that feeling."

Bea put her little hand on top of mine, and squeezed sympathetically. The gesture brought a lump into my throat that I had to swallow against.

"But this isn't about me, sorry," I apologized. "What does Asteria have to do with this?"

"At first, I just... *felt* her," Bea said. "I would be doodling, and I'd look down, and there she was. I'd draw her without really meaning to. And then, today, at the cafe... I told you that I started sketching Veronica. Well, this is what happened when I started doing that. It's why I didn't want her to see it." She flipped a few pages forward in her sketchbook, and held it up again for me to see. This time, the image was of Veronica Meyers, somewhat rough, as though it had been done quickly, with no time to go back and refine it. But it was clearly her—her swanlike neck, her aquiline nose, her slender figure, but she was not alone. Asteria stood beside her, almost hovering over her, and her expression was anxious.

"You saw Asteria with Veronica?" I gasped.

"Well, no. I didn't *see* her. But I felt something, and when I tried to draw what I felt..." And she gestured somewhat helplessly to the drawing, like it had sprung to life on the page in spite of her efforts, rather than because of them.

I wasn't totally sure if I understood, but I nodded as though I did. So Asteria wasn't here only to communicate with me. She'd been following Veronica Meyers around. Why? Had she known what Veronica was up to? Was she trying to stop her? Was she trying to warn me? My head was spinning.

"There's more," Bea whispered, and I pulled my attention from the sketchpad to look at her again. "When I went down to the festival... well, it wasn't exactly my idea to disrupt the festival."

"Whose idea was it?" I asked.

Bea pointed to Asteria's image. "It was her. She was there, at the festival. I was so scared, and I was crying, and then I heard her call my name. I looked up, and she... she smiled at me. She told me not to be afraid, and that I could break the spell if I stopped the words of the pageant. And then she... she was just gone. Vanished."

Again, I was rendered speechless. Asteria was still protecting me—protecting all of us. But why? Why hadn't she moved on after her clifftop send-off? Had the events of the last week pulled her back from beyond the grave? Or had she been here all along, undetectable, silent, and invisible among us? My head was beginning to ache with the pressure of unanswered questions.

Still, at least, the biggest question seemed to be answered at last. I'd proven I could connect with the other elements: earth, fire, air, and water. And now, with the sightings of Asteria, it seemed I could connect with spirit as well. Or at least... one spirit in particular. Still, it seemed like it might be enough. It seemed I might really be the pentamaleficus the Darkness was looking for. Five elements. Five points of power.

After weeks of wishing for some sign of power, I suddenly found myself wishing I had none at all. Once upon a time, I'd have thought magic the solution to all my problems, and now I knew that it was, in fact, the cause. What a bitter pill to swallow.

"Wren?"

It took a lot of effort to drag myself up out of those thoughts, but I managed it. "Yeah, Bea?" I asked.

"Are you okay?" she asked, looking at me with a skittish sort of wariness, as though she thought I might explode unexpectedly.

"Sorry, Bea. My head's kind of spinning with all of this. I'm okay. I guess I'm just... I'm wondering about my grandmother. I'm wondering why I can see her, why she's here. And I don't know how to answer that question."

"Oh, I do," Bea replied mildly.

I blinked. "I'm sorry, what?"

Bea looked puzzled. "You said you wanted to know why your grandmother was here, right?"

"Yeah, but—"

"Well then, that's easy. You go to see Xiomara. She can tell you."

Her words felt like a slap to the face. All I could do for a few seconds was sit there and blink at her, my brain slowly turning sounds into words, and words into thoughts. Finally, I managed, "Has... has Xiomara seen Asteria, too? Did she tell you that?"

"No," Bea said, shaking her head. "But she has a steadier connection than any other witch in Sedgwick Cove. If you want to communicate with a spirit around here, you call Xiomara."

"I... wow, I knew she was sensitive to spirit, but I didn't know it was... do you think she could help me?"

"I know she could. She could have helped me, too," Bea said, her voice and chin dropping suddenly. "But I didn't tell her. I didn't tell anyone until right now."

"What do you... oh!" It suddenly occurred to me that, once Bea had started sensing spirits, she'd had the perfect person to confide in right there in her house, a person she was close to, who had enough experience to answer all her questions. Then...

"Why didn't you tell Xiomara?" I asked. "Didn't you think she would understand?"

Bea swallowed. "I was too scared," she whispered.

"Of Xiomara?" the words came out more skeptical than I'd meant them, and Bea flinched a little. Luckily, she still answered my question.

"Shh!" Bea hushed me, and I pressed a hand over my mouth automatically. "And no, I'm not scared of *abuela*. But I am scared of..." She sighed, a sigh much too big and heavy for such a little girl. "I know Eva told you about the trouble I was having finding my affinity."

I flushed, ready to apologize, but she plowed on, "It's okay. Really, Wren, I don't mind that she told you that. But you should know that it's not true. Well, Eva doesn't know it's not true," she added, chewing on her lip, "and neither does anyone else in my family. The truth is that I've been lying to them about my magic."

"Lying? Why?" I asked, dropping my voice even lower.

"It's true that my affinity revealed itself a little later than most people," Bea said. "That part wasn't a lie. But then all of this started happening with my sketches." She waved a hand at the sketchbook, looking at it like it was a beloved pet that had lashed out and bitten her. "I'd draw a picture of our house, and without meaning to draw it, there'd be a man sitting on our front steps. I'd try to draw the beach, and it turned into the image of a woman standing up on the cliffs. I wasn't seeing them... only drawing them. But I could feel them, too, sometimes."

"How did you feel them?" I asked.

"Their feelings. They sort of just... came over me. Like I'd be doing my homework, and suddenly I'd feel really sad, like I was going to cry. But it didn't make sense, because nothing was happening to make me want to cry, even if it was math." She made a face. "It was so weird. So when it happened, I would pull out my sketchbook and then... well, I would usually be able to draw who was making me feel that way." And again, she flipped through the pages, stopping to point at certain sketches to show me that they were of spirits, rather than living people.

"How long has this been going on?" I asked.

"It started right after my ninth birthday. That was in April."

"And you were scared."

"Yes."

"But you didn't tell your family? Even though you knew they would understand?"

"I didn't want them to understand," Bea whispered. "I didn't want it to be true."

I shook my head. "Bea, I'm sorry, but I still don't underst—"

"*Abuela* is very strong. But the spirits weigh on her. I can see it sometimes, the way they wear her down. And then Bernadette... she's the other most powerful spirit witch in our town, and she..." Bea shuddered. "Her gift drove her mad. They had to lock her up."

"Bernadette sees prophecies of the future, though, doesn't she?" I asked. "That's very different than what your gift seems to be."

"But it's her connection to spirit that allows her to see the future. I was afraid, Wren. I'm still afraid. I don't want to be a spirit witch. I don't want to feel all those feelings that don't belong to me. I just want to... to shut it off. Like a light switch. Just... click." She pressed an invisible button in the air, her little finger trembling.

"Keeping it a secret won't make it go away," I told her, keeping my voice soft. I didn't want her to think I was chiding her.

She sighed again. "I know. But I also know that when I tell *abuela*, she'll say it's time to start my training. She'll say I have to start practicing. Instead of waiting for spirits to find me, I'll have to go out looking for them to build my skills. But... they aren't all nice. Some of them are..." Bea shuddered.

I didn't need her to elaborate. It only made sense that spirits were as varied in their nature as living people were. There were a lot of kind and wonderful humans in the world, but not all people were good.

"What do you say we both go down there, and you talk to Xiomara about it?" I suggested. "Maybe it won't be so bad. Maybe it will even be okay."

Bea hesitated. "Will you hold my hand while I tell her?" she asked.

I smiled at her. "Only if you promise to hold mine when it's my turn."

She considered this. "Okay."

I took her hand to shake it, but she didn't let go. Instead, she flipped it around, so I was holding hers in mine. She picked up her sketchbook with her free hand, and tucked it under her arm. Then she stood up with a grimace.

"Okay. Let's go."

23

When we finally arrived at Lightkeep Cottage that night, I was sure I'd be up for hours, hyped up on anxiety and unanswered questions. So imagine my surprise when I flopped down on the couch next to my mom, and immediately fell into such a deep sleep that I didn't so much as move for almost ten hours. It was as though my body knew I had to unplug, before I short-circuited. Like a glitching gadget, I needed to be turned off and then turned back on again, if I had any hope of functioning properly.

The sleep may have been deep, but it was full of nightmares, a vivid but confusing collage of images that made little sense: Asteria's spirit wandering across a stage full of entranced performers. Flowering vines bursting through my walls and winding up my legs like snakes. Bea drawing a sketch of Veronica Meyers, which immediately leaped off the page and pulled a gun from her pocket to point at my face. The Gray Man, with Sarah Claire standing on one side and Veronica Meyers on the other, all three of them gesturing at me to join them, to wear the crown they offered...

I jolted awake.

My mom was no longer lying against me. At some point, she had extracted herself, placing a pillow under my head, and a blanket over my curled limbs. Before I could panic about where she had gone, I heard her voice from the kitchen. She, Rhi, and Persi were talking quietly together at the kitchen table. I could smell a pot of Rhi's herbal tea. I supposed I didn't blame them for not waking me. They certainly had an awful lot to discuss. I wondered if they were still feeling as calm as they'd seemed last night while Bea, I, and the others had given them all the details we could about what had happened to us that night. It was true that my mother held my hand tightly the whole time I was speaking, true that my fingers were numb and tingling from the pressure she placed on them at times, but overall, she'd taken it all in her stride. I had to admit, I'd been worried that she would pack us up and leave town again, maybe even leave the country, but I should have given her more credit. I knew she'd learned from that mistake. She was scared, sure, but she was also stoic. She'd made her choice, and she was sticking to it. As I listened now, the tones of their voices were serious, but calm. It helped me feel calmer, too, for the moment. Calm enough for their voices to lull me back to sleep.

Another dream found its way into my slumber, but it was not one of the chaotic ones I'd endured in my first stretch of sleep.

I was standing in my mother's garden. I could hear Asteria calling to me. I looked and looked for her. Her voice was playful at first, then worried, like she'd expected me to find her by now. I began to call her name as well, unease growing in me. At last, I saw a scrap of flowing purple fabric fluttering from the shadow of a nearby willow tree. The fronds waved in the breeze, obscuring the figure who stood there. I paused, uncertain.

"Asteria?"

There was no reply. I almost turned to run. Then...

"Wren?"

It was Asteria's voice, but though the figure stood only a few feet from me, the voice sounded very far away.

"What is it?" I asked her. "What do you want to tell me?"

Another pause... and then...

"I don't know. I don't remember," came the faintest reply.

"Please, Asteria! It might be important!"

"I... don't remember."

I stepped through the fronds in a surge of frustration, but instead found myself falling down, down, down into pitch-black darkness, and then...

It felt like I hit the couch as I jerked myself awake again. I managed not to cry out, smothering my yelp of surprise with the pillow under my face. I sat up. The kitchen was dark, the table silent. A cup of tea had gone stone cold on the table in front of me, beside a plate of untouched cookies. The dream felt like it had lasted only a brief moment, but I'd clearly been asleep for hours once again. I glanced at the clock. It was after midnight.

Screw it. I didn't care how late it was.

I'd woken from that dream not only with a physical jolt but a mental one as well, as though waking up had jostled loose a decision I hadn't even realized I'd made. I could no longer wait passively for Asteria to find me. I had to reach out to her. I had to forge a connection strong enough that she could finally tell me whatever it was she was trying to say. And there was only one person I knew who could help me.

As I flew along the road to town, my legs pedaling furiously beneath me, I prayed that my mother wouldn't wake up, and that if she did wake up, she wouldn't absolutely murder me for sneaking out like this. Part of me knew it was stupid, of course—after all, there was still no sign of Veronica. Before I'd agreed to lay down, I'd made my mother promise to wake me up if Veronica had been found. I definitely shouldn't be out alone at night with that woman on the loose. At the same time, though, something very powerful was propelling me forward. I couldn't confidently say what it was, but I thought... well, I thought it might just be my magic.

For weeks, Rhi had been trying—and failing— to convince me to trust myself. *It's the key to everything, Wren. You sabotage yourself with doubt and skepticism. If part of your brain intends for you to fail, then that intention will interfere with your abilities. It's a self-fulfilling prophecy.* And she was right. Every time I'd felt an instinct, I'd questioned it rather than trusted it, and so I'd burned, undercooked, overcooked, or in some other way ruined every magic recipe I'd tried. All that self-doubt that started in the kitchen had left me paralyzed with indecision in the cavern, unable to save my friend. I no longer had the luxury to take my time. I had to take my magic by the horns, to embrace what I was now realizing I feared. I didn't want my magic. I'd been running from it all along, like my mother before me. Even when I thought I was trying my hardest to find it, I'd been hiding from it.

I was scared. But I wouldn't be scared anymore. I was going to listen to my magic when it spoke to me. I wasn't going to second guess, or defer, or delay. My magic was telling me this was what I needed to do, and damn it, I was going to do it. I felt my fear fall away like the moon-bathed road stretching away in a ribbon behind me. I felt so much lighter, that I was surprised the bike didn't become airborne.

I skidded to a stop in front of Xiomara's garden gate, sending sand and pebbles flying. I didn't bother with the chain, just resting the bike against the fence before charging up the stairs and, before I could lose my newly acquired nerve, lifted my fist to knock sharply on the front door.

Instead, I stumbled forward as the door fell open, and almost fell face-first into Xiomara's living room. I steadied myself, and looked up to see Xiomara herself holding the door open, not a trace of surprise on her face that I was standing on her front steps at nearly one o'clock in the morning.

"I thought I might see you tonight," Xiomara said, stepping back from the door and gesturing me inside.

I didn't move. "You did? How?"

Xiomara didn't answer, just cocked her head toward the living room. I swallowed hard, and walked past her. She closed the door behind us, and then gestured for me to follow her. Memories of the previous night tried to overwhelm me as we walked through the very room where I'd relived every detail for the Conclave. I shoved those memories aside. They would only slow me down and cause me to lose focus.

We walked through the living room to the kitchen, and then to a small back room that looked like it had been converted from a three-season porch. Windows looked out over the back garden on three sides. The windowsills were lined with a staggering assortment of candles, bottles, statues, and stones, and yet nothing about it was cluttered; on the contrary, each item looked as though it had been carefully, mindfully chosen, positioned just so as to compliment all the other objects around it. I stared in fascination, feeling a sort of calm wash over me.

The room had a round table in the center, with a red tablecloth draped over it, and two wooden chairs pulled up to it, directly across from one another. Above the table, an ornate gold lamp with multi-colored glass shades hung from the ceiling, bathing the room in a warm, patchwork light. Xiomara gestured to the closest chair, and I sank into it without thinking. It felt natural. Xiomara moved to the chair opposite me, and settled herself into it with a creaking groan. Then she placed her hands on the table and looked me in the eye, waiting.

"How did you know I would be coming?" I asked.

"Because I've sensed what I imagine you've been sensing," Xiomara replied. Her features were relaxed except for her eyes, which had a sharpness to them, almost like a bird.

"What I've been..."

"You have an energy attached to you, *mija*. But you know that."

I nodded, swallowing hard.

Xiomara nodded solemnly in return. She didn't ask me who I was talking about.

"She came to you."

I nodded again.

"In a dream."

It hadn't really sounded like a question, so it felt strange to contradict her. "The first time, I thought it might have been. I thought I imagined it. But then I saw her again during the day, and I knew it couldn't be a dream."

Xiomara's eyebrows shot up. "You saw her?"

"Yes."

"How did she appear to you? Can you describe it?" The urgency in her voice made me edgy, but I answered truthfully.

"She looked... solid. Alive. If I hadn't already known she was dead, I would have thought she was really standing there, waiting for me. Well, except for her voice."

"You heard her as well?"

"Yeah, but it didn't sound like her voice was coming from her. It didn't sound far away. It sounded like it was coming from... from inside my own head, but also from outside it? Sorry, it's kind of hard to explain."

But Xiomara didn't seem to have any trouble understanding what I was trying to say. In fact, she almost seemed to expect the words, like there was only one correct answer and I was repeating it back to her in class. She nodded along as each word dropped neatly into place. Her expression was grimly satisfied.

"Is that normal?" I asked. "To see or hear a ghost like that?"

Xiomara snorted. "*Mija,* we don't traffic in normal here. Now, you said 'the first time.' Does that mean you've seen her more than once?"

"Yes."

"Where?"

"Once in the garden at Lightkeep Cottage. And then again, standing in the garden at Shadowkeep. And then, finally, tonight. This time, it was a dream, but the dream took place in my mother's garden."

Xiomara grunted in satisfaction. "Asteria was a green witch. It follows that she would manifest in places, not only that she is tied to, but that she can draw power from."

"But I don't understand why she's manifesting at all!" I said. "I thought... I thought after her funeral, she would have... I don't know, moved on? Crossed over? Is any of that even true, or have I just watched too many movies?"

Xiomara smiled gently. "Yes. There is a spirit realm. And yes, when a spirit is ready, they cross into it, and there they remain."

"So, you're saying Asteria hasn't crossed yet?"

"That's what's troubling me," Xiomara said slowly. "I knew your grandmother well. I knew her energy. And I knew when it left this world. I felt it."

"But then...how can she be here now?"

"How, indeed? That's what we must discover, *mija*. Shall we try together?"

Xiomara reached a hand across the table, an invitation. I hesitated.

"Is there any chance I've just been imagining it?" I asked, almost hoping it was true. "Is it possible I'm just... just fixated on her and..."

Xiomara didn't have to answer out loud. I could read the answer in the depths of her eyes, where it burned, pitying but bright. However, she spoke anyway, her hand still extended toward me. "Do not be afraid, Wren. Asteria has reached out to you. If she has something to say to you, do you not want to know what it is?"

I couldn't answer right away. Was it possible I both wanted and didn't want to know? I didn't know much about ghosts, not really, mostly because I'd never believed in them before, but even I'd heard the well-known stories and urban legends about tortured spirits, unable to move on until they'd found resolution for their unfinished business. Was any of that true? Because if it was, I didn't think I wanted to know. I didn't want to imagine Asteria desperate and trapped. Surely, that couldn't be the case. And yet, if it wasn't something vitally important, why wasn't she resting peacefully, or was that just a story, too?

Xiomara watched me patiently as all of these thoughts chased each other through my brain. I realized she must do this all the time —guide people through experiences like this. Bea's drawing of her flashed across my mind, and I was able to appreciate on an entirely different level just how accurate it was. Though she did not speak, waiting for my permission to begin, I could see the curiosity burning in her eyes, the fire that seeks truth and knowledge.

"You want to know as badly as I do, don't you?" I whispered.

"Her presence here troubles me. If she has something to say, I think we owe it to her to discover just what it is."

That was apparently exactly what I needed to hear. I placed my hand in Xiomara's and told her, "Okay. What do I do?"

Xiomara smiled encouragingly. "Simply close your eyes, child, and try to feel your connection to her. You can connect to spirit, just as you can connect to the other elements. Trust yourself."

"I've never—"

"*Try.*"

I did as she told me, letting my eyelids fall shut, and trying to clear a hundred other thoughts that were bounding loudly around in my head, so that I could create a mental space for Asteria, and only Asteria. At first, it felt impossible. How could I focus on something so tenuous, on something that I knew was real, and yet in no way understood? How did you grab a hold of something so ephemeral?

"You're doubting yourself, Wren. It's blocking you," Xiomara said, after a silent minute.

"I know, but I don't know how to get rid of the doubts," I said, my teeth gritted in frustration as I battled with my own brain.

"You don't need to dispel them. Just push them to the side. Imagine a box in the back corner of your mind, and place everything in it, like a child putting away toys, until the room is clear."

The metaphor was concrete, and suddenly, I felt like I had something to hold onto, something that felt more real than anything we'd said up until that moment. I visualized the box, and one by one, every other thought that tried to crop up, I shoved it inside. I did it over and over again, and when I began to worry that my brain would simply produce a never-ending supply of distractions, I took that worry and shoved it away as well. It took what felt like a long time, but Xiomara showed no signs of impatience; and soon, I found, for perhaps the first time in my life, that my brain felt... empty. An empty stage, with a single spotlight, waiting for someone or something to make its entrance.

Perhaps it was the energy coming off of me or the fact that I seemed to have gone unusually still, but Xiomara recognized the very moment that I'd achieved what she'd requested of me. Her hand tightened around mine, and she said, "That's it, *mija*. Now, into that space that you've just cleared, I want you to picture your grandmother. Just place her there and picture her just as she appeared to you out in the garden, both at Shadowkeep and at Lightkeep. If there's a detail you can't remember, fill it in until she's like a picture you've drawn for yourself."

I began to do as she asked, and then started in surprise as Asteria popped into my head, fully formed. Every detail was exactly as I remembered it, and I felt myself taking mental stock of it, trying to commit it all to memory. Her hair cascaded over her shoulders in shining, gray-streaked waves. Her greenish eyes twinkled out from her lined face—I wouldn't have called it wrinkled. Each line was simply a memory of smiles and frowns and deep concentration, a permanent incarnation of the joys and sorrows and accomplishments of her earthly life. She wore the dress she had worn the very last time I'd seen her alive, a bell-sleeved confection of jewel-tone patchwork, with crocheted lace dripping from the collar, cuffs, and the handkerchief hem. I felt Xiomara's hand twitch in mine.

"She's here," we both whispered at the very same time.

"Asteria, my friend, why do you linger?" Xiomara was asking, her voice soft but insistent. "What message do you have for us?"

Wren. I need Wren. Wren Vesper.

It wasn't like hearing a human voice. I didn't seem to hear it with my ears, but with my brain.

"Wren is here, Asteria. She can hear you," Xiomara insisted.

Wren. I have to speak to Wren. I have to warn her.

My pulse sped up. I opened my eyes to sneak a look at Xiomara. She was frowning intently, her head cocked to one side, like she was trying to identify a distant sound. As I watched her, she muttered, "She's confused. I'm not sure why. She's got a direct connection to you, and yet she doesn't seem to know it's you."

"What am I doing wrong?" I whispered. The other thoughts rattled away against the confines of my mental box, but I kept them at bay. I was doing what Xiomara had asked, and yet something still wasn't right.

"You aren't doing anything wrong," Xiomara insisted. "It's Asteria. She's... something is off."

"What do we do?"

"You speak to her this time. Perhaps my guidance is interfering. I'll try to observe without inserting myself," Xiomara said. "Try again, *mija*, try again."

I shoved my fear and doubt aside, and focused all my energy on the Asteria standing in my mental space. I moved myself closer to her, mentally walking toward her so that I could have touched her if I tried. "Asteria, it's me. It's Wren."

I need to talk to Wren. My little bird.

"It's me, Asteria. I'm Wren Vesper. Your granddaughter."

Something flashed across Asteria's face, a blip of recognition, followed by confusion again. But she was looking at me now. It was startling, like an actor breaking the fourth wall unexpectedly, and speaking directly to an audience member. Xiomara reacted to it as well; I heard her stifled gasp, and felt her hand tighten again around my cold, numb fingers.

Wren?

"Yes! It's me!"

She still seemed unsure, but at least she felt the direct connection. She shook her head, her eyebrows knitting together like she had a sudden terrible headache. I felt a wave of something unpleasant—not quite nausea, but something akin to it.

She has to know. I have to tell her.

"Tell me! I'm Wren, and I'm listening!"

The girl. The girl will bring the book.

"What girl? What book?"

She understands the source. You must trust her. Everything depends on it.

"Asteria, who are you talking about? What girl?"

The source. She's connected to the source. She will bring the book. Trust her, little bird.

The spotlight was fading on my little mental stage. Asteria's voice was fading, slipping out of my hearing. I tried to reach for her, but my hands closed around the absence of her instead. When I opened my eyes, I found that my hands were reaching out into the empty air in front of me, that Xiomara had let go of my hand, and that the connection was broken.

I looked at Xiomara, and she looked back at me, her expression inscrutable.

"Did you break the connection?" I asked her, lowering my hands.

"No. Asteria did," she said. Her brow was still furrowed. "It was not a clean break; she couldn't hold on any longer."

"Couldn't hold on to what?"

"To you."

Tears were pricking the corners of my eyes, but I blinked them back. "Could you hear what she was saying?"

"Yes."

"And?" I asked. There was an impatient snap in my voice, but Xiomara didn't seem to mind. She shook her head slowly, grinding her teeth together in her frustration. "I have no idea. I was hoping her message would make sense to you."

My heart sank like a stone in my chest. "You don't know what girl she's talking about?"

"I do not. Nor do I know what book she's talking about. Is this not something you and Asteria have discussed before?"

I threw my hands up in frustration. "Xiomara, I haven't so much as spoken to Asteria since I was ten years old. She's said more to me since she died than she did in the last six years of her life, and I have no idea what the hell it means!" The tears won out now, and I let my head flop down onto my arms on Xiomara's table. Xiomara didn't coddle me or try to placate me while I cried. She got up, made me a cup of tea, put it down in front of me, and waited quietly until I'd cried myself out. Finally, I raised my head, took a sip of the tea, and tested my voice. It was hoarse, but it sounded steady again.

"Sorry about that. I'm okay now."

"You have nothing to apologize for, Wren. Sitting with your feelings is strength, not weakness. You have been heaped with the troubles of your ancestors. That is a heavy burden."

"You know a little something about that, don't you?" I asked, thinking again of Bea's drawing of her grandmother.

Xiomara smirked knowingly. "Perhaps. But there are degrees of troubles, are there not?"

I took a sip of tea to fend off another wave of tears. Yes, there were.

"I admit I am troubled," Xiomara went on. She tapped her stubby fingertips on the tabletop as she spoke. "Not about the girl and the book. No, I believe they will reveal themselves in time. My worry is about the source."

The hot tea scalded my throat all the way down as I swallowed it too quickly. "Asteria said the girl was connected to the source. That she understands it."

"Yes. In many ways, I wish I could say the same of myself," Xiomara said. She pressed her palms flat against the table, spreading her fingers wide like she was bracing herself against her own words. "We went there, you know. Last night, after you had gone back home to Lightkeep Cottage. The Conclave went down to the playhouse, and we saw it for ourselves."

I hadn't known this. I wondered if my mother or my aunts knew. Maybe that was what they'd been whispering about in the kitchen while I'd slept.

"I believe," Xiomara said, "that the source is tied somehow to the element of spirit. I say this because I am the only one of my fellow

Conclave members who felt deeply drawn to it, and I am the only spirit witch among us. I felt presences there. Whispers."

"I felt it, too," I murmured, my breath scattering the swirling tendrils of steam rising off my mug. "And Veronica... she sensed something. She must be a spirit witch, too."

"Does that not worry you?" Xiomara asked.

I laughed, though nothing felt particularly funny. "Everything about the source worries me. I'm worried that we know where it is. I'm worried that people like Veronica will continue to seek it. I'm worried someone will learn how to tap into it. I'm worried the Darkness will gain access. But probably most of all, I'm worried that we don't understand it. We're trying to protect something we don't understand."

"But that has always been the case, from the earliest days of witchcraft on this shore. The source has always been a mystery to us," Xiomara said. "We have never known exactly why this place has such an effect on our magic, and most of us have accepted that we may not be meant to know. We only know that it must be protected, never sought, never exploited."

"But now someone is coming who does understand it. Someone who is connected to it, somehow," I said.

"So Asteria has warned us."

"And Asteria also said we should trust this girl, whoever she is."

"She did."

"So then... maybe we won't have to do all of this in the dark, you know? Maybe this girl, whoever she is, will be able to help us—to help me—so that I know what I'm facing."

Xiomara looked at me long and hard. It was an appraising look, one that brought a flush of self-conscious pink to my cheeks, but I didn't let myself look away.

"If it is true, Wren. If you are the pentamaleficus the Darkness seeks, it means that, in some way, you are the key to that door. And if there is someone who can tell us what's behind that door... well, then let us hope she's already on her way."

Epilogue

I was so sure, as I laid down in the pre-dawn light of the morning, that Veronica would return for me within hours. That the Gray Man would be standing beneath my window, within days. That Sarah Claire would haunt my waking steps, before a week had passed.

But the hours passed. The days passed. The weeks passed. Nothing.

Well, I really shouldn't say nothing. After all, that would be doing a serious injustice to the best summer of my life.

I worked at Shadowkeep, mostly dealing with the tourists downstairs. But on those little lulls and breaks, I could sneak upstairs, where the real magic lived. I began to learn every nook and cranny of the shop. I learned to differentiate the dried herbs and flowers, first by sight and then by smell, when Persi declared she would blindfold me. Soon, I knew what each and every apothecary drawer contained without reading the labels.

Back home at Lightkeep, I divided my time between the gardens, the kitchen, and the library. I read every book I could find on elemental magic, on the pentamaleficus, on the moon, and the witch's calendar. I learned the properties of the plants in our gardens, helped Rhi dry and crush them, and wrote little labels on them, before storing them carefully in one of our pantries. It made my heart happy to see my slightly messy handwriting alongside Rhi's neat square hand, Persi's languorous scrawl, and Asteria's flowing script. It felt like completing a family photograph; I was finally in the frame.

I started to get the hang of baking—not to say it would ever be my forte, but I learned my way around the kitchen, learned to listen to myself, to what I needed, and incorporate it into my cooking. I learned to observe my aunts and my mom, to read their moods, and adjust my recipes to nurture their needs—a bit of vanilla for tranquility. A pinch of allspice to soothe sore muscles after a day of weeding. A bit of cardamom for courage after a hard day. I would never be a true kitchen witch, but I could do my part. I was finally starting to understand intention. I knew now that when I took the focus off myself and onto others, intention wasn't so hard after all. I learned to get out of my own way... most of the time.

I spent time with my new friends and my old ones, too. I went back to Portland for the 4th of July, and had a blast at Charlie's block party barbeque, and down by the water eating ice cream and cotton candy while watching the fireworks over the bay. I invited Poe and Charlie for the weekend in August, and took them all around Sedgwick Cove. I even took them to the playhouse to see the summer's flagship production, a revival of Sweeney Todd, during which Poe required physical restraint to keep her in her seat at the end of each musical number. They met my aunts, who kept the full extent of their witchiness under wraps, and we walked the beach to the lighthouse and ate lunch at Xiomara's Cafe. It meant a lot to share the parts of my life that I could with them—the secrets didn't feel so heavy when I knew they could picture my house, the inside of Shadowkeep, or the faces of my new friends.

It wasn't all sunshine, though. Stewing just beneath the surface of this beautiful summer was the fear, and the expectation, and the questions, the constant questions of why nothing had happened yet. Where had Veronica gone, and why hadn't she returned yet? What had become of the Darkness? Was it simply biding its time? And though she searched and reached and grasped deeply into her connection with the spirit world over and over again, Xiomara could find no trace of Asteria. So many questions, and each week that passed without any answers only magnified them.

And then there was Luca. My heart sank every time I thought of him.

It wasn't only that Luca had no idea what was going on. I didn't see him as often once I no longer had a reason to be at the playhouse (and about a million reasons to stay away). I'd heard that he and his uncle had had to file a missing persons report with the Sedgwick Cove police department, but we all knew that was a mere formality. If Veronica Meyers didn't want to be found, not even a police department as uniquely skilled as ours was likely to find her. The town itself had drawn back from the Meyers, even more so than before. After all, there were outsiders, and then there was a family harboring a dangerous enemy, and though they had done it unwittingly, a safe distance had to be kept. I knew Luca could feel it—I knew he was probably hurt by it. But there wasn't much I could do. I wouldn't let him get drawn into this. I wouldn't put him in danger.

The fact was that Veronica had exploited even my budding schoolgirl crush on Luca. She had used him to get to me—or at least, used his image to get to me. But I knew she was capable of far worse. I wouldn't have put it past her to put her own stepson in real danger if she thought it would lure me into doing her bidding. And so, when he stopped by Shadowkeep and asked if I wanted to hang out, I made an excuse. I kept making excuses, and soon, he stopped asking. And when the summer season at the playhouse ended, he didn't even bother to say goodbye before he left for Manhattan again. It made my heart ache, but I had to let it go. He was safer without me in his life, at least for now.

When September came, a wave of sadness overtook me. Even though I loved my new life in Sedgwick Cove, it was strange not packing up my backpack and heading back to Portland High, to the familiar hallways and the theater, answering excited texts about the fall musical, knowing they'd be putting it on without me, knowing that each day that passed, each rehearsal I wasn't there for, every inside joke I missed, was another inch of string that I let out, distancing myself from my old life. It was necessary, but it was not easy. On paper, I was officially enrolled in Sedgwick Cove High School. In reality, my education going forward would be a hodgepodge of a few in-person classes, a smattering of online courses, and a lot of homeschool witchcraft. Our schedule revolved around the witch's calendar and the phases of the moon, rather than arbitrary things like local holidays and breaks. Kids came and went at all hours of the day and night so that it seemed, to an outsider, that there was no rhyme or reason to the school at all. And speaking of outsiders, I was walking out of one of the school buildings in the middle of the morning, three weeks into September, when I first spotted her.

She was a young woman who looked to be in her mid-twenties. She had long black hair with purple streaks in it, and she wore an oversized black sweater over a pair of shredded jeans, and black boots. As I glanced at her, she appeared to be spouting a stream of colorful language under her breath as she glared, first at the school buildings, and then down at the phone in her hand. I wondered if she was lost; I had certainly been confused when someone first pointed out a row of tall, stately Victorian-style houses and told me they were, collectively, the local high school. I very nearly stopped to offer my assistance, but she looked too aggravated to accept a stranger's help, so I kept walking.

As I turned the corner to head downtown, I chanced a glance back toward her. She was marching up the front steps of the first building. I decided that she looked determined enough to find whatever it was she was looking for, and put her out of my head as I walked toward Shadowkeep. An hour later, from my perch by the shop window, I spotted her again, this time examining one of those trifold maps of town you could find in the Visitor Center. Occasionally, I watched as she stopped and spoke to people. She looked like she might be asking for directions. She had that overtly goth look that made me think her next stop would be the tourist level of Shadowkeep, in search of gaudy pentagram jewelry, or notebooks with Edgar Allan Poe quotations on the covers. But despite my expectation that I'd see her walk through the door at any moment, she disappeared down the street, and didn't reappear.

That afternoon, I rode my bike along the road back to Lightkeep Cottage. I was supposed to be reciting a list of gemstone properties I was trying to memorize, but I kept trailing off, entranced by the scenery. The first of the leaves were just beginning to change; little pops of red and orange and yellow bursting in the trees, heralding the coming of fall. Though I'd lived in Maine all my life, I never got tired of watching the change of the seasons, each one beautiful in its own way, transforming the landscape in its own unique style. I was so distracted that I didn't notice the woman in front of the cottage gate until I was almost next to her. I braked hard, swerving a little to ensure I wouldn't bump into her as she whirled and saw me coming.

"Hi," I said as I dismounted from the bike and leaned it up against the fence. "Can I help you?"

"I'm looking for Lightkeep Cottage," the woman said, running a hand through her slightly wild hair. "And since the road ends just up there at the cliff, I'm assuming this is it?"

"Yeah, you found it," I said.

"And do the Vespers live here, do you know?" the woman asked. Now that I was seeing her up close, I could see dark circles under her eyes, and an almost sallow paleness to her skin. She looked exhausted.

"Yeah, they do," I hedged. I felt some uneasiness. I didn't know this woman—had never seen her in Sedgwick Cove before today. It made me anxious, not knowing what it was she was here for. My words brightened her expression at once, though, and her face lit up with a relieved smile at my affirmative reply.

"Thank God," she said, sagging a little. "I don't think I could have walked much further. Did you know this place isn't on Google Maps? And no one in this town gives information very freely."

So, she wasn't local. And she was here solely to find us. My heart began to pound. Should I call for my mother or my aunts? Was anyone even home?

"What do you want with the Vespers?" I asked, playing for time.

"I'm actually just looking for one. Her name is Wren. Wren Vesper."

My heart leaped into a gallop as the woman stared at me, her eyes full of expectation. I swallowed hard, choking back first one answer, then another. What should I say? Should I lie? How could I know what to do if I didn't even know who this woman was?

She noticed my strange hesitation, and she narrowed her eyes. "Is that who I've found? Are you Wren Vesper?"

"I... I am," I finally managed to stammer.

The young woman's face split into a smile so genuine that I felt my body relax slightly. Maybe I was reading into this all wrong. Maybe my anxiety about Veronica had me seeing enemies in perfectly average strangers.

"Wren Vesper," the young woman repeated, still smiling. "I'm not sure I've ever been so happy to see anyone in my life. I have something for you." And she pulled a black backpack around onto her hip, so that she could unzip it and dig around inside.

"Sorry, but... who are you?" I asked, taking half a step back from her as she pulled something from the bag, something large and rectangular, and wrapped carefully in a swath of velvet fabric.

"Oh, I'm sorry. I should have introduced myself first," the young woman said. She unwound that fabric from the item in her hands to reveal a very old and tattered book, which she held carefully out to me. "My name is Jess Ballard, and I've traveled a very long way under strict instructions to give this to no one but you."

About the Author

E.E. Holmes is a writer, teacher, and actor living in central Massachusetts with her husband and two children. When not writing, she enjoys performing, watching unhealthy amounts of British television, and reading with her children.

To learn more about E.E. Holmes and *The World of the Gateway*, please visit www.eeholmes.com

Printed in Great Britain
by Amazon